FRAGILE
PUBLISHING

THE MADISON
CHRONICLES

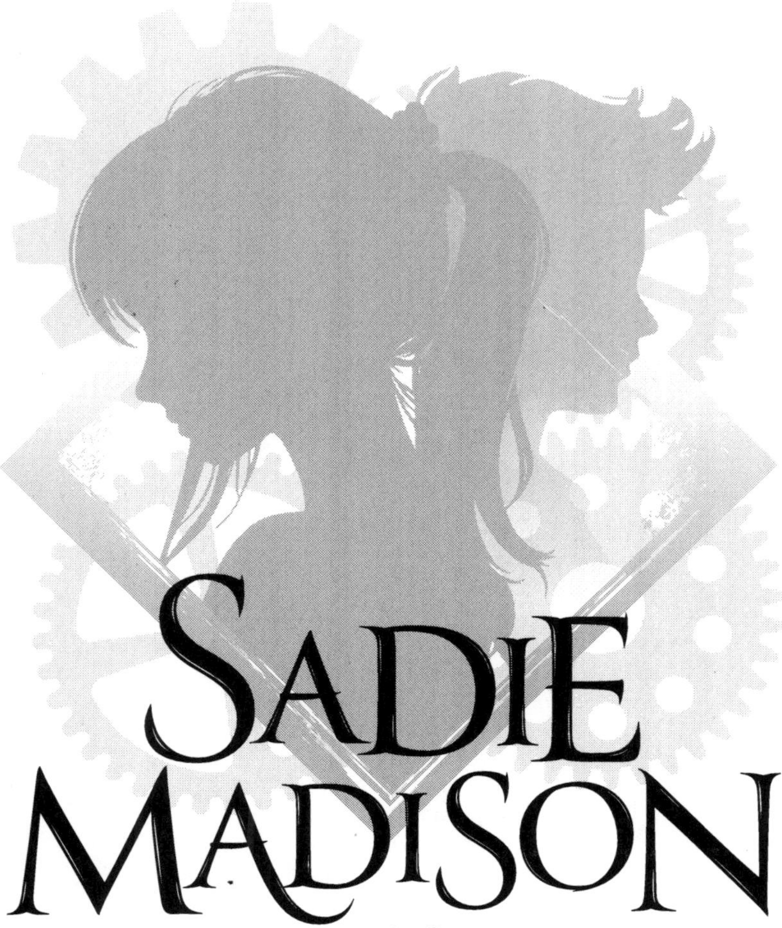

SADIE MADISON

and the
BOY in the CRIMSON SCARF

NEIL J HART

First published worldwide in 2024 by Fragile Publishing

Copyright © 2024 Neil J Hart
Edited by Manda Waller | www.mandawaller.co.uk
Cover design and layout by Neil J Hart

This is a work of fiction. Names, places, events, and incidents
are either products of the author's imagination or used
fictiously. Any resemblance to actual persons, living or dead,
is purely coincidental.

A CIP catalogue record of this book is
available from the British Library.

ISBN: 978-0-9554832-4-0
Also available as an ebook

www.neiljhart.com

For Mulder, Roger, Thor, Ozzy, Scully, and Jake.
Wise cats, one and all.

SECRETS

Everyone lives with secrets.
Most are small and inconsequential.
Tiny ripples on a giant ocean.

But some secrets should never have been.
Secrets so unfathomable that even the faintest
whisper could tear your mind apart.

And if these secrets were to see the light of day,
the world would change forever.
A meteorite flash-boiling the Sapphire Seas.

PART ONE
AWAKENINGS

"The stars do not fear the darkness.
For it is the darkness that makes them shine."
—FATHER MORQASH DAVIDIAN
Iron Bridge, Norland, 1900

THE SHADOW VALLEY

Fire Wolves and Frost Bears fled for the Carcassus Mountains while Silver Squirrels and River Badgers retreated to their frozen hollows. Sightings of Goofang, Cactus Cat, and the Winter Witches were becoming less common than the summer sun.

And in the stillness of the trees, a dark mist spread.

Flowing like water over stone, it brushed against bark and twig, leaving ash and dust in its wake. At the base of the foothills, where the vast canopy of evergreen sandaracs thinned, it waited.

Silently, purposefully, the mist gathered.

It swirled into a ball of black, then morphed through corrupted shapes, twisted and broken. Finally—as if deciding, settling on an idea—the mist became a strange, curious girl.

She smoothed her long dark hair with cadaverous fingers, squared her shoulders, and flattened her white linen dress. The girl glared at a mighty sandstone wall that rose between her and the peaceful town of Iron Bridge.

A sharp eyebrow flickered.

A rotten grin cracked her face.

Sadie Madison stuffed her hands into the deep pockets of her black, threadbare cardigan. She lingered in the hallway of Number 5 Leviathan Crook, surrounded by a horde of

11

mismatched antique furniture, dog-eared books, and gruesome paintings. Some depicted people, places, and things Sadie understood. But most were surreal and strange. Gloomy paintings of war and bloodshed, distorted realities, monsters, and broken, frightened things.

Before her hung *Battle For The Clockwork Universe*. It depicted a barbaric scene from the Divine Wars where the armies of Earth stood screaming, thrusting weapons over their heads. High above, lightning cracked a nightmarish sky. A gigantic hand hovered over the battlefield. Upon its palm, an army of angels with furious wings rode raging stallions towards the fight.

It was Sadie's favourite painting.

A window into the past.

History.

Memory.

Her mother's voice shattered her daydream, through fire and brimstone and chaos and death. "Dinner's ready!"

Tucking her unruly black hair behind her ears, Sadie followed her nose through the cluttered hallway and into the dining room. Amber lamplight warmed a long wooden table laden with thick steaks, cheesy mashed potato, carrots, peas, parsnips, runner beans, cauliflower, and several boats of delicious-smelling gravy. Crystal decanters filled with golden Tokay, plum wine, and blood-red ziela dowsed the dark walls with a spectrum of shimmering diamonds.

Sadie's brother sat in a high-back chair, scribbling furiously in his notebook. As she entered, he snapped it shut, jamming several yellow envelopes between the leaves.

Nine-year-old Eli Madison had the same dark, untrustworthy hair, and profoundly blue eyes as his sister. However, pushed onto the top of his head sat a pair of odd-looking spectacles made from copper and brass, ordained with all manner of tiny levers and dials.

Eli called them his Monster Magnifiers.

Natalia whirled down the wide staircase and joined them at the table. Smelling of winter flowers and spiced fruit, she took her seat and tossed her golden, tangle-free hair over her shoulders. She stared thoughtfully out the window. Sadie wondered what her sixteen-year-old sister daydreamed about. Boys, probably. Well, one in particular.

The front door yawned. Snowflakes drifted into the Madison house.

Atticus barked, emerging from the library.

From her seat in the dining room, Sadie watched her father wrap his arms around the loveable old wolfhound.

"Evening, soldiers!" said her father. He was in good shape for his years, she felt. Slim, bookish, a constant fidget. He'd parted his hair to one side. A pair of tortoiseshell spectacles nestled beneath thin, arching eyebrows. "Attention!"

All three children stood straight. Hands raised to their temples.

Michael Madison chuckled. "Excellent, excellent." Like any good drill sergeant, he paced around the table. Buttoning his cardigan. Inspecting his children. "Good turnout this evening," he went on, saluting back. "As you were!"

"Have you had a good day, General?" Natalia asked, continuing the charade.

"Tip-top day! Received word from our troops on the front lines," he replied, looking around conspiratorially. He leant in, whispering, "Dragon Riders are congregating in the Carcassus Mountains, while the Winter Witches draw their sinister plans in the south. Trouble and unrest brew in every town, village, and hamlet from Hüntesgaard to Fort Campion but, most worrying of all, a shadowed evil stirs in the east—something ancient, as old as time herself. I fear for our future. And our lives!"

Sadie's eyes sparkled with excitement.

Can I go to the front line? Eli signed, his hands forming the words.

Michael straightened, looking over his spectacles.

"Perhaps," he replied, a comical eyebrow raised. "But tell me, Eli. Do you fight for the Gods or the Godless?"

The Godless, Eli signed enthusiastically.

"Quite right, young man," Michael said. "There is no place for the Gods at this table. Their kind has been driven from our world. Eradicated in the Divine Wars. Exiled to the far reaches of the universe. Death to the Gods!"

Death to the Gods, Eli signed as his mother arrived carrying yet more gravy boats.

"Death to the Gods!" Sadie and Natalia cried, punching the air.

Larissa Madison cast the gravy boats onto the table. "Michael." Her voice a half-whisper. "What *are* you doing?" Dashing around the room, she closed the curtains on the snow-capped world beyond. "You don't need me to remind you what the Eighth Day Assembly will do if they hear!"

They all nodded, but none of the Madison children were entirely clear on the details. They had been warned, on more than one occasion, to never acknowledge the Gods outside the house—*not a whisper, nor a thought*—for the Eighth Day Assembly had eyes and ears everywhere.

"It's been almost seventy years since the Divine Wars, Michael," Larissa went on, distributing plates. "Yet you carry on as though you're eager for their return."

"But ma'am!" Michael Madison exclaimed, thrusting out his skinny chest. "To serve one's country is a great honour." Larissa opened her mouth to object, but Michael continued, waving a hand at a collection of paintings above the sideboard. "My father, the great Field Marshall William Madison—"

He seemed to freeze as the name escaped his lips.

The Madison children spun to look at the paintings. Michael could only have been referring to one in particular. The other paintings were of a blue-skinned demon, a bowl of rotten fruit, and a horse stampeding across a field of broken corpses.

The painting in question depicted a man in his later

years wearing a pith helmet and desert camouflage. Seated on a campaign stool in a brightly coloured canvas tent and surrounded by barrels of fruits and caskets of wine, he drank from a posh cup and saucer. Grandfather William's fine white hair flowed over his collar, where a proud little monkey sat holding a strange jewel.

"Michael!" Larissa exploded. Her hands slammed against the table.

Serving spoons and gravy boats jumped with surprise.

"Is that him? Is *that* Grandfather William?" Sadie asked, pointing with her knife.

"Yes," Michael nodded after a moment. "That's your ... grandfather."

Eli wrinkled his nose. The Monster Magnifiers slid over his eyes.

The painting had been there Sadie's entire life. It had always been just another weird painting, but now it felt different. Now it had meaning. Sadie's eyes traced every inch of her grandfather, consigning his image to memory.

"Why didn't you say before, Father?" she asked.

Michael looked lost, far away. "He's been ... on my mind of late."

"Tell us about him," she urged, hungry for one of her father's wondrous stories. "Did he fight in the Divine Wars? Did he kill any Gods? Why does he have a monkey on his shoulder? What is it holding? It looks shiny."

"There is nothing to say," Larissa hissed, pouring herself a glass of Tokay. "He was a silly old man, with silly ideas, and a head for ... well, goodness knows what!"

Michael stared at his plate. His shoulders turned in.

"It's a horrible painting, Michael. I've never understood why you insist on keeping it. Why we must keep *any* of them. They're all ... ghastly."

A pink rash had begun to bloom on Larissa's neck. She fussed with a dark-red cuff bracelet that had stained her skin green. "We'll have no more talk of that man at this table. Stories of William Madison, like those of the Gods, are *never* to be uttered again. Do you hear me? Well, do you?"

Silently, her children nodded.

Michael straightened his cardigan.

Larissa sipped her wine.

Despite the tension, Sadie wolfed down her dinner, enjoying an extra-large helping of banana toffee crumble and cream. However, something lingered on her tongue that could not be satisfied by food. She tried to imagine what kind of stories her grandfather would have told. Tales of fighting, camaraderie, and adventure, no doubt. Tales of the Divine Wars and the forming of the Eighth Day Assembly. She wondered what sort of man he was. Where he'd been? And why he'd sat for such an unusual painting?

Snapping a hand to her forehead, she saluted her dead grandfather before skipping through the hallway and into the library for the most anticipated part of her day.

THE
GATHERING

Books. Thousands of books. A bastion of knowledge. The Madison family had accrued one of the largest personal collections of encyclopaedias, novels, grimoires, anthologies, diaries, biographies, and autobiographies in the Shadow Valley. Every centimetre of wall space had been filled with book spines, a reprieve from Michael's gruesome paintings.

Amidst the towering shelves, the Madison family stood in a tight circle.

Michael's eyes roved suspiciously over his wife and children. Then, without warning, Eli grasped his throat and silently collapsed to his knees, struggling for breath.

Natalia died next. "The pain, the pain," she gurgled as she dropped to the floor. "The unrelenting pain!"

Michael surveyed the remaining players. He'd have to make an accusation soon or the game would be over. Pointing theatrically, he turned to his wife. "I declare that you are the Murderer—"

But Larissa's shoulders were already shuddering. Coughing and groaning, her hands clawed at her throat. "It burns, it burns," she informed her husband, with rather less conviction than normal. "I'm burning. Someone help me. I'm burning up!"

And with that, she carefully lowered herself to the ground and died.

Michael looked at his victorious daughter. A smug grin

plastered her face. Light from the fire flickered on Sadie's skin. Her chaotic black hair shimmered with bolts of electric blue.

"I win, I win, I win!" she squealed, hopping from one foot to the other.

"Sadie is wink-murder champion!" declared Michael, nodding his approval.

"We're all still dead," mumbled Natalia.

"Oh, yes. Silly me. Of course." Michael cleared his throat, closed his eyes, hands raised, fingers entwined. "By the power of the Ancients … The Old World and the New … As Souls return to Bodies … Life begins anew!"

Like fresh zombies, Natalia and Eli pretended to wake from their deathly slumber. Larissa, her patience clearly worn thin, got straight to her feet. "Well done, Sadie," she said, flattening her skirts and fussing her hair. "Very well played."

"And, as a reward for your murderous cunning, you can entertain us with some music," announced Michael, turning to a grand piano that lurked beneath the library window, polished and reflective, a hunk of chiselled black glass.

Sadie trilled with delight.

She slid onto the piano stool. Her gaze drifted to the long window. The sun dipped behind the Carcassus Mountains. Shadows shifted uneasily. Below, Ryndai patrolled the street. Strange light from their crystal lanterns flickered blue and green in the gathering dark. One stopped and turned towards the Madison house, her face hidden beneath a dark hood.

Quickly looking away, Sadie returned her attention to the piano. She took a long breath and pushed all thought of the Ryndai and the Eighth Day Assembly from her mind. She levelled her shoulders. Steadied her hands.

Music spiralled into the air. Pleasant and melodic, it stuttered in places and lacked emotion, dynamics, flair. However, Sadie performed without mistakes and, more impressively, with no score to guide her.

As the music played, Sadie's mind soared.

She floated across the hallway, past *Battle For The Clockwork Universe*, over the pristine dining table, and came to rest on the painting of William Madison. She studied her grandfather's face, his wispy white hair, the barrels of fruit and wine, and the curious monkey on his shoulder. Slowly, the image morphed into something more like a pictogram than an oil painting. Smells and sounds from the image invaded her senses. Honeyed dates and blackberry wine. Pipe smoke, chatter, laughter. Her grandfather turned his head and looked directly at her. He smiled, winked, and fussed the monkey with his little finger.

Focus shifted to the curious jewel in the monkey's hand.

The music changed.

Michael sat forward in his chair.

Larissa's shoulders dropped. The Tokay almost slipped from her grasp.

The Madison library became filled with wonder. Something majestic, something divine. But, as swiftly as it had arrived, it withered away.

Sadie found herself staring down at the keys. Her fingers slowed to a halt. The music gently resolved.

Gathering themselves, Michael and Larissa erupted with vigorous applause. Eli joined them. Atticus barked, rolled onto his back, and pin-wheeled his legs in the air. Natalia stared disbelievingly at her little sister.

The melody lingered in Sadie's mind for a moment. She traced each note, turning them over and over like curiosities in an antique shop. They felt strange, forbidden. "Sorry," she said finally. "Got a bit stuck in the middle."

"Don't be so critical," Larissa encouraged. "You did a fantastic job."

Michael adjusted his spectacles. "A marvellous performance," he said. "Rudolf Petrov has nothing on you."

"Don't be daft, Father," Sadie told him. "Petrov is a master."

"One day, Sadie," he enthused, his voice low and wistful. "One day."

Sadie closed her eyes and looked for the melody again. She'd never known anything quite like it. It moved through her mind, twisting, turning, with a will of its own. Where had it come from? Who did it belong to? It certainly wasn't hers.

She closed the piano lid and joined her brother on the sofa.

Eli coiled his hand around his ear and signalled towards the wireless. Michael theatrically checked his pocket watch, then bounded over to a large wooden cabinet in the corner of the room. Humming quietly to himself, he flung the doors wide, flicked a switch and the Electro-Magnetic 850 Wireless Radio burst into life. Static buzzed from a fluted speaker cone while he adjusted the dials. Eventually, the theme for the National Broadcast erupted into the room.

With smiles on their faces, the Madison family sang along as they settled down to listen. Soon enough, the unmistakable voice of Bernard Benjamin Brooker floated on the airwaves. "Good evening, Norlandians. Good evening to you all."

"Good evening," said the Madisons in unison.

Eli waved.

"It is Thursday the twenty-first of December eighteen ninety-nine. The time is seven o'clock. We have an excellent show for you this evening. But first, I implore you to sit back, relax, and enjoy the inconceivable, incomprehensible, incredible sound of the prodigious violinist Gerald Kaylock."

Gerald's performance sounded effortless, beautiful and soaring. Sadie drifted into her imaginary world once more. She flew over fields and villages, her arms powerful and majestic, transformed into feather angel wings. She swooped between sandarac trees and rose above the mouth of the River Myr as it broke on the Sapphire Seas.

"Fantastic, fabulous, fanciful, and phantasmagorical!" declared Bernard Benjamin Brooker. "Quite the master, wouldn't you all agree?"

The Madisons nodded.

Next, Bernard introduced a string quartet from Los Kralice,

a flautist from a small village in the Northern Territories, and finally a pianist from Hüntesgaard.

Afterwards, while rustling his papers, he announced the news headlines for Norland and surrounding territories. He started, as usual, with the National Warning from the Eighth Day Assembly, followed by news of Lorntide preparations throughout the Shadow Valley and the much-anticipated invitations to the Winter Festival at the Palace of Light. To finish, Bernard Benjamin Brooker read a local news story.

"After completing her studies at the Fort Campion School of Elements where she achieved their highest honours, Miss Chimera Falsom has been accepted to read Advanced Alchemy, Thermatology and Electricity at the University of San Cristophe under Professor Dwight Nightingale. Earlier, Miss Falsom told me, 'For hundreds of years we've been calling these areas of study Magic, but the world has moved in giant strides. It's amazing to be at the forefront of this scientific revolution. I'm so thrilled. I can barely believe it.' Professor Nightingale only accepts one student each year. This is quite the prestigious placement for our very own Chimera."

Sadie turned to her father. "A girl from the Shadow Valley is going to study at the University of San Cristophe. That's amazing!"

"Yes. It is," replied Michael. "I'll bet there were thousands of candidates from all over the world. Proof that hard work and dedication can take you anywhere."

"I shall double my efforts!"

"You'll do fine."

"It's now seven-thirty," the broadcaster continued. "Please stay tuned throughout the night for intoxicating back-to-back performances. And I'll be here at the same time tomorrow. Goodbye, Norlandians. Goodbye to you all."

"Goodbye."

Eli waved.

Bernard Benjamin Brooker vanished from the airwaves

and a delicate violin sonata returned. Michael clasped his hands together enthusiastically.

"So, what are we playing next?"

✴ �‿ ▦ ⚔ ⛲

After several rounds of fictionary (a game rooted in deception and lies), snap dragon (a test of risk), elephant's foot umbrella stand (a word association game), charades (Eli's favourite), and two hands of black gimlet (an elemental card game played with dice which, at Lorntide, Michael let them wager the outcome against coins and secrets), Sadie sat on the window seat in her eaved bedroom, reading the horror grimoire *The Hangman's Last Words and Other Terrible Fates.*

She leant against the arched picture window and fanned her fingers into Mischief's soft, tortoiseshell fur. Known as the three wise cats, Mischief—along with Fable and Puzzle—had joined the family almost thirteen years ago. The cat purred happily, blinking her mesmerising cerulean eyes.

Far below, the town of Iron Bridge twinkled and gleamed with a million faerie-lights and lanterns. Sadie had faerie-lights of her own. They flashed in gentle reds and yellows and greens around her picture window. Snow drifted past the glass. It moved through gaslamps along the promenade by the River Myr, settled on roofs, and automobiles, and the gigantic factory chimneys of the industrial district.

She tried to return to her disgusting tales, but her mind reeled with thoughts of her grandfather, the little monkey, and that strange jewel. She pictured the wonders he must have seen, what terrors too, where he'd travelled, out there beyond the Shadow Valley and across the Sapphire Seas.

As she daydreamed, she searched for the melody but found nothing more than a haunting echo. Frustrated, she looked harder, desperate to recall it. But the harder she tried, the more the melody seemed to evade her. Not gone, simply hiding. A childish prank.

A soft knock at the door preceded her father. "What have you got there?" he asked, indicating the book on her lap. "Any good?"

"Diabolically gruesome," she said, hopped off the window seat and headed for bed.

"Well, goodnight then," he said, before adding in a sing-song voice. "Sleep soft and sound to avoid the hell hound. Don't wake late at the demon's gate!"

Sadie bared her teeth, forming demon horns with her index fingers.

Michael chuckled and dimmed the lamps.

"Father?" she said, slipping beneath the bedclothes. "Do you think I'll be able to study at the University of San Cristophe when I'm all grown up like Chimera Falsom?"

"Of course," Michael replied, sitting on the bed. "Anything is possible. Truly."

"She's going to study Advanced Alchemy, Thermatology and Electricity. What are they?"

"They're calling them the new sciences, but they've been around for hundreds of years, thousands maybe. Until now we haven't understood them properly."

"I know about Electricity. It makes things work. Like the wireless in the library and the cinefilm projector at school. What are the others?"

"Alchemy is the discipline of turning one thing into another."

"Like bread into toast?"

"Yes, I suppose so." He chuckled. "But also on a far grander scale. Like morphing base metals such as iron, lead or nickel into gold and silver. Or combining plants and herbs together to make medicines or potions. That sort of thing. And Thermatology is the study of fire. Some people use it for medical remedies and therapies. But there are those who would harness fire for more *unconventional* means."

Sadie chewed her lip. "How do you know all this?"

"From books …" He looked strung out, disconnected for a moment, quietly humming a tune. "And my parents."

Sadie frowned, listened. The melody. Almost. But he'd changed it, hadn't he? Or had she forgotten it? She shook her head. Impossible.

"Fah-ther?"

"Ye-es?" he mimicked.

"Tell me more about—"

"Grandfather William?" Michael guessed. "There's not much to tell. He was a good man, no matter what your mother says. She has her reasons." He smiled. "You would have liked him very much. You have his inquisitive, adventurous spirit. And the same curious blue eyes."

"Who was he? What did he do?"

"I know a good story about the Witch Tree at San Cristophe," Michael said, attempting to deflect her questions. "It's quite scary … and completely true, one hundred per cent. I swear it! Or perhaps the tale of the Princess in the Threadbare Gown?"

"You've told me those," Sadie said, folding her arms. "Many times."

"How about the Relentless Squirrel? King Jeremy the Wicked? Or the Ice Pirates?"

Sadie shook her head.

"The Beautiful Death?"

"Heard them. All of them."

Michael hummed the melody again. His eyes melancholic and faraway. "Such a fantastic piece of music," he whispered. "Old, powerful, filled with … memory." He tiptoed to the door. "Grandfather William," he muttered, his back to her. "It's an incredibly grown-up story, Sadie. I'm not sure you're old enough."

"I am," she said. "I'm almost thirteen, Father."

Michael's entire body tightened. "It's getting late," he said, opening his pocket watch. The melody played on his lips once more. His body softened.

"Just a little," she pleaded.

The door closed. Michael returned to the bed.

"Don't say a word to your mother! She'll have my guts for garters!"

Sadie zipped her mouth shut. Michael dimmed the bedside lamp. Shadows swamped every stubborn corner of the room. Sadie wriggled beneath the bedclothes.

"It all started billions of years ago. Before the creation of the universe. Before earth and sky and planets and stars and anything you can name. Suddenly, there was an almighty flash and everything we know and see and hear and feel sprang into existence. Now, a lot of people know about these things, mostly scientists and learned men—"

"Like Professor Nightingale," Sadie added helpfully. "From the university."

"Yes, like Professor Nightingale," Michael agreed. "But few know about …" He paused for dramatic emphasis, then whispered, "… the Gathering."

Sadie's skin rippled.

The melody flashed into view.

It sang in her mind, vivid and glorious, like a choir of angels. Sadie thought her father must be hearing it too. But it was for her, and her alone.

"Grandfather William was part of the Gathering all those billions of years ago," Michael continued as the music boomed in Sadie's head. "A Narrower, he was. A spirit, a collector of forgotten memory, a protector of the Vents! For billions of years he lived within the Vents, collecting everything that had been forgotten, vouchsafing it for all time. For there is a Vent for every life ever lived, where all the forgotten things reside. But, as the universe entered the time of man, Grandfather William fell in love with a beautiful girl named Karolinja. Now, at this time Grandfather William was a spirit, a thing of particles and dust, not flesh and blood like you nor I. His heart ached to be with Karolinja, to live a human life. But his soul was bound to the Gathering."

"What did he do?"

"He renounced his heritage and his power. Leaving the Narrowers and the Gathering behind, he transcended the spirit world and took human form."

Michael's hands crossed his chest, holding himself as though he were naked in the snow. He hummed the melody, stuttered, drifted into silence.

"How?" Sadie gripped her bedclothes with both hands. "How did he become human?"

"He had … help," Michael replied awkwardly. His face became ghostly pale. His lips quivered. "But that is for another time."

"But Father—"

"And not a word of this to anyone! Not one word. Promise?"

"Promise," she mumbled.

Michael left the room.

Sadie buried her face in a pillow and closed her eyes.

The music exploded in her mind as she imagined her grandfather rocketing through the universe, made of energy and light and space dust and all manner of wondrous things. She pictured the Vents where the forgotten thoughts and memories of every living thing were kept. She saw all types of Vents. Not just those of men and women and children, but those of dinosaurs and algae and whales and gorillas and trees and flowers and faeries and dragons. She imagined the memories stored in gigantic vaults, in knobbly chests-of-drawers, buried underground in wooden boxes and metal tins, pressed inside the pages of enormous books, written in blood, or trapped inside the smallest, most delicate locket.

But what did the Vents actually look like?

She had no idea, but she could dream. Dreams coated in the most beautiful music she had ever known. She dreamt of the Vents, the Narrowers, and the Gathering. She dreamt of Grandfather William crashing to Earth like a fiery meteorite and emerging as a man ready to live and love and make Karolinja the happiest woman on Earth.

Michael Madison had told hundreds of audacious stories. But none of them felt like this one. None of them felt as *real*. Something in the story made Sadie believe.

Something in the way he told it.

Something in his voice.

Something … *melodic*.

Millions of children would have laughed if they were told they were descendants of the Narrowers, collectors of all forgotten memory.

But Sadie believed her father's story completely.

She knew it was true, for she had never forgotten a single thing in her entire life.

Not one thing.

THE BROKEN MOON

Sadie woke the following morning with a head full of moonbeams, monsters, and magical-memory-make-believe. She draped her favourite threadbare cardigan over a long dress, knee-length stockings, and hard-wearing boots, and bounced downstairs, fizzing with excitement.

She found Eli at the kitchen table.

Her mother at the stove.

"Smells amazing in here!" tooted Michael, entering the room. He snapped his heels together and ordered, "Attention!"

Sadie and Eli stood and saluted their father. "The hell hounds were kept at bay then. I don't see any life-threatening claw marks."

Larissa tutted disapprovingly.

"I trust you slept well," Michael continued. "And you too, Eli."

"Very well, thank you," Sadie replied. "I had the most wonderful dreams."

Larissa handed out plates piled high with pancakes.

Sadie beamed and fought Eli for the syrup.

Natalia wafted into the kitchen, smelling of cucumber, coconut, and apple blossom. Late for breakfast as usual. Michael shook his head comically as her perfumes surrounded the table.

"Crikey me! Is Dimitri about?"

"No Father," Natalia blushed. "He's coming for dinner this evening."

Michael flicked his gaze towards his wife.

"Please tell me you didn't forget!"

"Of course not, darling," Larissa said smoothly. "Everything is in hand."

The doorbell chimed.

Sadie took her pancakes and skipped through the hall. "Danver's here," she announced, beckoning her friend inside.

Eli focused his Monster Magnifiers at the arched oak door.

Sadie and Danver talked in the hallway while the Madisons finished their breakfast. Larissa stuffed school bags with sandwiches wrapped in brown paper and tied up with string.

At the door, Eli wrestled his arms into his winter coat.

The girls laced their boots.

Larissa knelt beside them, helping with their bootstraps. Sadie studied her mother's face. She looked drawn and pale, as though sleep proved a hard-fought battle. "Are you okay, Mother?"

"Of course, dear," Larissa replied. "What makes you—?"

"Nothing," Sadie replied.

Her gaze drifted towards the door and the glistening snow beyond.

Larissa smiled. "It's a magical world out there, Sadie. A world filled with adventure and mystery, opportunity and endless possibilities." She took Sadie's arm and spun the girl to face her. "But a world filled with danger and darkness too. It's the season of River Wraiths, Fire Wolves, and the Winter Witches—"

As Larissa spoke, a knowing look bloomed on her daughter's face.

"You don't actually believe Father's stories," Sadie said. "Do you?"

Larissa bit her lip. "No ... but I *do* believe in your father." She attempted to fix Sadie's hair, but quickly gave up. Kissing her mother's cheek, Sadie fastened her amaranthine coat and waited on the porch.

The Madison children, accompanied by Sadie's friend

Danver, ambled past the family jongelier and waited silently beside the automobile. Eli peered through the filthy windows with his Monster Magnifiers. He adjusted the dials and scribbled his findings into a notebook that peeped out the top of his school bag.

"Can we take the automobile today, Father?" Natalia asked. "It's been months since we used it. And it's so cold."

"I'm sorry, Natalia. I ... I think there's something wrong with it." This wasn't a lie, despite sounding like one. "I'll have a tinker with her at the weekend. Then perhaps we'll go for a trip ... or something."

Natalia looked crestfallen but shrugged it off. Michael led the way down Leviathan Crook, past frosted trees and bushes, descending the snowy streets of Iron Bridge towards the River Myr.

Across the street, Danver's father stood smoking a pipe on his whitewashed porch. Arnold Tomes was a tall man, quiet and reserved, with onyx skin and wiry hair. Around the top of his arm he wore the Broken Moon. A red fabric band embroidered with a shattered orb in dark velvet and thread.

Everyone who believed in the Gods, no matter what denomination, wore the Broken Moon by order of Minister Craven and the Eighth Day Assembly. The Broken Moon was seen as a symbol of shame. An emblem for tarnished souls who clung to the old world. A brand that deprived them of the rights and privileges everyone else enjoyed.

You didn't see the Broken Moon too often. Not anymore. Michael assured Sadie that most people had forgotten about the Gods. Or pretended to. Others hid their beliefs behind closed doors, worshipping in secret and shadow.

Danver wore one too.

The Madisons were a Godless family. Always had been. But her father had hundreds of stories about the Gods and the Divine Wars. He told them to her like all his other tales, but these were whispered, and forbidden, and came with a heavy price.

Stories of the Gods and the Divine Wars were terrifying and violent. War always was, Sadie supposed. For, as the final story went, *The women and men of Earth stared up at the Gods, their faces filled with contempt and hatred. And then, as the sun rose on the Eighth Day, they took up arms against the Gods and vanquished them all.*

Sadie smiled and threw a cheerful wave at Danver's father.

Arnold Tomes did not wave back.

☀ ☪ 🎞 🦅 🏛

Iron Bridge elementary school had been built as a hospital during the Divine Wars and was erected on the bank of the River Myr at the same time as the famous bridge itself. Made of rough stone and crumbling plaster, the school and playing fields were encompassed, like most of Iron Bridge, by Darachna Forest. The vast woodland snaked along the base of the Carcassus Mountains for thousands of miles, covering the entire Shadow Valley from the spring of the River Myr—high above the town of Hüntesgaard in the northern mountains—to the mouth of the Sapphire Seas at Fort Campion.

The Madison house backed on to Darachna Forest, separated by a large sandstone wall. At night, Sadie had heard noises in the trees—mostly Fire Wolves and Frost Bears with their noses to the wind, but some nights there were other noises. Sounds she could not explain. She'd told her father about them and he, in turn, told her stories of Goofang, Cactus Cat, the Winter Witches, Axe-Handle Hound, Glawackus, Hodag, Wendigo, Ratchet Owl, and hundreds more. All her father's stories thrilled her, but they never consumed her in the same way as the one about Grandfather William, the Narrowers, and the Gathering.

"Alright, Sades!" hollered a voice. It came from a group of boys watching her salute the monument to the Victorious Dead in the schoolyard.

"What are you doing?" Danver said in alarm. "Best not hang

around, Sadie. Let's get inside where it's safe!"

Sadie squared her shoulders.

The boys approached.

"Now we're in trouble," grumbled Danver, frantically pulling Sadie's sleeve.

"Well, what do we have here?" one of the boys said. "A last stand before the winter holidays?"

Sadie stared, hard. The boy fidgeted, laughed, and turned to his friends. "What you getting for Lorntide, Tobin?"

"Model railway."

"And you, Xander?"

"A wireless for my room."

"Verden?"

"Either a steam motorkart or an air rifle. Not decided yet. What about you, Cale?"

Cale Boswick was unusually large for his age. He had a thickset jaw, close-cropped hair, and shark-like eyes that shone with honey and green fire. "Well, I'm getting my own boat," he said. "Top of the line. No expense spared." He glared at Sadie. "What about you, Sades? What are you getting?"

She continued to stare.

"Are you going to build a time machine and go back to the Divine Wars so you can stand and salute all the troops as they march to their deaths?"

Sadie didn't respond.

"And what about your brother? Eli, isn't it? What's he asking for?" Cale leant forward, cupping a hand around his ear. "Oh, silly me!" he rasped. "He can't ask for anything, can he? Poor little Eli can't ask for anything because he hasn't got a voice."

Cale smiled, wide and cruel.

"It's not her fault Eli doesn't speak!" Danver yelled, but Sadie held him back.

"Leave us alone," she said, finally.

"Leave *us* alone!" Cale sneered. "What are you going to do if I don't? Insult me with your sign language?" The boys roared with laughter. "I've got a Lorntide gift for you."

Cale grabbed Sadie's hair. She struggled for a moment as his grip tightened. He pushed her to the ground. The snow bit her face, sharp and cold.

"Get off me!" she yelled, thrashing around. "Get your wretched hands off!"

The school bell rang. Cale grumbled. "Not long until lunchtime, Sades," he said, his lips almost brushing her ear. "Be seeing you then!"

Laughing and jeering, the boys retreated inside.

"I hate him," Danver said. "I hate Cale Boswick with every fibre of my being."

Sadie rolled onto her back and smiled. "Only another six months and we'll be rid of him forever." She grabbed Danver's hand, pulled herself up and hurried inside before they were late for their first class.

✴ ☻ ▤ ✾ ⛩

Lunchtime was inevitable. The hands of the classroom clock moved towards it like a pendulum-axe descending on its ill-fated victim.

"Where shall we hide today?" Danver asked, the moment the bell tolled.

Sadie led him out of the classroom and into a busy hallway.

"Let's go outside and find Eli," she said.

"No. Let's run and hide."

"Why?"

"Because we always run, and we always hide. Why is today so different?"

Sadie studied her friend.

"Plus, I saw Ryndai in the schoolyard earlier," he added urgently.

"Okay," Sadie said and threw him a mischievous smile. "Just for you."

Down two flights of stairs they ran. Along a dark corridor filled with framed paintings of lecturers and professors. They skidded to a stop outside a door emblazoned with a large letter *M*.

Most pupils presumed it stood for the room's current use.

Music.

But Sadie knew differently.

This had once been the morgue.

She put her ear to the batwing doors while Danver stood on tiptoes to peer through the circular window. "Don't see anyone."

A virulent damp swirled through the music room. Odd-shaped instruments lurked against the walls, cast in long shadows. The windows—positioned where the subterranean room met ground level—were caked in frost and heaped with snow.

They swept across the room like fleeting spirits, lifted the edge of the dust sheet, and slipped beneath the grand piano. Sadie imagined they were adventurers sitting in an expedition tent somewhere deep in the Winter Continent, tracking the Wampus Cat, or a Chupacabra, or a scamper of Bogeymen.

"What's with you today?" Danver asked.

Sadie gathered her thoughts. "Something happened. Something ... *amazing*."

She told him the story of Grandfather William. About the Narrowers and the Vents and the Gathering. He sat in silence, his eyes wide in the faint light.

"So, everything we forget is taken to these ... Vents ... for all time?"

"Yes."

"And your father is the son of a billion-year-old spirit?"

"Yes."

"Making you the daughter of the son of a billion-year-old spirit?"

Sadie smiled. Her eyes gleamed. "I believe it does."

"Come on." Danver laughed. The worry in his voice vanished for a moment. "Your father is always telling crazy stories. There's one about a woman who labels all her possessions and another about a tree and some witches and—" He faltered, the stories escaping him. "This one is no different."

Sadie frowned. "It's true. All of it."

"Yes, of course," he said, chuckling. "Spirits steal into our houses—like the Urisks, or the Soul Fairy, or Gruselmann—and take away the things we forget and store them in some mystical unfathomable dimension! It's nonsense, Sadie."

She pointed at the Broken Moon on his arm. "You believe in the Gods. What's so different between that and the Narrowers?"

Danver shook his head. "You and I are not allowed to discuss the Gods, Sadie. You know that. And you know what the Eighth Day Assembly will do if they find out."

"Something horrid, I should imagine. But I'm not afraid of the Eighth Day Assembly or Minister Craven. She's thousands of miles away in San Cristophe, sitting in some high castle. No one can hear us here."

"She has ears everywhere," Danver said, his voice a hushed whisper. "Ryndai."

Sadie sniffed and cradled her chin in her hands.

Danver fiddled with the armband. "Why?" he asked suddenly. "Why do the Narrowers take away what we forget? Why do they keep them? What possible reason could there be?"

Sadie didn't know. She hadn't thought to ask.

"If it were true," Sadie said. "What do you think happens to people who ... cannot forget?"

"Everyone forgets, Sadie. As sure as everyone lives and everyone dies."

"But what if someone couldn't forget? Can you imagine?"

Danver took a moment. "If that *were* true, then it would be as amazing as the idea of the Narrowers themselves. If it were me, I'd be top of the class ... like you! It'd turn me into some kind of supernatural, magical entity, right? I'd be a titan or a ... God!"

Sadie knew *exactly* what it felt like.

It didn't feel like a supernatural power to her, and she certainly didn't think of herself as a titan or one of the Gods. Her mind had always been busy, complicated. Memories fought for every square inch. But the idea of truly forgetting something—*anything*—felt terrible, agonising, like leaving a favourite toy on a steam train bound for distant lands.

"Then again," Danver continued, "wouldn't a person who remembers everything run out of space? Eventually, I mean. Sooner or later, their brain would become full ... and overflow! It'd be like my mother and her apples. She's always buying too many and they end up spoiling on the larder floor."

"Rubbish," Sadie exploded. "Overflowing brains? That'd never happen!"

"They'd go mad," Danver went on, chuckling. "Driven mad by overflowing brains. All spoilt and rotten!"

"Stop it," she said. "You're talking utter drivel!"

Danver stopped laughing. Fear had, for the first time today, appeared on Sadie's face.

"Are you okay?" he asked.

She lowered her head, avoided his eyes, and wrapped her arms around herself.

"What is it?" he asked again. "Tell me."

She glanced up at him. "I'm one of those people."

Danver wrinkled his face. "What?"

"You said it yourself. 'If it were me, I'd be top of the class ... like you!' And I *am* top of the class. Always top of the class."

"I thought you were incredibly smart," he replied. "I mean, you *are* incredibly smart." His imperfect mind appeared to contemplate the magnificence of hers. "It's impossible though, right?"

"Test me," she told him quietly. "Ask me anything."

Danver put a finger to his lips. "What's my middle name?"

"Easy. Jaguan. Next."

"Where was my father born?"

"Still easy. North Holt. The eastern border of the salt flats, near San Cristophe. And his name's Arnold and he works at one of the copper mills, and he collects coins, and he believes in the Gods and the original creation story. Next. Make it as hard as you can."

"How many times, in our entire lives, have we hidden beneath this piano?"

"Eighty-four times. Including today."

Danver sat back, aghast. "That's amazing. But there's no way to prove it."

"Then why did you ask?"

He chewed his lip and ventured one final question. "What am I thinking right now?"

"I'm not a mind reader," Sadie groaned. "I can only remember the things I've seen, or heard, or read, or … experienced. I can recall every word of my father's bedtime stories. I can remember the smell of the delivery room where I was born: jasmine, lemon root, and turpentine. I can see every sunrise, every smile, and every frown. I can taste every meal. I can hear every song that has played on our wireless or been sung to me as I drifted off to sleep—"

A single pair of feet padded into the room.

The music room doors flapped shut.

Sadie and Danver held their breaths.

Was it Cale Boswick?

Or perhaps Professor Kassonoff preparing for his next class?

Could it be the Eighth Day Assembly come to punish them away for discussing the Gods?

Whoever it was, if they were discovered, they'd be in trouble.

Outside of class, the music room was strictly off limits.

Instruments moved aside. The door to the store cupboard creaked open. A clock ticked. Their heartbeats thudded in their chests.

The stranger's feet crept around the edge of the piano.

Closer.

Closer.

The dust sheet rippled, moved.

Danver put his arm around Sadie. He closed his eyes as if an atomic blast might detonate and reduce them both to cinders. But as the dust sheet rose, a pair of odd spectacles filled the gloom with phosphorescent light.

Sadie exhaled and grabbed her brother's hand.

What are you doing here? she signed to Eli.

Looking for you, he answered. Found you.

Eli nestled beside them. The eerie light from the Monster Magnifiers made their faces look ghoulish and forsaken. For as long as anyone could remember, Sadie's brother had been afraid of the dark. To remedy this, his father had built Eli his very own spectacles—out of magical materials from another dimension, so Michael's story went—and if Eli focused them in the right way, the spectacles would enable him to see any kind of monster, ghost, critter, or demon.

What are you doing? Eli signed. Hiding from Cale again?

"Yes, alright," Danver replied. "I'm a big coward. Your sister is too."

"No. I'm not. Not anymore," she said. "Not today."

Eli shrugged.

"Oh yes, Eli. For some reason, today is different. Something has happened—"

Sadie silenced him with a finger.

What happened? Eli asked.

"Nothing," Sadie lied. "I feel different. I'm not afraid of Cale anymore and I don't need to hide!" She crawled out from under the piano, tore the dust sheet to the floor, and flicked on the lamps. "And I don't care if he finds us. I refuse to live in fear of a school bully for one more day. I welcome a confrontation!"

She paced back to the piano and, lifting the lid, hammered on the keys with her fists and forearms, flooding the room with a thunderous, atonal din.

"Someone will hear you!" cried Danver.

Sadie continued to smash the life out of the keys.

Danver grabbed her by the wrists. "Stop it," he implored. "He'll hear you. He'll come for us! I'm begging you, Sadie. Please stop hammering!"

But Sadie was overcome by a melancholic, dreamy sensation, as if floating outside her body. All the days of anxiety and suffering at the hands of Cale Boswick were present in her mind, but they no longer dominated her.

Her fingers reached down from Danver's grip and pressed the piano keys. Sadie watched it happen, feeling utterly disconnected. She started to play. Slowly at first, one note following another. Her fingers worked effortlessly over the keys. Danced on the smooth ivory. Conjured a beautiful song. She didn't need to try. She didn't need to concentrate. It was as if her fingers were under the control of a master puppeteer.

The melody from last night suddenly returned.

Music filled the room with heat and colour. It pirouetted through the air and into her heart. Images bloomed in her mind. Strange images of people she did not know. Places she had never been. They felt like cinefilm versions of her father's monstrous paintings. She shook her head. Desperate to sweep them away.

But everything changed.

New notes rang out.

Something ill-fitting, something dark and malevolent, discordant and biting.

Eli grimaced as though Sadie had hit a wrong key, but Danver leant back, opened his mouth and breathed in the dark notes. Her friend's entire body began to shake and judder. His eyes filled with menace and mischief. The dark notes darted around the room, enveloping him like a swarm of locusts.

And then—he ran.

The melodies chased him through the batwing doors like a legion of demons across the Plains of Hell. Sadie and Eli tore after him. Down the corridor, up the stairs and outside. Their feet beat into the white earth.

"Well, look who's come to play—" Cale Boswick snorted as

they approached at an alarming rate. But his words were quickly silenced by Danver's whirring fists. Cale fell into the snow, whining like a trapped animal. Danver pounced.

Sadie and Eli came pounding across the schoolyard. They dived headfirst into the melee, grabbed Danver and pulled him away. Sadie's breath came in heavy and ragged spurts as they landed clumsily on the reddening snow.

THE GIRL WHO
COULD NOT FORGET

Sadie dreamt of black grass and stone towers. Bloodied arms and screaming voices. Magicians and conjurors with twisted faces and rotten teeth. Grit and sand and dirt and smoke. Three wretched faces, distorted and venomous, peeled through the dark towards her. Fields of fire where men and beasts burned. Angels with red flickering eyes. Warriors and witches and seers. Wind and water and earth. The white sun and a red moon collided in the heavens. A screeching, hissing crone. Cages of wild animals, gnawing and lashing at their captors. Amber light and shrouded figures. A monster with glinting talons and leathery wings, its face hidden beneath a thick cowl, enveloped in a dark, swirling mist.

And, amidst the chaos, came a voice. A constant voice, dim and soft and crying out. "I want to go home. Please take me home." Sadie saw her own face. Not a reflection, but the face of a girl who looked like her in every way—save for a ring of dark cryptic symbols around her scalp. "Beware," the girl whispered. "Murder sleeps soundly. They are close. Do not forsake me." She turned to ash and drifted away in fragile flakes of grey.

Sadie shuddered.

Her eyes opened.

The voice seemed to hang in the air, whispering, haunting, fading into the walls of the eaved bedroom.

I want to go home. Please take me home.

Sadie looked at the brass and chrome clock atop her bookcases. Early evening. Six forty-seven. She turned the dream over and over and over in her head. This wasn't like any dream she'd had before. There was something different about this one.

It felt real.

Less like a dream.

More like … a memory.

But not her memory. Someone—or *something*—else's.

Yawning, she shuffled to the window seat and rested her head against the glass. She stared at the snow-covered street below. A long, black, important-looking automobile had parked outside Danver's house. An unfamiliar vehicle, one she'd never seen before. Sleek and expensive. Old yet pristine. Somebody clearly loved it. Sadie did not. It didn't feel right. Not right at all.

Mischief leapt up beside her and let out a discontented yowl.

Sadie weaved her hands through the cat's fur. Most of Cale's blood had come off after a hard scrub, but there were still stubborn deposits lurking beneath her fingernails. She dug at them irritably with her teeth. A thin trace of copper wriggled on her tongue.

Larissa's voice rattled through the house, calling them to the table.

Sadie pulled on her cardigan, happy that it was time to eat.

Halfway down the stairs, the doorbell chimed.

Natalia rushed out of the library and swung the door open. There, silhouetted against the snowy moonlit world and the jagged Carcassus Mountains, stood a tall, athletic young man with neat golden hair and serious eyes. They whispered conspiratorially to one another, making their way to the dining room. Hands intertwined. Eyes sparkling.

"Evening, soldiers!" Michael Madison said, arriving late to the table. "Attention!"

Sadie and Eli stood up. Hands raised to their temples. Dimitri gave Natalia a quizzical look. She blushed and whispered an explanation.

Michael circled the table. He stopped behind Dimitri. "This must be a new recruit. Comrade Rubinov, if I'm not mistaken."

"Father," Natalia began. "Perhaps Mother could use your help in the kitchen."

Michael caught Natalia's drift, but Larissa had already started ferrying trays of food onto the table. Her face flushed and anxious, her rash in full bloom. Michael moved to help, but Larissa batted him aside with her oven gloves. Soon enough, they sat around the slightly under-baked, over-boiled meal, trying to avoid each other's gaze.

"This looks fantastic, Mrs Madison," Dimitri said. "Thank you for inviting me into your lovely home."

Five pairs of arms attacked the serving spoons while Michael reached for the plum wine. Beneath the table, Mischief joined Fable and Puzzle as they awaited the inevitable avalanche of crumbs and scraps.

"Tell us more about yourself," Michael said to Dimitri. "All I know about you is your work in my history class—which is exemplary, by the way—and Natalia says you're keen on words."

"Well, Mr Madison—"

"Call me Michael. We're quite informal here."

"Well … Michael," Dimitri started again. "I'm the oldest brother of three. My father, Alexsy, as I'm sure you're aware, made his money from imports and exports. As for me, well, I'm interested in writing. Poetry, mostly. Nothing too romantic, mind you, nor too dark. Sort of expressionistic. People, places, colour. Light and shade."

"Right," Michael replied, sloshing plum wine into Larissa's glass. "And you plan to pursue that for a living?"

Natalia frowned.

"I'd like to," Dimitri said, lifting a pile of withered-looking carrots onto his plate. "If time allows. Father wants me to—"

Natalia couldn't hold her tongue any longer. "You do know who his father is, don't you?" she exploded. "Rubinov? Alexsy? *Anyone*?" Natalia turned from her mother to her father and back again. Her fingers clawed the tablecloth.

"What?" Larissa replied. "Not *the* Alexsy Rubinov?"

"Alexsy Rubinov?" Michael echoed, turning the name over on his tongue. "Why do I know that name?" He snapped his fingers. "Not ... the billionaire?"

"How many Alexsy Rubinovs do you think live in Iron Bridge?" Natalia groaned.

"*The* Alexsy Rubinov. Good gracious," Michael said, looking at Dimitri. "So, you live in the ... Palace of Light with—?"

"With my father, mother, and younger brothers?" Dimitri said helpfully. "Of course."

Sadie opened her mouth in a silent yawn.

Eli trained his Monster Magnifiers on the billionaire's son.

Michael ignored them and began to fidget, unable to decide if he should sit or stand. "Well," he said, pressing his hands together. "We appear to have royalty for dinner, Larissa. Break out the fine china!"

"You should have said something, Natalia," Larissa muttered, boring a hole in her daughter's head. "I wasn't expecting such *important* company." She looked at the food on the table, glanced down at her clothes and shuddered. "I'm so sorry about dinner, Dimitri. It's been a trying day for our family. I'm usually far more meticulous with my preparation and I sincerely hope you don't—"

But Dimitri smiled and raised his hands. "Mrs Madison, it's okay."

"Larissa. Please call me Larissa," she said, over-smiling, her body as rigid as stone.

"I don't expect to be treated differently to anyone else."

Larissa's shoulders relaxed a fraction.

"What happened today?" Dimitri asked.

"An altercation at the school," she told him. "Sadie and Eli were—"

"Danver started the fight," Sadie cut in. "Not us."

"Perhaps you would like some wine," Larissa said, refilling her own glass.

"With regret, I must decline," Dimitri replied. "My father does not permit it."

"I could use some," Natalia said sourly.

"So, tell us more about your father," Michael encouraged. "If you don't mind."

"What would you like to know?"

Before Dimitri could say another word, Sadie sat forward and popped a blood-encrusted fingernail from her mouth. "Alexsy Rubinov is one of the most important and celebrated men in the Shadow Valley. Born in San Lundkvistburg, in the heart of the Winter Continent, on seventh of April, eighteen fifty-one to Nickolai and Irina Rubinov—a poor family—and joined by a sister, Svetlana, three years later. He worked as a deckhand from the age of five, alongside his father, until he turned eighteen. Even at a young age, Alexsy had a keen mind and began trading goods and contraband on a small scale while he sailed the world. His unlawful endeavours were discovered by the Winter Continent Border Authority and, instead of him disappearing into a frozen gulag, the government harnessed his talents for global import and export negotiations. After years of success—including National Honours—he set up his own business, opening offices in every major port. Alexsy met and married Helene Voronin in eighteen eighty, who later bore him three sons: Dimitri, Branislav, and Erik. During his adventures, Alexsy Rubinov fell in love with the West, in particular Fort Campion and the Shadow Valley, and commissioned the Palace of Light to be built overlooking the town of Iron Bridge and the River Myr. Constructed between eighteen eighty-five and eighteen ninety-one, the grand palace is a masterpiece of neo-classical architecture expressed in sandstone, mortar, and stucco. The Palace of Light is fronted by one hundred and twenty-four panes of intricate stained glass—each depicting a historic scene from the Winter Continent's vast history—illuminated by brass oil lanterns that burn day and night."

Five pairs of eyes stared at Sadie.

"Sorry," she said, a forkful inches from her mouth. "That's all I know about Alexsy Rubinov. I'm sure Dimitri can tell you the rest."

Dimitri's mouth opened and closed like a goldfish. "I think that covers it."

Michael sipped his wine. "Where did you learn that, Sadie?"

"He's listed in one of your encyclopaedias," she mumbled, her mouth full of food.

"And you just ... *remembered* all of it?"

She stopped chewing. Danver returned to her mind. The music, the fight, the blood. Overflowing brains. She placed her cutlery down gently. "Yes, Father," she said. "He's an interesting man. I guess it just ... stuck."

"What about all the parties?" Larissa asked, moving the attention back to Dimitri. "I hear you've entertained the rich and the famous."

"Yes," Dimitri replied. "Father has many friends—and many more clients—so we are frequented by thousands of important faces. Perhaps you would like to come to the palace sometime. The Winter Festival is only a week away. I'll ask Father. I'm sure I can get you an invitation."

Larissa nearly dropped her wine.

"Too kind, too kind," Michael replied. "But we shan't hold our breath. I'm sure your father is a busy man and invitations to the Winter Festival are like gold dust."

Larissa kicked Michael under the table.

"I'll let you know," Dimitri said, jabbing his knife into his food. "This turkey is quite excellent."

"Thank you," Larissa blushed. "I believe it's chicken."

"Oh."

"I'd better check on pudding ... I mean, dessert."

Sadie sat quietly through the rest of the meal, thinking about Danver. Her mind wandered back to the music room and the schoolyard. She pictured Cale Boswick lying in the snow, blood jetting from his nose, an ugly wound open down the side of his face.

Danver's hands were covered in Cale's blood. His breath vented into the cold air. His eyes flicked erratically as he whispered ghostly words in some strange tongue. And through it all, the music played. It brought new images, spliced them into her memory, mixed with the blood and snow.

Snapshots from her dream weaved their way in too. Strange beasts and shadowy characters lurked at the edges of her sight. They watched with burning eyes as Danver threw his fists into Cale's helpless body. But as she watched, and the music played, Danver became faint. The monsters inched in and blocked her vision. And then, she lost him.

With dinner done, Sadie scampered back to her bedroom and shut the door.

Dropping onto the window seat, she stared at Danver's house. The lights were on in the dining room. His bedroom cloaked in shadows. The long, black, important-looking automobile had gone, leaving nothing but a dark rectangle in the snow.

Sadie shivered. Something was missing, stripped from her, stolen. The most unusual feeling. What had she seen in her daydream? Had monsters truly come to take Danver away? She looked at the spot where the automobile had parked.

Something inside her broke. Tears flooded her eyes. She slumped against the wall, pulled her knees under her chin and rested her head against the frosted glass.

Was this what it felt like to forget?

Downstairs, the FarSpeaker whirred and buzzed.

Sadie jolted upright.

The device reverberated through the walls of the house.

The muffled sound of her father taking the call rose from his study below.

She dropped to her knees and crawled into the middle of the room. Pulling at the carpet, she prized open a hidden section and removed the boards. In the secret cavity, she hid old diaries, a box of trinkets, her bunny Fergus (a toy she was too old to admit to keeping, but too young to throw away), an ornate switchblade, and other treasures. Pushing her most precious objects aside, Sadie lowered her head into the dark.

"Blood. Yes. Everywhere," she heard him say in a grown-up, serious voice—not the usual sing-song timbre of his fanciful tales and bedtime stories. "I didn't see what happened. I got her out of there as soon as I could … I spoke to Cale's father this afternoon … Shocked and angry … Yes … I understand … No. Nothing … Very well. I'm sure you know what's best … Goodbye for now."

Sadie rolled onto her back. She replayed her father's words. Tried to fill the gaps. Who was on the FarSpeaker? Danver's parents—Arnold and Fisher? It *had* to be.

Quickly, she returned the floorboards and smoothed the carpet down at the edges.

She ran the events of the day over in her head.

Breakfast, Cale pulling her hair, hiding beneath the piano in the music room, the story of Grandfather William, the Narrowers and the Gathering—and talk of the Gods.

Minister Craven.

The Eighth Day Assembly.

The Ryndai.

They were always watching Danver's house, watching any family who wore the Broken Moon, patrolling day and night with their strange lanterns and curved blades.

Had they heard them talking beneath the piano?

Had they come and taken Danver?

A knock at the door.

"Sadie. Are you okay?"

She sat up and nodded briskly, then shook her head.

Michael shuffled into the room and helped her to the

window seat. He leant forward and looped her impossible hair behind one ear. "Sadie," he said in his best storytelling voice. The melody from her performance followed her name. "I have news of your friend."

"What happened?"

Michael swallowed. "He's gone away. To Hurtmore House. Not for long. Just … for now. Just until—"

"Hurtmore House," Sadie exploded, and Michael nodded. "But that's where they put the madmen and lunatics. That's where all the monstrous psychotics, and schizophrenics, and criminally insane villains come from in your stories, Father."

Michael massaged his palms. "Those are just bedtime stories. But Hurtmore House is a real place, where real children with real illnesses go to get better. A good place. A safe place." He shook his head disbelievingly. "Criminally insane, eh? Goodness gracious!"

"Danver isn't mentally ill," she said. "Just scared of Cale Boswick. Like I used to be."

Michael paused. "You're not scared of him anymore?"

"No. Not since—" She turned to the window.

"Since Grandfather William?"

She nodded.

Michael sighed. "I wish I'd never told you that silly story. I suppose you blame yourself for what happened."

"Should I?"

"No."

Her head fell into her hands.

"If you have to blame someone then you should blame me for telling you such a ridiculous tale," Michael said. "You've never believed any of my stories before, Sadie. They're just fantasy. Nonsenses and faerie-tales. Trivialities to ease you into sleep."

"I believe *all* your stories," she told him. "There's a thread of truth in every single one. I can … *feel* it." Sadie shook her head. "But the one about the Narrowers is completely real, Father. Every last word. The Vents, the Gathering, Grandfather William.

It's all true. I *know* it is."

Michael stared at her.

"Who did the automobile belong to?" she asked. "The one outside Danver's house."

Michael twisted his head and glanced at the space where the automobile had been. "Doktor Merrick," he said, stroking his stubble as the melody returned to his lips.

"A doktor?" Sadie said. "What kind of … Oh. I see. Hurtmore House."

He brushed Sadie's tears aside. "It's late. Bedtime. You need sleep. We all do."

Reluctantly, Sadie lurched across the room and slipped into bed. She pulled the bedclothes over her head and screwed up her eyes as tight as they would go.

Anger surged through her.

She wanted to run down the road, kick down Danver's door and discover if he truly had gone.

Screams clogged her throat.

She wanted to find the long, black, important-looking automobile and burst its tyres with her switchblade. She wanted to push it into the River Myr and hold Doktor Merrick under the water with his arms and legs flailing helplessly until his body expired.

Sadie took a deep breath. Where had all these brutal emotions come from? She'd never felt anything like it before. They were powerful and twisted, wriggling like snakes through her belly, coiling up her spine, seeping their venom into her brain.

Hurtmore House. The words floated, disembodied, in her mind.

What would they do to poor Danver in that horrible place?

Her mind ran riot.

Tears soaked her pillow.

Shadows stretched around the room. Sadie couldn't sleep. She wrapped herself in a ball beneath the bedclothes. A bitter chill nibbled her flesh.

My best friend—my only friend—gone. Driven away down the Shadow Valley by an evil doktor, in his evil automobile, to his evil hospital, where he'll do evil things.

"Danver," she whispered. "Gone."

Uttering the words aloud made them seem more real, more heartbreaking.

She felt naked and alone.

A prisoner in the dark.

She thought of herself. A terrible, selfish thought. An emotion so alien that it snapped right to her bones. She wriggled beneath the bedclothes, trying to rid herself of it, but it proved a futile game.

What was she going to do without Danver?

Her mind turned to the winter term. She'd have to face Cale Boswick single-handed. Would he be out for revenge? Or would he stay away? Whatever happened, she'd be completely alone. No one to play with and no one to bully her. She couldn't decide which was worse. She'd have to stand alone in the schoolyard and wait for the next class to begin, for term to end, for Eoster to pass, for summer to rise and wither and then—

She'd wished away half a year in half a minute.

There was something else at work. Something bigger than the story of Grandfather William, and Danver's rage, and the music. Something strange was happening in her miraculous mind. Odd places and nameless faces accompanied the music again. Images from her dreams flickered in her mind, torturous and disturbing. Sadie grabbed the bedclothes, pulled them tight and formed a cocoon around her quivering body.

She wanted to cry, then felt stupid.

I need to get Danver back. I need to get to Hurtmore House and bring him home. But I'll never manage it on my own. I can't ask Eli. He's only interested in checking for monsters and scribbling in his notebook. Natalia? Forget it. This is hopeless.

Sadie blinked.

Her eyes widened as a long, thin shadow crept across the ceiling. It moved like swaying branches, reaching towards the window.

She jerked onto her side.

Froze.

She wasn't alone.

A strange shape had formed beside the picture window. Images of Danver spun inside her head. Horrible, distressing images. The field of fire, the cages, the warriors, the witches, and the haunting voice.

Take me home. Please, take me home.

She pulled the bedclothes tighter.

I have to save him. I have to get him out of Hurtmore House. But I'm only one girl. One frightened little girl.

"But you were not frightened in the schoolyard," said a boy's voice, young and etched with a cold shiver.

Sadie's skin prickled. "No, I wasn't," she whispered, not daring to look. "I stood up to Cale Boswick. I felt different. I was different."

"I know." The voice trembled. "I was with you then. As I have always been. In the darkest corners of your mind. Waiting."

Sadie peered over the bedclothes.

He stood there now, fully formed, staring directly at her.

The light from the moon cast the side of his face with brilliant silver. His hair hung straight and dark, parted on one side, and swept over the opposite eye. As he moved in the moonlight, Sadie noticed a thin flash of white hair—a dozen or so strands—all clumped together in his swaying fringe. Under a long dark coat, emblazoned with copper zips and buttons, he wore black from root to leaf, save for a knitted crimson scarf that flowed round his neck like a river of blood.

Cautiously, he moved forward and sat on the bed. His eyes bored into hers. They were large, grey-blue in colour, surrounded by dark rings, aching, tired. He held out a pale, cold hand and touched hers. His fingers, like his arms and legs, were elongated, as though stretched on a rack and tinted the colour of ash.

"Who are you?" she asked.

"I am part of you."

"Which part?"

"I thought you might be able to tell me."

Sadie shook her head.

"I guess we will find out together."

THE BOY IN THE CRIMSON SCARF

Lorntide excitement had been building ever since the first snowflakes had fallen on Iron Bridge. Sadie and Danver had planned to fill their days with adventure and enjoy the time away from Cale Boswick and his worshippers.

But now everything had changed.

Danver had gone.

And this strange boy had arrived.

Sadie watched him approach the window and placed a tentative hand on the frame. A gentle wind blew through an opening at the top. His hair rustled. Its white strands sparkled. He pulled the crimson scarf over his mouth and gazed down at the Shadow Valley, tracing the stars with his wide eyes and long fingers.

"Are you okay?"

"I believe so," he replied, jerking slightly at the sudden sound of her voice.

She joined him by the window. "I do not know where you came from, but I'm glad you're here."

"I came from you."

"Yes, you said. But—"

"You needed me. I am here."

"Will you still be here in the morning?"

He sat on the window seat and nodded.

"Then you're going to need a name."

"Of course."

"I take it you don't have one already."

"I do not believe so."

She considered the boy for a moment. What was he? A ghost, a hallucination, an imaginary friend? And what sort of name could she give a person like that? Sadie had no idea. Instead, she turned to her large bookcase. With eyes closed, she spun in circles and jabbed her index finger against the spine of a random book.

"*Complex Inherited Wisdoms of the Dragon Riders,*" she read. "By Domingo Oliveria." She looked at the boy. Her eyes thinned. "How about Domingo?"

"If you like," he replied.

"Dom?"

"Sure."

"Not a chance," she told him. "But Oliveria isn't right either."

The boy shrugged.

Sadie smiled. "Hello, Oliver. I'm Sadie."

"Hello, Sadie," he replied and took her outstretched hand.

"This isn't a dream, is it?"

"I do not believe so."

"Good."

Sadie sat beside him and looked out the window. "This is Iron Bridge."

She described the coiling residential streets of Leviathan Crook, Hydra Drive, and Kraken Walk. The caves and foothills beside the River Myr. The commercial and industrial districts beyond the Glade of Remembrance in the south, and the sandstone quarry and the Palace of Light in the north.

Before long, the sun began to rise.

Oliver seemed fascinated by it.

"The world is an amazing place. You simply won't believe it," Sadie told him.

Oliver took her hand. His touch tender, yet cold as ice.

"What shall we do first?" she asked eagerly.

Oliver fiddled with his scarf. "I thought I was here for a purpose. To find somebody."

"My friend. Yes. Danver."

"Who is Danver?"

"Danver was, I mean, Danver is my best friend. Like you, but you know ... real."

Oliver's eyes widened. "Am I not real?"

"I'm not sure what you are."

Oliver blinked. He stroked the scarf and swallowed hard, letting out a deep, calming breath.

Sadie wrapped the silver bedclothes around her shoulders and ambled across the bedroom to a scuffed box at the end of the bed. "This is my dressing-up trunk. I've had it for years. It used to have Father's old shoes and walking equipment in it, but Mother forced him to throw them out. Once upon a time it belonged to Grandfather William who won it at a circus ... so the story goes."

Made of teak and burnt umber, the trunk had large brass hinges and a chunky locking mechanism. Sadie flipped the catches and heaved the lid open. It creaked excitedly. Oliver appeared at her side and stared down into its depths.

"Danver and I have been on so many adventures," she told him, pulling clothes and props out of the trunk. "We've battled the Ogre Horde, escaped the vile clutches of the Winter Witches, launched a space mission to the moons of Kelsyn, and joined the ranks of cut-throat Ice Pirates, scavenging and plundering the Sapphire Seas!"

Oliver nodded. "So, where is Danver? Where did he go? Did he ... you know ... die?"

"He's not dead," she corrected quickly, tossing a wooden cutlass back into the trunk. "He's at Hurtmore House. A brain hospital. I played the piano, and he went a bit ... weird ... and he had a fight with Cale Boswick. There was all this blood and then Doktor Merrick carted him off like a sick animal."

"A brain hospital? Where?"

"I don't know. I have no idea. But it's a horrible, terrifying, disgusting place."

"How do you know?"

"Father told me lots of stories. And they talk about Hurtmore House at school. The teachers use it as a threat if we misbehave. They promise us that Hurtmore House will rid us of our childish ways using techniques, and theories, and equipment, and all manner of wicked devices. To be honest, I thought it was a hoax—a joke amongst the teachers to scare us straight—but learning that Hurtmore House is real, and my best friend Danver is there, makes me cold inside. I have to find him. I have to get him back."

Oliver looked terrified. "You *want* to go there?"

"I *have* to," she told him. "Danver needs me."

Oliver pulled the crimson scarf up so high only his eyes peeked over the top.

Sadie giggled. "You look like a highway man from one of my grimoires." She paused for a moment. "Or a Ryndai."

"What is a Ryndai?"

"The guardians of the Eighth Day Assembly."

"What is that?"

She grabbed her cardigan. Her eyes sparkled. "It's probably easier if I show you."

✷ ☽ ☷ ⚰ ♨

Sadie idled by the front door, zipping and buttoning her knee-length amaranthine leather coat. Fastening the top clip, she pulled her hair out with both hands and let it fall down her back. She grabbed her canvas shoulder bag, threw it nonchalantly over her head and stepped outside.

On the porch, Oliver darted away from her, pointing at a strange figure hanging from a length of rope.

Sadie laughed. "It's only a jongelier," she said, prodding it playfully.

The creature twisted on the rope, clicking and clacking tunelessly to itself. The Madisons' jongelier was three foot tall, made of broken wicker, worn out jacket sleeves, old socks, and stuffed with rags and spices. Sadie had drawn a crooked smile on its face. And cold, dark eyes.

"It's an effigy of the infamous Doktor Edvard Mistery. Everyone in the Shadow Valley hangs a jongelier in winter." Her eyes narrowed. Lips curled into a dark smile. "It keeps the River Wraiths at bay."

Oliver shuddered.

"Come on," she urged, leading him through the front gate and out onto Leviathan Crook. "So, what do you think? About finding Danver?"

"I do not understand why you want to go to Hurtmore House. It sounds like a frightful place."

"But Danver is my best friend. If the situation became reversed, he'd find a way to rescue me."

Oliver nodded. He seemed to understand. "Do you love him?"

"Of course," she replied instinctively. This admission flooded her senses, making the endeavour a hundred times more painful and a thousand times more important.

"Then we shall find this hospital and bring your friend home," Oliver said, looking up into the cool, morning sky. "Whatever it takes." Three birds soared overhead, spiralling through the threadbare clouds. "You think the music invoked his reaction."

"I think so. Maybe," Sadie said quickly. "To be honest, I don't understand what happened."

"Is it normal for people to react in strange ways when they hear music?"

"Whenever I hear beautiful music, I start to daydream. I imagine I'm soaring above forests and mountains, or sat in great halls surrounded by kings, or sailing a trawler across a storm-ravaged ocean."

"Then it is completely possible the music did something to him, changed him, made him attack the other boy."

They followed Leviathan Crook to the school gates by the bank of the River Myr. The schoolyard sat empty, save for a handful of hardy leaves encrusted with ice and hoarfrost. "Do you want to see my school?"

"I can see it," he replied, pointing to the sign by the gates. "Over there."

"No, Oliver," she snorted, playfully punching his shoulder. "I mean, do you want to go inside and snoop around? There's a museum and a huge library. It seems as good a place as any to find clues to Hurtmore House."

"It appears to be closed."

"Don't worry. I know ways. It can be our first adventure, Oliver. The first of a thousand great adventures!"

Sadie didn't wait for a reply. She scaled the iron gates and dropped down onto the icy cobbles beyond. Oliver waited for her as she landed. "Show off," she sneered, jokingly. "How did you do that?"

"I was there, and I wanted to be here." Oliver shrugged. "Then I was here."

"Amazing!"

"Is it?"

"I can't teleport myself from one place to another. Nobody can. That counts as amazing, Oliver. Magic, even."

They saluted the monument to the Victorious Dead as they passed and crept up to a green wooden door behind a parade of industrial waste bins. "Janitor's entrance," she told him, winking. "There's always someone guarding the school, so we have to be careful."

"What sort of guardian? One of those ... Ryndai?"

"No," she said. "Not Ryndai."

"A minotaur, then. A hell hound. Or a multi-headed phantasm?"

Sadie laughed. "Hang on, I'll check and see what multi-headed phantasm is on lookout today." She pushed a fingertip through the door and peered inside. Dust rose to meet her. Wafts of stale tea invaded her nostrils. Through the dark she could just make out an old man in brown overalls sitting on an armchair trying to tune a wireless.

"What is it?" asked Oliver. "Is it the multi-headed—?"

"Yes," Sadie said, her voice rippling with mock terror. "It's Hobbsworth!"

Oliver froze. "Hobbsworth? I have no knowledge of such a creature."

Sadie giggled. "Don't worry. He's an old man. And dead easy to trick. He only has one head, after all."

Sneaking behind the waste bins, Sadie rocked one on its wheels.

"Push!" she urged, but Oliver's hands passed straight through the bin as if it wasn't there. Carrying on alone, Sadie shook the bin until it pitched forward.

"It's going!" she squealed. "Keep pushing, Oliver!"

Shrugging, he pretended to help.

Crashing into the snow, the bin sent glass bottles, ripped cardboard, and stinking leftovers tumbling onto the ice. Hobbsworth came trudging out. He clasped a mug of tea in one hand while rubbing his stubble with the other. He squinted, stumbling towards the fallen waste bin and reeled at the stench. He muttered to himself and took a noisy slurp of tea.

Sadie seized Oliver's hand. They took their chance and slipped through the unguarded door.

Inside, Hobbsworth's wireless fizzed and wheezed in the gloom.

They moved through a frosted glass-panel door, along a corridor, and down into the bowels of the school. Tunnels of shadows, speared with slivers of light, filled the basement. At the end they were met by a pair of double-height wooden doors. Sadie pushed gently and the doors whispered open.

An arched ceiling of white stone was held aloft by evenly

spaced columns. Between them, towering bookcases dissected the room into corridors and gangways. A labyrinth of words and knowledge.

Sadie strolled confidently, looking down each passageway.

"Do you know what you are looking for?"

"Not a clue," she replied. "The doors to the museum are way over there, at the eastern end of the library." She stopped, turned to her strange friend. "But we should start here, in the library. If Hurtmore House is real, there must be a book or reference guide or map showing us where it is."

Oliver scanned the library. "This could take a while."

"Come on," Sadie encouraged, grabbing his hand. "The librarians have a detailed codex of every book." She marched swiftly over the polished stone floor. Oliver followed her to a long wooden desk, piled high with books, date stamps and ink pads, paperwork and soiled teacups. Behind stood a high cabinet filled with scores of tiny drawers. Sadie ran her fingers along the cabinets until she arrived at the letter *H*. She filed through several drawers, inspecting each little white card dwelling within.

Hurtman Diaries, The ... Samuel B. Gonne

Hurtmora & Grace ... Prof. Alixander Metrollax

Husskrieg: Norlandic Myths and Fables ... Bronwyn Tallinn-

Yikes.

Frowning, Sadie worked her fingers through the cards again. "What is it?"

"It must be a mistake," she said, slamming the drawer shut. "Not one listing. Not one book."

"You said Hurtmore House is a mysterious place," he replied. "Perhaps—"

"Perhaps what?" Sadie spat. She took a breath. "Sorry."

"It is okay. I understand."

Sadie slumped against the codex cabinet. Her gaze roved the library, hoping a book on Hurtmore House would magically float across the room and drop in her lap. When any kind of sorcery failed to materialise, she smiled at Oliver, rolled her shoulders, and headed towards the museum.

They walked between high bookcases, around research tables dressed with reading lanterns and inkwells, and approached more double doors.

Pressing her fingers to the solid wood, Sadie could feel her hope beginning to dwindle. If a library stocked with hundreds of thousands of books had nothing on Hurtmore House, then what could the museum possibly hold?

Painted white throughout, low lamps hung over rows of cabinets, mannequins, and artefacts. Strips of red carpet snaked between displays. Sadie shivered with excitement as they approached a mannequin dressed in a desert camouflage uniform and pith helmet. "This looks identical to the uniform my grandfather wore for the painting in our dining room."

"Was your grandfather a soldier?"

"I'm not sure. After he fell from the Vents, he became an explorer and an adventurer."

"The Vents?"

"Yes, Grandfather was a Narrower. A memory collector from the beginning of time. Father told me about it. Although he later told me he'd made it up to help me sleep."

Sadie sauntered down one of the aisles, recounting her father's bedtime story. Oliver listened intently as she spun the tale. "So," she concluded. "He found a way to renounce his heritage and his power. He left the Narrowers and the Gathering, transcended the spirit world and took human form!"

"How?" Oliver asked. "How did your grandfather become human?"

"I asked my father the selfsame question, and do you know what he said?"

"No. I do not."

"He had ... *help*," Sadie replied, shrugging. "Help? What kind of person can help one of the Narrowers transcend the Vents and take human form?"

"Again, I do not know."

"It was rhetorical," Sadie mumbled, feeling the magnitude of the story was somewhat lost on Oliver.

"I imagine it would take a creature of great power to achieve such a feat," Oliver said. "A senior Narrower, a titan, or some sort of God."

Sadie bit her lip.

Perhaps he was right.

"Come on, you have to see this." She dragged him over to a large celestial globe. "It's a map of the heavens," she told him. "Professors from San Cristophe studied the skies and plotted all the stars and planets and their distances from the Earth. Well, the ones they can see anyway." She spun the globe around. "Amazing, isn't it? Makes you consider how tiny and insignificant we all are. Come on, let me show you—"

"No," he said. "I do not think these are stars."

"Of course they are. Scientists have done thousands of experiments. I've read all about it. They're finding more every day. What else could they be?"

Oliver paused, his large eyes transfixed on the globe.

Sadie hooked her arm through his and led him to a bookcase built into one corner of the museum. Before them were row upon row of large tomes. Their spines adorned with metalwork and intricate inlays. Titles written in strange, foreign tongues.

"Father told me all the books in the museum are either priceless, or banned, or sealed by magic, and filled with devilish mysteries from the beginning of time!"

"I do not see anything on Hurtmore House."

Agreeing, she took him to another bookcase. Then another. And another. Finally, they came to a much smaller set of shelves. Pamphlets and leaflets and a handful of slim books were positioned beneath a glass display.

Sadie cast a cursory glance at the contents before switching her attention to the sacred relics and artefacts beyond the glass. Oliver, however, remained on his haunches and studied the spine of each book. There were many odd titles, most made no sense, and one had no markings at all. The spine was so dark he could easily have missed it, thinking it nothing more than a shadow. He moved his hand towards it and, as his long grey fingers brushed the dark spine, something amazing happened.

Oliver fell back.

His fingers knitted into the crimson scarf.

"What is it?"

"A book," Oliver whispered. "A strange book."

"Where?"

"Here."

Sadie sighed. "There's nothing—"

"Watch," he told her and tentatively waved his fingers against the book once more.

Golden letters materialised on the spine. They danced from end to end, spelling out a series of words. Sadie's heart skipped with wonder.

Hurtmore House: Remedy Through Torment.

She dug her fingers into the shelf and prised the book free.

The lettering disappeared the moment it fell into her hands.

"Where did the words go? Bring them back."

Before Oliver could oblige, the museum door clattered open. Hobbsworth mumbled incomprehensibly to himself as refracted lantern light bounced off a dozen glass cabinets.

"I know you is in 'ere," he said, his voice like wet sand.

The janitor paced slowly up the first aisle.

"Is that you, Cale Boswick?" he mumbled. "If I've told ya once, I've told ya a fousand times. This museum ain't your playground."

Sadie dropped the book into her bag and crawled down the aisle on the opposite wall.

Hobbsworth reached the far end of the museum. Sniffed and snorted like a bull. He spun on his heel and turned towards them.

"Let us get out of here," Oliver whispered.

"He'll hear the door," she replied. "He'll chase us. And he'll catch us. I'm convinced he knows secret passageways."

She crouched, frozen, undecided.

Her vision flicked between the door and Hobbsworth's approaching lantern.

"Come on, Sadie. He is going to see us."

"I know."

"He is coming. He is almost here!"

THE SHOP THAT
WAS NOT THERE

Hobbsworth crept by. Six feet away. Sadie could hear the squeak of his boots, the coarseness of his breath. "There's nowhere to hide, ya little monster. Hobbsworth'll find ya. You can count on it!"

She led Oliver down another aisle, moving as quickly as she dared.

Hobbsworth turned. "I hear ya, little one," he barked, dislodging some dirt from his teeth with a yellow fingernail. "Hobbsworth's gonna git ya!"

Sadie stifled a giggle at the janitor's tired patter.

Oliver, however, was a different story. He'd dropped to his knees beside a suit of polished armour and started rocking frantically. He clasped his hands together. Kneaded the palms like raw pastry. With his entire body shaking, Oliver's head bobbed around on his shoulders like a marionette.

Sadie tried to pull him to his feet but failed miserably.

Slowly, Oliver's eyes closed.

His body froze.

Tick, tack, tick-tick, tack.

Sadie spun.

The strange sound came from the other side of the room.

Grunting, Hobbsworth lumbered towards it.

Tick, tack, ticketty-tack, tack.

Light from the janitor's lantern seesawed around the room.

Tick-tack-tack-ticketty-tack-tack.

Sadie followed Hobbsworth. She swept nimbly between the display cabinets, moving in and out of the shadows. And then, peering around a carved sarcophagus, she saw it.

Moving rapidly, without the assistance of human contact, were the keys on an odd-shaped typewriter. It looked like a leather ball, cut in half, and punctured with forty or more large brass pins branded with letters, numbers, and symbols. A slim tray sat beneath, surrounded by thick brass where engraved words read:

~ Gladstone Writing Ball ~
1808, Patent Pending. Gladstone Brothers
Warrior District, Circle 5, San Cristophe, Norland

Previous visits had taught her that the Gladstone writing ball had been damaged beyond repair in the Divine Wars. But somehow, here it was, working perfectly.

The janitor shook his head as if the ancient keys moving of their own accord were some sort of illusion. He waved a hand over the typewriter to check for strings or some such trickery. He leant closer. His lumpy nose almost touched the bouncing keys when it let out a piercing—*Bing!*

Hobbsworth shot up. His arms flailed. The lantern crashed to the ground.

Sadie stifled a laugh.

The janitor steadied himself and, grabbing the writing ball with both hands, shook it wildly above his head. Failing to have any effect, he wedged his grotty fingers under the keys to stop them tick-tacking.

The machine resisted.

Hobbsworth dumped the machine down and tore a sheet of manuscript protruding from the slender mouthpiece below the writing ball. He staggered back, holding the parchment to the lamplight. Hobbsworth's face turned pale. A childlike whimper escaped from his lips. The terrified man darted for the door, throwing the manuscript behind him on the museum's red carpet.

With Hobbsworth gone, the tick-tacking eased, stopped.

Sadie crept forward to retrieve the manuscript.

She angled it into the dim light and gasped.

Leave Me Alone. Leave Me Alone. Leave Me Alone.
Leave Me Alone. Leave Me Alone. Leave Me Alone.
Leave Me Alone. Leave Me Alone. Leave Me Alone.
Leave Me Alone. Leave Me Alone. Leave Me Alone.
Leave Me Alone. Leave Me Alone. Leave Me Alone.

Oliver was still sitting motionless, his eyes shut, when Sadie returned to him. "How did you do this?" she asked, brandishing the inky page.

Slowly, Oliver opened his eyes. He peered at the words. "How did I do what?"

"You were panicking, shaking all over, and then you froze." She looked across the room at the writing ball. "And then it started typing."

"You are describing magic," Oliver insisted. "I cannot do magic."

Sadie held the manuscript at eye level. "This proves otherwise."

Oliver turned away.

"I don't know how and, by the looks of things, neither do you, but you *did* magic." She folded the paper carefully and concealed it inside one of her many zipped pockets. "And then there's this," she added, retrieving the black book on Hurtmore House from her bag.

It had an odd feel, like chalk or ash. Any trace of the magical lettering had utterly vanished. Steadily, she moved it towards Oliver. At first nothing happened but, as she got closer, the golden words exploded down the spine and across the cover. The edges of the pages glowed blood-red. "So," she said, raising an eyebrow. "Explain this?"

Oliver fidgeted. "I cannot."

Sadie gathered up the book and returned it to her shoulder bag. "Hobbsworth is gone for now, but he will return."

"Do you know a way out?"

Sadie nodded and crept towards the museum door. She could hear the janitor ranting and raving in the dark far ahead, his boots squeaking on the linoleum. "We'll circle around and climb out through the music room windows."

Oliver followed her through the labyrinth of corridors. Once inside the music room, Sadie positioned a chair by the wall and tried to reach the windows to the schoolyard. "I'm not tall enough. Here, help me move the piano."

The piano proved harder to move than she had imagined. Sadie put her entire weight behind it, wedged her shoulder beneath the keyboard and pushed from her knees. Once she got some momentum, the instrument glided slowly, wheels groaning.

Oliver skittered around the edge of the piano, pretending to be of some use.

With the piano butted up against the wall, Sadie climbed on top and yanked the window open. A mini avalanche of snow and ice tumbled into her face.

Behind them, someone choked, spat.

The batwing doors flapped open and a nervous figure emerged.

"Ah, there you is!" groaned Hobbsworth through the gloom. He barrelled across the music room, tripped over some chairs and went careering into several empty cello cases.

"Quick!" Sadie yelled, grabbing Oliver's hand, and hauling him onto the piano.

They squirmed through the narrow window and slid like penguins onto the icy schoolyard beyond. Sadie turned and kicked the window as Hobbsworth's face appeared at the glass.

He caught her boot in one hand.

Sadie wriggled on the snow, thrashing wildly, trying to shake him loose.

"I see ya, Sadie Madison!" Hobbsworth grunted. "I saw what you did back there, ya wretched little witch! Your hocus-pocus and childish magics won't fool me next time. Mark my words!"

With his face squashed against the shallow windowpane, Hobbsworth swung his other arm towards her leg. His nicotine-stained fingernails scratched against her boots. She kicked again and caught the janitor's knuckles. He howled in pain as a ribbon of flesh tore loose and stained the snow red.

Sadie pulled her leg free and scuttled away. "I'm sorry," she said, staring at his bloody knuckles. "I'm so very sorry. I didn't mean to hurt you."

Hobbsworth stopped struggling and caught his breath. His unblinking eyes locked on her. "I see ya, Sadie Madison," he whispered again, cradling his wounded hand. "I know what you is. What you is inside. Dark and ugly and full o'maggots!"

"Lies and falsehoods," she protested. "What a horrible thing to say!"

"We'll see. I'll be going straight to ya father with this," Hobbsworth sneered, biting his bottom lip. "Then we'll see who's right."

Hobbsworth disappeared into the shadows.

The window swung shut with an icy crunch.

"We should get out of here," she told Oliver as the pair scrambled to their feet. "We can hide in Iron Bridge. Hobbsworth won't find us there. I know places."

✷☺▦☆血

A frenetic mix of activity, noise and aromas spilled from the traders and merchants across Iron Bridge Plaza. Sadie and Oliver dived into the sprawling marketplace, sidestepped frostbitten sellers in rough-spun aprons and well-to-do shoppers in top hats and dark winter dresses. Oliver's eyes bulged at the sights and sounds, frantically trying to take everything in.

But his attention was drawn to an obsidian obelisk that towered above.

"What in creation—?"

"That's the Steam Totem," Sadie told him. "Famed through the Shadow Valley and beyond."

"Has it got ... faces?"

"Yes, five of them. The Witch, the Angel, the Warrior, the Oracle, and the Companion. Father says there's a complex series of cogs and mind-boggling engineering that make the faces rotate, signalling the minute, hour, day, month, and year on that large copper dial in the flagstones."

Above them, the five faces of the Steam Totem tooted melodically, erupting with streams of hot vapour. Oliver dived behind Sadie for cover.

"It's ten o'clock," she told him. "The Steam Totem always signals the hour. You should see it on New Year's Eve when the steam is replaced by fire!"

"Are we safe here?"

"Iron Bridge? Of course."

She nodded towards a man and woman dressed in dark blue uniforms. Silver emblems adorned their chests. "Those are the wardens. They keep us safe against thieves and murderers and scoundrels and undesirables."

"And who's that?" Oliver said, his eyes meeting those of a woman standing in the shadow of the Steam Totem.

Quickly, Sadie spun away. She led them out of the plaza and up the highstreet. "She's Ryndai," Sadie whispered after a time. "Don't stare at her."

"Why not?"

"They're the ones I was telling you about. The guardians of the Eighth Day Assembly." Images of Danver toppled into her mind. "They keep an eye on anyone who believes in God, the Gods, any Gods. Big, small, vicious, harmonious, human, crocodile, wolf, turtle. You name it." She shook her head irritably as Oliver jogged to keep pace. "There are nine stationed in Iron Bridge, overseen by the one known as Storm—a ferocious-looking woman who has command over the entire Shadow Valley. Father says she carries poison arrows and fights with no concern for her own personal safety. But they're *all* strange, odd and unsettling. They don't belong here."

Sadie ushered Oliver behind a table selling spiced cakes and savoury loaves. Across the street, the eyes of another Ryndai found them. She stood in a passageway between two buildings, trampling propaganda posters into the ground. She wrinkled her nose beneath her shemagh and disappeared into a thick cloud of steam, her black silks rippling behind.

Sadie scanned the highstreet for additional threats. Her attention came to an abrupt halt on a small shop, no more than eight feet wide. The door alone took up almost half the frontage. A slim window displayed a cramped suit of armour, a selection of plates, cups and saucers, tired flags, bunting, and a host of other clutter.

"What is it?" Oliver asked. "More Ryndai?"

Sadie rubbed her forehead. "This shop," she said, inching towards it. "It's new. Yet ... old."

"That is illogical."

Sadie sighed. "Look at it. It's old and tired and looks like it has been here forever." Oliver agreed. "But it's never been here before. Never. I would know." She looked at the worn, ice-encrusted sign above the door.

Doktor Puttock's Apothecary of the Bizarre.

Mysteries of the Myr—part shop, part museum—stood to the right. *Margery Fitznell*—milliner to the valiant and the wise—to the left. Somehow, *Doktor Puttock's Apothecary of the Bizarre* had squeezed itself between these two buildings.

Sadie bit her lip, examined the brickwork, guttering and roof tiles. Nothing looked forced or out of place. It was—implausibly—perfect.

"How can something that has never been, suddenly—?" Oliver asked.

Sadie raised an eyebrow.

He looked down at himself and fussed his scarf.

"It's a junk shop," she told herself, now at the window, fingers spread against the glass. Cold, solid, *real*. "Let's take a look."

"Are you sure?" Oliver asked. "Looks ... creepy."

"It's a junk shop," she said again, heading for the door. "Mother loves these. We've spent countless hours trawling through places like this. There'll be lots of weird stuff. And dust. But sometimes"—she smiled playfully at her anxious companion—"there'll be treasure!"

The door swung open.

A bell chimed happily.

It felt even smaller inside. The cabinets on either wall bulged with curios, teacups and teapots, plates, vases, pressed flowers, painted eggshells, porcelain figures, babylon candles, miniatures, silver-plated cutlery, a brace of alethiometers, stuffed creatures in glass boxes, cauldrons of all sizes, mirrors, silver talers, costume jewellery, second-hand clothes, mounted insects, chess pieces chiselled from bone, lamps, swords and rifles, monstrances and masks and helmets, and a battered wooden trunk with dozens of feet.

It smelt of printers' ink and stewed tea.

A figure loomed at the back, silhouetted against curtains suspended between two large glass-fronted cabinets where objects of all shapes and sizes glimmered in the faint light—jars, bottles, vials, and lockboxes—labelled and forbidden.

"Dark in here, isn't it?" Sadie called down the shop.

"You think? I rather like it," came a woman's voice, young and confident.

"Are you Doktor ... *Puttock*?"

The woman giggled.

"What's so funny?"

"There is no Doktor Puttock. I made it up. Has a nice ring

to it. Better than *Rhiannon's Apothecary of the Bizarre*, don't you think?"

"Both sound fine to me," Sadie said, approaching the woman. "Rhiannon? Is that your name?"

"Indeed," the woman said leaning over the counter. Matted blonde hair swung out from behind her ears. "And *you* ... are Sadie Madison."

☿ ☽ 🗒 🜍 🏛

"Cup of tea?" Rhiannon asked, stretching to full height. Not waiting for an answer, she disappeared through the velvet curtain.

"She knows who you are?" Oliver said. "I do not understand."

"Snap."

"We should leave," he decided. "Immediately."

"Don't be hasty. The owner of a magically appearing shop could know lots of things. Like, where Hurtmore House is for a start."

"Seems impossibly convenient to me."

Sadie sank her fingers into her shoulder bag and brushed the chalky cover of the strange book. "Or a huge stroke of luck."

Oliver shook his head impatiently. "Where has she gone?"

"To make tea."

Rhiannon returned holding a tray. She slid it onto the counter. Several biscuit tins toppled onto the floor. Rhiannon theatrically poured tea into three cups. "This is a blend of green tea, lemongrass, seaweed, and coconut. Sounds horrible, right? Wrong! It's amazing. Try some. Both of you."

She pushed the cups forward.

"The other is for your friend," Rhiannon explained.

"His name is Oliver," Sadie replied before she'd realised what had happened.

"Hello, Oliver."

Sadie froze. "Can you ... see him?"

"Not yet," Rhiannon said, sipping her tea. "But everything becomes clear with time."

"Like this shop."

Rhiannon wiggled her nose. "Quite so, Sadie Madison. Things come and go all the time. More often than you think. People don't pay them any mind, too wrapped up in their own business."

Sadie took a cup and sniffed it suspiciously.

"Talking of which," Rhiannon added. "What business brings you to my mysterious little shop?"

"We are escaping the guardian known as Hobbsworth," Oliver said.

"We're looking for Hurtmore House. My friend Danver's there. I need to rescue him."

Rhiannon moved into a sliver of lamplight. She had a thin, sharp face and eyes of shimmering ocean blue. Her matted silver-blonde hair—entwined with beads, wooden blocks, and lifeless gems—swung playfully as she moved. But it was her temples that focused Sadie's attention. They were horribly scarred, like someone had stubbed cigars out on the skin.

"What happened to your friend?" Rhiannon asked.

Sadie told her about Danver, and the piano, and the fight in the snow. Rhiannon listened carefully, munching loudly on a ginger biscuit and nodding.

"You see," Sadie pressed. "He's not mad. He doesn't deserve to be in some horrid place."

Rhiannon finished her biscuit, considering Sadie's story. "I'm sorry," she replied, "but it sounds as though he's in the perfect place. He is safe. Right now, safe is good. Yes?"

"Right now? Safe?" Sadie exclaimed. "Hurtmore House isn't safe."

"Of course it is. Whatever makes you think otherwise?"

"Stories. Terrible stories."

"From your father, I'll bet."

"How do you—?"

"Trust me, Sadie. Hurtmore House is the safest place for Danver. It would be far more dangerous for him to stay here with you, do you not agree?"

"I'd never hurt Danver. He's my best friend."

"Glory in the Vents!" she whispered. "Your father hasn't told you, has he?"

Sadie offered a puzzled look.

Rhiannon moved closer. Ropes of dreadlocked hair fell across her face. The beads and gems rattled like a jongelier. Her eyes shone in the darkness.

"The child that wields untold power and dominion will be the firstborn, of the firstborn, fallen from the highest."

The words danced off her tongue like rising steam, searching, lingering.

"Have you heard those words before?"

Sadie shook her head. The words sluiced inside her brain, their meaning out of reach. She slid her hand into Oliver's.

"Is it something to do with ... the Narrowers?"

"Rhiannon smiled, a finger raised. "So, you're not completely in the dark. Your father has told you something. It's a start, I suppose."

"You're scaring me. What's going on? And how do you know my father?"

"You're a child of the Foretelling. You're not *the* child. Well, not definitely, anyway. There are others to consider."

"The Foretelling?"

"Well, it's a sort of ... *prophecy*," she whispered, "but we don't like to use that word. Has so many confusing connotations, not to mention what the Eighth Day Assembly would make of it."

"I don't understand."

Rhiannon sighed sympathetically. "No one does. Not really. That's the trouble with ancient words written down millennia ago. It's all just hopes and beliefs. Possibilities. Nothing definite. Nothing set in stone. Not yet." She took a bite of a second biscuit. "But you should know you are *one* of *many* possibilities."

"In a prophecy where I will *wield untold power and dominion*?" Sadie looked at Oliver. "That cannot be true. I'm just a girl from the Shadow Valley."

"But we all grow up to become something," Rhiannon said expansively. "That's why Danver is safer at Hurtmore House. For the time being. Safe from those who might use him to get to you."

"Who is this woman?" Oliver said. "What is she talking about?"

"You're the firstborn, of the firstborn, fallen from the highest. Your Grandfather, William, was once a Narrower. He fell to Earth and had a child. The firstborn. Your father, Michael Madison. And then Michael had you. Sadie Madison, the firstborn, of the firstborn."

"How do you know all this?"

Rhiannon smiled.

Ginger biscuit crumbs fell to the floor.

"Because I was sent to kill you."

THE WOMAN
IN BLACK

Artefacts blurred as Sadie sprinted through the shop. She clattered into the front door. Fingers pressed to the glass. Oliver appeared on the other side, beckoning her into the snow-lined street. Sadie rattled the cold handle, but the door wouldn't budge.

She spun. The handle pressed into her back.

Rhiannon breezed towards her, skirts blooming.

In the light from the street, Rhiannon seemed older than the story her face told, as though wearing away at the seams. The woman wore thick black cotton ankle-length skirts edged with tassels and a flowing blouse whose sleeves, embroidered with shimmering dragonflies, were rolled to the elbow. "You silly thing," she said, smiling at Sadie. "You should've let me finish."

"Get away," Sadie warned.

Oliver appeared and took her hand.

"I'm not going to hurt you," Rhiannon said. "Not anymore."

Sadie travelled back through every year of her young life. To the hospital and the moment of her birth. To the night her parents brought her home. To her first images of the Madison house and her eaved bedroom.

The words of the Foretelling echoed through her.

"I'm not the first," Sadie whispered. "I'm not the firstborn, of the firstborn."

"Yes," Rhiannon said. "Yes, you are."

"Natalia is. My sister. Natalia is the firstborn."

"I'm afraid not, Sadie."

"But she's my older sister. She must be!"

Rhiannon's hands sank into her pockets. "For all intents and purposes, she *is* your sister, Sadie. She'll always be your sister. Your big sister. But she is not your blood."

"Liar!" Sadie cried. She rattled the door handle again. "That's a horrible, cruel lie."

"What reason would I have to lie? You are the firstborn, of the firstborn."

Relinquishing the handle, Sadie crumpled into a ball on the dusty carpet. "Stop. Just stop. Danver. Hurtmore House. The Foretelling. Natalia. It's … too much."

Rhiannon sat cross-legged in front of Sadie. "I know a lot of things. Some useful, some not so much. I know about bric-a-brac, trinkets, bibelots, and objets d'art. I know about tea and biscuits. I know about the history of all life." Rhiannon paused for a moment. "And I know *you* cannot forget a single thing."

Sadie stared at her.

"To be honest," Rhiannon continued, "I cannot understand how that's possible. I believe it *is* possible, but I don't know *how* it works, how *you* work. You probably remember far more than me and you've been alive for a fraction of the time."

"How do you know?" Sadie said. "No one knows except … Danver."

"It's part of the Foretelling."

This strange ability she had lived with every day was no longer a private, personal thing. It had been stripped from her, thrown into some ancient riddle, into the Foretelling. She pictured mysterious scribes and sorcerers writing prophetic words about her on weary manuscripts with curled corners, thousands and thousands of years ago in the towers of some dank, stone fortress on the other side of the world.

"Fine," Sadie said, pushing herself up against the door and straightening her jacket. "Tell me about the Foretelling."

Rhiannon fixed her with a hard stare. "Your father should

have told you."

"He told me about Grandfather William. About his fall from the Vents. The Narrowers and the Gathering, too."

Rhiannon's eyes glistened. "The Foretelling is the oldest story in the universe, Sadie. It all started with the Vents, a place to put the forgotten thoughts and memories of every living thing. The Narrowers knew, even then, that a child would be born whose thoughts and memories could *not* be taken."

"Me?"

"Perhaps," Rhiannon replied. "As I said, there are others to consider. The Foretelling talks of this child bringing apocalyptic destruction and utter desolation to the world. To the entire universe as we know it. This child's mind will connect with the Vents, accessing everything, every Vent, every thought and memory ever forgotten." Rhiannon turned her hands nervously. "This child will know everything that has ever happened. Have access to every happiness, every desire, every evil deed, and every secret ever told."

"Everything?"

"Everything."

Rhiannon's words were cold and edged with fear.

"What am I supposed to do?" Sadie asked.

Rhiannon rubbed her forehead. Her fingers skimmed the edges of her circular scars. "There are three paths open to the child of the Foretelling. The first is the path of the Narrowers. Their plan was to destroy the child, as I was employed to do thirteen years ago."

"But you didn't. Why?"

"Things ... changed," Rhiannon replied. "A deal was struck. You were given thirteen years. I do not know the details." Sadie opened her mouth, her tongue loaded with more questions, but Rhiannon continued, her voice a whisper. "The second is the path of the Balance. They hope to teach the child to forget, to destroy that connection to the Vents and deny the Foretelling."

"The Balance?"

"They live amongst the Narrowers, working in secret. A resistance, a band of rebels. They must never be discovered or all they have done will be for naught."

Rhiannon tucked a cord of matted hair behind her ear.

"And the third?"

"The path of the Unknown."

"What is that?"

"*Who*, you mean," Rhiannon corrected. "Once a creature of the Vents, the Unknown was exiled billions of years ago. The Unknown would seek to harness the child's power for himself, radiating misery and destruction from this side of the universe to the other."

Oliver coiled his arms around Sadie, his head on her shoulder.

"And I'll have to choose?" she asked. "The path of the Narrowers, the Balance, or the Unknown?"

"Potentially. Eventually," Rhiannon said. "As I said, there are … others."

"Who?" Oliver asked immediately and Sadie echoed him.

"They're called the Candidates," Rhiannon went on. "I know, this is a lot for you to hear but you must. You are one of five. One of you will be the child of the Foretelling. Right now, nobody knows which it will be. Only time will tell."

"And my father knows this?" Sadie said sadly. "Why would he keep it from me?"

"He is involved," she admitted. "He struck the deal to keep you alive thirteen years ago. At what cost, I know not. But, on your thirteenth birthday, when you leave childhood behind, all will be revealed."

"But that's only a week away!"

"I know."

"But I have to find Danver."

"Leave him where he is. Where he is safe."

"No. I have to help him. Do you know where Hurtmore House is?"

Rhiannon sighed. "I cannot simply tell you. It's not that easy."

"She does not know," Oliver suggested.

"Is it hidden?"

"Yes. And for good reason. There are many ways to get there, but they change. Even if you find a way in, the way out will be a mystery. Sadie, despite all your knowledge and all the things you've read and learnt, you'll need to discover the secrets of Hurtmore House on your own."

"I was right, she has no idea where it is," Oliver said bluntly.

"Sometimes you'll find things where you least expect them," Rhiannon continued. "Everything is close, within reach. You just have to know where to look. You must learn to see things *differently* if you are to find the way."

"How do I see things differently?"

"Give it time, Sadie. The world is about to change. And you'll change, too." The lock on the shop door clicked open. "It's time you were off. I'll see you again soon. I promise."

Sadie stepped out onto the snow.

The Narrowers, the Balance, the Unknown, the Candidates—

There was too much to take in. Too much to understand. Just ... too much.

The firstborn, of the firstborn, fallen from the highest.

Michael had made a deal.

Rhiannon had let her live.

But Sadie wasn't the first.

Natalia was ... wasn't she?

Sadie's skin prickled at the thought of her—*adopted?*—sister.

In the biting cold of Iron Bridge highstreet, Sadie removed the dark book on Hurtmore House from her bag and hurried into an alleyway beside the Iron Bridge Hotel to brush the gathering snow from the golden letters.

Sadie and Oliver huddled together and turned to the first page.

A Concise History of Hurtmore House

Built upon a vast open plain, surrounded by impenetrable mountains, Hurtmore House served as the colonial residence of the Winter-Smith family. For over one hundred years, and three generations, the family inhabited the house, until one fateful day, the 4th December 1832. Hershel Winter-Smith had returned from the Divine Wars some weeks earlier. His mother, father, and sisters—Lillian and Frances—were thankful to see Hershel unharmed, yet found him to be quiet and brooding, a dark reflection of his former self. The Divine Wars had changed the young man beyond measure. As the days passed, and the winter skies drew dark, Hershel became more reclusive, locking himself within his quarters, moaning and screaming and causing all manner of disturbances. One night, three servants vanished without a trace. Those remaining called for Hershel to be brought forth and made to answer for what had happened. But the Winter-Smiths denied their request, refusing to believe their son responsible of such atrocities. The following night three more souls disappeared. The servants abandoned their positions and left the Winter-Smiths alone in the big house. Hershel came to them at night, wailing and screeching, his eyes washed with black, hands dripping with blood. With abnormal human strength, he brutally murdered his mother, his father, and his sister Lillian. But his youngest sister, Frances, survived to tell of her ordeal. Having made their way across Longridge Fell and into the mountain towns, the servants told the authorities of the events at Hurtmore House. Hershel Winter-Smith was finally arrested, tried, and hanged on the grounds of Hurtmore House after a long and bloody manhunt. His body was buried beside previous generations of Winter-Smiths, his murdered family, and servants, in the Quadrangle Gardens. To this day black roses bloom on the graves of the fallen, but no life grows on Hershel's grave. His sister Frances remained at Hurtmore House, cared for by the grieving staff for two years, until she

83

signed the property over to Doktor Robey Merrick on her thirteenth birthday. The doktor turned Hurtmore House into a Psychiatric Hospital. He updated the buildings, creating laboratories, treatment rooms, therapy centres and a vast, sprawling pleasure garden for the patients to enjoy and aid recovery. Doktor Merrick's professional interest covered many areas but focused primarily on memory loss and dementia. Above his office door, engraved on a dazzling plaque, were the words: Something Forgotten Is Never Lost. But all was not well at Hurtmore House. Despite the summer sun that shone above the plain, the house never warmed, and, at night, the windows cracked with frost, as thunder rattled the walls, and lightning struck the rooftops. A villainous storm gathered over the house, low and fierce. Reports were made, by staff and patients, of a dark presence that stalked the corridors—

"I am not sure I want to read any more of this," Oliver said as they huddled over a stinking steam drain.

"I thought it was just getting interesting. Did you see that name?"

"Which one? There were so many."

Sadie ran her finger beneath the black lettering.

Doktor Robey Merrick.

"He came the other night in a long black automobile and took Danver away."

"Says he took over Hurtmore House in eighteen thirty-four, two years after the murders."

"So?"

"Well, that is sixty-six years ago. Making the doktor more than ninety years old."

"So, he's old. What—?"

"Incredibly old ..."

"What difference does that make?"

"Seems unlikely he is still running a hospital, that is all."

Sadie snapped the book shut and pushed off from the drain.

"Come on," she said. "I've been an idiot. I know how to find Hurtmore House."

Oliver dutifully followed Sadie down the highstreet, through the sprawling market beneath the Steam Totem, across the iron bridge and up Leviathan Crook.

The Tomes' ramshackle residence was smaller than most of the houses on Leviathan Crook. It rose three floors with large, shuttered windows and a porch that wrapped around like a ribbon. Sadie nudged the broken gate open and traipsed up the uneven cobbles to the front door. She yanked the bell-rope. A series of discordant chimes rang inside.

Arnold Tomes appeared. "Yes?"

"Sorry to disturb you, Mr Tomes."

"It's okay, Sadie. What can I do for you?"

"Who is it?" rattled a woman's voice.

"It's the Madison girl," Arnold replied over his shoulder. "From number five."

Fisher Tomes appeared beside her husband. They both wore the Broken Moon on their upper arms. "What in heavens do you want, Sadie?"

"I need to find Danver," she said bluntly. "I need to get him back. Hurtmore House is a horrible place. I cannot believe you agreed to send him there."

Arnold looked confused.

"Are you okay?" Fisher said, lowering herself to Sadie's eye line.

"Tell me where Hurtmore House is. Please—Arnold, Fisher—let me and Oliver get your son back. Or better yet, let's all go and fetch him."

"Our son?"

Sadie began to shake. "Yes. Your son. Danver Tomes."

Something moved inside her. The same something she'd felt the night before. A slithering, venomous thing. Anger and rage and helplessness.

Fisher put a calming hand on Sadie's shoulder.

"We have no children, Sadie. You know that."

The words reached Sadie's ears, but they made no sense. "But ... Danver," she bleated, turning to Oliver. "They do. You do. He loved adventure books and ancient heroes, aircraft and puzzles and those hot apple and vanilla turnovers you make. He wanted to become a Zeppelin pilot and join the Air Command. He wanted to live up high in Hüntesgaard, near the clouds and the spring of the River Myr, with a wife and two children. He was going to name them Molly or Miriam or Marcos or Mim and run a sanctuary for stray and injured birds. He wanted to—"

"Sadie, stop this."

Her face tightened. "How could you forget? I could *never* forget. Not Danver. Never."

"I should fetch your father."

"No," Sadie said, the word hard and urgent. "We'll be fine."

She stepped away from the front door and stumbled down the steps. Danver's parents called to her from the porch, but she couldn't bear to look at them for one moment longer.

✳ ☻ ▦ ⚔ ⛩

Michael Madison paced in circles around the library. A cup of coffee wobbled in his hands. Sadie could sense his eyes on her the moment she came through the door. Dropping her bag, she unstrapped her boots, slipped the coat from her shoulders and hung it on a series of mythical-animal-themed coat hooks.

"I trust you've had a good morning," Michael began, trying to sound casual. "Tell me, what have you been up to?"

Sadie studied her father's face. He looked the same as always, but everything had changed. There were so many secrets locked behind those tortoiseshell glasses, those arched eyebrows and knitted brow. Sadie wasn't sure who stood before her anymore.

He'd hidden so many things from her.

Huge secrets.

Apocalyptic secrets.

Secrets destined to change everything she knew, everything she cared about.

And secrets about—Natalia.

Michael sipped his coffee. A trickle ran over his chin. "Where have you been? I don't remember you leaving. Must have been early," he said quickly, before taking a breath and asking. "Were you at the school today?"

Her heart quickened.

Hobbsworth.

"Did you go to the museum?" her father pressed.

Sadie nodded. There seemed little point denying it.

Michael dumped his mug onto a low wooden end-table and paced the room again. He rubbed his face with both hands, slipping his fingers beneath his spectacles to massage his eyes. "You shouldn't be breaking into the school, Sadie. Much less the museum! They have all manner of dangerous things in there. And the Eighth Day Assembly have it under close watch."

"I know," she mumbled. "I'm sorry, Father. It's Danver. I *need* to find him—"

"Danver?"

"I was looking for something to help me find Hurtmore House."

He stopped pacing and spun to face her. "Well—?"

"Nothing," she said. "Just Hobbsworth and—" She thought of the Gladstone Writing Ball, the words Oliver had made appear on the parchment. She glanced to her left. The boy in the crimson scarf stood beside her, worry etched on his face.

"And that's it?" Michael asked. "Nothing else happened?"

Sadie swallowed. "We went to see Arnold and Fisher," she admitted. "The Tomes."

"Yes, I know who Arnold and Fisher are," Michael said agitatedly. "And what did they have to say for themselves?"

Sadie wanted to tell him everything, but something stood in the way. Something that hadn't existed when she woke this morning. She tried to push all knowledge of the strange little

87

shop, and Rhiannon, and the Foretelling, and the black book from her mind.

"Nothing much," she lied. "They don't know where Hurtmore House is."

Michael dabbed his upper lip with a handkerchief. "Danver does not need to be saved, Sadie. Please do not worry about him. I'm sure he's safe where he is. Believe me, Danver is in no danger at all."

"How do you know?" she pried. "Have *you* been there?"

"No. Never," Michael said. "The location of Hurtmore House has always been a mystery. That's what makes it so safe. So *mysterious!*"

"How can an entire hospital be hidden?"

"I have no idea."

His gaze lifted and met hers. A smile forced its way onto his lips.

"Perhaps magic and sorcery and otherworldly wonders," he said in his bedtime story voice.

Instinctively, Sadie leant in. The same way she always did when a good story was in the offing, but Michael snapped out of it.

"You'd better run along," he told her. "And don't go thinking I've forgotten about your trespasses at the museum. And the fight with Cale Boswick. There will be repercussions for your actions, Sadie Madison. That is the way of things."

She grabbed her bag and hurried to her room. With the door firmly shut, Sadie sat beside Oliver on the bed and thumbed the corner of the dark book. They flipped through the covering pages, ignoring the rest of *A Concise History of Hurtmore House* and found a Table of Contents, split into four headings: Torment, Remedies, Case Studies, Buildings.

Sadie turned to Buildings.

Beneath the heading sat a murky monochrome pictogram. A huge mansion of dark stone, timber, and glass hunkered upon a lush lawn surrounded by finely clipped trees and bushes.

Mighty towers, five or possibly six storeys in height, rose at each corner of what Sadie decided must be the Quadrangle Gardens, the resting place of Hershel, his victims, and the other Winter-Smiths.

Several structures reached out from the Old Building like mutated arms. At the end of one sat a circular building with an enormous domed roof made of metal plates. The plates had been retracted in one area where a long tube projected into the air. Beneath, it read: *Hurtmore House, as viewed from the south, January 1883.*

Sadie turned the date over in her head. January 1883. Four years before she was born and six months before Natalia.

The book fell from Sadie's hands.

She'll always be your sister, your big sister.

But she is not your real sister.

She is not your blood.

Pushing off the bed, she turned for the door.

The black book fell open on the bed.

A cool breeze ruffled the pages until they settled on a pictogram of a group posing for a portrait in a wood-panelled office. But the people in the pictogram were changing, blurring, shifting. One minute there were five, then four, six, one, none. The words printed below the pictogram altered too, stretching and shrinking, whirring through all manner of symbols, numbers, letters, and hieroglyphs. Finally, the pictogram settled on five faces—two seated and three standing. The letters slowed and formed legible words. *Hurtmore House Medical Staff circa 1884. Standing (left - right) Counsellor Moira Vasquez, Doktor Wolfgang Deeds, Doktor Rosemary Collins. Seated (left) Doktor Robey Merrick and (right) Professor Michael Madison.*

MICHAEL   MADISON'S

THE WITCH TREE
AT SAN CRISTOPHE

The legend of the Witch Tree began more than two thousand years ago. To hear it, we must travel great distances, through time and space.

Over the River Myr we fly, leaving the safety of Iron Bridge far behind. We skim the western treetops of Darachna Forest. Crest the Carcassus Mountains. Sharp stone and rock spread beneath us for hundreds of miles. Holdfasts and crumbling castles perch on cliff tops and take root in barren vales. Beyond the mountains we fly, across the Snake Plains, towards distant Western Waters. And here, at the edge of the world, lies the mighty circular cities of San Cristophe.

And now time slips away.

Back and back and back we go.

Somewhere in the swirling sand and withering heat outside the walls of San Cristophe, stood three sisters.

Dressed in black.

Bound in iron.

The first, no older than sixteen, shielded her vivid blue eyes from the sun. The second grunted listlessly, digging her work-worn hands into her wide hips. The third raised her gnarled head towards the battlements and muttered the ancient Words of Shadow.

Now, they were not sisters in the way you and I think of them, for they were not born of the same mother.

They belonged to a wretched sisterhood.

A sisterhood of witches.

The king looked down on the three. From his sandstone tower, they looked like harmless desert beetles. Beetles he could crush beneath the heel of his boot. But they were far from harmless and, even at this distance, he did not feel safe.

"Harridans!" the king bellowed. His voice vanished into the desert. "Your time is at an end. San Cristophe is a city of peace and justice, of learning and knowledge, of truth and honesty. A city built for all time. There is no place for your magics and sorcery. Your malcontent. Your Words of Shadow!"

The old witch spat on the ground in disgust. Her spittle sizzled, smoked, spawning hundreds of black scorpions that wriggled and fought before melting into a steaming tar.

The king turned to his advisers, their faces white with fear.

The archdeacon approached and demanded the witches be banished from the city, cursed never to return. But the king silenced him with a hand and commanded they be put to death.

"Death?" said the archdeacon. "Do you seriously believe death will be the end for these women? They're witches, sire. Harridans, sorceresses, necromancers. Their power is beyond anything death can contain."

"My order stands," the king growled. "Cut them down. All of them."

The king's Golden Warriors took the witches one thousand paces south of the city and ended their mortal lives. Their bodies were burned in camphor oil, the bones covered in soil and sand and salt, and placed in a communal grave beside the Kings Road. The archdeacon gave a short benediction. No marker, cross or headstone was erected. And, after the wind had worked its magic, no trace remained at all.

An opalescent moon rose above San Cristophe that night. It turned the Snake Plains into a shifting pale blue sea. But the stars seemed diminished, as though afraid to show themselves.

The king stared across the city, towards the gate where he

had condemned the three, and said a prayer to the Night Gods.

But his prayers went unanswered.

For across the city, beyond King's Gate, one thousand paces south of the city walls, the ground stirred.

A shoot sprang from the desiccated earth. It writhed and flicked like an earthworm. Within minutes the shoot broke into two, then four, eight, and stretched towards the sky. It grew and built and spread, becoming a mighty tree with twisted branches and gnarled bark, black as night. The tree grew twenty, thirty, forty feet high, swaying gently in the cool night air.

Alerted by the cries of his advisers, the king went to the site of the black tree, accompanied by a host of Golden Warriors, clerics and men-at-arms.

"I warned you about the witches," cried the archdeacon, seeing the king's pale expression. "I warned you and now look at what has happened!"

The king turned to his Golden Warriors. "Cut it down. Immediately!"

"But sire!"

"Silence. Proceed!"

With longswords in hand, his Golden Warriors approached.

The tree shifted and moved in an unearthly way.

Fear swirled through the thin morning air.

The Golden Warriors hesitated as black branches planted themselves in the ground around the trunk. The tree groaned and creaked and wailed like an injured beast.

"Cut it down!" the king bellowed, becoming impatient.

They advanced once more, weapons raised, but the tree defended itself. Branches whipped and lashed and threw them into the sand. Again and again they attacked, rallied, attacked again, but the tree brushed them aside like buzzing pests.

The king, tired of the Golden Warriors' attempts, took his Moonblade Axe and approached the Witch Tree. To his surprise, the branches parted to let him pass. With his feet planted beside the huge, blackened trunk, the king arced his axe through the air.

Instantly, the branches seized him.

They tightened around his waist like the coils of a deadly serpent.

The king went reeling into the air, screaming and yelping.

The tree pulled him close.

The faces of the witches appeared before him in the burned bark, knotted and angry.

"Foolish man," chuckled the maid. "You are no match for us."

"Even in death, we are more powerful than you can imagine," said the mother.

The crone laughed, dry and sickly. "And now it's time you *joined* us!"

The king hung suspended above the tree. A branch around each limb. A fifth whipped forward, coiled itself around his neck, and killed him stone dead.

But that wasn't the end for the king.

His body hung limp and loose in the branches as the witches muttered and chittered gleefully inside the bark. Smoke rose from the trunk and swirled in chaotic skeins. Arrows of blue and white light bloomed across the sky. Sparks dropped to the sand like dive-bombing fireflies.

The king's body landed cruelly on the sand, twisted and broken.

The archdeacon moved to help his king, but there was nothing he could do. As he sat weeping, he could have sworn he heard his king's voice, smothered, wailing in the distance.

He turned to the tree.

And there, in the bark, sat the wretched faces of the three. But, most horrible of all, etched in the black bark of the Witch Tree was the king. His eyes shook with horror, wide and aching. He opened his mouth to scream but thirty long, wicked fingers reached over his face and dragged him deep into the roots of the tree.

Following the king's death, a sandstone tower was built

around the Witch Tree, and eventually engulfed by the expanding city. To this day it is guarded by descendants of the Golden Warriors. Its true location, an ancient mystery. But, they say, if you're able to find the Witch Tree at San Cristophe, and you possess the courage to creep close enough, you can hear the screams of the king from inside, begging for forgiveness.

PART TWO
REVELATIONS

"Struggling with a friend through shadows is better than strolling alone in the sun."

—EMBER VAN DEUX,
Evenlight Festival, Los Kralice, 1894

THE BRIGHTLY PAINTED DOOR

Natalia's room was predominantly white with accents of pink and gold festooned here and there. She adored a crisply made bed with clothes and shoes stored away neatly beneath and books colour-coded upon the shelf. It was the only room in the Madison house where all evidence of Michael's peculiar paintings and Larissa's clutter had been surgically removed.

Natalia sat at a dressing table brushing her golden hair. She hummed almost inaudibly as Sadie entered with Oliver in tow.

"Hello, Natalia," Sadie said, trying to sound normal but failing.

"Oh, hello," her sister replied. She put her hairbrush down and spun to face Sadie. "Where have you been all day? Father's been pacing. I don't like it when he paces."

Ignoring Natalia's question, Sadie fired off one of her own. "What do you remember?"

Natalia tightened. "How do you mean?"

"What's your earliest memory?"

"Why do you—?"

"Please."

Natalia paused, folding her hands. "I'm not sure if this is my first memory, but I remember you being born. I mean, I remember Mother and Father bringing you home. I remember being jealous of the amazing nursery Mother decorated for you. There was an awful storm that night. And the moon was blood-red. The river and most of Iron Bridge consumed with a strange mist. I remember fearing the noises from Darachna Forest ... barking, screaming, howling. But Father told me about the River Wraiths and how we're protected by the jongeliers. I think he was trying to get me to sleep, but that story is not meant for bedtime ... or children. Someone should tell him."

"What else?"

"A visitor came to the house. A woman. I don't remember her arriving. I must have been asleep. But I got woken by raised voices—Father and the woman—and there was a loud noise, like a door slamming and then books falling off a shelf. And then ... silence."

"You have a good memory, Natalia."

"It was a frightening night. An odd night. I guess that's why it stuck."

"Do you remember anything from before?"

Natalia flicked her hair over her shoulder. "I have memories of riding a bike, flying a kite, Atticus arriving one Lorntide, the cats in the new year, picnics, the Candlelight Parade, the Steam Totem, but I don't know if they were before or after you were born, Sadie. They're snippets, I suppose. Moments. Like pictograms."

"I remember the woman being here," Sadie said, her eyes soft and faraway. "The one Father argued with."

Natalia laughed. "Impossible. You were only a few hours old. I was almost four and I barely recall it." Natalia reached out and stroked her sister's arm. "Seriously. Are you okay? You're acting strange. Just like Father. Some weird old man came to see him. He smelt awful. What's going on?"

I can't tell her. I just can't. I don't know if I believe it myself.

"Sadie? What happened?"

"Nothing, Nat. Nothing at all," Sadie lied. "Everything is ... fine."

Evening descended. Dinner passed slowly. Michael told no jokes, played no characters, and saluted half-heartedly. The Madison family sat in relative silence feasting on pork belly boiled in Eden Rock Cider, Silverwater potatoes, creamed carrots and parsnips, broccoli, kale, and buttered peas. Afterwards, they retired to the library for parlour games and the National Broadcast.

Except Sadie.

The punishment due.

Instead, she returned to the shadows of the eaved bedroom. The faerie-lights around her window were dark and still. Muffled chatter and music seeped up from the library below.

Sadie sat at the window and set her gaze on the distant mountains. "You're out there somewhere, Danver," she spoke to the night. "Out there somewhere amongst the trees and rock. Your parents may have forgotten, but I'll find a way to save you. I promise."

She left the curtains open so the night could send her an answer before padding over to the bed and pulling the bedclothes around her chin.

Oliver perched at the end of the mattress. His eyes gleamed in the moonlight. "And I will be with you the whole way."

Sadie pulled *Hurtmore House: Remedy Through Torment* from beneath the covers. But, before she'd read more than a handful of pages, sleep took her.

✷ ☟ ▦ ⚰ ⛩

Sadie woke in a dark room. Shafts of light sliced the air. An iron-frame bed lay beneath her. Across the room sat a small wooden desk, a wardrobe with lopsided doors. Shelves held coloured-glass bottles stoppered with corks.

The air smelt full and close. A confusing, overpowering blend of aromas.

Her hands found a heavy wooden door. It led to a hallway and a vaulted communal chamber. Three men sat at a table, dunking bread in warm broth. They looked up as she entered and nodded a greeting.

A red fire roared in an enormous hearth. Flames rippled on her skin, but she couldn't feel the heat.

A fanfare of trumpets erupted.

The men looked at one another then jumped from the table and barrelled past. Sadie followed them up three flights of stairs. Pure, brilliant sunlight hit her face as she emerged on a cobbled street. Huge sandstone walls towered above, criss-crossed with lines of rippling laundry. At the top, flags cracked in the wind.

The trumpets fired again.

Here on the street, people were moving with purpose. Sadie watched for a moment. "What's happening?"

"It's the tree," a woman said, rushing past.

"What tree?"

The woman laughed. "The Witch Tree, of course!"

"The Witch Tree?" Sadie said. "The one from Father's stories?"

"Yes, dear. The Witch Tree at San Cristophe!"

Sadie shook her head. "What about it?"

"They've found it!"

✻☽▦☆⛪

Sadie sat up. Her skin glistening. Her head pounding.

The moon floated high above the Carcassus Mountains. Oliver watched it from the window seat. "You were having a bad dream," he told her, not taking his eyes off the view.

"I think I was in San Cristophe," she said. "They were firing the trumpets for the Witch Tree. I thought it was nothing more than a bedtime story. Father hasn't told it for years."

"What were you doing there?"

"I woke up there. In my bedroom. I mean, not my real bedroom, but it felt like my own. People seemed to know me."

Oliver quietened. "Sounds like a vision."

"A vision …? Of what?"

"Of the past, the future."

"Don't be silly."

Oliver stood. "Perhaps that is what Rhiannon talked about."

"Seeing things in a different way," she said, nodding. "Could that really be what she meant?"

"I have no idea. How could anyone? It could be one of a thousand things, a million. But the ability to see the future? Well, that is definitely different."

Oliver wandered past and stared out the window to the back garden. The endless snow nestled on Darachna Forest and the towering mountains beyond. The world seemed so huge, unfathomable and endless. A chill shook Sadie's bones. "I have to get to Danver."

"Why have his parents forgotten him?"

"The Narrowers," she replied. "I thought about it during dinner. It seems like the only explanation. They must have taken away all their memories of their son."

"Why?"

"Something to do with me. Probably. Or the Foretelling. Or both. I don't know."

Oliver nodded grimly.

"I don't care what Rhiannon says, I know Danver isn't safe at Hurtmore House. We *have* to do something. We will find a way."

Below, in the back garden, something moved. Oliver's eyes followed a white creature, the size of a small dog, as it dug in the snow then bolted out of sight.

"What's that?" he asked, reaching for his scarf.

"I'm not sure," she replied. "Looks like a white fox."

She pressed her nose against the small window. Beyond, the Madison garden stretched steadily uphill. A sandstone wall rose at the back, entwined with brambles, vines, and creepers, keeping the marauding Darachna Forest at bay.

The white fox sprang into the middle of the lawn, running to and fro in the deepening snow. He jumped in the air and landed with his front paws pressed together. Heading over to the swing set, he nosed the seat which arced pleasingly on its rusty chains.

"Where did it come from?"

"I don't know. Perhaps—" But Sadie's gaze had been stripped from the fox and focused on the forest wall. "Do you see that?" she said, grabbing Oliver by the shoulder.

"The white fox? Of course. I am pretty sure it is real."

"No," she said, her voice glazed with disbelief. "The door."

"What door?"

"The door in the wall."

Oliver stared down the garden. "Yes, what about it?"

"Well, it's never been there before. Never. I'd remember if it had, and it definitely has never—*ever*—been there before."

"Like Rhiannon's shop?"

"Yes."

"And me?"

Sadie took a long breath. "Quite so."

The white fox had stopped playing and sat staring directly up at the window. His eyes sparkled. His nose twitched. Then, he spun in the snow and trotted up the garden and disappeared through the door, leaving it slightly ajar.

Sadie got dressed in record time.

"What are you doing?"

"We have to shut the door," she explained, searching beneath the bedclothes for the book on Hurtmore House.

"Why? What's out there?"

"Darachna Forest is out there. It's full of terrible things. Goofang, Glawackus, Hodag, the Cactus Cat, the Winter Witches, Axe-Handle Hound, Wendigo, Ratchet Owl, and loads of others. Father told me all about them. I've heard them too. Howling, wailing, screaming in the dead of night. The last thing we need is one or more of them coming into the garden. Or into the house!"

Oliver moved for the door. Sadie crept after him, along the corridor, round the landing, down the stairs, and into the hallway. Silently, she pulled her boots on and slid into her amaranthine coat.

The grandfather clock in the hall began to chime midnight as Sadie stuffed the strange black book into her shoulder bag.

Disturbed by the commotion, Atticus raised his head from a pile of blankets beside a withering fire. "No, boy," Sadie whispered. "You stay." The wolfhound whinnied like a horse, his ears stood to attention. "No," she said again, crouching next to him and ruffling his fur. "You stay right here and have a good long sleep. Oliver and I will be back before you know it." Atticus made soft, contented noises, then rolled over as Sadie slipped through the shadows and into the garden.

Outside, the cold snapped right to her bones. She trudged up the garden, ironing footprints in the snow, following the delicate impressions made by the white fox.

She brushed the thick brambles and creepers aside, stopping six feet from the wall.

Ahead hung a brightly painted door.

"Where did you come from?" she asked, inching forward and prodding the solid, wooden door. The paint shimmered in the moonlight, the colour subtly changing like oil in a puddle. Slowly, she wrapped her fingers around the iron handle.

Then froze.

"You should probably close the door," Oliver reminded her, his voice quick and urgent. "Goofang, Ratchet Owl, the Winter Witches ..."

Sadie stared at the handle.

"Are you okay?"

Sadie looked at her friend. "Perhaps *this* is what Rhiannon meant. And if the existence of this door is me seeing things differently, should I just close it and walk away?"

"Maybe," Oliver said, sounding more anxious than usual. "Who knows? I am confused about the whole thing. Rhiannon could have been making it all up. Ancient riddles, strange hospitals, assassination orders, this magically appearing door, her odd little shop. It is not right. Any of it." He paused for a heartbeat. "And I am including myself in this list."

Sadie stared at the handle again and, instead of closing it, pushed the door wide.

"What are you doing?" The terror in Oliver's voice tore through the night.

Sadie smiled reassuringly. "Well, this door is not a dream or a vision. This door is real. If I can see this door, and feel this door, then it's for a reason."

"Somebody built this enormous wall for a reason too. You should close the door before all the horrors of the forest come flooding through," Oliver urged, his fingers at his crimson scarf.

"Yes, Oliver. You're right. I *am* going to shut the door."

He relaxed a little. "Thank the Gods."

"But we'll be on the other side when I do."

THE FIRE
WOLVÊS

The two friends stared into the imposing forest. Beneath the vast canopy of branches and evergreen leaves, grew the charcoal bark of sandarac trees and a sea of grey shrubs with bright red leaves, edged with a bloom of sulphuric yellow that surrounded the base of each tree, like children clinging to a mother's leg.

And then Sadie noticed the noise.

A distant murmuring. Like a steam engine, throbbing away somewhere in the depths. A ghostly breeze carried the whispered words of every bird and beast. A yawning of bark and branches, bending and straining. A faint rhythm, a heartbeat far beneath the earth, at the edge of hearing.

"This is a magical place, Oliver. Don't you think?" she asked, the sounds of Darachna Forest playing together in the moonlight.

"It is definitely not what I expected," he replied. "But what do we do? Where do we go? It is just trees … everywhere!"

Sadie wasn't sure. She'd hoped to feel something or see something—the way she'd seen the door—to tell her what to do next. "The door!" she exclaimed, turning and pressing her hands against the sandstone wall. "Where's the door?"

"It is gone," Oliver moaned. "You shut the door and now it is gone!"

Sadie's heart pounded with excitement. The call to adventure and the threat of danger registered in equal measures, but she held no fear. "There's no way back," she smiled. "So, we go onwards."

"Onwards? Into the weird and terrifying forest?" Oliver sighed. "With no guide and no idea where we are going?"

"The white fox," Sadie said, mostly to herself.

Oliver carried on regardless. "Honestly, this is irresponsible."

"You can go home anytime you like," Sadie told him. "Just do that zip-zap, tele-transporting thing and you're golden."

Oliver faltered. He turned from Sadie to the wall and back again.

Was he seriously considering it?

"I cannot leave you out here on your own," he said in the end. "You will freeze to death."

He had a point. Sadie's teeth were chattering and it would definitely get colder before the morning sun appeared.

"We should keep moving. I'm far more likely to freeze if I stand here all night. If we keep the wall on our right, we'll come to the Glade of Remembrance. There's an entrance in the north wall we can use if nothing else. At least, there is on all the maps."

"The Glade of Remembrance?"

"It's an enormous graveyard, Oliver," Sadie told him, setting off through the trees. "Biggest in Norland."

They hiked through the deepening snow, leaving the Madison house behind. Sadie kept the sandstone wall within touching distance at all times. Blue-grey tendrils of smoke spouted into the night from chimneys beyond the wall, reminding her Iron Bridge was close at hand.

The wall curved to the left, away from the houses, deeper into the forest and meandered over uneven terrain. Sadie stumbled several times, using the wall and the soot-coated trees for balance. At the top of a steep mound, she fell while negotiating a black root crossing their path. The snow cushioned her fall, but her knee and chin stung from the landing.

Oliver dropped beside her. "Watch where you are going. If you get seriously hurt out here, we will be lost forever."

She shook her head to clear the pain. "Oliver. Look. There."

The white fox perched before them, his dark eyes watching through the trees.

"What's he doing?"

The fox twitched its nose and darted into the gloom.

"We should follow him."

"You are serious?" Oliver said. "Follow the white fox? Into the forest of doom? Come on, Sadie. What about sticking to the wall? What about the North Gate to the Glade? That is the plan. Let us do that."

But Sadie had already taken several steps into the forest, through the sandarac trees, towards the white fox, away from the wall. In turn, the fox scuttled deeper into the forest and turned to watch. "See," she said excitedly. "He *does* want us to follow him!"

"To what possible end?" Oliver moaned. "Where is the white fox going to take us? He is luring us into the forest. Further and further we will go, until we are utterly lost and exhausted, and then the much larger, more terrifying foxes—and goodness knows what else—will tear us to shreds and feast on our remains."

"Are you quite finished?" Sadie snapped. "The white fox has come to help us."

"You are wrong. You are mad," Oliver muttered to himself. "You are going to get us both killed."

Sadie glanced beyond him, to the safety of the wall, the perimeter of Iron Bridge.

Safety.

Home.

Things were different now. Everything she'd known and loved had been turned on its head. Once she had dreamt of studying at the University of San Cristophe, learning the piano, falling in love, and raising a family like her parents. Now the future seemed nothing more than a clouded mystery.

Did she have any kind of future at all?

Her mind replayed Rhiannon's words. The Foretelling. An

ambiguous prophecy about the end of all things. With her and the Candidates at the centre.

But most of all she thought about Danver.

And, as they turned and marched through the snow, Sadie hoped and prayed she'd find him soon.

❋ �‿ ▤ ⚔ ⛩

The sandstone wall retreated. The world had become an endless blanket of white, stabbed with sandarac trees and the splatter of red leaves. Despite Darachna Forest stretching for thousands of miles in every direction, the terrain remained unchanged. It seemed as though they were walking the same fifty yards over and over and over again.

With her strength ebbing, Sadie leant on a nearby tree. The world spun. Trees and bark and branches rushed past, blurring in and out of focus. Oliver stood beside her, his face pained and helpless.

"I told you this was a bad idea."

She wavered for a moment, then half-sat, half-collapsed.

"Where's the white fox, Oliver? Is he close?" she asked, waving a hand. "Find him. Please find him."

"He will be around somewhere," he said, but Oliver's assurances were dashed by an awful noise. Not the strange churning sound of the forest, nor the thrumming rhythm in the deep. This was a guttural moan, pained and angry, that ricocheted through the trees.

Sadie tightened.

Hairs pricked on her neck.

The horrid sound died.

A hush fell over the forest.

But it came again.

Louder this time.

Closer.

Much closer.

"What is it, Oliver?" she whispered. "Can you see it?"

No more than ten feet away, a pair of pitiless eyes materialised, glowing in the dark. Then another, and another. Sadie gripped a tree with both hands and inched herself up the bark. Before she knew it, a dozen pairs of eyes surrounded her, floating in the darkness.

"What are they?" she asked, but Oliver said nothing.

The boy in the crimson scarf was flickering and stuttering like a dying gaslamp. He looked down at himself. "What is happening to me?"

Sadie could feel the blood draining from her face, her lips and cheeks turning pale, her legs weak and promising to fail. One pair of red eyes moved closer, revealing a snout, pointed ears, thick autumnal fur, and the drooling mouth of a deadly Fire Wolf.

He moved closer. Steadily circled the tree. His back arched.

A snarl curled from his mouth.

"Oliver?"

But he did not answer.

Oliver had vanished.

Without warning, the Fire Wolf put its nose to the wind and let out a blood-curdling howl. The other wolves joined their pack leader in a moonlit call, filling the night with shrill, haunting voices.

Just stand still, Sadie. Be still and all of this will soon be over.

At first the voice was her own, and then Oliver's. A blend of the two. Sadie's heart thumped in her chest. She could feel it against her ribs. Her head reverberating to the rhythm of her lifeblood. The rhythm of the forest.

Is this it? Is this how it all ends? I'm sorry, Danver. I've failed you. Too impetuous. Far too impetuous. Teeth. So many teeth.

The Fire Wolf approached, inches from Sadie's face. He sniffed her flesh, her hair, her blood. His snout wrinkled, displaying the full arsenal of vicious incisors. His breath stank of blood and decay and a multitude of things Sadie didn't care to think about. She squirmed, forcing her head round the tree, away from the first bite. But the teeth never came.

I need you, Oliver. I need you now. Help me. Please.

Sadie risked one final glimpse and discovered the Fire Wolf sat on his haunches, staring curiously. She sensed herself rising, her back to the tree, her legs pushing her body to full height.

And then she felt his cold, frail hand.

His long, grey fingers wrapped around hers.

"I am here," Oliver whispered.

Hearing those words forced a tsunami of emotions to cascade through her. She could do anything: climb a mountain, lead an army, fly a rocket ship to the moon and back, even rescue a troubled friend. With Oliver by her side, she could do anything. Be anything. The strength to overcome it all.

Steadily, Sadie reached out.

"What are you doing?"

She touched the top of the wolf's head.

"Sadie?"

He growled initially, pushing her away, but she persisted. Sadie stroked his head and ears, the same way she did with her beloved Mischief. Letting out a playful yowl, the wolf nuzzled up to her and wrapped its tail around her legs. Sadie buried her fingers in his thick auburn fur, going face to face with the wolf, their noses touching.

The pack materialised from the darkness, padding softly around the two friends. Most of the adult wolves had the same markings as their leader—a fierce burning umber—while older creatures were brandished with tufts of black, grey, or white. A handful of cubs waited nervously, their fur a spiralling mix of them all, like living fire.

"They're no different to Mischief or Atticus," she insisted. "Obviously bigger, leaner, more dangerous, but somehow—"

Sadie put her hands on either side of the Fire Wolf's head. Their eyes met. Sadie felt a sudden rush, like being flushed down a drain.

She ran, hurtling along at great speed. Skimming the ground, driven by hunger and a nameless shadow. She could feel it behind her, keeping pace, observing, chasing. The shadow moved in an unearthly way, flowing like water, curling like smoke, edging ever nearer through the endless wood. Her nose found powerful scents. Blood, fear, death. Her eyes were sharp. A thousand things darted and scuttled away as she ran. She dodged through trees, hurdled discarded logs, vaulted shards from the mountains, fallen and shattered. With the pack around her, they waded through shallow streams and tore up the earth as they fled into the wilds. The shadow following them at every turn.

Her hands swung to her sides. "He's frightened."

"He *told* you?"

"No," she answered. "I saw ... something. It's out there. In the forest. Something the wolves are afraid of. Something ... evil. Something ancient. A swarm of darkness." Sadie stood, searching through the gloom. "We should keep moving."

Oliver worried at his scarf. "But which way? We are utterly lost."

But there, trotting out of the darkness, came the little white fox. He hovered by a nearby tree, no more than six feet away. The Fire Wolves turned to look, then moved aside to let him pass.

Sadie smiled. "I believe it's this way."

Oliver gathered himself. "How are we still alive?" he asked. "How did you do this?"

"It wasn't me, Oliver. I told you," Sadie said, following the white fox deeper into the forest with the pack of Fire Wolves at her side, "this is a magical place."

✴ ☡ ▦ ☫ ⛫

Sadie staggered, exhausted. She had no idea how long they'd been walking. The Fire Wolves stopped, their tongues lolling, at the lip of a starlit clearing. Sadie looked up into the night sky. Billions of stars twinkled brilliantly above the swaying sandarac trees and the icy tips of the Carcassus Mountains.

Before her, the clearing formed a crude circle, cut by hand. Tree stumps lingered at the perimeter with axe marks embedded in each. At the centre rippled a small lake, no more than fifty feet wide. Mist hovered on the water, concealing the edge of a tiny island. A slim bridge, edged with eerie lanterns, stretched across, leading to the smallest house Sadie had ever seen. Its door hung at a jaunty angle, the roof lopsided and bowing. An amber light burned within.

"This is it," Sadie said. "This must be where the fox is leading us."

A thin tendril of smoke stretched up from the house's crumbling chimney stack.

"Who lives in such a place?" Oliver asked, pointing towards the tumbledown pile. "Nobody normal, I promise you."

"I'll bet an interesting soul lives here," Sadie decided whimsically. "Someone who has lived deep in Darachna Forest their entire lives. Someone who talks to the trees, and walks with the animals, and embraces the horrors of the night. Someone who knows the location of mysterious places ... like Hurtmore House."

"You said the same of Rhiannon's mysterious shop and look what happened there."

Sadie strode into the clearing, scowling at Oliver.

"Are you sure about this?" he said, shadowing her. "Sadie. This feels all wrong. Please. Let us retrace our steps, find our way back through the forest, down to the wall. Back home." Oliver grabbed Sadie's arm, spinning her around. "Look, even the wolves do not want to come any closer."

True, the Fire Wolves seemed unsure, choosing to remain by the tree line. Shrugging, Sadie pushed on towards the edge of the lake.

Mist crawled off the water.

The island flickered in and out of sight.

Sadie tested the slim bridge with her boot. Wooden slats

creaked under her weight as lanterns swung back and forth. She took another step, and a third, and soon she was on the far side, standing before the strange little house.

A rusty knocker, shaped to resemble a fox, protruded from the middle of the wonky door. Without hesitation, she rapped three times.

"Maybe the white fox is their pet," Oliver ventured.

Slowly, the door swung open.

A velveteen voice rumbled. "Enter."

Sadie obeyed.

Inside, dimmed lanterns and soft candles burned on an upturned crate. Silence choked the air, as if all the strange ambient noise of the forest had been switched off, deleted.

"Please sit," the voice continued.

It sounded close, emanating from the darkness several feet ahead.

Oliver faltered in the doorway, his hands pressing against the lopsided frame.

Sadie crossed her legs in front of the crate. She felt serene and relaxed, as if she were reading horror novels and grimoires in her eaved bedroom.

She searched the darkness for who, or what, sat opposite.

Oliver gasped as a figure moved into the candlelight.

A man's head emerged. Smooth as an egg. Chalk-white with blue veins criss-crossing his skull. He grinned, causing the black paint around his eyes to crack into deep crow's feet. His head sat atop a thin neck surrounded by wreaths of dark feathers. Purple, blue, and black silk garments shimmered with embroidered curlicues of gold and silver.

"Sadie Madison," he said, smiling. "What an honour. Please, let me introduce myself. My name is Vulpes."

"You know me?"

"Of course," he answered plainly. "We all know you."

"We?" Sadie huffed, this familiarity becoming increasingly unpleasant. "You and Rhiannon?"

He beamed wide and exposed his teeth. He still had several of his own, but most were glittering precious gems. "You are known to many in the Vents."

"The Vents," she said, looking around. "Are we in the Vents?"

Vulpes laughed darkly. "Goodness, no. This is Darachna Forest, Sadie. A handful of miles from your home in Iron Bridge. Yes?"

"And who *are* you?"

"As I said, my name is Vulpes," he said, his teeth glittering. "Conjuror, magician, alchemist ... friend." He stretched his smooth hands across the crate, displaying long fingernails painted with bright, apotropaic symbols.

"Do you own a little white fox?"

"He's an Ice Fox, Sadie. But he is not a pet. Far from it."

"An Ice Fox," she said, her eyes widening. "How did he get to Norland?"

"How indeed?" he answered. "I think that mystery is just as bewildering as a pack of Fire Wolves deciding to shadow *you* all the way here. I've never seen the like of it."

"They're afraid of—" Sadie began.

Vulpes held up a finger, silencing her momentarily.

Oliver shuffled into the tiny house.

The door closed behind him of its own accord.

Curling his long fingers around a brass handle, Vulpes flipped open a cap on the end, pressed a button and yanked the lever down. Somewhere in the ground, cogs began to churn and grind. A virulent hiss erupted, sending hot plumes of steam rocketing all around.

It reminded Sadie of the Steam Totem.

It reminded her of home.

"Hold tight," Vulpes said calmly.

The house began to spin. At least, that was Sadie's first instinct. She dug her hands into the crate as Oliver curled his fingers around her shoulders. The house appeared to turn and rise into the air, leaving Sadie, Oliver, and Vulpes in its shadow.

But, as she came to realise, the house had not moved at all. In truth, the floor had rotated—with them on it—descending into the darkness beneath the island.

THE
ALCHEMIST

The revolving platform stopped with a splutter of machinery and the hiss of pistons. All trace of the strange little house had gone. In its place was a low room full of mismatched workbenches. Each table was mounted with a complex system of pipes that led to vials, pots, and bubbling tubes. Crude scribbles on old parchment were plastered to curved stone walls between wonky, disorganised bookshelves. Hanging lanterns swung over an unmade bed. A wireless buzzed with static.

Vulpes hopped off the platform and swept around the workbenches, gathering items in his pale fingers. He came to an abrupt halt in front of Sadie.

"Chin," he requested.

"Huh?"

"You are bleeding."

"I fell," Sadie said. "I thought it had dried."

Vulpes produced a fine cloth and, after dipping it in a clear substance, dabbed the wound. It stung at first, but quickly faded. He ran the cloth over the cut, making Sadie wince. "You will live," he declared, smiling brightly. "Try not to prod it or it will never heal."

"Thank you. That was very kind."

Vulpes waved away her thanks. "Do not mention it."

"I do not trust him," Oliver told her, inspecting her chin.

"You are right," Vulpes called as he walked briskly around

his laboratory, collecting more items, and dumping them on one of the workbenches. "The Fire Wolves. They *are* afraid."

"Afraid of what?" Sadie said, desperately resisting the temptation to prod her chin.

"The dark mist," Vulpes replied ominously. "At least, that is my theory."

Sadie could hear Oliver swallow.

"You saw it." Vulpes grinned. "It is okay. I can tell."

"Yes. Through the wolves. It follows them, watching, waiting for something."

Vulpes plucked a large blue bottle from a top shelf. He opened several vials and small boxes, sprinkling unmeasured amounts of one powder and liquid into a silver goblet. "Not something ..." he started, popping the blue bottle open and filling the goblet to the brim. "Some*one*." He pushed the goblet towards her. "Here. Have some of this. It is cold, but it will warm you through. Sounds backwards, I know, but it works wonders."

Sadie swung her legs off the lift and approached the table. She stared down at the dark contents swirling in the goblet.

"Do not—" Oliver said.

"It is quite safe," Vulpes assured her.

"Who is it? The dark mist, I mean."

Vulpes steepled his fingers and ran his tongue over his priceless teeth. "He is a shadow. I say *he*, could be a *she*, could be all manner of things. Been in the trees east of Iron Bridge for as long as I can remember. Watching, waiting—for what, I have no clue. But searching for something. Or someone."

"How do you know all this?"

"Sadie Madison, you are not the only one in tune with the animals of the forest," Vulpes informed her. "What did you see through the eyes of the wolves?"

"Running mostly. Through the woods, scared, terrified. A choking, smothering darkness. Chased and chasing at the same time. Locked between the two things. It was painful, sad, and angry all at once."

"It is called skin-walking," Vulpes told her. "The ability to see through another's eyes."

Sadie's forehead wrinkled. "How did I—?"

Vulpes tightened. "You do not know?"

"I was alone. Terrified. Convinced the wolf would tear me to pieces. But Oliver returned and I was suddenly calm, like I wasn't afraid anymore."

Vulpes inched the goblet towards her. "Interesting," he said. "It would appear Oliver is quite the accomplice."

Sadie wrapped her fingers around the goblet. "He's my … friend."

"Oh, I think he's far more than that. I am not sure exactly, but he definitely has more than a modicum of power."

"Power?" Oliver whispered.

"Now, tell me, what are you doing up here in the forest in the middle of the night?"

Sadie wasn't sure. "We're … looking for Danver," she told him. "He was taken to Hurtmore House after a fight with Cale Boswick. I asked his parents how to find Hurtmore House, but they had completely forgotten about him. Forgotten they had a son! He's been my friend forever and ever. I have to get him back. I have to."

"Is that so?" Vulpes waved his bejewelled fingers towards the silver goblet. "Well, drink up, think of your friend, think of … Danver. Hope can be a powerful ally."

Sadie lifted the goblet.

Images of Danver rose through her mind.

Oliver shook his head and mouthed the word *no*.

But the edge of the goblet had touched her lips. The cold liquid seeped between her teeth, smothering her tongue.

"Think of Danver," Vulpes encouraged. "Think of your friend."

The liquid tasted sweet, rich and, as it slid down her throat, invitingly warm.

"Think of all the memories you shared together."

The effect spread across her chest, like a strong cough remedy or a glass of warmed ziela.

"Good girl. Now, give me your hands," Vulpes instructed, taking the goblet from her and slinging it over his shoulder.

He wrapped his hands around hers and closed his eyes.

At the end of the table, a large black candle—stuffed into an empty bottle of DarkHeart—burst into life. The flame licked excitedly as Vulpes' hands grew hotter and hotter and hotter. The heat surged up Sadie's arms and into her chest, mixing with the liquid from the goblet.

"Think about Danver," the Alchemist said. "Recall your best, happiest memories of him. Think about your long-lost friend. Your best friend. *Dan-ver.*"

Sadie became drowsy.

The heat wrapped her in a soft cocoon.

The black candle danced on the workbench and erupted like a firework, shooting tiny flames into the air.

Sadie's eyes fought to stay open. Around her, the room brightened, revealing more ornaments and possessions of Vulpes' mystical life: glass-vials, sand-timers, match-grinders, tinder-boxes, flint-keepers, weather-books, charts, and medicines in an army of labelled pots and jars. Three archways led off the main room. Each revealed a series of root-lined corridors stretching under the forest.

A labyrinth of wonders.

Vulpes shut his black-rimmed eyes.

His hairless head rocked slowly from side to side like a pendulum.

"Watch," he whispered.

The candle diminished momentarily. Then, several faces sprang from the flame and danced in the air, wreathed in colourful light. First, were three young women. They spiralled towards the roof of the underground laboratory and faded into withering embers. Next sprang a winged child, a centurion, an old man, an elvish girl, and finally a young boy—Sadie could have sworn he looked just like Oliver.

She ripped her hands away. The room descended into darkness. The faces fizzled out like damp fireworks. "What was that? What did you do?"

Vulpes' hands scurried away like spiders under a sofa. "It is a future, Sadie."

"A future?"

"Of sorts."

Vulpes seemed agitated. He shook himself and then, turning skyward, spoke aloud to someone else. Someone who was not there. "It's unclear ... I cannot see for sure ... Some of it is missing ... You know why."

Sadie sat and listened to Vulpes' side of the conversation, attempting to fill in the blanks as she had with her father on the FarSpeaker. "Trying again will make no matter ... What is seen, is seen. Even with one eye ... Very well." He turned his attention back to Sadie. "I'm sorry. That was impossibly rude of me."

"Who were you ... talking to?"

"A friend," he answered. "Just like Oliver."

Vulpes' eyes were now on the boy in the crimson scarf.

Sadie's hand flew to her mouth. "You can ... see him?"

"Naturally," Vulpes replied. "Things that exist in the veil between life and death are common to me, for I often dwell there myself. Oliver is as clear to me as he is to you. Perhaps more so."

Oliver shifted nervously. "He can see me?"

"You are different to what I had imagined, more *human* looking than the others, but you are finally here, and that is the most important thing of all."

"The others?" Sadie asked. "You mean the Candidates, don't you?"

Vulpes pursed his lips and pulled a silver watch from his pocket. He studied it for a moment then snapped the lid shut. "Goodness, have you seen the time?" he said, jumping up from the table and rummaging around in a clothes trunk beside his bed. "I am terribly sorry. I have to go."

"What?" she said. "Where?"

"And you should be going too, Sadie. Morning light will soon be upon us and, with it, the crawl of the dawn feeders."

Oliver shuddered.

"But we've only just arrived. We've only just found you. You have to tell me who the Candidates are. You have to help us find Hurtmore House. That's why I saw the door in the wall. That's why the fox led us all the way here."

"Is it?" the alchemist said, lobbing clothes onto the floor.

"Vulpes?" Sadie wailed desperately.

"I do not know why or how you managed to find your way here," he answered. "Do not get me wrong, I am glad you did. But I know nothing of Hurtmore House—beyond the tales and the rumours—and it is almost light. A girl your age should be at home with her family."

Sadie could smell the promise of dawn, fresh and innocent. She kicked the nearest table in frustration. Glass tubes tipped over. Oliver shot to her side and squeezed her hand.

"How do we get back to Iron Bridge?" she asked irritably. "We're lost up here."

Vulpes looked up from his trunk and smiled curiously. "Head downhill, of course," he said, wrinkling his face. "Let the Fire Wolves guide you. Or become a wolf yourself and use your nose. I am sure there will be something tasty cooking in your mother's kitchen when you return. Scratch that, I know there will be."

🪲 🌙 🗄 🐕 🏛

The Fire Wolves followed Sadie and Oliver downhill for over an hour, sniffing the air and rubbing themselves against sandarac trees.

Sadie wandered playfully, arms stretched, her gaze flicking between the trunks.

It was Oliver's turn to hide.

Sadie's to seek.

A fraction of her attention focused on the game. The rest dwelt on her encounter with Vulpes. At first it had seemed like an utter waste. Not unlike her time with Rhiannon. Both had come about under the strangest of circumstances. Just when Sadie thought she'd found answers to the Foretelling, the ground was ripped from under her.

Rhiannon and Vulpes were both incredibly strange. Different from the sort of people living in Iron Bridge. Except the Ryndai. They were all from some other place, Sadie concluded. Somewhere magical.

A figure moved to her left.

A shadow on the snow.

The wolves growled, snarled.

"It's only Oliver," she whispered, but they formed a circle around her. Their fur changed, shining with a fiery autumn-gold.

Sadie stepped forward.

The Fire Wolves moved with her.

She scanned the trees and shrubs, straining to see what the dawn haze veiled. And then, through shards of brilliant morning light and dazzling snowflakes, appeared a girl. Swirling above a white linen dress whose edges curled like smoke, was a torrent of black, chaotic hair. Dark markings etched her forehead. Eyes, sad and lonely. She held out a frail, quivering arm and whispered, "Take me home. Please take me home."

Sadie's blood ran cold.

The voice from her dream. Her nightmare.

The Fire Wolves scattered, fur turning white, bounding, screaming, howling.

The girl couldn't be here. She wasn't dreaming, was she?

Sadie looked at the dark markings on the girl's head. They were symbols. Writing of some kind. A language she did not know.

A single tear of black ink ran from the girl's crown, across her cheek and pooled by her feet.

"Take me home," she whispered again. "Please take me home."

They held each other's gaze for what seemed like forever.

Sadie froze, her body still, lifeless.

A hand grabbed her shoulder, spinning her like a top.

"Are you okay?" said Oliver. "I have been hiding for ages."

Sadie snapped out of her reverie.

She looked at Oliver for a moment, then back at the girl.

But she had gone.

Sadie spun in circles, scanning the forest.

"You scared her away."

"Scared who away?"

"Her. The girl. The one from the dream."

Oliver paused. "The one with the dark markings and ...?"

"Yes," she said, her voice ghostly, hollow.

"She was *here*? In the forest? But—"

Sadie crumpled to the snow. She ran her hands through her tangled hair. "I thought I could deal with this, Oliver, but I'm not sure. I'm so utterly confused by everything, and nobody will give me a simple, straight answer. The girl in the dreams, the Vents, Vulpes and his dancing candles, the dark mist, Rhiannon and the Foretelling, the music—"

"And Danver," Oliver added.

Sadie turned her head.

Her eyes thinned as a frown scarred her forehead.

"Who's Danver?"

THE MAN WHO COULD
SEE IN THE DARK

The sandstone wall appeared between the trees like a giant wave breaking the early morning mist. Relief washed over Oliver's skin. His heart skipped in his chest. The outlines of Iron Bridge had returned.

Ahead, Sadie staggered from side to side, her body shaking in the cold morning air. The temperature appeared to have no effect on him whatsoever. However, a deep worry coursed through his veins like a virulent poison.

"What do you mean?" he'd said back in the depths of the forest. "Danver. Your closest friend. Your best friend."

"You're my best friend, Oliver. No one else matters."

"But what about Danver? And Hurtmore House? We have to save him. Right?"

"Save him? I don't even know him." She smiled at Oliver then. "What's gotten into you? Don't tell me you've started creating people out of thin air too!"

Sadie giggled and Oliver had to resist the urge to pursue the matter.

Now, standing at the wall, Sadie stared in both directions. Sandstone bricks, vines and creepers blocked their path. She closed her eyes and seemed to concentrate. Oliver wondered if she could conjure the brightly painted door with her mind or think up some marvellous way to scale the wall. But nothing happened. Oliver knew he could return to the house whenever he wanted. The simplest thought and *whoosh!* he'd be there. But Sadie was not like him. She was flesh and blood and bone and all manner of things he did not understand.

"I suppose we'd better head for the Glade. It can't be too far," she said, and Oliver nodded.

The sun had cleared the top of the Carcassus Mountains when the North Gate appeared. Sadie's pace increased as she half-walked, half-ran towards it.

The North Gate was bookended by two stone gargoyles. Chipped, cracked, and smothered in a patina of moss and filth. One had the body of a bird and the head of a crocodile. The other, a lion with the tail of a serpent.

"What are these?"

"That's a harpy," Sadie said, pointing at the bird with the crocodile head. "In Menzani myth they have the head and torso of a woman, but I think this is a Hiero-Menzan hybrid, the head of Balek, the Crocodile God, brother of Abnar."

"Is that so?" said Oliver, not keen on the history lesson. "And the lion with the—"

"A chimera," she answered. "Specifically, in this case, a fire-breathing monster of Menzani origin. Sometimes there'd be a goat in the mix too."

"How do you know all this stuff?"

"Books."

"Of course," he said. "You cannot forget, can you?"

Sadie raised an eyebrow. "Not one thing."

Oliver's worry deepened.

Sadie strode through the North Gate, negotiating the broken cobbles. Inside, the forest thickened. Sadie hopped over low-hanging branches and nests of thistles, skirting between the dark bark of the sandarac trees. Tombs, headstones, crypts, and sepulchres nestled amongst the trees and weeds, designed with a myriad of religious connotations. Angels and demons and birds and beasts, carved from stone and wood and bone and iron, stared down at the two friends.

Save for the rustle of leaves, the yawning wood, and the distant vibrations of Darachna Forest, the Glade remained silent.

But they were not alone.

Ghostly shapes moved with them through the timberland. Oliver watched nervously as they peered out from behind trees, and crypts, and stone monoliths. Their eyes seemed cold and heartless, empty of anything resembling life. They flickered too, invisible and barely there. Failing, faint, promising to vanish forever.

"Who are all these people?" Oliver asked, the crimson scarf rising.

Sadie turned through three hundred and sixty degrees, her skirts billowing out like a ballerina. "What are you talking about? There's no one here."

"No," he corrected her. "There are lots of ... *things* here."

"You mean the figures and statues and grotesques? They're not real," Sadie replied cheerfully. "Just, you know, carvings for protection in the afterlife." She inched in close, her cheek next to his. "You know, this place is full of mummified bodies. Thousands upon thousands of them. All bound and gagged and locked in stone caskets."

Oliver tried to ignore her. "No, it's not the carvings. Or the mummified bodies. These things are real," he insisted. "They're ... moving."

They ducked beneath a tangle of fallen trees and emerged onto a wide cobbled road. Oliver found himself surrounded by hundreds of spectral entities. Some were human, some were animals, some birds, reptiles, beasts, and monsters. They didn't seem to be paying him any attention. Most stood still, looking into the distance, thoughtful and melancholic. But others walked, slithered, rolled, or flew along the cobbled road, darting between graves and crypts.

Oliver pulled the scarf up to his eyes.

"Seriously?" Sadie asked him. "You're seeing ... ghosts?"

"Do you not?"

"No, Oliver. Not one soul. I can only see you."

"Then how can *I* see *them*?"

"I've no idea," Sadie said. "I've no more idea than how you made the writing ball print your thoughts on a piece of paper." She tapped her pocket. "Or the way you can jump from place to place."

"The veil between life and death," Oliver muttered, repeating Vulpes' words.

Sadie put her hands on his shoulders. Their eyes locked. "It's okay," she told him. "I'm here. Everything is fine." He nodded several times. The white strands amidst his black hair became prominent. He didn't feel safe. He didn't feel soothed by Sadie's words at all.

They set off again. Sadie's feet dragged on the long grass and knotted roots that pushed through the broken cobbles. Oliver watched his friend as she took one stumbling step after the next. Running on empty, tired and cold.

He knew they should never have left the wall and gone after the little white fox. The Ice Fox. Oliver pictured the thick forest and Fire Wolves. The circular clearing, the tiny house, the laboratory, the candles, and the silver goblet filled with that strange, dark liquid. He saw Vulpes' chalk-white head and black, painted eyes. A dark sneer curled onto the alchemist's lips as a cruel laugh echoed through the dawn light.

The invading forest forced them off the cobbled path, through a maze of gravestones and sepulchres. Oliver trailed after Sadie, reminding her of the rising sun and the trouble they would be in if her parents woke to find her missing.

Eventually, the western path emerged from the tree line and took them south. The sun climbed in the winter sky, making the snow beneath their feet sparkle like diamonds. From time to time, Oliver gripped Sadie's hand as awful shrieks and wails came from the marauding forest.

But they kept to the path.

One foot in front of the other.

Onwards, always onwards.

A few ghosts remained, staring with hollow, lifeless eyes. Here, the spectres were mostly soldiers. Some could have been from the Divine Wars, but others were much older. Foreign-looking campaigners in ancient garb who sported strange headdresses and crude weapons.

They came upon a large stone building at the western tip of the Glade. A three-storey sandstone structure, encircled by a colonnade and topped with a bright-green domed roof. Large wooden doors sat ajar.

Oliver pointed to a sign beside two ethereal horses. "The Temple of the Living."

"That's right," Sadie replied. "There are five temples in all. The Temple of the Living, the Dead, the Forgotten, the Temple of Solitude, and the Temple of Enlightenment. I've only ever been to this one and the Temple of the Dead, but one day I'll see them all."

"The dead?" Oliver whimpered. "Do people worship the dead here?"

"Of course not. Well, thousands of years ago, sure. They would embalm the dead before putting them in the ground, to preserve the flesh. It's a library now. So is this one. A warm, cosy library. They usually serve tea."

Oliver inspected a map on the wall by the entrance. He saw the Temple of the Dead set in the south, the Forgotten in the east, the Temple of Solitude back up in the overgrown north. In the dead centre hid the Temple of Enlightenment, larger than the other four combined.

"I'm going to warm up," she told Oliver, stumbling inside. "Just for a few minutes. There's still time. We can make it back before they notice we're gone, right?"

Oliver stood between the gigantic wooden doors and

watched the ghosts. There didn't seem to be any order to what they were doing.

They ambled and wandered listlessly.

Lost.

Disconnected.

His eye caught the ghost of a young man by the temple railings, attempting to light a thin cigarette. He tried again and again, pulling one match after the next from a battered tinderbox and striking them against a rough stone.

The match sparked, smoked, died.

"You wanna give me a hand, son?"

The man's voice seemed to scratch in his throat.

"Yeah, I'm talking to you, the boy in the scarf," he said, turning to face Oliver. "No point askin' one of these lot to give me a hand, is there? As pointless as tryin' again meself. But you … well, youse different, ain't ya? Not a human. Not a ghost. Somefin' else, eh?"

"I guess so," Oliver replied tentatively. "To be honest, I am not entirely sure what I am."

"Well, don't matter, does it?" The man snorted. "You're here now and that's all that matters. Better to be here than to be no place at all."

Oliver frowned.

"Better to be here. In the Glade. Remembered by someone. Who knows who? I surely don't." The man walked over. His eyes were sunk into his skull. The pupils large and dark like those of a shark. "Better than not being here at all. Better than being forgotten." Placing the tinderbox in the crook of his arm, he held up ten grimy fingers, slowly coiling them into his palm until they'd all vanished. "Forgotten by everybody who ever knew you. Gone. Forever!" He spread his hands suddenly, wiggling his fingers through the air like falling snow. "Into nuffingness. Like you never existed in the first place." He paused, considering Oliver. "You alright, son?"

Oliver gathered himself. "Yes, of course. I am fine."

"Tell ya face. Looks like you've seen a ghost!" He cackled and snorted to himself. "I'm AppleGarth," said the young man, proffering an outstretched hand. "And you must be—"

"Oliver," he said, looking at AppleGarth's hand.

"Go on. I'm not gonna break your fingers or nothin'."

AppleGarth's hand felt warm and surprisingly solid.

"I can ... touch you," Oliver said.

"Course you can, Oliver," he said, shaking his hand vigorously. "We're one and the same, you and I. Only, I'm dead and you're, well, who knows. But basically, the same. You see?"

It didn't make any sense. "What sort of name is AppleGarth?"

"What sort of name is Oliver?"

"It is just a name."

"Exactly."

"Sadie named me," Oliver told him. "Sort of."

"And my parents named me. Toseland Jeremiah AppleGarth, to be sure," he said with a short bow. "But, if you please, AppleGarth will suffice. Or TJ, if ya like. 'Sup to you, son."

"I am simply Oliver. Nothing more," he replied. "Do you still want a hand with your matches?"

"Oh, yeah. T'rrific."

Oliver plunged his fingers inside the tinderbox and, to his surprise, took a match first time and held it up. It appeared faint and ethereal, like AppleGarth, but solid in his grip.

"Well?" the ghost said.

Oliver struck it against the rough stone. It lit first time. AppleGarth eagerly held the end of his cigarette to the ghostly flame and took a long drag. "That's better," he wheezed. "Been a while."

"How long have you been trying to light that thing?"

AppleGarth hacked and convulsed, slapping himself on the chest with his free hand until the effects of the smoke cleared. "Ah, dunno. Maybe a hundred years, more or less. You lose the sense of time when youse dead. When you're alive you know you've got sixty, seventy, eighty years—if you're lucky—to do everyfin'. When you're dead, you're dead forever. There's no endpoint. There's no purpose. It's a whole different shooting match. What year is it anyway? Ah, never mind. It makes no matter."

AppleGarth took another noisy drag on his roll-up.

Oliver waited for the inevitable coughing fit to subside. "Did you die in the Divine Wars?"

"The Divine Wars? Nah, never made it that far. Taken out by an unhappy client." AppleGarth settled himself against the railing, clearly happy to be telling his tale. "Used to be a hawkshaw in Los Kralice. The underground city. You heard of it? I'm surprised I survived as long as I did, to be sure."

"A hawkshaw?"

"A detective, privately hired. I'm a bit of a curiosity as it goes," AppleGarth continued. "It's these eyes. Excellent night vision. Absolutely no idea why. No history of it in the family. Not a dickie-bird. But livin' in the underground city of Los Kralice, where daylight is somefin' you soon forget, my unique skill gave me an advantage. An advantage that a certain client became tired of. And"—AppleGarth snapped his hands together—"boom! I'm a goner. Dead as a doornail. Kaput. Over."

"But, if you died in Los Kralice, how come you are haunting the Glade of Remembrance in Iron Bridge?"

"I didn't die there, son. I died here. Down by the river. Rifle shot to the head. Not pretty. I'd been on the run, but they found me and, well, I'm dead. And as for hauntin'... I'm not hauntin' nothin'. I'm just livin', well, not livin'. Remainin'. Forever. You understand, right?"

Oliver looked at the other ghosts shambling by. "What about the rest of them?"

"I dunno. The same? Probably. Shufflin' about. Waitin' for whatever it is they're waitin' on."

"Sounds pointless."

"Well, as I've said already, son, it's better than the alternative."

AppleGarth took a drag on his cigarette.

"I am not sure I agree."

"And how would you know anyfin' about it? You're not *really* dead."

"Well, I am in the veil between life and death. Apparently."

AppleGarth grumbled an acknowledgement.

"Oliver?" Sadie said, emerging from the temple. "Who are you talking to?"

Oliver thumbed towards his new friend. "His name is AppleGarth. He is a private—"

"Detective! Yes, TJ AppleGarth," Sadie cut in, skipping down the steps. "Toseland Jeremiah AppleGarth. Father told me a story about him. And I've read about him too. Famously assassinated by Doktor Edvard Mistery, in eighteen hundred and five, over the abduction of the doktor's daughter. Are you really speaking with TJ AppleGarth?"

"You make him sound like he is famous."

"I'm famous?" AppleGarth asked.

"Did you abduct someone's daughter?"

"Not at all! We was deeply in love," AppleGarth corrected, dropping his spent roll-up to the ground where it vanished. "Her father was an overly protective man. He didn't care much for the likes of me. If we wanted to be together then we had to run away. Don't suppose your friend knows what happened to her? To my love. To Alice Mistery?"

Oliver turned and asked Sadie.

She hesitated for a moment. "I … um … no, sorry. I don't know what happened to Alice. Father told me that story a long time ago. I always get it mixed up with the one about the Ice Pirates, or the Relentless Squirrel, or the Beautiful Death."

Oliver glared at her.

"Oh. Shame," AppleGarth said, a little crestfallen. "I know she'll be dead now. Just wish I knew what patch she's shufflin' about on."

Sadie wandered over to the railings. "We have to go."

"If I find out anything about Alice, I'll come back and let you know," Oliver told the hawkshaw.

Sadie shot him a dark frown and yanked him by the arm towards the cobbled path.

"Nice meetin' youse anyways," AppleGarth called, as they headed for the South Gate.

"What happened to Alice Mistery?" Oliver asked when they were out of earshot. "And do not pretend like you do not know."

"Horrible things. Disturbing things. Things we should never tell him."

Passing through the South Gate, they walked silently across the playing fields, through the school grounds, and onto the streets of Iron Bridge. They snaked up Leviathan Crook, past row after row of houses adorned with jongeliers and faerie-lights, to the very top.

Danver's house stood on their left. Dark and seemingly empty.

Sadie strolled passed, showing no interest in the house whatsoever. She headed straight for number five, the Madison family house, looking to sneak in unnoticed.

But outside, watching the sunrise from the porch swing, sat Michael Madison.

THE HALL OF
GLASS AND MIRRORS

Michael Madison watched the pan boil. The three wise cats eyed him curiously from the trapdoor above the meat cellar.

"What are you lot doing here?" he whispered, but the cats did not reply.

Popping a filter into a brass funnel, Michael spooned a heap of coffee on top. He placed the funnel over a large clear jug and topped it up with boiling water. As the water mingled with the coffee and filtered down into the clear jug, a rich aroma filled the entire kitchen. The smell of morning.

But it wasn't morning. It was a minute after midnight.

Michael shifted his eyes to the kitchen window.

Sadie Madison was standing by a brightly painted door at the back of the garden, wrapped in her winter coat, her bag slung over her shoulder. She seemed to be talking to someone, but Michael couldn't see who.

He took a porcelain mug decorated with hand-painted dachshunds and filled it to the brim. Michael blew on the coffee. Sipped eagerly. Then, glancing back down the garden, he noticed both Sadie and the brightly painted door had vanished.

Michael took his coffee into the hallway, through the library, and placed it on the desk in his study. Two coloured-glass lamps burned low, casting long shadows of clocks, and metronomes, and globes, and collections of copper and silver colonial figurines in dark reds, purples, and greens. The embedded aroma of cigars, and cinnamon, and ziela, infused with the fresh coffee.

He swept around the desk and slid purposefully into a high-backed leather chair. Pushing a drift of papers aside with one hand, he stacked books—riddled with bookmarks and cuttings—into a neat pile with the other. Michael produced a small silver key from beneath his shirt and unlocked the bottom desk drawer.

Inside was a great leather tome.

Blood-red and bound with iron.

The desk yawned under its weight. Dust plumed at the sides.

Hovering over the book, Michael's hands quivered.

And there, branded onto the cover in lavish, sweeping script, were the words *Book of Whispers*.

"What are you doing, Michael?" came a voice from the shadows.

"Her journey has truly begun," he responded, unfazed.

"And there is no stopping it."

"Yes, I know." Michael's hands grazed the sides of the book. The leather was soft and warm under his fingers, ancient and priceless. "I've read it hundreds of times. Maybe a thousand. There must be something else."

The arched study window crystallised.

Frost methodically filled each pane.

Shadows on the porch gathered. They swarmed against the window, testing the edges for a way in, faces appearing and dissolving in shifting shadows.

"There is nothing more you can do, Michael," said the voice. "You made your choice."

"It was hardly *my* choice."

"Do you think you are being treated unfairly?"

"Unfair? Of course it's unfair. It's been unfair for the past thirteen years, but here we are. I have nowhere to go, no options other than ... *this*."

He placed a hand gingerly on the book.

"The Foretelling is not an option, Michael. The Foretelling is truth. The Foretelling is all."

Michael's blood rose.

"We have sent three to watch her," the voice said. "Do not fear them."

"Three?" Michael replied. "You've sent agents?"

"Naturally," the voice said. "The Gathering Order has been compromised. They seek to deny the Foretelling. They are among us, concealed, fighting from within. The Balance," it whispered. "We will weed them out. Their fate will be as that of the Unknown."

"The Unknown?" Michael hissed. "I've read that name, in these pages. Malmortem, they called him, amongst other names. But he was destroyed, his spirit exiled to a place beyond all comprehension."

"That book was once his," the voice said coldly. "It is more powerful than you could possibly imagine, Michael. Keep it safe. Always." Shifting shadows coalesced in the centre of the window. Drawing the frost to them, they formed a crooked icy branch that stretched across Michael's study and touched him lightly on the forehead.

★☽▦𖤐𝍢

Michael found himself surrounded by darkness. The fringes of night. Smoke and glass. Whispers and silence. A hall of mirrors with floors of stone. Black and marbled. Endless and cold. A world of stars. Pin holes in the sheet of night.

The *Book of Whispers* sat on a stone plinth before him. Three figures of tumbling shadows watched Michael as his eyes adjusted. The first thrust out an arm and turned a crumpled page. Paper scraped as it turned, whispering its secrets to the dark.

"The Foretelling," it announced, as the page presented itself before him. "Its time is upon us once more."

Its voice was a low whisper, neither woman nor man. The

second and third shadows nodded. The first ran its fingers over the ancient manuscript. "Read it, Michael. Read it aloud so we can all hear. So everyone can hear."

At the edges of darkness, in the boundless hall, countless shadows appeared. Dancing like black fire, they huddled together until Michael was surrounded by a wave of faceless transient entities.

Steadily, he approached the plinth and looked into the cowl of the first, trying to find its eyes, but saw only endless night. Reluctantly, he scanned to the manuscript, adjusted his spectacles, and cleared his throat.

"All wickedness begins this way; small and helpless, naked and alone. The fifth and final child will come into the world. A child that should never have been. A child of untold power. A child of limitless knowledge. A child that will wield dominion over all. When the blood moon rises and the sea's mist crawls across the land, when the Fire Wolves leave their forest homes and the Redkites head to the sea, when friendship appears lost and love seems an unobtainable promise, the child will come forth." As he spoke, the stars seemed to darken. "The child that wields untold power and dominion will be the firstborn, of the firstborn, fallen from the highest. For the child that takes everything we hold dear, and locks it away for all time, is the child that puts her fear aside and leads the others into darkness." The words echoed around the mighty hall, disappearing into mirrors, and glass, and the endless night above.

"So it is written, so it shall come to pass," said the first.

"As it has before," replied the second.

"As it always has," added the third.

"And, as always, we have our part to play," the first told them.

The book thundered shut in Michael's face. "Remember," the voice pressed, a whispering rasp, eyes suddenly burning white inside the shadows. "Nothing shall stop us this time!"

The entire congregation, hundreds of thousands of voices, suddenly bellowed, "NOTHING!"

Michael's skin turned cold.

His stomach lurched.

The figure landed an evanescent hand onto the book, fingers spread. Whispering an incantation, orange and purple flames licked the edges of the book. Michael put up his hands to shield his eyes and, when he risked a second glance, found he was back in his study.

The red leather book sat before him on the desk.

Golden filaments crackled and died around its edges.

Michael Madison reached for his coffee, but it had gone cold.

✹ � ▦ ✺ ⛩

Larissa stirred as Michael returned to bed. "Where have you been?" she asked.

"I couldn't sleep," he said. "I read for a while."

"And drank coffee, by the smell of it."

"Go back to sleep. No point us both being awake."

Larissa sighed haughtily and rolled over. Michael sat against the headboard and watched his wife's body rise and fall like a sombre wave.

Time slipped away. Golden rays flooded the bedroom floor.

Cursing under his breath, Michael swiped his pocket watch from the bedside table and flicked it open. He glided out of bed and tiptoed around the landing and down the corridor to Sadie's room.

He stopped outside the door for a moment, hoping against all hope she had returned. Tentatively, he peered through the crack. A sorrowful cry rose from Mischief, who rolled around on the bed, hair flying everywhere.

"Get off there," Michael said, shooing the cat away.

His stomach lurched again.

Sadie had not returned.

He sat on the window seat and let his vision wander along the sharp ridges of the Carcassus Mountains. A huge world spread beyond the Shadow Valley. A strange world. A complicated world.

She'll be fine. She has to be fine. They won't let anything happen to her. Not now. Not her.

Michael galvanised himself and retrieved his coffee cup from the study. As he orbited the desk, an icy chill rippled against his skin.

He spun.

Nothing.

He was alone.

Straightening his papers, he lifted a crystal decanter of ziela and returned it to its rightful place on a high shelf.

The dark-red liquid had been routinely outlawed throughout Norland. The Gods were famed for their obsession with ziela and desired it above all else. Yet bottles appeared from time to time, in contraband and black-market sales, away from the watchful eyes of Ryndai and the Eighth Day Assembly.

As the decanter slid onto the shelf, Michael stopped.

Beside it, a thin green glass bottle rolled from side to side on the shelf. A tattered label had been stuck to the side, the corners peeling away.

Michael turned it over in his hands, removed the cork stopper and wafted the bottle under his nose. It had no odour. And, on the label, were words in black ink, written by a flowing, artistic hand.

Michael knew the handwriting. He'd seen it many times. And every time he had, nothing good followed.

He adjusted his spectacles to read the tiny words.

Nepenthe. Administration: Sadie Madison. Three doses. Evenly spaced.

🦟 ☻ ▥ ☪ ♨

Michael took a seat on the porch and sipped a fresh cup of coffee. He stared down at the winding curves of Leviathan Crook as the

Madison family jongelier clicked and rattled to itself in the early morning breeze. Almost an hour passed before a figure emerged around the bend. Michael sat forward on his chair.

Is it her? Is it Sadie? Please. Please let it be her.

Sadie ambled up Leviathan Crook, negotiating the thick snowdrifts.

She looked exhausted.

Michael stood as she approached the gate.

"Hello, Father."

Thank goodness she's home. Out of the forest and home. Safe.

She looked so small, so fragile.

But not safe from me. Not safe from the Nepenthe.

She smiled awkwardly and trudged up the steps.

"I'm sorry, Father. I was—"

"Later," Michael said, raising a hand. "You look like you could use some breakfast."

Sadie smiled.

"Get yourself in bed and I'll bring it up. What would you like? Pancakes? Porridge?"

"Porridge," Sadie replied, "with brown sugar."

Michael had only made porridge a couple of times before. He heated milk and mixed in oats until it formed an incredibly thick paste. He added more milk. Too much milk. More oats. Too thick again. He gave up. He ladled the substance into a porcelain bowl, shovelling a spoonful of brown sugar on top, and loaded it on a tray with a beaker of warm redcurrant cordial.

He lifted the tray.

Then placed it down.

Can I do it? Should I? She knows nothing of this world. No, it's for the best. This has to happen. We have to know—one way or another—for all our sakes.

Michael pulled the green glass bottle from his cardigan. He stood over the porridge and, taking a quick look around, dispensed a small amount of the thin, clear liquid. It disappeared instantly into the gloop, but Michael stirred it several times to be sure and dusted it with more sugar.

Too much? Not enough? What constituted one dose?

Michael panicked. The green bottle shook in his hand. He poured another glug into Sadie's redcurrant cordial before stoppering the bottle and slipping it away.

By the time he arrived upstairs, Sadie had fallen asleep.

Michael placed the tray on her bedside table.

"Sadie," he whispered. "Sadie. I've got your—"

Poison. Porridge. Poison. Porridge.

"Porridge," he managed.

Sadie's eyes yawned open. She mumbled something inaudible, then pulled the tray off the bedside table and balanced it on her lap.

"Sorry. Not my best work. Looks like wallpaper paste, like glue, like something used to build houses," he said, and Sadie giggled. "But at least it's hot."

Michael stared at his daughter.

He could stop this. Half of him knew he should stop her from eating the porridge but the other half knew he had to let the Nepenthe do its work.

"Are you okay?" Sadie asked.

Michael smiled and fidgeted with his spectacles. "Yes, everything is exactly the way it needs to be."

Sadie tilted her head. "Father?"

"I think I need some coffee," Michael announced and strode through the door, pulling it to behind him. He turned, frozen, his eyes watching Sadie through the crack. His heart stampeding in his chest. Guilt and worry bubbling in his gut.

His daughter placed a spoonful of the porridge in her mouth and, minutes later, had devoured the entire bowl and sucked down the hot redcurrant cordial.

"I don't feel so good … It's probably a headache, Oliver … No, not at all … I think I need to lie down for a while."

Beyond the door, Michael's eyes widened.

"You keep watch for the Winter Mitches, or FooGang, or

Snatchet Owl, or … yes, of course, Oliver … Grufflemann and Gromlits too," she snapped, sliding beneath the bedclothes, muttering as she went.

Michael blinked disbelievingly.

Oliver? Who is Oliver?

He pulled the Nepenthe from his pocket and looked at the label again.

I've done this. The Nepenthe has done this.

Michael felt eyes on him and that chill against his skin.

"It is not of my doing," came a voice.

Michael spun, scampering away from Sadie's room.

"I am not here, you fool." Vulpes' voice rang in Michael's head.

"What have you done to her? She's seeing things!"

"The Nepenthe has not created Oliver. Although, he is another matter altogether. It's important now that she forgets about the boy taken from her. This … *Danver.*"

"And the Nepenthe will banish every trace of him?"

"That is the idea."

"It has to, Vulpes. I have to prove to the Narrowers she is able to forget, that she has nothing to do with the Foretelling and the darkness that promises to follow."

"Do not doubt my skill, Michael," Vulpes hissed. "If she is able to forget, the Nepenthe will succeed. Two more, Michael. You must give her two more doses of the Nepenthe … and then the truth will be revealed!"

THE GREEN
GLASS BOTTLE

As Sadie slept, Lorntide bloomed throughout the Madison house. With Natalia's help, Larissa dragged boxes full of decorations from the attic, pinning silver moons and stars to window frames, running gold and green tinsel between the bannisters and Michael's horrifying paintings, hanging coloured paperchains from ceiling roses to cornices, suspending Anmer and evergreen garlands to each door, and draping the porch with a cornucopia of bunting, stars, tinsel and flare in gold, silver, red and green.

Natalia dusted off two dozen oil lanterns and hung them beneath the porch awning while Larissa retrieved a small army of sowing mannequins from the attic and dressed them in traditional outfits. She positioned the mannequins throughout the house, as though they were attending a fancy party. A strange, static, headless Lorntide party.

Exhausted by all the activity, Michael took Eli on the family sledge into town looking for a mighty tree to adorn the hallway. People were out in their hordes. True, Lorntide had once been a religious festival, but the people of Norland had long since stopped celebrating it in the name of one God or another. A celebration of winter, of the imminent new year, of family and friendship and hope for the future, people called it.

Even so, the Ryndai remained vigilant and every year their numbers swelled on the streets of Iron Bridge.

Michael held out a variety of trees to Eli, who weighed up

their suitability, discarding one after the next until they arrived at a solid blue spruce with waxy grey-green leaves and a scaly grey bark. By the time they returned home, Michael's hands were sore, his knees and back shot. Larissa and Natalia rushed to help him lift the tree through the front door and secure it in a large decorative planter.

The tree was quite a specimen. It stretched up through the hallway, touching the edge of the stairs and finishing in line with the bannisters on the landing. Michael admired the fantastic decorations Larissa and Natalia had displayed and could feel their excitement to start on the enormous tree that dominated the hallway. Eli sunk his hands into the nearest box and pulled out armfuls of tinsel.

"Wait a minute," Michael said. "Let me see if Sadie wants to join in."

As he climbed the stairs, the wonder and magic of Lorntide seemed to drain from his body. Was he too old for this? Did he lack the strength required to deal with the coming moments?

Sadie sat by the window as Michael craned his head around the door. He adjusted his spectacles with his middle finger. "Sadie?"

She turned and smiled.

"How did you sleep?"

"Fine."

"No hell hounds or devils to speak of?"

"Not one."

Michael faltered for a moment. "Tell me again," he began, swallowing hard. "Why did you go to the museum yesterday?"

Sadie bit her lip. "The museum?"

"I won't be angry," he said. "It slipped my mind, is all."

"I was ... looking for something."

Michael's eyes thinned. "For what?"

"I'm ... not sure," she shrugged. "Adventure, probably."

"Not a person?"

"No."

"Not a dear friend?"

"No."

"One you'd do anything for?"

Their eyes met. "I've already got one of those."

"Oh." Michael's shoulders tensed. "Danver."

Sadie frowned. "No, Father. Oliver."

Michael took a long, slow breath. "Well, I hope you found the adventure you sought," he asked, smiling. "My father, William Madison, would always say"—Sadie joined him, speaking in unison—"life without adventure is an empty journey."

She nodded. "Yes, yes we did."

"You and ... *Oliver*?"

Sadie looked at the empty space beside her on the window seat. "Yes. Me and Oliver."

"Well, I'm glad you're *both* home safe," Michael said. "We're about to decorate the Lorntide tree. Would you like to help?"

Sadie looked distracted, melancholy. "I feel ... I'm not quite sure what it is. Sort of ... *strange*. I think I'd rather play the piano," she said, standing and wrapping her arms around her father. "Can I?"

"We'd love to hear you play."

"Thank you," she whispered close to his ear. "Thank you for not getting angry. Sorry for going to the school yesterday and disappearing all night. It was foolish of me. I'll never do it again. Ever."

"Promise?"

"On the old Gods and the new."

✷ ☽ ▤ ⚕ ♨

Something moved through Sadie's mind, turning, writhing. Something dark, something wrong. Some malicious thing. She could feel a black curtain being drawn across her thoughts and memories. If this was forgetting, she hated it.

Her skin shivered. A pale sadness.

A sharp spear of pain lanced her scalp. It lingered, throbbing. Ebbed away.

Slowly, she rose the piano lid. Smooth teeth, in ebony and ivory, smiled at her. Sadie slid her fingers over the cold, hard keys.

Oliver appeared at her side, watching her prepare.

Delicious vapours of vanilla, cinnamon, cloves, citrus fruits, and rich red wine weaved through the house from a vat of Silverwater scorch—a local Lorntide speciality—that Larissa had made.

Eli and Natalia paced in thoughtful circles, cradling shiny decorations while trying to decide where to place each one on the enormous tree.

Michael watched them all, silently sipping his coffee.

The pain clawed at the inside of Sadie's skull.

Trying to find a way out.

And the music called to her, that melody, a remedy, something to soothe her mind. Something to help her find those lost, hidden things.

Her thoughts wandered arbitrarily. Her hands rested on the keys. She saw faces. Happy faces, sad faces, faces filled with joy and laughter. Sorrowful faces filled with rage. She heard voices. Laughing, giggling voices. Earnest voices invested in heavy dialogue, screams and cries, warning barks and deathly whispers. She smelt smoke, and ziela, and cinnamon, and something rotten—like putrefied eggs, sulphur—and hot, fresh coffee.

As the afternoon sky smudged with yellow and pink, Sadie played her first notes. The music caressed her ears, it flowed up her arms and filled her heart with beauty. Hearing the delicate music, Michael settled into one of the armchairs while Larissa, Natalia, and Eli abandoned their Lorntide duties and stood, clutching each other, beneath the library arch.

The power of her melodies twisted through the corridors and hidey-holes of number five Leviathan Crook, like columns of smoke seeking an open window.

People began to congregate, huddled in the snow-lined street, mesmerised by the sound. Neighbours abandoned their afternoon chores and joined those on the street. A handful of familiar faces became a dozen and, before long, Sadie glanced through the window to see more than a hundred awestruck faces huddled outside.

Pushing out of his armchair, Michael floated across the library and gazed at the gathered crowd. Further away, people trudged up Leviathan Crook. Whole families clung together in the falling snow, their faces bright and beaming, pulling themselves towards the euphoric sound. He looked towards the mighty iron bridge. More were swarming over the river. Like an invading army.

Michael hummed Sadie's melodies.

His feet carried him into the hallway.

His fingers swung the front door wide.

Respectfully, the people of Iron Bridge filed into the Madison family house. Fifty or more stood shoulder to shoulder in the library—ringside seats—as Sadie played. Bodies bulged out of the library, up the stairs, around the landing. They crossed the hallway into the living room, dining room, and kitchen, surrounded by the twinkling Lorntide decorations, the enormous tree, and Larissa's headless mannequins. Many more stood on the path, along the porch and lawns, and down Leviathan Crook. Even Atticus and the three wise cats perched courteously by the door to Michael's study, listening to the beautiful sound.

And, as Sadie played and she gazed through the window, many faces became pressed to the glass, their eyes wide and intoxicated.

Most she did not recognise, yet two were familiar.

The first, Cale Boswick. The bane of Sadie's existence, the boy guilty of ruining her school life. A horrible scar wove along the side of his face, held together with stitches and dark congealed blood. She wondered how he had received such a vicious injury. Despite the scar, his face looked different. No hate, no malice, no malcontent. He looked like a twelve-year-old boy should look. Happy, keen, and filled with the wonders and possibilities of the world.

The second, an older man, around fifty. Despite his wide smile, his face looked worn and ill. His eyes hinted at a life of tragedy. A loss of desperate proportions. It was her neighbour, Arnold Tomes. Something familiar echoed in the contours of his skull, the knowing in his eyes, the Broken Moon displayed around his arm. The throbbing and the scratching against the inside of her skull started again in earnest.

Sadie shook her head, but the pain endured. It built and built until tiny specks of black invaded the edges of her vision. Knives of white pain sliced her scalp, building and building. Her music intensified but the pain was equal to it. Sharp, insistent and foreboding.

Sadie wrenched her hands away from the keys.

Her audience gasped in horror.

Emotion bloomed everywhere as her music hung in the air, real, tangible.

Then, as quickly as it came, the music vanished.

Sadie closed the lid.

People stood frozen.

No one moved an inch.

Disbelief on their faces.

"I need to stop. Just for a while." Sadie spun and looked at a hundred or more people tightly packed into the house, like a communal grave. "I have to lie down."

Sadie dug through the bodies, up the stairs, round the landing, and into her room. She forced several people out into the hallway, shut the door, and collapsed onto the bed.

What caused the horrible pain now pushing at the back of her eyes? Small dark flecks skittered the peripherals of her vision again. She attempted to chase them but, no matter how hard she tried, they always darted out of reach.

"So tired," she said softly.

"I know," Oliver replied, sitting next to her. "Sleep now, Sadie. I will keep an eye on things here."

Her eyes rolled back into her head as she whispered, "Thanks, Danver."

🐛 ☺ ▦ 🎪 🎠

Sadie stumbled through black grass and fields of fire, past caged animals and onto a smooth flagstone corridor. A large flag-topped marquee appeared. A Ferris wheel. Jugglers, clowns, magicians, and conjurors with twisted faces and rotten teeth, cackled and roared with masterful fervency. The girl in the white dress with the dark markings flickered in and out of sight. "Take me home," she whispered. "Please take me home." She danced in circles, her dress blooming like a flower. Suddenly, she swept forward, her lips brushing Sadie's ear, and whispered, "Beware!"

Sadie sat upright.

Her skin glistened with sweat.

Gently, she shuffled across the room and stood in front of the mirror.

In the reflection, a dark liquid began to flow from her fingertips, dripping like black blood onto the carpet. She looked at her hands, but they were white and clean. Glancing back to her reflection, Sadie stepped back.

In the mirror, the liquid no longer dripped on the carpet. Instead, it fell into long, dark grass swaying rhythmically as if under the spell of the wind. Colourful snakes wriggled dangerously amongst the deceitful blades, thrusting out their forked tongues and hissing dreadful warnings.

The walls of the eaved bedroom began to disappear—brick by brick—until her reflection stood in the middle of the dark field surrounded by tents and fire and circus performers. From her crown, dark liquid flowed across her face like a cracked rotten yolk. It trickled over one eye, down the bridge of her nose and onto her lips where it slithered between her teeth and coated her gums. Sadie screamed, but the reflection did not. Instead, the ink-stained girl showed a caliginous smile and whispered, "I want to go home. Please take me home. I'm so close now."

Sadie shut her eyes and, when she opened them again, found herself standing before the mirror in the early morning light. She turned from side to side and examined her head, then her hands, and just about every part of her, before taking a deep breath and collapsing on the window seat.

Oliver sat on the bed, watching.

Beside him, lay an enormous stocking.

Sadie gasped.

She couldn't believe it.

She'd slept for an entire day and missed the Lorntide Eve celebrations.

☀ � ▦ ✖ ⛲

From the stocking, Sadie pulled a bag of hazelnuts, a lemon-scented soap, three pencils bound with lace, two oranges, a carefully folded native Norlandian headdress, a lined notebook, and a hardback book.

Iron Bridge: A Pictographic History.

She flipped through the book, rapidly scanning the pictograms of the town before, during, and after the building of the iron bridge.

The sound of Lorntide verse broke out on Leviathan Crook. Sadie dropped the picture book and went to the window. To her amazement there were still hundreds of people on the twisting street. Many of them were singing at the tops of their voices, passing round cups of Silverwater scorch.

"I think my mother has gone a bit mad."

"Really?" Oliver replied.

"She's down there somewhere, beneath the awning, dishing

out scorch in her sacred, collectable—supposedly priceless—antique cups. No one's allowed to touch them, never mind drink hot, scented, highly stainable scorch out of them!"

They sat and listened to the singers for a while. Sadie examined each face. There were so many. She found it hard to believe they'd all come to the house to hear her play. But the music had called to them, as it had to her. The thought made her skin ripple, her stomach churn.

Was this another strange facet of the Foretelling—like Rhiannon's shop and the brightly painted door? The Ice Fox and Vulpes? She gripped Oliver's arm. "Was it weird?" she asked. "The music, Oliver. Was the music weird?"

"It was beautiful. Magical," he said. "It did something to them. Like it was speaking to them. Like you were speaking to them."

Sadie held her face in both hands. Her cheeks flushed beneath her cold fingers. "I saw Cale Boswick in the window, but he looked different. He looked calm, as though all the anger in him had gone. And there was Arnold Tomes, too. His face looked strange, like a sadness was leaving him."

Oliver gave her a sideways look. "That is Danver's father."

Sadie laughed. "The Tomeses don't have any children. Don't make stuff up."

"You called *me* Danver. Right before you fell asleep."

Sadie took a moment to recall it. "Yes. Sorry. My dreams were so strange. I saw the field again, the circus, fire, clowns, animals. And that … girl."

"The one who looks like you … but with the black markings?"

"She called out. Asking me to take her home."

"Did she say where home is?"

Sadie shook her head, nibbled a fingernail.

Michael appeared around the doorframe. "Good morning, Sadie," he said spritely. "And a Merry Lorntide salute to you and your troops!" He swung his hand up to meet his forehead.

Pushing off the window seat, Sadie inched herself to full

height and slowly saluted back, grimacing from the pain that gripped her body. "Merry Lorntide, Father. I can't believe I slept through the entire night and missed the Lorntide Eve celebrations."

Michael smiled, but his eyes glistened with a hollow sadness. "You were exhausted from your adventures. You needed sleep. Not party games and cake."

"But I love party games and cake!"

"There's always next year," Michael said, his eyes evading hers. "And every year to come."

"Thank you for the stocking," Sadie tried, pointing at the detritus on her bed.

"Not my work, the work of St Nicholai."

Sadie raised an eyebrow. "Thanks, St Nicholai, then. No sign of Gruselmann, I take it?"

"Well, I haven't seen your brother yet this morning. Perhaps Gruselmann has thrown him in a sack and smuggled him away to the Slitherland during the night."

Sadie gave him a half-smile and moved to the bed, tidying her gifts into a neat*ish* pile.

Michael's face changed then, like the elastic string on his mask had snapped. "I've got some more of that … porridge you liked so much yesterday. Thought it might be, you know, a nice Lorntide treat." He disappeared behind the door and returned holding a tray. He put it beside her, smiled awkwardly, then hurried out of the door. He wasn't gone for more than a second when his head reappeared. "There are lots of people outside, Sadie. They're all dying to hear you play again."

"Dying?" she repeated, dryly.

"You know what I mean," he countered. "It'd be a marvellous Lorntide treat for everyone—including your mother and I—if you were to give a small recital. Do you feel that is something you might …?"

Yes, the music pushed the pain away for a while, but it seemed to come back stronger, more vicious, spiteful even. Michael's face loitered, expectant and hopeful. The pain shifted position, moving from the back of her eyes to the top of her spine. "Yes, yes. Of course," she said. "Sorry, I'll be down soon."

"Fantastic. I'll let everyone know. And ..." He looked ill, tortured. "Don't let your porridge go cold."

THE
INVITATION

Every nose in the Madison house sniffed joyously at the aroma bleeding from the kitchen. The smell of Lorntide drifted to the landing, where Sadie and Oliver stood, peering over the bannister at all the people below.

"Ah, here she is," Michael announced. "The remarkable, the sensational, the miraculous and talented ... Miss Sadie Madison!"

Sadie felt like the main attraction at a circus.

A performing seal, a dancing pony, a sad little clown.

Descending the stairs as gracefully as she knew how, Sadie edged past her ardent admirers while awkwardly balancing the breakfast tray. She passed it to her father who looked down at the empty bowl and gave her a half-smile.

Hundreds of eyes followed her into the library.

Sadie settled her skirts, licked both hands and attempted to flatten her tousled hair.

As she nestled onto the piano stool, a brilliant light flashed, disorientating her, angering the throb in her head.

A pictographer, with a wide moustache that curled up at the edges, smiled playfully. "He's getting a shot for The Iron Bridge Illustrated News," said a middle-aged woman, emerging from the crowd like a funnel-web spider.

She wore a vivid purple suit over a lime blouse that was buttoned tight under her chin. Her white-gold hair had been scraped back in a topknot, her face long and sharp, her mouth a thin dark line. In her small hands, whose nails were decorated with dark green polish, she held a bundle of papers, a pencil poised.

"I'm going to be in the newspaper?" Sadie asked, still dazzled by the flash.

"Of course," the woman replied. "Take a look around. Quite the sensation. We're not sure whether to list you under *Entertainment* or *Miracles*." She laughed, scribbling furiously. "Cassandra Monkford-Corpse," she said. "Reporter. Nosey parker. Your new best friend."

She held out a hand. Sadie shook it softly.

"Now, tell me. Any plans to perform on the wireless? Perhaps the National Broadcast?"

"New best friend?" Sadie echoed, her voice a whisper.

Murmurs of discontent rumbled through the house. Cassandra waved a theatrical hand to silence them. "How did this all happen?"

"What do you mean?"

"Practice? Natural ability? Talent? Magic?"

"A story," Sadie answered cautiously, looking past Cassandra for her father's reassuring face. "Grandfather William."

"Ah, so your grandfather taught you?" Cassandra concluded. "He *must* be a magician!"

Sadie shook her head. The black flecks were creeping round the edge of her vision. Sickening pain surged through her. "I've never met him," she answered, which made Cassandra stop mid-scribble.

The audience mumbled their discontent more forcefully. "I'm sorry," the reporter muttered, clearly annoyed she'd got precious little from Sadie. "Not to worry though, I can fill in the blanks." She stared at Sadie, her eyes hard and penetrating. "Mustn't keep you from your audience. Oh, and have a magical Lorntide and a wonderful New Year, my lovely."

Cassandra vanished into the audience as another flash

erupted from the pictographer.

Sadie rubbed her eyes with the heel of her hand. She wanted to collapse into her bedclothes, coil herself deeper and deeper into their embrace. But the audience pressed in.

She could feel them shuffling closer.

Could sense their anticipation, their desire.

Their potential disappointment.

And their anger.

Her head was primed to detonate. If she could find the music, perhaps the pain would abate for a time. She stretched her fingers onto the keys and looked out over the Shadow Valley. A calm swept through the house, like a well-deserved yawn. Sadie took a deep, goose-infused breath, and began.

Images bloomed. Strange foreign places, forbidden places, private and personal. They spoke to her. Sang to her. Sadie let them surround her, smother her, drench her skin with their magnificence. The mood in the house shifted through pleasure, joy, glee, euphoria, and into exaltation, as her fingers worked their cryptic mastery. A spellbinding performance.

But Sadie struggled.

Despite the beautiful music she made, something rotten festered inside. It scratched and clawed incessantly, ten times harder than before, and with more purpose.

Burrowing, destroying, shredding, tearing, ripping.

She brought the performance to a considered finale before resting her hands calmly on her lap. Her head dipped forward as her last drops of energy spirited away.

Applause broke across Iron Bridge.

Her audience appeared more disorientated this time, swaying rhythmically, their eyes gazing into the middle distance like an army of clapping automatons.

Rising, she pushed her way out.

They clawed gently at her clothes, her hair, her skin, desperate for a keepsake, raining praise and words of admiration into her ears as she fled. With the bedroom door shut, Sadie collapsed on the bed, holding her throbbing skull with both hands, the pain intensifying with each passing moment.

＊◡▦☆𝍐

As the music subsided, Michael retreated to his study. He needed a minute to himself. A moment to sit and think. The music left him coated with elation and joy, but something less magnificent loitered in his mind.

He pulled the Nepenthe from his pocket. A thimble's-worth left. One last dose. The last memories of Danver.

His fist shook. Glass wrapped in flesh.

Closing his eyes, Michael tried to picture a different path, a different outcome. Some way to make everything okay. Some way to save his daughter without destroying her best childhood memories.

He opened his fingers and let the bottle fall. Landing on its side, the Nepenthe rolled across his desk and stopped against a pile of books. Michael drew both hands down his face and let out a deep sigh. He snatched up the bottle again, thinking he'd throw it against the wall, smashing it into a thousand pieces. Instead, he flicked the cork out with his thumb and stared at the last traces of liquid. Michael Madison lifted the Nepenthe into the air, aiming the open bottle towards his mouth.

I'll just wash away my own thoughts, my own memories, my own stupid life.

He tipped the bottle.

The Nepenthe bubbled at the rim.

Dammit.

He slammed the bottle down on the desk, his thumb over the top.

She has to forget him. She has to. And she will.

An authoritative fist rapped on the door.

Michael snapped his head towards it.

Natalia stood in the doorway accompanied by a man dressed

in a smart, dark uniform, stripes and gold pendant hanging from his lapel.

Michael corked the Nepenthe and slid it onto his lap. "Yes," he said, aggravated by the intrusion. "What is it?"

Natalia's playful smile faded. "Oh, I'm sorry, Father. There's a ... man here to see you."

"There are hundreds of people here," Michael replied, gesturing towards the library. He nodded grimly at the man in uniform. "Who's this one?"

"He's from the Palace of Light, Father. He works for Alexsy Rubinov, Dimitri's father," she said sheepishly. "He has a letter for you ..."

"Yes, yes." Michael sighed, waving a hand at her dismissively. "What does this letter say?"

The man moved forward and gave Michael the traditional salute of the Winter Continent—two fingers pointing to his temple, three folded below—before proffering a folded card, embossed with ornate lettering and tied with green lace.

The man turned and left.

As Natalia looked on expectantly, Michael untied the bow and flipped the card open.

In three days hence,
the 28th of this great month of December,
Alexsy Rubinov and his glorious wife Helene, invite
Michael and Larissa Madison, and family,
to the Palace of Light for their Winter Festival.

Attractions, festivities and performers will be in attendance for your delectation and amusement.

The adventure begins at 6pm.
We look forward to seeing you then.
Alexsy and Helene Rubinov

On the back of the invitation was a handwritten message:

Dearest Sadie,
We're looking forward to seeing you at our party
on the 28th December. We would be eternally in your debt
if, after enjoying the festivities, you would honour our
distinguished guests and members of state with a small recital.
We await your response with anticipation,
Alexsy and Helene Rubinov

Michael sat back in his chair.

"I think Dimitri had something to do with it," Natalia said, studying her father's face.

Michael gave a shallow nod. "Go and show your mother," he replied, tossing the invitation towards his daughter.

As he moved, the Nepenthe slipped from his lap and rolled along the carpet. The green glass sparkled as it stopped by Natalia's feet.

"What's this?" she asked, bending to grasp the bottle.

"Nothing," Michael replied hurriedly, holding out a hand. "Give it here."

"Ne-penth-ay," Natalia read. "Is it alcohol? A Lorntide spirit?" she smiled, seduced by the gleaming bottle.

"Yes!" Michael lied. "A spirit, of sorts, but quite strong. You shouldn't—"

Natalia had already whipped the cork out and waved it under her nose. Michael launched forward, hands flailing for the bottle, but it was too late.

Natalia tipped the last dose down her throat.

"No!" Michael cried, knocking the bottle from her hands. It hit the wall and smashed into dozens of pieces. "You stupid girl! That was not for you. The Nepenthe—the spirit—you're far too young for such drinks!"

"Father!" Natalia shrieked, her hands trembling. "What's gotten into you? It's Lorntide!"

"Get out of here!"

Natalia grabbed the invitation and turned for the door. She stopped suddenly. A hand reached for the frame. Her body began to shake. Her face turned pale.

"Nat?"

Her eyes rolled back.

Her legs buckled.

Michael launched himself round the desk and caught his daughter before she struck the floor.

"Nepenthe, Nepenthe, Nepenthe," she whispered, her eyes glowing white orbs.

Beside her, broken glass lay on the study floor. A large green chunk still clung to the label. Michael traced a finger through the last remnants of the Nepenthe as it soaked into the carpet, ruined and lost.

Eli appeared in the doorway.

"Nepenthe. Nepenthe. Nepenthe."

"Find your mother," Michael told him, unable to sign. "Quickly!"

Eli disappeared.

Michael hoisted Natalia into his arms and carried her through the busy hallway and up to her room. As he placed her on the bed, Natalia's lips snapped open, spouting strange words in some foreign tongue.

Larissa burst through the door, heading straight for her daughter. "What's going on?"

Eli loitered in the doorway, Monster Magnifiers over his eyes, notebook in hand.

Go to your room, Michael signed, noticing his curious, silent son. Immediately.

Eli scanned the room, adjusting the levers and dials. Nodding satisfactorily, he obeyed his father and departed.

"Natalia?" Larissa urged, sitting on the edge of the bed. "What happened?"

"She came to deliver an invitation."

"Invitation?"

"To the Winter Festival."

Larissa fixed Michael with a cold, unblinking stare.

"And then she ... collapsed. The stress, probably."

Larissa didn't flinch.

No point in lying to his wife, she could sniff it a mile away.

"She had a *small* drink."

"A drink? Vodka, gin, brandy ... what? You didn't give her any ziela, did you? It's far too strong. Outlawed across the entire continent. And for good reason!"

"Nepenthe. Nepenthe. Nepenthe."

Larissa's mouth hung open. "Michael Madison!"

"It was Vulpes," he admitted. The words were out of his mouth before he could stop them, the same way the story of Grandfather William had sprung its cage.

Larissa's face darkened. "Vul-pes? Here? That creature was in my house?"

"Things are happening fast, Larissa. It's hard to stay focused when the music is playing," he admitted. "You must know that. I *know* you feel it."

"Yes," she admitted. "Sadie's music is remarkable. It does strange things. It changes me—inside."

"She's changing everything, the way we feared she would. She was talking of going to Hurtmore House. I had to do something, Larissa. I had to take steps to ensure—"

"Steps?" Larissa's eyes became wild, vengeful. "With Vulpes?"

"It was just a Nepenthe," he confessed. "I'd given her two doses. She just needed the third. One more dose. In her cordial or on her Lorntide pudding. One more dose, but—"

Realisation washed over Larissa's face. "Natalia drank it!" She put a hand to her mouth. Her red cuff bracelet slipped down her arm.

"It wasn't meant for her."

"You don't say?" Larissa pointed to Natalia's prone body, her lips still spouting unintelligible sounds. "You've poisoned both our daughters."

"*Poisoned?*" Michael exclaimed defensively. "Never. A remedy. A solution."

"You're her father. You're the one that's supposed to be there for her—for us—above all others! If we cannot rely on you, then we're all doomed. You're a monster, Michael Madison. A monster of the worst kind!"

A sudden rush of cold air filled the room, as though someone had opened a dimensional window to an arctic world.

"Vulpes," Larissa hissed, turning to look at his round white head, inky-black eyes, and dazzling teeth.

"Larissa," he whispered. The dark feathers around his neck ruffled as he spoke. "How wonderful to see you. You look … weary."

"Look at her. Look at my daughter. Look what you have done!"

"She's sleeping," he replied sarcastically. "A perfectly normal activity." He moved a step closer, listening. "And she's speaking Gyznian—no, Totchi. A bit of both."

"She drank the poison," Larissa exploded, her fingers flexing like claws. "She drank your Nepenthe!"

Michael struggled to hold her back.

"Get off me!"

"A poison?" Vulpes laughed, crude and sharp. "A cure, to be sure. A way to reveal the truth. A way to save Sadie from all the things you fear. The Foretelling, the Narrowers, Hurtmore House … the Unknown. Should I go on?"

"To what end?" Larissa growled.

"If the Nepenthe destroys all memory of Danver, it will prove your daughter is able to forget. That she is *not* the child of the Foretelling. And it would eradicate her desire to locate Hurtmore House too." Vulpes turned to Michael. "Stop me if I'm going too fast."

Larissa struggled, but Michael's grip held fast. "And what of Natalia?"

"It was made specifically for Sadie. With her own blood."

"You bled my daughter?"

"I have no idea what the side effects could be"—he looked down at Natalia—"for this one."

"Natalia!" Larissa burst out. "Her name is Natalia. You—" She whipped her head over her shoulder and looked at Michael. "And you, are to blame for all of this! You *must* know what will happen to her. You simply must."

"La-rissa," Vulpes purred. "My dear. Don't take me for a conjuror of party tricks and misdirection. A Nepenthe is old magic, robust and complex. Your daughter could suffer anything from disorientation and headaches to a complete psychological break, even slip into a coma." Vulpes spread his hands expansively. "But she'll probably have a good, long sleep and be as right as rain come the morning."

"You'd better pray to the Gods she is!" Larissa warned. "Now, get out of my house. You are not welcome here. And never … *ever* … come near me or my family again. Do you hear me? Do you?"

Vulpes' face remained expressionless. Her fury seemed to have no effect on him whatsoever. "You should watch your tongue," he replied. "Talk of the Gods will have you taken far from your precious family and everything you care about."

"Vulpes!" she wailed into the stillness of Natalia's bedroom, but he had gone.

Dropping to her daughter's side, Larissa put a hand on her forehead. Natalia's eyes moved erratically beneath her eyelids, secret dreams swarming through her mind. Without looking, Larissa held up a hand and Michael took it.

"I'm sorry," he whispered. "I'll fix this. Whatever it takes."

"There's no way to fix this, Michael. We've always known this would happen. That things would get beyond our control. But that was *our* decision. Neither of us could stomach the alternative." They remained still, silent. "Do you remember a time before all this? When it was only you and me rattling around in this big old house? We were young, fearless. We could have done anything, gone anywhere, been whatever we wanted. If you could go back now and make a different choice, would you?"

"No. I'd never give back the thirteen years we've had with Sadie. Despite all that's happened, and all that is to come. I wouldn't change a thing."

Larissa braved a smile. "Good," she said. "Things are far worse than we ever imagined. I thought I knew what we were doing, where we were heading, every step planned out. But the future is clouded and unclear. The music, and Vulpes' meddling, and *you*."

"I'll find another way," he promised. "Another Nepenthe perhaps—"

Larissa swallowed hard. "There is no other way, Michael. A thousand Nepenthes won't make a blind bit of difference. Don't you get it? We've failed. The Foretelling is coming. It's only a matter of time."

✸☺▤☆𝍊

Nepenthe? Sadie spelled the word back to Eli with her hands. *She said Nepenthe?*

Eli nodded, flipping through his notebook with one hand and adjusting his Monster Magnifiers with the other.

They stood on the landing by the arched picture window that looked out over the Shadow Valley. Fable perched on the ledge watching them lazily with one eye. Sadie turned away from her brother who had returned to scribbling in his notebook and leant against the bannister.

"Do you know what Nepenthe is?" Oliver asked.

"Yes," she replied. "It's in one of my encyclopaedias."

"Well?"

"Nepenthe. A potion used by the ancients to induce forgetfulness of pain or sorrow," she said. "What's Natalia doing drinking something like that?"

Oliver's eyes darkened. "The Nepenthe was not meant for Natalia."

"Then who?" Sadie frowned, then, "No. Don't be ridiculous. Who would want to give *me* something like that?"

"You are the one who cannot forget," he reminded her, as if he needed to. "You are the one able to recall every moment of your life. You are the one producing this strange music which has the whole of Iron Bridge under its spell. You are the one—"

But she silenced him with a cold stare.

"Me?" she whispered, leaning over on the bannister. Exhaustion rose through her. People mingled in the hallway, laughter and joyful chatter rising through the house. "You really think—?"

"Of course," he urged. "They are trying to make you forget something ... or everything!" He froze. "Like they did to Danver's parents," he cried, grabbing Sadie by the shoulders and shaking her gently. "Danver! It is all about Danver."

"You keep saying that name like it should mean something to me."

"Exactly."

"Who was he?"

"He is your friend. Your best friend."

Sadie scowled. "You're my best friend. Not this ... Danver."

Her eyes turned sad, veiled in tears.

"What is it?"

"Nepenthes are delivered in doses," she explained. "The number of doses depends on the amount of pain or sorrow that must be forgotten. Or so the description goes."

"So?"

"Someone would have to give it to me. They'd have to put it in my food, or drink, disguise it somehow." A single tear left her eye. "There are only two people—"

"They are your parents," Oliver whispered. "They would never do such a thing."

Sadie removed the tear and smeared it into her dress.

Larissa and Michael emerged from Natalia's bedroom.

"There you are," her mother said, shifting round the landing and taking Sadie in her arms. "Are you okay?"

Eli pulled a white envelope from his notebook and handed it to his mother. Found this, he signed, tucking the notebook under his arm. Downstairs.

Larissa turned the invitation in her hands. She traced a finger over the Rubinov crest embossed on the crisp white card. Flipping the invitation open, she read every word aloud, including the personal message to Sadie on the back.

A curious smile appeared on her lips.

Her emerald eyes sparkled.

"The Winter Festival, Sadie. The Palace of Light, dear. And they want you to perform! They want to hear your music. The Rubinovs—*and their distinguished guests and members of state*—want to hear you perform. Isn't that amazing? Isn't that the greatest thrill of all?"

Listening to her mother's outpouring made Sadie swallow her sadness and anger. She knew then her mother had no part in the Nepenthe. Her gaze shifted to Michael. He'd hidden the Foretelling from her. She'd almost forgiven him for that. But now this. Everything she'd known and loved about him, everything he'd taught her and everything he stood for—even the bedtime stories he weaved for her night after night—turned to ash.

"That *is* amazing." Sadie smiled joylessly. "That's the most amazing news I've ever heard."

"This is going to be the best Lorntide ever," Larissa insisted. She slid an arm around her husband as he idly stroked Fable's ice-white fur. The cat hissed, unimpressed.

"That's right," he concurred. "The best ever."

Michael looked at the Lorntide garland hanging beside the picture window.

He plucked a sprig of Anmer.

Larissa inched away at the sight of it, Michael's face looming beyond. But she relinquished, moved forward, and kissed her husband tenderly on the lips. He turned to Sadie, crouching before her, the Anmer raised over her head.

"Come on, Sadie. It's traditional."

Sadie did her best to sweep all emotion aside.

She leant forward ... *the porridge. Of course. It was in the porridge* ... and planted her quivering lips on his cold, shallow cheek.

THE
DUNGEON

Far beneath the earth, in a room of grey stone and iron bars, stood a boy. A bucket lingered in one corner. A rotten bed with filthy bedsheets lurked against the wall. Fire-torches burned.

His clothes and skin were covered in dirt.

His eyes, like black pools, strained in the firelight.

He reached through the iron bars.

He could sense her.

"Help me," he whispered, snatching at air. "Please help me."

"Who are you? Where are you?" she asked, but found herself drifting down a corridor, away from him, passing more and more cells, until she climbed a long windowless staircase.

His voice followed her, pained, whispering tormented words.

The dream vanished.

Dashing across the room, she pulled a notebook and fountain pen from her dressing table drawer. She closed her eyes and tried to see his face again, but it faded, drifted away. She squeezed the pen tight and began to scribble.

She wrote four words.

The sun broke its cover from behind the Carcassus Mountains. It had been years since she had seen a sunrise, far more content to sleep and dream. She'd forgotten how beautiful the Shadow Valley could be.

Natalia closed the notebook and smiled.

Knuckles rapped softly on the door. Sadie rolled over and looked at her sister's face.

"You awake?" said Natalia.

"I am now," Sadie replied, kicking back the bedclothes and rolling her shoulders. "Are you okay? Eli said you collapsed, and your eyes went ... weird."

"Something happened," Natalia replied, clutching a notebook. Her eyes looked normal. Emerald-green, naive and confused. "I had a dream," she started. "A strange dream. I was in this prison, or maybe it was a dungeon. Cold and wet and dark. There was this small, dirty boy. I couldn't make out his face, but he spoke to me, calling out in a whisper. He said four words. I wrote them down."

Natalia flipped through the pages.

The dream sounded like the one Sadie had had about the Witch Tree in San Cristophe. A vision? A premonition? Something unnatural. "What words?"

"Here," Natalia said, flattening the notebook and pointing to her inky handwriting.

Danver Tomes. Hurtmore House.

Sadie frowned at them.

"He's your ... friend, isn't he? I feel like I know him too, but in an odd way. He feels like one of those people you hear about in one of Father's stories, but never actually meet. I have an idea of his face but it's ... out of reach. Does that make sense?"

Natalia reached out and put a hand on her sister's arm.

Sadie's skin fizzed with static.

Her mind exploded with images.

Rolling onto her side, she curled herself into a ball and shook like a frightened mouse.

"Sadie?" Natalia tried, kneeling beside her on the bed. "What's happening? Who is Danver Tomes?"

When Natalia said his name aloud, something burst

through. Sadie's heart quickened, her stomach flipped, her mind flooded with emotion. Exploding like a show-stopping firework, his face returned to her.

"Danver," she whispered. "My friend."

There was almost nothing of him left, a face, a lingering outline. Memories filled her mind, emerging like bubbles on the surface of a dark ocean.

"I have to save him," Sadie said, her lips trembling. "I have to save him, Natalia. He's in a horrible dungeon, a disgusting prison. He needs me, Nat. I have to go to him."

"But where? Where is …" Her sister looked at the notebook. "Hurtmore House?"

"I don't know. I mean, nobody does. Not really. I guess … maybe … the doktor."

Natalia looked baffled.

"You remember the fight?" Natalia nodded. "Afterwards, Doktor Merrick came and took Danver," Sadie explained. The long, black, important-looking automobile stationed outside the Tomes' house came to her, the Gladstone Writing Ball, Hobbsworth's grubby fingers, the mysterious black leather book.

Steadying herself, she opened the secret compartment beneath the floor where she'd stashed *Hurtmore House: Remedy Through Torment.*

More memories returned to Sadie. They came thick and fast. It felt like a blackout curtain being torn down allowing voluminous light to illuminate all that had been lost. Sadie gulped for air as the images of her life with Danver filled every inch of her mind. Every conversation, every game, every secret, and every argument swirled into her, filling her up, making her whole, like a demolished house rebuilding itself, brick by brick.

Natalia shook her. "Sadie?" she cried. "What's happening?"

But Sadie smiled. A smile filled with every good thing she could think of.

"I'm fine," she said. "I'm better than fine. I'm great. Amazing."

Natalia's dazzling green eyes sparkled. "I don't understand."

"You shouldn't have to," Sadie said. "This is something Oliver and I need to do."

"Who is Oliver?"

Sadie's gaze shifted a fraction, focusing on something over Natalia's shoulder. "He's standing right behind you."

Oliver stepped forward as Natalia's head swivelled. Her hand shot to her mouth, gasping. She toppled backwards and let out a stifled scream.

"He's real?" she said, gripping the wall for support.

Sadie and Oliver froze.

"You can see me?"

"You can see him?"

Natalia nodded. "Who is he? Who are you?" She struggled to stand, her legs clearly refusing to answer the instructions of her brain. "What are you doing in our house at this hour?" She skittered across the room like an upturned beetle. "Where did you come from?"

"Sadie made me. At least, she needed me, and I was here."

"She *made* you? Out of what? Thin air? How is ...? That's not possible." Pinning herself against the window, Natalia forked her fingers through her golden hair.

"I don't understand either," Sadie added, sitting beside her. "But he's part of me. He's real. As real as he needs to be."

"This is a dream, isn't it?" Natalia said, looking down into Sadie's secret compartment. "This is another dream, like the boy in the prison. I feel strange. Is this what being hungover feels like? What was in that drink?"

"Yes, Natalia," Sadie replied, bouncing on the mattress. "The Nepenthe! Of course. That's why you can see him."

Natalia's hands flopped to her sides. She looked at Oliver again, taking long blinks, whispering incomprehensibly to herself. He stood awkwardly in the middle of the room, his long limbs coated in black from head to toe. The red scarf ribboned around his neck.

"I am here," he told her. "Blinking will change nothing."

"So, what's your story?" Natalia said. "Where were you before Sadie … *made* you?" After the words came out, Natalia's face looked offended by their very nature.

"I am unsure," Oliver replied. "I am still not *one* thing." Natalia wrinkled her nose as though she'd smelt something awful. "I think I am a collection of things. Some old, some new, some happy, some sad. I am an amalgamation. It is hard to describe."

"I suppose it's like asking you how all the atoms in your body feel," Sadie added. "Where they've been, and what they were before they were flesh or blood or bone or—"

Natalia looked horrified. "My body was something else before it was me?"

"Of course," she said. "And you'll be something else after you die, too."

"I think I need to go back to bed. This is … All of this is …"

Sadie nodded.

"I cannot believe she saw me!" Oliver exploded as Natalia left the room.

Anger prickled Sadie's skin, bitter and cold. "Vulpes made it," she said through clenched teeth. "He wasn't cleaning the cut on my chin, he was stealing my blood. And that goblet of strange liquid must have been—" Her eyes found Oliver's. "I know, I know. You told me so."

She slammed her fists into the window seat. Michael's betrayal ached. Sadie found it hard to think of him without her blood boiling over into a feverous rage.

Tears pressed on the corners of her eyes, promising to fall.

Her fists shook.

"You are scaring me," Oliver said.

"I know."

A crisp winter dawn enveloped the Shadow Valley. Joy flowed through the people of Iron Bridge as they opened their eyes on a welcoming world. The music that had filled their hearts sang on through their dreams, encompassing every hour of daylight.

But every heart longed for the next performance.

Together, the people of Iron Bridge prayed for the music to begin. They went about their business in a new way. Everything brighter, more colourful, exciting. They seemed to float through the day, consumed by their euphoria and their love for all that was good and just.

In the eaved bedroom, the words of the Foretelling floated through Sadie's mind. She could feel them scratching at the back of her eyes, lurking, reminding her.

The child that wields untold power and dominion will be the firstborn, of the firstborn, fallen from the highest.

And she thought of the three paths described by Rhiannon.

The Narrowers wanted her dead.

The Balance wanted her to forget.

The Unknown wanted her power for his own.

She wondered—if the day ever came—which she would choose, which she was destined for, or if any of this truly involved her at all. She didn't want it, any of it. She wanted to read her scary books, play let's pretend, discover the secrets of the Glade of Remembrance, and dream of a future where she became a student at the University of San Cristophe, striding forth into the world: fearless, adventurous, and filled with love.

With the pain of the Nepenthe washing away, Sadie took to the piano and played her heart out. She rang joy and beauty from every note. Bliss and rapture from every chord. Delivered heavenly, enchanted melodies with every touch of her fingers. Happiness in her music kept the darkness surrounding her father at arm's length, kept the dark notes from her masterful fingers, and the three choices from gaining any ground.

And all because Danver was back in her heart.

But Sadie ached.

Ached for Danver to be close.

The distance between them was impossible to fathom, but somehow palpable. She could taste his absence, as though in some other dimension. A sidestep away.

She lay awake in the early hours of each morning thinking of him. She scoured the library and her father's study for books and pictograms, journals and ornaments, anything leading to him, anything that might produce a clue, a path, a glimmer of hope.

She found nothing. A crushing blank.

With Oliver close, she studied the black leather book on Hurtmore House, but every time she read it the words and pictographs changed. Reluctantly, she stowed it beneath the floorboards for safe keeping, frustrated it had failed to provide all it had promised.

But she had Oliver.

She had the music.

And as she played, she drifted away, seeing new places and faces, days long ago, events occurring in real time. She transitioned from one joyous event to the next, the images blurring and refocusing themselves, colour melting and swirling, sounds and smells forming around her and ebbing away. Each scene personal and unique, bursting with happiness and contentment. They were like dreams, but no dream Sadie had ever experienced before. These felt real. True, they weren't hers, but somehow, she could see them. Everywhere she went the music carried her, powerful and safe, as though riding a mighty dragon.

The days ticked by.

Iron Bridge came to a halt.

Sadie's music filled every soul with euphoria and contentment.

Stories of good deeds, humanitarian work, and modern miracles filled the local press. Families and businesses opened their doors to any who needed shelter, food, a kind ear.

Iron Bridge buzzed with happiness and good will to all.

Increased numbers of Ryndai materialised on the streets.

Oliver sat through the night watching them patrol Leviathan Crook. From the Palace of Light all the way to the River Myr. Their dark suspicious eyes, shrouded in shadow behind thick cowls and crystal lanterns, were now trained on the Madison house.

Despite this, people left the sanctuary of their homes and wirelesses, and were out on the streets singing and praising the glory of the world. Their hands reached for the heavens as their hearts swelled with the bliss and joy fizzing in their blood. A sight not seen since long before the Divine Wars.

Sadie's music overwhelmed the entire town. It washed away their selfishness, their greed, and their fear. They held their lives in their hands, seizing each moment as though it were their last. Smiles and cheer and thanks threw out the cold, and the warmth of human kindness blanketed the town like the gently falling snow.

THE WOMAN WHO LABELLED EVERYTHING

In a majestic house, on an immaculate street, opposite the Royal Park in Ville de Feuilles—the City of Leaves—lived a wealthy woman named Estelle Gautreau.

Split over five floors, her house was packed with books, paintings, ornaments and antiques, glamorous clothing and costumes, jewellery, shoes and wigs, flawless wooden furniture, couches, armchairs and chaise longues, tiny silver thimbles, spoons, pill coffers, snuff boxes and cigarette cases, and every type of possession and collectable you care to mention.

Sitting in her house, surrounded by her belongings every day, made Estelle happy beyond all imagining. But a sadness lingered in her heart. Something was missing. Something she coveted more than anything else in the world.

Now, the City of Leaves was famous throughout Norland for its New Year celebrations.

One year, the Royal Park opposite Estelle Gautreau's house had been chosen to hold the festivities. She watched with fevered anticipation as the carnival arrived and an army of roustabouts worked tirelessly to rig tents and fairground attractions.

When the fateful evening arrived, Estelle dressed in her finest clothes and wandered through the canvas avenues. Glorious sounds and smells swirled through the night air, filling her with wonder. She sampled whiskey-glazed pork skewers; toffee-flavoured tea coated with fluffy cream and chocolate flakes; fried potatoes dripping with cheeses from all over the world. And, to her astonishment, found herself outside a fortune teller's tent, considering if she should enter.

Now, Estelle was a cautious woman, not one to be taken by frivolous notions such as fate and destiny on the turn of a card or glimpsed in a crystal ball. But she soon found herself sitting in a candlelit tent with a stranger's hands on hers.

"Why have you come?" the fortune teller asked.

"I felt … compelled."

"What is it you seek?"

"Nothing. I have everything. More than I need."

"Yet there is something missing," the mystic told her. "In your heart, Estelle. A longing. A need. Something money cannot buy."

Estelle pulled her hands away. "How do you know such things? How do you know my name?"

The fortune teller's hands slipped beneath the table. "Do not be afraid. Speak from your heart."

Estelle's bottom lip quivered. "Love," she said, finally. "I wish to be loved."

The fortune teller stared at Estelle for a moment. "To find love—true love—you must let people into your life. Relinquish the hold on your material things. Collect memories and experiences, not possessions. Talk to every stranger. Accept every invitation. Live in a way you have never lived before. Do this, and love can be yours."

Back home, Estelle swept through every room and admired her belongings. She brushed her hands against furniture, ran her fingers over rugs and silver jewellery, smelt the polish and incense and the wealth packed into every corner. Finally, at the stroke of midnight—as fireworks erupted in a storm of colour above the Royal Park—she hauled the bottom drawer of her armoire open and lifted out a nickel-plated dymograph.

A dymograph, if you didn't already know, is a compact typewriter that prints onto small strips of parchment while coating the reverse in a mild adhesive. She spent the entire night printing dymograph labels and sticking them to everything around her.

Item #00001: Bedside tables (pair). Mahogany, two drawers.

Item #00002: Hand-forged, wrought-iron bed, dragon-size, brass bed knobs.

Item #00003: Rug, Persian, labyrinth design.

And so on.

As she dymographed each item, she measured the dimensions and noted them in a large, leather-bound journal. She took a pictogram of each item and developed them in her dark room. After almost two days of typing and measuring, pictography and scribbling, Estelle had done her entire bedroom—six hundred and fifty-eight items.

She spent the following thirty days and thirty nights cataloguing every item in her enormous house. In total, she dymographed and recorded seventy-four thousand, eight-hundred and forty-three items which included everything from an oak dining table made to seat twenty to the tiniest pair of silver sugar tongs in her doll's house.

As the final item—the dymograph itself—was recorded, Estelle collapsed onto her bed and slept for days.

She woke to a man shaking her gently.

"Madame?" He wore a pine green City Warden's uniform. "For a minute there, I thought you were dead."

"Dead?" she replied, sitting up.

"You haven't been seen for days," he told her. "People have been worried."

"People?" she replied. "What people? I have no—" The word *friends* stuck in her throat. "Who are you?"

"Officer Leroux. August Leroux," he told her. "Madame? Do you feel alright?"

"I'm fine. Just tired."

"You have a fantastic home."

"It's been my life's work. I wouldn't change it for the world."

Estelle stopped, frozen.

The last thirty days and nights bloomed in her mind.

She looked at the bedside table. The dymograph sat silently. Its label curled around the side. "But ... I have to get rid of it. All of it."

August looked amazed. "Whatever for?"

"I have so many things but nothing more. Collections, objects, possessions. That is all my life has become. An abundance of treasures I cannot take with me when I leave this world."

"Most people would covet what you have," he said. "You should enjoy them."

Estelle nodded, but her face looked sad. "I have. For many years. But now my possessions are bereft of enjoyment. The things I own have ended up owning me."

And so, from that day, Estelle Gautreau dragged her dining table out onto the cobbled street at midday and, for one hour, covered it with box after box of her worldly possessions. As people passed, Estelle studied them and gave her treasured possessions to those she felt suited them. Some people were unsure, confused by her actions. But, as word spread, hordes flocked to the house opposite the Royal Park to see if Estelle Gautreau would bestow one of her treasures upon them.

Officer Leroux returned to see Estelle from time to time. He stood and watched as she gave away the things she had spent her life collecting. One day, as the last item left the table, he approached Estelle and invited her for coffee, and then dinner, and then for a stroll in the Royal Park. In turn, Estelle invited him to watercolour classes, book swaps, a steamboat trip down the Blackbrook beneath the withering trees and the white-painted bridges of Le Tigre.

And, as sure as summer follows spring, Estelle and August were wed in the Royal Park opposite her house and news of a baby followed. Throughout her pregnancy, Estelle continued to distribute her possessions, one by one, to people gathered outside her house. She refused to take a day off, even when August begged her, fearing she looked unwell. Her addiction to ridding herself of every possession took precedence over all else. With each item leaving her hands, she became lighter, transforming into someone new, someone better.

Estelle drove forward, day after day, until she had nothing but a single box.

It contained a pair of bronze bookends in the form of playful cats, a handful of framed oil paintings, a jar of mixed buttons, and the dymograph itself. But, as she headed out onto the street to free herself of her last possessions, her child sprang forth into the world.

Estelle gave birth to a baby girl at the foot of the stairs of her enormous house with August and a troupe of nurses surrounding her.

The following day she took to the street, determined to complete her task. With her daughter beside her in a basket, Estelle relinquished the bronze bookends to an old man in a grey suit, the oil paintings to a young couple hopelessly in love, and the jar of buttons to a gang of children playing in the park. The dining table itself, over which every item had been passed and countless lives were changed forever, fell into the possession of the local museum and was heralded as an icon of modern culture.

Estelle took the dymograph and the leather-bound journal containing every listing and pictogram and placed them on the cobbles.

Her hands shook.

August came to her side. "Two to go," he said. "And you'll be free."

"I need a minute."

Nodding, he left Estelle on the street and disappeared into the huge empty house. The afternoon passed slowly, and Estelle did not return. Eventually, August went in search of his wife and found her sitting on a bench at the centre of the Royal Park. He smiled with relief as she came into view, cradling their daughter.

But, as he approached, his relief shifted to terror, for what she held was not their daughter at all. "What have you done?"

Estelle stared into the distance.

A muted breeze caressed her hair.

"What are you doing with that?" August demanded, pointing. "Where's our daughter?"

"I couldn't do it," Estelle said slowly, looking at her panic-stricken husband.

Her eyes drifted to the object in her lap.

The leather-bound journal containing all the things she had once owned.

"I'm taking them all back." Her hands gripped the soft leather as her voice rasped a desperate whisper. "They're mine!"

August looked lost.

With tears in his eyes, he wrestled the journal from his deranged wife and rifled through the pages. Estelle's fingernails rent the air, desperate to retrieve the huge tome, but August forced her aside and ran a trembling finger down the last page of the manuscript.

He flashed past the bookends, the oil paintings, the jar of buttons, the dining table.

And then—

Item#74843. Dymograph. Nickel-plated. 6 inches x 2.5 inches. Well-used.

Item#74844. Baby. Female (unnamed). 18 inches (approx). Hair: Blonde. Eyes: Green.

PART THREE
METAMORPHOSIS

"Music is the sixth magic.
A power that rivals tears and memory."
—SANTA LYANA,
Temple of the Moon, San Lundkvistburg, 1669

THE
STARTRAIN

Wisps of ivory cloud formed in the early evening sky.

The world turned from blue to gold as the three wise cats congregated to watch Larissa dress Sadie in a heavily embroidered ballgown. The tight bodice shimmered with copper and bloomed like a luscious mauve flower as it floated towards the floor, ensconced in fine silver lace.

Sadie frowned solemnly.

Her mother laced the back and fastened a safety pin to stop it slipping. The dress had once belonged to Natalia, but Sadie had yet to fully grow into it.

"I look stupid," she complained bitterly. "I want to wear my black skirts. And my black tights. And my black cardigan. I look like a Lorntide tree. I'll never be able to perform wearing this!"

"Tonight is important, Sadie," Larissa said, dismissing her daughter. Jabbing several pins between her teeth, she mumbled, "Please hold still."

Despite this, excitement about the Winter Festival fluttered in Sadie's heart. Thoughts of Vulpes and her father—thoughts that lurked beneath a rattling trapdoor, fingers rising through the cracks, promising to break free—were kept to one side.

The grandfather clock chimed six. It made Larissa jump, then sigh. Her fingers worked faster. "We're out of time," she said. "I suppose this will have to do."

Sadie shrugged, lifted the dress off the floor and trudged onto the landing.

Below, Michael fastened his bowtie and slipped his arms into an old dinner jacket. His outfit had been handed down too—from Grandfather William no less—and, at one time, had been quite resplendent. Staring at himself in the hall mirror, Michael attempted a smile, a mischievous raised eyebrow.

Natalia and Eli joined their sister at the top of the stairs.

Eli was buttoned up to the chin in a black suit, crisp white shirt and green velvet bowtie. His hair had been slicked off his face, making him look like another person altogether. But, true to form, his Monster Magnifiers hung round his neck, notebook in hand.

Natalia had coiled herself in pink and silver—a floating cough sweet—her hair swept up in a mind-bending algorithm and fixed with hand-carved sandarac hairsticks whose jade terminals twinkled like distant moons.

Sadie and Natalia floated down the stairs. Their dresses brushed each step with a gentle *shwoosh*. Eli trudged behind, a look of mild irritation on his face. Michael took him into the library to adjust his bowtie while Sadie and Natalia waited for their mother in the living room.

Sadie sat on the green velvet couch next to Oliver. Natalia gave him an awkward smile before picking up a copy of *The Iron Bridge Illustrated News* and skimming the pages for anything remotely interesting.

"Have you seen this?" Natalia said, suddenly waving the newspaper. "This article on you is wonderful." Sure enough, Cassandra Monkford-Corpse's gushing editorial dominated the centre spread beside a pictogram of Sadie at the piano. "Great pictograms," Natalia went on. "You should cut them out and put them in the family album."

Sadie finished fastening her heavy black boots, which she hoped to conceal beneath her dress, and stomped across the room. She took the newspaper from her sister and, kneeling on the floor, spread the pages before her.

Winter Wonderchild Wows the Shadow Valley.

She turned her attention to the pictogram opposite which dominated the entire page. Sadie's sunlit face shone with concentration, her fingers a blur upon the keyboard, her tangled hair thrown over her shoulders. The faces of her audience hung like ceremonial masks on a museum wall. She found Atticus and the three wise cats curled up by the fireplace, the faces of Cale Boswick and Arnold Tomes pressed to the window.

Danver.

Sadie's head dropped as the magic of the Winter Festival stepped aside and thoughts of her lost friend took centre stage. Scouring the pages of *Hurtmore House: Remedy Through Torment,* she'd found nothing except a series of horrifying techniques and procedures—the kind designed to make your skin crawl, your teeth ache—fashioned to cure and mend. But all Sadie saw on those pages was pain and suffering and hopelessness.

The book was peculiar.

Every time she opened it Sadie noticed something different. A pictogram of several scientists she kept returning to. And never the same twice. One day there would be three men and two women, another day they were all women, another all men. Some days there were five people, other days three, six, eight, one. A dog sometimes and once, a parrot. All the articles shifted position too. Half the time it was impossible to find what she was looking for. The story of Hershel Winter-Smith kept leaping around inside the book and mixing itself in with all those torturous remedies that Sadie could barely stomach.

She'd tried to use the music to find Danver, drifting in and out of those strange, personal visions, looking for clues to Hurtmore House. But there were no filthy dungeons like Natalia had described. No hospitals or treatment rooms. Nothing but the happiest of things.

"Ladies and Gentlemen," Michael announced ceremoniously, appearing at the arched doorway wearing his winter greatcoat.

It looked far too heavy for his slender frame. Sadie glanced up from the newspaper as Eli sprung onto the green velvet couch. "Please be upstanding for Larissa Odessa Madison."

Their mother glided into the room. Her ballgown shone in vibrant silver-teal, adorned with black lace, gleaming crystals, and sleeves—like that of a sorcerer—that hung impossibly low. On her head, a cluster of black feathers erupted from a mound of swirling blonde hair.

To Sadie it looked like an upturned pail of sand snakes.

Checking his pocket watch, Michael announced, "It is time."

☀ ⌣ ▤ ⚹ ♨

Michael had exhumed the Madison automobile from the snow and spent several afternoons with his head under the bonnet. Finally, with the help of enthusiastic volunteers, he'd got the machine running and scrubbed the dented bodywork until it shone like onyx. Despite his best efforts—which included several attempts with hot lemon, mild detergents, and even a squirt or two of Larissa's most pungent perfumes—he still hadn't eradicated an unspeakable smell that loitered inside.

Ignoring the bothersome aroma, the Madisons bundled in.

Michael fired the engine, released the handbrake, and launched the automobile onto Leviathan Crook. Natalia and Larissa squealed with excitement as the threadbare tyres squirmed on the ice.

Michael drove uphill, beyond the last houses on Leviathan Crook. The entire family held their breath as he guided the automobile between the forest wall and the plunging depths of Iron Bridge Quarry. At the crest of the hill, the road widened. Turning towards the forest, they drove for several minutes until the road narrowed again. The old automobile snaked and climbed between the trees until they fizzed along the gravel approach road and through the mighty gateway to the Palace of Light.

Hundreds of lanterns flickered between the sandarac trees. Sadie got an eyeful of the historic scenes depicted in the coloured-glass windows—Vasilisa and Baba Yaga, Father Frost, the Armless Maiden, Yuri and the Bloodspider, and hundreds more—as Michael slid the automobile to a graceful halt on the flagstone courtyard.

A young man in dark uniform stepped forward. He opened the door and peered inside. "Welcome, Mr Madison, to the Palace of Light. Welcome to the Winter Festival."

The young man walked to the opposite side and opened the door for Larissa. "Mrs Madison," he said, nodding his head formally. He reached for the backdoor, but Sadie had already booted it open and jumped out.

"Good evening, Miss Madison," he said, bowing generously. Sadie giggled and saluted him. "The attendees are looking forward to your recital with much anticipation," he added. "You are quite the talk of the festival."

Sadie gave him an informal thumbs-up which made every muscle in Larissa's body tense. Natalia and Eli slithered out and followed their parents up the palace steps. Two enormous arched doors were swung wide. Snowflakes danced in delightful spirals as they drifted over the threshold. Beyond lay a colossal hallway filled with people in expensive suits and lavish ballgowns. Beautiful music and excited chatter filled the night air.

Glasses *clinked*.

Champagne corks *thwocked*.

The main hallway rose through four storeys with stone stairways criss-crossing overhead. Huge oil paintings of the Rubinov family dominated the walls with strict, severe faces. Rosewood tables, monk seats, bureaus, display cabinets, and card tables were mounted with priceless ceramics and silverware from San Lundkvistburg and the far reaches of the Winter Continent.

Sadie thought of Rhiannon's little antique shop and how the Palace of Light was at the other end of the interior-design spectrum.

Perfumed oils and incense swirled around the hallway, warm and inviting. Sadie's heart began to sing. The Palace of Light made her feel as though she'd walked into another land, into an alien world, an alternate reality.

Somewhere truly mesmerising.

Somewhere filled with magic and wonder.

Dimitri Rubinov came bounding towards them. He slipped on the polished marble floor as he swerved to avoid a full-bodied collision with the other party guests. "Come quickly," he said, gathering himself. "Father finished it this afternoon. He wants you to be the first!"

✹☉▦⚟🏛

Dimitri led them across the vaulted hallway, beneath the circling stairways, through an archway wider than the entire Madison house, and into the palace gardens. They passed two giant marble fountains—one of swans and ganders, the other griffins and dragons—down a long flight of stone steps to a paved courtyard bustling with guests.

The smell of rich food, winter flowers, and assorted perfumes danced all around. Sadie's feet skipped on the flagstones as she made her way beneath a hedgerow arch and into the infectious hubbub of activity resonating beyond.

Dimitri beamed at Natalia, half-dragging her by the hand.

"What's going on?"

"You'll see."

The Madison family emerged on the most baffling sight any of them had ever seen. A gigantic construction of red iron and wood towered before them. It twisted and weaved around itself, bolted together with mighty pins, stretching hundreds of feet in every direction. Surrounding the construction, an endless stream of lanterns doused the structure and scores of elegant guests in warm amber light.

"What is it?" asked Natalia, aghast.

"Don't be so silly," Larissa bustled in, trying to save her daughter's blushes. "It's … well, it's art, isn't it?"

Dimitri smiled at Larissa. "In a way," he said. "But it serves a far more exciting purpose."

"Are those railway tracks?" Natalia asked, pointing into the air. Dimitri smiled.

"And that's a train," she said, almost robotically, her eyes unblinking.

"It's a railway?" Michael uttered. "On stilts?"

"Father!" Dimitri called, beckoning to a man at the centre of everyone's attention. "The Madisons are here!"

Alexsy Rubinov raised a hand and waved theatrically. The Madisons waved back curiously, one eye on their host, the other on the railway in the sky.

"Os rivolta!" Alexsy cried in perfect Lundkvistanese as he bounded over. "Parvelle, parvelle, parvelle! Welcome to the Palace of Light … and the Winter Festival! It's lovely to finally meet you all. Do excuse my attire. I've been breaking my back trying to get this blasted thing finished. I'll wash up shortly. Do you have a drink? Sjonta exemplar, Dimitri! Fetch some refreshments for our guests at once. And where are your brothers?" He turned and gestured towards the huge structure. "What do you think? I've been working on her for almost a year. Now, I know Natalia, and I'm guessing you're Eli—and Michael and Larissa, of course—and where is our esteemed guest? Ah, Sadie Madison, there you are!"

Sadie had not expected billionaire business mogul Alexsy Rubinov to be dressed in engineering overalls and coated from head to toe in axle grease.

She stared wide-eyed at him as he turned from one Madison to the next, talking at a hundred miles an hour. "It's called the StarTrain. A working title, at least. It's a thrill ride, vin? You know, like the Ice Slides in San Lundkvistburg. Only this one runs on rails like a steam train. And, you know, up amongst the stars. Mr Madison, are you okay?"

"I ..." Michael said. "I've never seen the like of it."

"And never will again!" Alexsy boasted. "I'm itching for a go. Who's with me?"

Sadie's hand shot up like a rocket, but Larissa forced it down.

"An adventurous soul!" Alexsy rasped, his eyes sparkling. "Exemplar! Who else? Come on, come on. This is going to make history. This *is* history!"

"It doesn't look particularly safe," Larissa muttered.

Alexsy turned to her. His expression changed. He gave her a faint, knowing smile.

"I can assure you, Mrs Madison—Larissa. Can I call you Larissa?—that I have taken the utmost care to ensure no one will be in danger on the StarTrain of Alexsy Rubinov. You, and your kin, will be in the safest of hands."

"Michael?" Larissa said.

"Come on, Michael," Alexsy encouraged, rubbing his hands together like a market trader. "There's no reward without risk! That's what I always say. Got to play the odds. Take a chance. Make a move. Dare to do. Proclamus dei! Come on, come on, come on!" Alexsy hopped from one foot to the other like a giddy schoolboy.

"How does it work?" Michael asked. "Does it run on coal, or steam, or petroleum like an automobile?"

"Nin, nin, nin. Not at all, Mr Madison," Alexsy replied, his arm around Michael's shoulder, leading him gently towards the StarTrain.

"Then how—?" Michael began, science failing him.

"Inertia, sir. Inertia."

"Really?"

"Vin! Oh, and gravity of course. It's all highly scientific." He wiped a sheen of excited sweat from his top lip with a dirty hand. "Once the StarTrain gets rolling it continues around the track, speeding up, slowing down, turning, descending and climbing, for all time—like a rock rolling down an infinite mountainside. The track moves and pivots to enable this process, much like a pendulum in a grandfather clock. Tick tock, tick tock, tick tock—"

"For all time?"

"Vin, vin, vin."

They'd reached the foot of a ladder that led to a loading platform. Michael took his eyes off the StarTrain and fixed them on his host. "You've achieved perpetual motion," he said in astonishment. "That's ... not possible. At least, not in this universe."

"Everyone keeps telling me so," Alexsy shrugged. "I don't know what all the fuss is about. It's just a bit of fun."

"It's a scientific marvel," Michael uttered. "Truly astounding."

"I have many questions," Larissa said. "Firstly, how do you stop it?"

Alexsy laughed. "You get someone to turn the brakes on! It's not that complicated. Well, it is, but you know what I mean."

"And if there's no one to turn on the brakes?" Larissa ventured, becoming more curious.

"Come now, Mrs Madison. La-rissa. No one would be foolish enough to ride the StarTrain of Alexsy Rubinov without a pilot on duty to operate the brakes." Alexsy laughed drily. "Hell's teeth! Imagine what would happen if someone were to get stuck. They could be on there forever." His eyes whirred manically, his brow furrowed, as though a million problems and solutions suddenly came to him. "Sorry ... off in my own little world! So ..." He clapped his hands together, shocking his audience out of their spiralling thoughts. "Sadie's in. What about the rest of you?"

✹ � 📰 ⚔ 🏛

Wind whipped through the loading platform. Alexsy seemed impervious to the weather. Sadie wondered if it was a result of being born in the north—in San Lundkvistburg, the heart of the Winter Continent—or whether he was just plain mad.

Both explanations held merit.

They were greeted on the platform by Dimitri's younger brothers Branislav and Erik. Sadie knew them from school. Branislav was in the year above, Erik the year below, and both looked like younger incarnations of Dimitri. Real-life matryoshka nesting dolls.

The StarTrain itself consisted of five carriages, linked together with iron chains and coarse rope. A cushioned bench, upholstered in black leather, sat inside each carriage next to an iron bar that came down over the knees. Each carriage was painted bright red with a smattering of glittering gold stars.

Sadie wrestled her ballgown into the front carriage. "Are you coming?" she asked Oliver, who had remained on the platform looking uneasy.

"I do not want to," he replied. "This is a deathtrap."

Sadie sighed. "Alexsy said I'm an adventurous soul. What does that make you?"

"Alexsy has clearly lost sight of his senses."

Sadie turned her eyes towards the track. It vanished in a vertical nosedive no more than ten feet ahead.

"Alright, alright. Move over," Oliver said, climbing in.

Alexsy sprang up next to their seat. "Room for one more?"

"I'm riding with Oliver," Sadie told him, slinging an arm around her friend's shoulders.

Alexsy cocked his head to one side, confusion flickering for an instant. He shrugged. "Fair enough. Dimitri! You're riding with me!" But Dimitri had already taken a seat next to Natalia behind Michael and Eli.

"Branislav? Erik? Who wants to—?" But his other sons were huddled together in the fourth carriage. At the back of the StarTrain sat Larissa, her face bone-white. "Looks like it's you and me, sister. Shuffle up, comrade!"

Alexsy stood in his seat and barked at the top of his voice, so the entire palace gardens could hear. "This is a momentous day. A day for science. A day for adventure. A day for fun. A day to be remembered for all time. Behold! The crew of the first mission aboard the StarTrain of Alexsy Rubinov! May their glorious names go down in history ... and may we all step off in one piece!"

He turned to Larissa and whispered, "Only joking."

"Is your wife—Helene—not riding with us?"

"Goodness, no," Alexsy replied. "She's far too sensible for this kind of devilment!" He raised his voice again, yelling with purpose and grandeur. "Pilot! Release the brakes!"

A huge crowd now swelled beneath them.

Excited, nervous chatter filled the night.

The pilot pulled on a large brass lever, causing something beneath the carriage to *hiss* and then *clang*.

The StarTrain's wheels trundled forward, grinding and scratching on the red iron tracks. Sadie suddenly felt as though she was no longer fixed to the earth in the usual way.

"This is an incredibly stupid idea—" Oliver began, but his words were thrown back down his throat as the StarTrain crept over the edge, hesitated for a moment, then plummeted into the night.

The StarTrain rocketed down the perilous drop, shaking and rattling horribly. The noise of the wheels against the tracks became ferocious. Sparks flew in every direction. *Oohs* and *aahs* from the crowd buzzed through the air as the train flashed past at breakneck speed.

Sadie could feel her eyes streaming. The cold night air smacked her in the face like a wet towel. They hit the bottom of the drop with an almighty crunch and the yawn of bending metal. The StarTrain threw them left, then right, then up towards the stars. The carriages began to slow as they reached the top of the first arc, but there was no time to take a breath or risk a scream, as the StarTrain hurtled back down again at monumental speed.

Sadie gripped the safety bar. Her knuckles burned white. Oliver had his eyes closed and one hand over his mouth. She tried to look behind at Eli and her father, but the acceleration of the train made it utterly impossible.

Up the StarTrain rose. The track moved beneath them, levering and pivoting on gigantic tripods that launched them into the heavens. The speed and noise abated for the briefest of moments before cracking with brutal direction changes at blinding velocity.

The StarTrain made one final blistering turn, the carriages almost at right angles to the world, the passengers gripping on for dear life, as they plummeted below ground, through a damp, pitch black tunnel, and then exploded back up into the sky, corkscrewing round and round towards the stars, the world turning over and over. The train rattled past the loading platform and the ride began once more.

Alexsy bounced in his seat as he marvelled at his achievement. "Exemplar! Truly amazing! What a thrill!" he screamed into the night, his arms waving above his head. "Vin, vin, vin!"

Larissa's face did not agree.

They endured three more laps on the StarTrain. The force of the turns squashed the riders from one side to the other, hips and elbows dug into ribs and shoulders, screams and wails rang through the landscaped gardens and the marauding tents of the Winter Festival itself.

Finally, Alexsy signalled to the pilot, who pushed the level back to its original position, and the StarTrain came to a grinding halt at the top of the track.

Bravo! A Triumph! Spectacular! echoed through the gardens.

"Mrs Madison," Alexsy said, raising the safety bar from his lap. "That was fantastic. Do you not concur?"

"Quite thrilling, Mr Rubinov. Quite thrilling indeed."

"Excellent!" he exclaimed, slapping her jovially on the back. "Successful human test!

THE WINTER
FESTIVAL

With their feet on solid ground, Sadie and Oliver dived into the crowd, heading for a sprawl of brightly striped tents. Sadie darted past tailored elbows and fashionable handbags, swinging umbrellas and polished walking canes. A large arch—constructed of wicker, twisted vines, and twinkling faerie-lights—marked the entrance to the festival where live music from various troupes and bands pumped within. A million glorious smells filled Sadie's nostrils.

As they approached, a slender man wearing a column of hats blocked their path. He tipped a hat from the top of the tower. "A mortarboard, right?" he asked, presenting it to Sadie. She nodded. He tossed the hat into the air and as it landed in Sadie's hands it became an impressive tricorn pirate hat, complete with Jolly Roger and the faint stink of rum.

"Gabriel Greenfold," he said bowing. The column of hats seemed to stick to his head. "Chapeaugrapher extraordinaire. The magic of hats, if you will."

Gabriel unfolded a small map, printed on crisp white paper, and edged with silver.

"Welcome to the Winter Festival. There's much to do and see and taste and hear. Why not get a tarot reading, or see a fortune teller, take a ride on a zorse, enter the goulash eating competition, lose yourself in the Tornado of Souls, get your face painted, stroke the Fox Bears and the Scaled Ligers, or get a bag of hot karamine donuts and watch one of the magic shows. It's time, Sadie Madison, for your adventure to begin."

Saluting Gabriel farewell, Sadie headed for the cobbled square in the centre of the Winter Festival where jewellers and merchants were selling everything from cakes to diamond rings.

In the centre stood three men in tight black bodysuits. As a fanfare roared, one of the men flipped his hands and produced a ball of flames. He ripped the ball of fire in two—the same way Sadie had seen her mother separate raw pastry—and threw one to each of his fellow performers. The process was repeated until there were more than twelve orbs of scorching fire. Juggling faster, they began to dance, jump, and somersault at the same time. Trails of fire linked one juggler to the next like a web of light. The intoxicating smell of sulphur, charcoal, and saltpetre filled Sadie's nostrils.

The audience began to applaud and holler.

"This is amazing," said Oliver. "How do you imagine it's done?"

"A lot of practice and hopefully some sort of gloves."

"Sadie!" The voice came from the other side of the square. "Sadie Madison!"

Michael hauled Larissa and Eli through the crowds, a hand raised high above him, waving frantically. Natalia and Dimitri drifted along behind, their fingers entwined.

"Sadie," he said, relieved. "Why did you run off? We've been looking for you for the past ten minutes. Please stay close to me and your mother."

Sadie shrugged but refused to smile. She still found it hard to look at him. She wasn't sure if any explanation or apology or amount of time would make any difference.

"So, what do we want to see?" he asked, unfolding his map, and staring at it intently.

"We passed a karmethian derby on the way," said Larissa. "Haven't played one of those since we were in the City of Leaves."

Eli signed frantically at Michael.

"Stripey donkeys?" Michael said.

"He means zorses," Larissa translated.

Michael turned to Natalia and Dimitri, but they were lost in each other's eyes. "Sadie, what about you? What would you like to see?"

She scanned the engraved signs and placards that hung above each tent. "There," she said, pointing. "The Tornado of Souls: An Experience for the Senses."

Michael bit his top lip. "What about the zorses?"

"No, Father. I do not want to see the zorses." Secretly, she did. "I want to experience the Tornado of Souls."

Larissa leant in. "I'll take Eli. You go with Sadie. Looks like just the ticket."

Michael grumbled. "Fine. The Tornado of Souls it is. It's not like I've had my innards re-arranged on the SkyTram or whatever it's called already this evening."

"The StarTrain."

"See you back here soon," he told Larissa, pointing to the ground as if to geographically mark it. "What should we do about ...?" He nodded towards Natalia and Dimitri.

"Oh, leave them. They'll be fine."

Agreeing, Michael looked Sadie in the eye. "Last chance," he tried. "We can still go and see those zorses with your brother."

Slowly, Sadie shook her head.

🜊 ☽ ▤ 🜋 ⛩

The Tornado of Souls took place in a large tent where benches formed a decagon at the centre. Michael and Sadie took a seat in the back row.

Three figures stood in the middle. Their bare feet entrenched in wood shavings. All were dressed in elaborate bird costumes. A wren, a hen, and a raven. With feathered wings and elaborate, oversized headpieces.

Michael thumbed his spectacles up his nose. He opened and

closed his mouth several times as though gearing himself up for something. Eventually, he said, "I've been meaning to apologise." Sadie said nothing. "It's well overdue."

People filed into the tent and took seats around them.

"I was trying to do the best for you. And, I'll admit, for me, too. For all of us." Sadie remained silent. "It was a Nepenthe," Michael admitted. "I didn't make it—not that I'm using that as an excuse—but I *did* administer it. I wanted you to forget all about Hurtmore House, and your friend Danver, and your notion of rescuing him." Despite his calm words, Michael seemed upset and frustrated. "If only you'd taken the last dose, then—"

"Then what?" Sadie said suddenly. "I'd have forgotten about Danver and that horrid hospital?"

"Exactly. Yes. If you'd completely forgotten about Danver then you wouldn't be hell-bent on finding Hurtmore House." He shook his head slowly. "And now we're no better off."

"We? Who's we? You and … Vulpes?" Sadie crossed her arms and stared incredulously towards the birds who were circling the edges of the decagon, pecking at popcorn, and candyfloss, and donuts, and children's fingers.

"Vulpes. Yes," Michael conceded. "He … felt it best—"

"I don't care about him," Sadie snapped. "Vulpes can go to hell for all I care. I only care about you … and what *you* did to me." Michael lowered his gaze, avoiding her hard stare. "You tried to harm me. You tried to take away something I love. Danver is my best friend, and you wanted to strip every memory of him from me. You betrayed me. And for what?"

"For answers, Sadie. I wanted to know one way or the other—"

"If I was part of the … Foretelling?" She spat the word like ejecting poison.

Michael's eyes widened. "You know about—?"

"Yes," Sadie replied. "A stranger told me. Not much, I'll admit, but more than you *ever* did." She folded her arms. "Almost thirteen years and you never mentioned it. Not once."

Half the seats were full now. A cauldron of excitement had started to brew.

"And if you had found out I was—or wasn't—this child of the Foretelling, then what would you have done? Would you have told me then?"

"I didn't want to burden you with the truth. Not unless there was no other choice, not until I knew for sure."

"And what does the Foretelling say about … this child?"

Michael took her hands in his. Their eyes met. The world seemed to close in. The edges of her sight littered with roaming black specks.

"All wickedness begins this way. Small and helpless, naked and alone. The fifth and final child will come into the world. A child that should never have been. A child of untold power. A child of limitless knowledge. A child above all others. A child that will wield dominion over all."

Oliver shrank behind Sadie as Michael recounted the words he'd spoken in the Hall of Glass and Mirrors. Words he'd read silently in the dark, late into the night, as ziela coated his tongue and lips. Words that spoke of a terrible future. A future that would make the Divine Wars look like a scuffle in a schoolyard.

"When the blood moon rises and the sea's mist crawls across the land, when the Fire Wolves leave their forest homes and the Redkites head to the sea, when friendship appears lost and love seems an unobtainable promise, the child will come forth."

"It speaks of the night I was born," Sadie uttered. "I remember the noise from the forest, the wolves, and the red moon."

Michael frowned, then continued. "The child that wields untold power and dominion will be the firstborn, of the firstborn, fallen from the highest. For the child that takes everything we hold dear, and locks it away for all time, is the child that puts her fear aside and leads the others into darkness."

Sadie's eyes flooded with tears.

Michael put an arm around her and pulled her close.

But Sadie resisted his embrace.

"I'm sorry," he said. "The Foretelling talks of unspeakable things. Many of which I shan't cast upon your young ears. The Narrowers believe the Foretelling is infallible. I believe there is ... another way. But there is much at risk."

"Tell me, Father. Tell me about the Foretelling." Sadie tried to catch her father's eye, but he evaded her. "You cannot hide it from me anymore. If there's a chance I'm part of it, we can fight. Together."

"I don't know," he said. "There's more to this than just you, Sadie. More than me. More than our family, more than every soul in Iron Bridge. This is about everyone—and everything— that has ever been."

The birds had moved to the edge of the decagon. Sadie could have sworn they were staring directly at her. The words of the Foretelling echoed through her.

All wickedness begins this way ... A child that should never have been ... When the blood moon rises ... When friendship seems lost ... The firstborn, of the firstborn ... The child that puts her fear aside.

It seemed like nonsense, like another of her father's bedtime stories. But recently she'd come to believe in those more and more. She wondered how prophecies came about and who took the time to write them down. They were the words of Gods, weren't they? Deities and supernatural beings, now driven from this world. She pictured strange scribes and prophets in long vestments, hunched over mighty tomes, quills scratching their inexorable way from one side to the other, as some omnipotent being loomed above bellowing prophetic riddles.

A cold wind whipped the entrance of the tent and pulled Sadie from her thoughts. A wave of snow sprinkled the wood chips. The gaslamps inside the tent fluttered and suddenly extinguished.

The entrance snapped shut.

Darkness fell.

From the fluted canopy descended a yellow-brown light that

spiralled with wisps of fog. Touching the floor, it formed a thin, revolving column. The birds turned their backs to it. Their wings spread, tips touching, as they began to sing, cluck, and croak.

Another sound joined them. An industrial sound, something powerful, grinding, like a steam train or the factories in Iron Bridge.

The column of light spread, enveloping the birds.

Oliver cowered behind Sadie.

The light and mist began to spin, slowly at first. The birds turned with it as they rose gently off the ground. The sound swelled as the column spun faster and faster and faster. The wind and light shifted gears, accelerating, throwing the birds around the tent in chaotic trajectories.

Genuine panic swept through those seated closest to the spinning mass. But there was nowhere to run. The entrance had long since vanished and a drowning disorientation had taken hold.

An almighty *crack!*

A blinding flash.

A rush of turbulent wind.

And then silence.

Oliver's fingers were like ice on Sadie's skin.

The storm still raged but it had swept through the audience and spun around the edge of what had once been the tent. All trace of the striped canvas and the fluted canopy had gone. A wall of rushing wind and light circled them, skimming the floor, and towering up into the sky where a handful of stars twinkled a billion lifetimes away.

Somehow, the birds were all in one piece. Sadie watched with utter amazement as they swooped overhead. She felt as though she was flying with them.

"Welcome to the Tornado of Souls," called a voice from high above. "Welcome to the eye of the storm."

Sadie craned her head back, searching for the voice.

Oliver shivered.

"Here, in this place of devastating power, there is tranquillity. Quieten your mind and drift. Think of your family, think of your friends, think of your hopes and dreams. For here, in the Tornado of Souls, you and the elements are as one."

Sadie shut her eyes and let her mind drift as the voice commanded. She thought of Michael telling bedtime stories. Larissa cooking, cleaning, packing lunches, detangling her hair. She thought of Natalia and Dimitri holding hands, and Eli writing furiously in his notebook, his Monster Magnifiers pinned to his scalp. Oliver's face beamed at her in the shifting shadows, his crimson scarf nestled around his chin like a woollen snake.

And then she settled on Danver. His kind, happy, harmless face. But Danver's face began to change. His eyes narrowed. His forehead wrinkled. Splatters of blood flecked his skin. Fists rose beside his face, then hammered down. Each time he pulled back they became redder and redder and redder, slick and dripping.

Stop Danver. Stop!

The three birds came to rest on Danver's head. They seemed to watch him as he threw his fists again and again and again.

Blood. So much blood.

Three pairs of beady eyes followed wherever she moved inside her mind, like one of Michael's creepy paintings. Sadie could barely watch as Danver pounded his fists into Cale Boswick's stricken body. Then, he stopped and lifted his head. Sadie almost screamed. The blood-stained face before her wasn't Danvers at all.

Instead, she saw her own.

The three birds landed on her head and ruffled their feathers. Dark cryptic writing seeped through her scalp, mixing with Cale's blood. Black ink pushed through her teeth.

Who are you? What do you want?

The birds began tearing the hair from her head in a crazed feeding frenzy.

Get off! Get off me!

"Get off—!" Sadie's eyes flew open as the words exploded

from her mouth.

Michael gripped her arm.

"Sadie!" he said, his breath short and heavy. "Thank goodness. I didn't think you were ever going to wake up."

"I was …"

"What?"

"Doesn't matter."

"Tell me. Where did you go?"

"The fight. With Cale. Danver. So much … blood."

Michael sighed. "That's all over now. Dealt with. No need to dwell on it."

Sadie scowled at him. "What about Danver? And Hurtmore House?"

"Of course."

"Where did the storm go?" she asked looking around. "And the birds?"

"I've no idea," her father said. "One minute we're in the eye of the storm, the next I'm daydreaming about Larissa and you, Natalia and Eli, then Mother and Father and—" Michael froze, his face darkening. Something moved through his mind. He blinked, adding, "Then I'm awake and we're sat in this tent, feeling a little foolish."

The tent opened with a slap. A triangle of amber lantern light poured in. The disorientated audience rose to their feet and shuffled towards the exit, exchanging their own unique experiences.

Following the crowd, Michael retrieved his pocket watch and angled it towards the light.

"What about you, Oliver?" Sadie said, whispering to her friend. "Where did you go?" Her question was met with silence. She turned to find Oliver's seat empty.

"We've got a little over an hour before your performance," Michael called. "Sadie?"

Sadie frantically scoured the tent.

"We should go," Michael told her, becoming a little impatient.

Reluctantly, Sadie stood and joined her father. Amber lantern light and the sprinkle of fresh snow coated his skin as he stepped back into the festival.

"What do you want to do next?"

"I don't mind," Sadie replied robotically, looking back into the tent one more time. "Although, I'd like it if you'd tell me about the Foretelling. All of it. Every last detail."

"I will," Michael said. "I promise."

Sadie waited.

Eyes wide.

"Perhaps now is not the best time. Wouldn't you like to see more of the Winter Festival before we run out of time?"

Sadie desperately wanted to understand what she had seen inside the Tornado of Souls, what it had done to Oliver, and what had moved through her father's mind. Was he truly going to tell her about Vulpes, and Rhiannon, and her grandfather, and all the other things written about her in the Foretelling—if it was written about her at all?

"You promise?"

"I do." Michael took a deep breath. "Tomorrow. I'll tell you everything tomorrow."

Sadie stared down the canvas alleyways, her eyes begging for anything resembling her friend in the scarf.

But she saw nothing.

Not a hint of crimson.

She sighed and took a glance at the tiny map. "Why don't we go and find Mother and Eli at the zorses?"

Michael smiled. "Excellent suggestion, Private Madison."

Sadie half-smiled and gave him a sharp salute.

THE MOST BEAUTIFUL ROOM IN THE WORLD

Music filled the air like stardust cascading from the heavens. It had colour, and depth, and passion, and innocence. Tangible, real. Sadie's fingers moved freely over the piano keys, as naturally as running them through water.

But something more than music filled the room.

Something spoken, uttered, whispered.

Mystical words floating on a hot, perfumed breeze.

But something ached deep inside.

Sadie's heart, her stomach, her soul?

She didn't know.

More than an hour passed. Oliver had not returned. Her mind drifted from the piano keys to the eaved bedroom, the museum, Rhiannon's shop, the StarTrain, and the glorious passageways through the Winter Festival. But every face that leant in to say hello or congratulate her musical mastery was not his.

Not Oliver.

Sadie sat in a small opera house. The sort of place she'd seen in one of her father's books but had never visited. Shaped like an egg, a stage had been positioned at the thick end with a proscenium arch towering overhead, engraved with frescos and figureheads from the Winter Continent. Lush curtains in deep red, purple, and green hung either side while golden gargoyles of mythical creatures from the Winter Continent's vast history stared solemnly at Sadie and the lavish grand piano beneath her fingertips.

The walls were decorated with red and black embossed paper, edged with white and punctuated by a dozen sets of double doors. Large paintings in elaborate gold frames hung in alcoves and recesses, dripping with amber lamplight, depicting strange beasts and historic scenes. A shallow dress circle—twenty or more feet in the air—spun around the ellipse of the theatre, filled with shadowy figures with gleaming eyes and twinkling jewellery.

From the centre of the ceiling hung the body of a mighty dragon, its mouth gaping with plumes of golden fire. Above, the beast's wings filled the ceiling. Sharp tips licked both edges of the dress circle while from its claws hung the chain to a breathtaking chandelier burning with hundreds of candles.

Below, an assortment of chairs, sofas, and chaise longues were positioned in irregular rows. Upon them perched an audience, their outfits as lavish as the room. Successful men and women in finery and priceless jewels drank from cut-glass tumblers and champagne flutes.

Dragging herself from thoughts of Oliver, Sadie revisited the memory of the masses on Leviathan Crook. She saw them standing in the street drinking Silverwater scorch and singing traditional verse. She saw their faces pressed against the window. Cale Boswick and Arnold Tomes and hundreds more.

Memories of Danver flooded around her heart. Together, they'd created new worlds from the dressing-up trunk, drunk tea, and read penny dreadfuls in the Temple of the Dead, walked in the Candlelight Parade, saluted the monument to the Victorious Dead, and hid beneath the piano in the music room.

Sadie's music reacted with each vision.

Happy, contented, and filled with promise.

But something ugly slithered through her mind.

Traces of the Nepenthe emerged. They reached up. Scratched and clawed at the inside of her skull. She tried to ignore them, but the pain and betrayal and loss endured. Sadie tried to think of Danver again, of happy times in the eaved bedroom, in the Glade of Remembrance, Iron Bridge, the music room at school.

But the darkness bloomed, spreading like a virus.

A ball of black fur and spikes appeared in her mind, floating against a brilliant world of white.

Sadie prodded it with a metaphysical digit. Raked her fingernails against it. Pulled and tugged until she made a ragged hole. Sinking her thumbs in like lettuce, Sadie started ripping and thrashing until the ball exploded into a thousand tiny shards that impacted on the insides of her skull with a deafening *crack!*

A figure emerged through a sliver of light.

He stood there, draped in black from head to toe. A ribbon of liquorice. Half of his black hair had gone. Replaced by silver-white. Peeking out from behind a red scarf, his face looked horrified, scared, desperate to avoid her stare. His chest heaved, bulged, expanding unnaturally.

Something was dying to get out.

He wailed in pain as whatever lurked inside smashed against his ribs, testing for a weakness, a way out.

And then—Oliver shattered.

Chunks of leather, blood mist, and puddles of liquid black flew in all directions. Splattering against the floor, they formed an amorphous vortex, swirling onyx and crimson. Faces rose to the surface. Vicious monsters and cruel nameless beasts. Then Vulpes, Rhiannon, Cale Boswick, Sadie's father, and finally the girl with the dark markings. Dripping with black, slippery ooze.

Their voices called out, laughing, sneering.

Blood gushed from the edges of the vortex. It pooled like a lake, thick and warm. Snakes, wolves, ravens, worms, bugs, and monsters with endless legs, and countless eyes, and vicious slicing pincers emerged from the black void and writhed in the sanguinary pool.

Sadie shivered.

Afraid.

Oliver?

And then she played it.

The dark notes.

Sadie wasn't aware what she'd done. But as she woke from her reverie and looked at the faces of her audience, she saw true horror.

Something lurked behind those faces.

Something hidden was being dragged into the light.

A veil of mischief and malice melted from their ashen skin, revealing grotesque and abhorrent faces. Vile, twisted, and rasping with vengeance.

One face stood out.

One face more loathsome than the rest. It had become bloated, the skin expanding to its absolute limit, like a balloon filled with fetid water.

Oliver? Where are you?

She looked down at her prancing fingers and begged them to stop, but they carried on spilling dark notes into the room, a flood of black water.

Why are you hiding?

In her maelstrom of fear, Sadie looked for her parents. Her doting, nervous mother and the father that had betrayed her. She'd take the reassurance of his embrace, after all he had done, if it made everything stop, if it took away the faces and the nameless terror burning within.

Michael Madison stood at the back of the room. His face had almost turned purple, bulging and throbbing, his head twisting on his neck like a corkscrew. Beside him, Larissa stood in her magnificent ballgown, her hands pressed together, her eyes teasing a tear.

But her face looked normal.

Sad, tired, but unchanged.

The music built to a dark finale. Sadie's fingers danced with dexterity and grace, flourishing with torturous notes. Her melodies hung for a moment, twinkled like dying stars in the sky, before descending into savage silence.

She closed the piano lid and collapsed on her forearms. The prestigious audience sat dumbstruck for a long breath. Finally, they put down their champagne glasses and applauded riotously.

Sadie chanced an open eye.

Oliver stood beside the piano, staring across the opera house.

"Oliver," she whispered. A tide of relief rose through her legs and filled her chest. "Where did you go? You shattered, exploded. I thought I'd killed you. You turned into ... horrible things."

"The faces," he said, his voice cracked and anxious. "The horrible, horrible faces."

"What are they?" she asked, turning. "They're everywhere."

"Secrets, dark secrets, hidden away."

The applause continued. Standing, Sadie bowed anxiously, then slumped down, exhausted, on the piano stool.

As the applause died, the faces brightened. The ghostly masks evaporated, returning to the tormented minds that bore them. Sadie shuddered and looked at her shaking hands.

"What happened?"

"It is the music," Oliver told her.

"Obviously."

"It does things to people, it speaks to them, controls them." His voice sounded serious, calm. "At first, it made them happy because you were happy. Because you were playing without fear. Free to express yourself without being afraid."

"I know," she replied slowly. "I've felt that way since the story of Grandfather William. Since Danver went away. Since ... *you* came."

Oliver nodded. "You have not been afraid of anything, not one thing," he told her. "Not the brightly painted door, or Darachna Forest, or the Fire Wolves, Vulpes, the dark mist, or the girl with the strange markings."

She shivered. Nervous, undone.

"Because you have been without fear, Sadie."

She stared at him, trying to keep up.

"And now you see what happens when your fear returns." He gazed around the room. "Your music speaks to them of terrifying things. It urges them, forces them. It drags their darkest secrets and their biggest fears to the surface. They are masks of guilt. Masks of lies, deception, hatred, and shame. The darkness in us all ... revealed."

Sadie's eyes clouded over as she recalled the words of the Foretelling. "For the child that takes everything we hold dear, and locks it away for all time, is the child that puts her fear aside, and leads the others into darkness."

She focused on Oliver again.

A quivering hand brushed her lips.

"You're ... my fear?" she stammered. "Aren't you?"

Oliver half-smiled, nodding. "You made me," he replied. "You took everything that frightens you, worries you, holds you back, and put it into me. I had to show you what you are capable of, what the music is capable of, if I was to return to you. It conjures horrible things, Sadie. Horrible, horrible things." He paused. "What did you see in the Tornado of Souls?"

A sadness crept over her. "I saw Mother and Father. Natalia and Eli. I saw you. And Danver. And ... her. The girl with the dark markings."

"The nature of your soul," he said. "Your family and friends. The people that make you who you are. But who is that strange girl?"

"What about you, Oliver? What did you see?"

"I looked into myself and saw all the things you fear. All the things that make me who I am. It was chaotic and terrifying."

Was Oliver trying to scare her?

But nothing could frighten her, not while he stood at her side.

Her friend.

Her fear.

Oliver, the boy in the crimson scarf.

✳ ☺ ▦ ☂ ♨

Michael Madison did a lap of the opera house, shaking hands and making small talk with the beautiful people. He seemed somewhat out of place in his ill-fitting dinner jacket. A jester conversing with kings.

Eventually, he strode over to Sadie.

Larissa joined them.

"I've been making plans," Michael told them. "Big plans. Lots of performances. Lots of faces to see. Lots of hands to shake. Tonight is the turning point. Tonight is the first night of the rest of our lives."

Larissa blew her nose, rolled up the handkerchief, and tucked it inside her red cuff bracelet.

"I sincerely hope you're not getting a cold," Michael snorted at her. "Best keep your distance for the time being. We don't want anything jeopardising our little *Winter Wonderchild!*"

Sadie looked at Larissa.

She wondered why her mother's face had not become distorted during the music. Was she truly afraid of nothing? Was she without guilt, regret, secrets? Her father's twisted purple face had been horrifying. She already knew the kind of things he was capable of.

But was there more?

"Fetch Natalia and Eli and wait for us by the automobile."

Larissa faltered under Michael's orders. A wave of defiance shook in her fists, but she nodded gently and departed.

"She'll only get in the way," he told Sadie off-hand. "There's little she can do."

Michael hunkered in front of his daughter and slipped an arm around her shoulder.

"It's okay. This is an amazing time for us. We'll be rubbing shoulders with the likes of Gerald Kaylock and Porcelina Chatburn before you know it. We have to seize the moment. Can you imagine the price people will pay to hear us play? Most people would give their right arm for what we have. Do you understand, Sadie?"

"What happened to you?" she asked.

"To me?"

"The faces. Didn't you see the faces?"

"Yes, yes. Everybody was filled with wonder."

"What about ... the faces, the dark masks, the wicked ...?"

"Stop that," he said. "This is no time for one of your childish games."

"Father ..." she tried, but Michael raised a finger in warning.

He led Sadie over to a man wearing a dark velvet suit beneath a close-fitting tunic of wonderful silver cloth embroidered with swords and cutlasses in gold thread. He wore a grand hairpiece, augmented by a solitary rose. His face was caked in white powder. His lips painted with a thick dark lacquer.

It was the man with the loathsome, bloated face.

The bag of fetid water.

"Os rivalto, Sadie," he said.

Sadie studied him, confused. His dark mask flickering in her mind.

"It's me! Alexsy Rubinov!"

Sadie squinted and tried to picture this man covered in axel grease, hooting and hollering at the top of his voice on the StarTrain.

Alexsy held out a white-gloved hand.

Sadie took it nervously and curtsied.

"Exemplar! Exemplar!" he enthused. "You were truly wonderful tonight, my dear."

Sadie tried to smile, but the horrible face stained her mind.

"Ah, my attire." He laughed, looking down. "Probably unrecognisable! And just a bit of fun. We like to dress up in the manner of our ancestors from time to time. Do you like to dress up, Sadie?"

She smiled shiftily and nodded.

"Of course you do," he went on. "Life's far too short to be

serious all the time. Isn't that right, Mr Madison?"

Michael forced his tight, anxious face into a fake smile. "Vin, vin," he said, making Sadie cringe. "Far too short."

Alexsy crouched. His eyes met Sadie's. "Between you and me, I think your father takes things a little bit too seriously."

Sadie smiled knowingly and looked at Michael.

He pretended not to listen.

"I mean, what is there to be serious about?" Alexsy went on. "He has a beautiful daughter with a wonderful talent capable of chasing away the shadows in his life. I know if you were my daughter, I'd be the luckiest man in the world."

Michael's nose twitched.

"How old are you?" Alexsy asked, his eyes narrow.

Sadie snapped all ten fingers open, fanning them in front of him, then added two extras.

"Have you lost your voice?" he continued, unfazed.

Sadie looked over at the piano, dappled in lamplight. Her tongue seemed unable to form any words. Was this how Eli felt all the time?

"Ah, music," Alexsy said. "A worthy language indeed. Far more delicate and infinitely more expressive than mere words. Perhaps you would like to come back sometime and delight us with another recital?"

Sadie began to shake her head, but Michael interjected. "We would like that. Very much. But we have many engagements over the coming months."

Alexsy drew himself up to full height. "That is a shame, Mr Madison. Perhaps when you have an opening in your busy calendar you would do us the honour of returning. I'm eager to hear what Sadie will *say* to us next … and let her have another go on the StarTrain, of course!"

Michael nodded, took Sadie's hand and moved for the door.

She stared back at Alexsy as her father led her away from the beautiful room and the beautiful people.

The billionaire smiled and arced his body in a long, low bow.

✹☺▦✖♒

Michael and Sadie made their way from the opera house, down golden corridors the size of train stations, through archway after archway, and out into the vaulted entrance hall.

Helene Rubinov came rushing towards them.

She'd dressed similarly to her husband. Her face powdered white, lips black, her dress a silk shock of bright pink and gold, twinkling with magnificent gems.

"My dear, you're not leaving already!"

"It is late," said Michael, swivelling to face her. "And Sadie is exceptionally tired. The Winter Festival and the performance have taken it out of her, I'm afraid."

"Well, let me at least get a pictogram with you," Helene pleaded. "It won't take a moment."

She clicked her fingers venomously.

A small man with a pictograph tripod emerged and scuttled over.

"Quickly now," Helene told him. "Sadie is very important. And very tired."

The man kicked the legs into position and fussed with the lens.

Helene wrapped a long arm around Sadie's waist and pulled her close. Tortured, grotesque faces flickered in Sadie's mind as Helene's spider-like fingers wormed their way over her hip. She shuddered. A sickness rose in her throat. The pictograph flashed, leaving bright bursts, like fading Rorschach fireworks in Sadie's eyes.

Helene released her. "Thank you—Rikta es—for tonight. You were sensational. I hope we'll have the pleasure of your company again soon."

"Yes, of course, but we must be going," said Michael, moving through the door and into the night.

They dropped down the long steps, climbed into the automobile—where Larissa, Natalia and Eli were waiting—and took off down the palace driveway.

The Madison family sat in awkward silence.

The automobile groaned and wheezed.

"You shouldn't listen to men like that, Sadie," Michael blurted. "It's okay for him to be happy. He has money, and social standing, and success. He has no binds. He has no shackles pulling him towards the darkness. He has—"

"Michael!" Larissa cried, breaking her silence. "You're terrifying the children!"

The automobile fizzed across the snow and gravel, undulating violently on the steep, uneven terrain.

"They need to be terrified sometimes," he went on. "We all need to be terrified, Larissa. It's what keeps us alert. Alive!"

"Be that as it may, Sadie's still a child. She's twelve years old. She should be shielded from horrors and fearful terrors, yet you yearn to thrust them upon her. Like your ridiculous bedtime stories—"

The faerie-lights and coloured lanterns of Iron Bridge floated in the darkness below.

"Slow down, Michael!"

The automobile slid. Michael swore. The back wheels fought for grip.

"Watch out!" Larissa wailed. "You're going to kill us all!"

"It's for her own good," he bit, fighting the wheel. "I cannot—"

A man stood in the middle of the road.

Michael slammed on the brakes.

The automobile slid wildly.

The back replaced the front.

Round and round and round they spun.

Michael's hands slipped from the wheel.

Larissa screamed.

The children huddled together in the back seat.

Tyres wailed, juddered, scraped against gravel and ice.

With a spine-rattling *crunch!* the rear of the automobile buried itself in a large snowdrift, saving them from plummeting into Iron Bridge Quarry hundreds of feet below.

Michael didn't check to see if his family were safe.

His eyes were fixed on the man in the road.

"No," Michael said, his voice shaken and cold. "It can't be. That's impossible."

THE STRANGER
IN THE SNOW

By the time Michael Madison had clambered out of the automobile, the man had vanished.

Cold, ragged breath jetted from his mouth in plumes of white cotton.

Larissa shook. Her hands spread against the window, watching her husband stagger across the snow.

"What happened?" she asked, stepping out of the automobile. "What did you see?"

"It's nothing." Michael grabbed his wife and forced her against the vehicle door. "Get back inside."

"You're hurting me."

Michael grunted. His grip softened.

"You look like you've seen a ghost."

Michael shot her a horrified glance. His eyebrows dug into the bridge of his reddening nose. "What did *you* see?"

Larissa struggled. "Nothing. Nothing at all. Michael, you're scaring me!"

"I'm scaring *you*?"

They stood for a moment locked in terror. The automobile engine spluttered and choked as it idled impatiently. Larissa inched forward and placed her head on his shoulder. She pulled him close, but her embrace did not soothe him. Instead, Michael became rigid and quivered like a leaf.

"You have to go," he told Larissa, swinging the automobile

door open and pushing her inside. "Now!"

In the distance, automobiles trundled along Leviathan Crook. Horns honked. Tyres juddered on the snow.

"What is it, Michael?" Larissa implored him. "There's … nothing here."

Across the gravel road, the man had appeared again, his greatcoat flapping in the wind.

"Drive," Michael hissed.

"But I don't know how—"

"Right pedal is faster, left pedal is slower, the wheel steers the damn thing," he barked, slamming the door. "Drive now and don't look back! Get her in the house. Get them all inside!"

Larissa squirmed into the driver's seat, gunned the engine amateurishly and fish-tailed in the snow.

The stranger didn't flinch as the automobile passed within inches of hitting him.

"Michael," he began, methodically fastening his greatcoat. "Where are they off to in such a hurry?"

Michael inched back. He could feel the dizzying emptiness of the drop into the quarry behind him.

"An excellent performance tonight," the man enthused. The Madisons' automobile turned out of sight, brake lamps flashing red on the white snow. "Most impressive, I have to say. It's been a long time since I've seen talent to rival hers."

Michael turned on his heel and sprinted through the snow. Emerging on Leviathan Crook, he skidded and breathlessly grasped a gaslamp, his lungs on fire.

The man stepped in front of him and frowned.

"You know," he continued. "The last time I heard a talent like hers, it wasn't under spotlights. Glitter, champagne, fame, fortune. Never had those sorts of things back then. Far more humble and … *private*. Probably for the best. Don't you agree?"

Michael spun, looking up the hill. His footprints were set deep in the snow. His and no others. He wanted to scream, but fear had lanced his throat. With a burning reticence, he turned and faced the man.

"I'm guessing this is all your fault," he continued, standing no more than three feet from Michael. He sounded agitated, as if fate had dealt him a cruel hand.

Michael straightened as he approached. "Leave her alone," he said. "Sadie has done nothing."

"Nothing!" the man spat. "Nothing? Come now."

Michael stumbled over the kerb.

"You and I both know Sadie has done *everything* ..." the man continued, his gloved fingers spreading like a fan, "she should *never* have done."

"That's not fair!" Michael countered, adjusting his balance. "Sofia was the first, not Sadie. We dealt with it. We dealt with it in the cruellest way."

The man leant forward. Gaslamps lit his broad face. A finely trimmed beard surrounded a thoughtful smile. His eyes were cloudy and meaningful yet filled with sorrow.

"Father?" Michael said tentatively. "Is it really you?"

"Yes, Michael. It's me."

"But you're ..." he faltered. "Dead."

William Madison smiled mischievously. "Yes. I suppose I am."

✻ ◡ ▮ ✺ ⛪

Michael stood and stared. Every mechanism in his body ground to a halt, his batteries flat. His father was here, in Iron Bridge, in the falling snow. Sure, there were days when he wished he could see his father again, ask his advice, wrap his arms around him and pull him close.

But William Madison was dead.

Dead and gone.

Like the Gods.

To most, this sort of thing was impossible.

But Michael knew differently.

A childhood under William Oscar Madison had taught him that the Dead were never truly gone as long as they were remembered by someone. Even the Forgotten had a chance of returning. And now, here he was, waiting patiently in the snow.

"We should get inside," William told him. "You'll catch your death."

"Still making jokes?" Michael said, pulling his coat tight. "So, what are you?"

"I'm a ghost," William said, doing a spin. "What else?"

Michael considered this for a moment. He'd imagined something more profound.

"Don't injure yourself, son. You've seen things far less believable than ghosts."

Michael nodded, but the sight of his dead father standing before him in the street, chatting as if no time had passed, knocked him off-balance.

"How about a nice warm bar?" William asked. "Don't know about you, but I could murder a drink."

Michael stared down Leviathan Crook. Furrows from Larissa's urgent driving cut into the snow. He crossed the street and stared down a precarious flight of steps that led to the far end of the promenade. There were one thousand and twenty-three steps in total—he'd counted them as a child—now covered in treacherous black ice.

"A bar?" he asked, and William nodded. "Right."

Michael lost his footing more than a dozen times but hung onto the handrail for dear life. By the time he'd reached the bottom, his shoulders and back were sore from supporting his weight, his knees ready to buckle. William waited patiently under a flickering gaslamp. The River Myr glided serenely by.

"Come on, son," he said. "Time waits for no man. I could have travelled to San Cristophe, Los Kralice—even Ville du Feuilles—eaten a hot dinner, and still had time to spare."

Michael wiped his nose. "I apologise for my mortality," he said stiffly. "There are no short-cuts in the real world."

William laughed and gazed up at the heavens. He took a long, deep, satisfied breath. "The real world. Yes, of course."

Michael strode nervously along the promenade, passing in and out of gaslamps.

William made idle small talk.

He ignored his father's patter for the most part, focusing instead on a handful of figures in the distance. They stood between the gaslamps, holding eerie blue-green crystal lanterns of their own. Each one stared up at the foothills. Towards the fleet of houses on the hillside, Darachna Forest and the Carcassus Mountains beyond.

"Ryndai," Michael hissed.

As they passed, heads turned but made no sound.

Michael pressed on.

The Ryndai faded into the falling snow.

Across the river, the Steam Totem stood before him. A pillar of mysterious faces, swirling with snowflakes and mist. Michael tugged his coat tighter as the cold bit into his bones.

William Madison had gone quiet.

Turning, Michael saw another Ryndai stood between the mighty iron pillars of the bridge. Like her comrades, she wore black, curved swords arced across her back, her colours scarlet and blood-red.

She dropped her heavy hood to reveal a pale face marked with crosshatched scars. Pulled back from her face, her hair was slick like black oil, save for a ruby curl that twisted to her shoulder.

"Mr Madison," she said, her accent seemed local, Norlandian. Michael had always believed Ryndai were trained from infants in the distant west, far beyond the Dustlands, at the edge of the world, where there was nothing but sacrifice and sleep and stone.

Michael took two paces towards her before stopping and slipping his hands into his pockets. "Yes," he said. "Is there a problem?"

Popping the lid of a small canister, the Ryndai took a long

draw on the liquid inside. "What's your business in Iron Bridge tonight?" she asked, licking her lips.

"Ziela," Michael said, sniffing the air. "Correct me if I'm wrong but I believe it's outlawed in these parts."

"Yet you can detect its aroma from ten paces," she said, a sharp eyebrow raised. Concealing the canister, she approached and planted the end of her lantern pole between two flagstones by Michael's feet. Her armour and weapons rattled ominously.

Michael's hands squirmed in his pockets.

"Again, where are you headed?" The Ryndai's eyes burned like embers.

Michael glanced at his father standing beside the Ryndai. She wrinkled her nose, inspecting the space William Madison occupied.

"Heading out for a drink. Night cap. Brandy, probably," he said. "No ziela for me. Obviously."

The Ryndai rolled her shoulders. Her neck cracked. "We're watching you," she told him. "You, and that daughter of yours … Sadie Madison."

A dryness gripped Michael's tongue.

"Naturally," he replied. "The Eighth Day Assembly is watching us all."

She traced her scars with a blunt fingernail. "Some more than others."

"That hardly seems—"

"She's becoming a nuisance."

"Who? My daughter?"

The Ryndai looked at the Steam Totem. "We've distributed the Broken Moon over three hundred times these past days," she said, her voice sounding sickened. "The Broken Moon has never seen such prominence. And I doubt this is the end. People are flocking to the Temple of Santa Lyana in Sepulchre Park." She shifted forward. The smell of ziela hung heavy on her breath, tobacco, and spiced onion goulash too. "They're praying, Mr Madison. Praying to the Gods."

"Worshippers?" Michael said, feigning disdain.

"More souls than we've seen since the Divine Fall."

"Disgusting."

"Is that so?"

Michael clicked his tongue against the roof of his mouth. "They're praying to the music. To ... your daughter."

A nervous laugh whistled between Michael's teeth.

The Ryndai pulled an armband from her layered garment. On the blood-red fabric sat the insignia of the Broken Moon. "Do you need one of these, Mr Madison? Your daughter too?"

"No. Never. Of course not."

"People need to know who they can trust," she said. "Who is loyal to the Eighth Day Assembly and who is ... lost. That's what the Broken Moon represents after all. Distinction between the sound of mind and those who wander alone. The right ... and the *wrong*."

"We're a Godless household. Always have been."

The Ryndai considered Michael for two breaths longer than was comfortable. The Broken Moon returned to the depths of the Ryndai's garments. She wiped her nose with the back of her hand. "Very well," she said. The heavy hood shot over her head. "Enjoy your ... *brandy*, Mr Madison."

"Thank you." Michael swallowed hard. "And goodnight."

The Ryndai caressed the hilts of her curved blades and swept away.

※ ☾ ▦ ⚔ ⛪

The Iron Bridge Hotel seemed as good a place as any for a conversation with his dead father. It was, after all, one of William Madison's favourite places.

"Just trying to make you feel welcome," Michael said insincerely as he opened the heavy glass door. A welcome warmth rose to meet him.

William sniffed like a wild animal.

The smell of liquor and cigars drew a shallow smile.

The expansive interior was made to feel claustrophobic by crowded furniture and oversized decorations. Pink carpets with gold asymmetrical patterns, worn and sturdy wooden tables, brass lanterns, and stacks of old books and board games occupied the irregular space.

Michael could not ignore the expression on his father's face.

"What?" he said, shutting out the cold. "What's the matter?"

"A Godless family?" William bleated. "Storm could smell your lies a mile away."

"Storm?"

"The Ryndai."

Michael sighed. "What was I supposed to do?"

"Take the armband, son. Take the Broken Moon. I've always worn mine. I'm not afraid."

"You're dead."

"Not because of my belief in the Gods! For all that's holy, we're their descendants. Earth-bound sons and daughters of the Divine."

"Stop," Michael urged. "Just …"

Several people looked up from their drinks.

They shifted into a booth that overlooked the plaza. The Steam Totem erupted, marking ten o'clock. Michael folded his collar down and sniffed violently.

A waitress glided up to the end of the table.

"Brandy, please. Double."

She turned to William. "And for you?"

"Tea. I don't mind what kind. Dealer's choice. And vodka. The best you have. One ice cube."

"Be right back," she said and disappeared.

Michael stared in bewilderment at his father. "She saw you." Part question, part statement. "How did you …?"

William Madison raised both hands. "Why shouldn't she see me?" he replied. "I am, after all, sitting here opposite you. You can see me. Why not her?"

"Why not? Because you're dead. Because you used to come here all the time. Some of the people in here went to your funeral. As did I. I imagine they'd think it a trifle odd to see us having a nice little posthumous drink, don't you?"

"Michael. It's okay."

"That … woman. Storm. She didn't see you, nor Larissa or the children."

"And rightly so," William added. "It would have scared them half to death, I shouldn't wonder."

Michael pointed at his own face. "But to do that to me is perfectly reasonable?"

"Enough of this," William snapped, his playful nature taking a backseat. "There is much to say and—as we're dealing with the *real world*—little time."

Michael folded his arms.

"The Foretelling."

"Of course." Michael sighed. "What else?"

"You know what is coming, Michael. You know the dangers the Foretelling will sow. Yet somehow you're sitting here like this has nothing to do with you."

Michael frowned. It wasn't true. He knew all too well what was upon them. For the most part, he feared the Foretelling. Everything it stood for, everything it said, everything it promised. But some small slice—a faint, lingering part of him— found it laughable, preposterous even. Nothing more than frightened words scrawled in an ancient book. But Michael had done horrible things in the name of the Foretelling. Things that would haunt him until the end of time.

"The music, Michael."

"What of it?"

"At first it filled Iron Bridge with joy and happiness. You heard it from the Ryndai herself. People are flocking to the Temple of Santa Lyana, praying, worshipping, outlawing themselves against the Eighth Day Assembly. But tonight, she played something different. Something laced with fear. It unveiled the deceit, the lies, the corruption, the darkness in the hearts of everyone in that room."

"Nonsense," Michael said, glancing at the distant glowing lanterns of the Palace of Light, high in the foothills of the Carcassus Mountains. Fireworks erupted from the Winter Festival, filling the sky with blooms of colour. "Alexsy Rubinov is one of the most respected men in the Shadow Valley, throughout Norland, and beyond."

William's eyes narrowed. "Show me a man of extraordinary wealth and I'll show you a man with darkness in his heart."

Michael attempted a laugh. "Enough of your fanciful worldly wisdoms."

"Son." William grabbed Michael's hand. His father's sudden touch turned Michael's skin to ice. Excitement and fear coiled and knotted together. "This is no bedtime story. This is happening right here, right now, and your daughter is at the heart of it."

"And it all stems from you, Father. It's all your fault." Michael pulled his hands away. "Why couldn't you stay in the Vents and collect memories like the rest of the Narrowers and avoid getting mixed up in this horrid business?"

The waitress appeared at the end of the table. She'd clearly caught the end of their conversation. She placed their drinks down and vanished once more.

"My fault?" William replied, picking up where Michael left off. "The Foretelling is an ancient prophecy. There is no avoiding it. The bones are already cast, Michael. I played my role. The way I was always supposed to play it. The way it will always be played."

"And what of my role? And the role of my daughter? Roles cloaked in shadow, dictated by words in an ancient book."

"You must play the hand you've been dealt … for good or ill. I don't make the rules, Michael."

"Oh, you're just a pawn in the big game, is that it?"

William laughed. "Stop playing the victim. I cannot change what has happened. All we can do is prepare for the future."

Michael drained his brandy then waved at the waitress for another. "What's the point?" he asked, spinning the glass in his hand. "You've spoken about everything being decided. The dice have cast. So ...? What ...? Are we supposed to sit back and let whatever is going to happen, happen?"

"Do something. Do nothing. Do whatever your heart tells you, Michael. Your actions are inevitable anyway."

Michael grumbled. "And what of you?"

"Me? I'll do everything I can. But you, Michael, you have to stop the music. Something lurks inside those notes. Something ... unnatural."

A fresh brandy arrived. Michael cradled it like a child, secretly wishing for the touch of ziela instead. "How? Forbid her from playing? Lock the piano shut? Destroy the damn thing?"

"Sadie must be stopped. She'll find another instrument. She'll find something else to play."

"Just like Mother did."

William wrinkled his nose and stared absently over Michael's shoulder.

"You could have done more, you know. You could have stuck around to help me prepare for this. And to help with Mother—"

"Leave Karolinja out of this," William broke in. "I warded the house, what more could I do?"

"We didn't see you for weeks, sometimes months. Always away on one of your selfish adventures. It began to feel like you were merely visiting, rather than coming home. And then you went and died."

"Ah, the greatest adventure of them all!"

"Stop making light of everything. Stop acting like this is one big cosmic joke."

William moved forward. The vapour from his tea rose around his face. "I don't joke about Karolinja. The love I have for your mother is bigger than anything in the universe, the Vents, the Nyx, and beyond! You leave her out of this."

"What did you do to her?" Michael asked. "What did you do

to my mother?"

"Michael!" William rose out of his seat. "Leave it!"

Heads turned.

"She was the reason you made the Transference, fell from the Vents, and started this chaotic pantomime of events. How could you …?"

William silenced Michael with a ferocious stare.

Returning to his seat, he took a sip of tea. "Her … *condition* … has nothing to do with me. Well, not entirely. But none of that matters now, son. What does matter is Sadie, and the music, and keeping her safe." William's face became hard and still. Nothing but his lips and moustache moved. "Michael, you must be careful. The Narrowers will return. Her thirteenth birthday is three days away. If they fail to extract a memory, they will know she is the one. You must prepare her for the choices she must make. You must guide her, Michael, or all will be lost."

"The Narrowers cannot get to her in the house. It's protected. You did it yourself."

"Wards and glamours will only work on the Narrowers themselves. Once she turns thirteen, flesh and blood will come to the door, Michael. In what form, I know not." His face darkened. "Agents are abroad in Iron Bridge. Things prowl the streets. Things far more terrifying than Ryndai, the Eight Day Assembly, or Minister Craven herself. There is a darkness sweeping through this town. Cruel souls filled with an ancient malice. They ride the bodies of one, then the next. It is a dark craft they weave. We're doing all we can, but they are like ghosts, phantoms."

Michael finished his brandy. "We?"

"The Balance," he whispered, moving closer. "Never utter their name outside my company." He took a moment and considered his son. "We are all that prevents the Narrowers from having their way with your daughter."

"What can they do against the Narrowers?"

"The Balance have more than a modicum of power. You

wouldn't send a fly to catch a spider, would you?" William smiled. "You know of one. She helped us before."

Michael gripped the table. "*Helped* us?" The word hissed from his lips. "Rhiannon."

"She is one. The second is known to me. The third, a constant enigma. We must put our trust in them and be ready at all hours."

Michael's eyes drifted. "Three," he said softly.

"There is incredible power in threes. You need look no further than the humble triangle." William smoothed his moustache with his thumb and index finger. "Michael, focus. Listen to me. These are dark times. The future will be decided in the coming days. Be mindful. Be alert. Be her father. Protect her against whatever comes. I'll be here, with you all, to whatever end."

Michael swallowed hard. "Did we do the right thing thirteen years ago?"

"You mean … Sofia?"

Michael nodded. His eyes glistened.

William sighed and wrapped his hands around his teacup. "Find a way to stop the music. Talk to Sadie. Tell her everything. Tell her nothing. Lock her in a cage. Do whatever it takes."

"I'm afraid for her, Father."

"You're afraid for yourself."

"That too."

William Madison looked grave.

"We're all afraid, Michael. Every last one of us."

THE RED
PAINT

Sadie sat up. Bedclothes knotted around her waist. Through bleary eyes, she glimpsed herself in the mirror. And almost screamed.

The girl with the dark markings sat beside her, smiling playfully.

"Come with me," she whispered, and ran.

Sadie leapt from the bed and hurried through the door as the girl's white linen dress billowed like a trail of ghosts. They whistled along the landing, swept downstairs, ignoring Larissa asleep in the living room. Sadie found circus performers and magicians drinking tea and eating cake in the kitchen. Long blades of grass burst through the flagstones. A wire-frame cage containing three strange creatures sat on the table. They hissed as she passed, displaying jagged teeth and leathery wings.

Sadie followed the girl out the back door and up the stone steps to the garden where a large tent had been erected. Jugglers and fire-dancers and acrobats milled about, stretching, rehearsing, watching. Alexsy Rubinov and a handful of his esteemed guests sat to one side on velvet sofas drinking champagne, their faces distorted, bulging, swollen.

Scampering towards the swings, the girl sank her black nails into her wrists. She let out a nightmarish war cry. Blood pooled on the ground.

The garden fence took the brunt of her fury.

She lashed at it with her hands, smearing blood against the stained beams. Red daubs gushed from her veins, arcing in the moonlight, peppering winter flowers and the snow-packed earth. Her screams became a low, inhuman moan as the strain of her endeavours took their toll. But some malice whipped at her heels, demanding more of her, pushing her to her limits and out the other side.

Sadie stood close, watching.

Together, their little hearts pounded like bolting hooves on a cobbled street.

The world fell silent, but for the girl's soft wheezing.

She slid down the fence. Blood stained her white linen dress as she repeatedly stabbed her hands into the hard white earth. Every face in the garden turned towards the fence, towards what the girl had written, applauding and raising their champagne glasses in celebration.

A word.

One single word.

But what did it say?

Sadie stepped back. Her head angled. The word slipped in and out of focus, as elusive as the wind. She stared, squinted, as the letters began to form.

✷ ◡ ▤ ⚔ ♨

The front door slammed. Vibrations echoed through the bones of the Madison house.

"Oliver?" Sadie whispered, waking sharply.

"I am here."

Sadie cleared the sleep from her eyes. "Is Father back?"

Oliver shook his head. "I think your mother took Natalia to look for him."

"I had horrible dreams, Oliver. Dark things. Distasteful things. A word scrawled in blood. And faces. Horrible faces. Alexsy Rubinov and his guests at the Palace of Light. There was fire, and clowns, and magicians. Strange monstrous beasts. But I wasn't afraid. I know I should be. But I wasn't."

"You are welcome," he said, smiling.

"How is that possible? How are you possible?"

Sadie stuffed her arms into her black cardigan and moved to the window seat. She placed a hand on the cold glass. Below, Larissa and Natalia trudged down Leviathan Crook.

"You made me," Oliver said.

"But I don't know how. Do you think …?" She tapped the glass. "Do you think I'm the child they wrote about in that stupid book?"

"Do you want to be?"

"What?" Sadie's eyes burned. "A destroyer of worlds? No. Of course not!"

Oliver shifted awkwardly.

"When Father returns, he's going to tell me all he knows about the Foretelling," she said, returning to the window. "He promised. I'm going to hold him to it. Whatever it takes."

"What did the word say?"

"Sorry?"

"The word scrawled in blood?"

"I don't know," she said slowly. "It was out of focus. Out of reach."

With Natalia and her mother gone, Sadie relocated to the front porch. The bench swing beneath her bedroom seemed the perfect location to sit and wait for their return.

Below, the River Myr journeyed south towards the Sapphire Seas. She'd spent hundreds of hours watching the water. She wondered where it had been, where it was going, what adventures it had seen, and what lurked beneath the surface.

She closed her eyes for a moment. The winter sun made the backs of her eyelids glow salmon pink. Sadie tried to picture the word from the dream. The word written in blood on the fence by the girl with the dark markings. But the dream had ended before she'd recorded it in her mind forever. She tried guessing what the word might be but, after a time, resigned herself to the fact she might never know.

Eli brought Atticus to join them on the porch. The dog spread himself by Sadie's feet. Sadie and Eli played an alternate version of black gimlet with an incomplete deck of tattered elemental cards and a single die. Eli's version made no sense to Sadie. She failed to understand how anybody could win at black gimlet when the scarlet jester, the copper knight, the sea sorceress, *and* the king of crystals were missing? But it passed the time and took her mind off a million burning questions.

Eli won three games in a row. The rules suspiciously different each time. Sadie's interest waned. With victory losing its shine, Eli packed up the cards and disappeared inside.

The sun was high in the midday sky when Michael appeared. He looked as if he'd walked to Fort Campion and back. Atticus barrelled down the garden, disturbing the fresh snow with his tail. Michael smiled wanly and ruffled the dog's fur.

"As you were soldier," Michael ordered. He gave Sadie a limp salute. Atticus followed him up the steps, turning in feverous circles on the porch and barking excitedly.

"Is your mother about?"

"She's out."

Michael frowned.

"Looking for you."

He nodded, vanished inside, then returned with a glass of ziela. Sadie folded her arms as her father stared absently into the middle distance.

"Oh, right," he said knowingly. "Here and there. Walking mostly. And thinking."

"Mother was mad with worry."

"Of course."

"Who did you see on the road?"

Michael took a breath.

"Was he from the Eighth Day Assembly?"

"No."

"Are we in trouble for discussing the Gods?"

"It's nothing like that."

"Oh. Okay."

"There is something I need to tell you." He took a sip of ziela. "The world is an amazing place. So much colour, so much beauty, so much happiness. But everything has a flip side. You are young now, but you will learn of these things. As every person who walks the earth has done. One day you'll see the other side of the coin." His eyes found hers. "Colour will become shadows, beauty will erode, and happiness will crumble into despair."

Sadie had never heard her father talk in such dark tongues before. Sure, his bedtime stories were the place for fright and horror, but he was a joyful storyteller, a conjuror of fantastic tales, myths, and folklore of the ghastly and the bizarre. Words summoned to enchant and thrill the eager minds of his children.

"The world has many secret places, Sadie. And I don't just mean ethereal, biblical places like heaven, and hell, and purgatory and suchlike, but places beyond comprehension, beyond space and time. Places that seem so far away, yet are so close. They surround us, dwell within us. Places where we hide our sorrow, our guilt, our betrayal, and our broken promises. These places aren't just thoughts and feelings, Sadie. These places are real. As real as you and I are sitting here on this swing." Michael drained his glass. The ruby liquid stained his lips. "Do you understand?"

Sadie nodded affectionately but her gaze was drawn to the boy in the crimson scarf.

"Ask your mother about Sofia. You deserve to know the truth."

He stood and returned to the house.

"Sofia?" she whispered, but the door clicked shut. "Who is Sofia?"

Oliver squinted down Leviathan Crook. "They are back."

Sadie waved as Larissa and Natalia trudged towards the house. Their faces drawn and pale from the chill. Noses red and dripping.

"Any sign of him?" her mother asked. "We've been all over town. The Steam Totem, the hospital, the railway station, Sepulchre Park, even the Ryndai garrison and back. No one's seen him since last night."

Sadie thumbed towards the house.

"He's here!" Larissa said. Colour flooded her cheeks. "Really? He's home?"

"Got back a few minutes ago."

"Thank the Gods," Larissa whispered under her breath.

Natalia hugged her mother and helped her to the front door.

✳ ☻ ▤ ⚑ ⛪

Michael Madison stood in the kitchen, heating a pan on the stove. Larissa appeared in the doorway and placed her hands on her hips. "Where the hell have you been?"

"I'm sorry."

"What is it?" she asked. "What happened?"

"It's all happening," he tried. "Everything we feared. Everything we hoped. Just … everything."

"Michael, please. Tell me. I need to know."

"William."

A hand shot to her face. "Impossible."

"I thought the same, but we both know differently," he told her evenly. "We always knew there would be a risk keeping Sadie."

"No. She was not the first. Sofia was. That's what the Foretelling says. In black and white. In that horrid book. There must be some mistake."

"Larissa," he said, placing his hands on her shoulders. "We both know Sadie wasn't the first, but they're two halves of a whole. Father says they'll come for her. He says the Narrowers are sending agents."

Larissa's eyes widened. "Agents?"

"Three of them."

"Here? In Iron Bridge? We must do something. Run away, far away."

"What do you propose?"

"We'll go to San Cristophe," she said. "We can hide in one of the five cities. There are more than a million people there. We can find work. We'll be fine. Yes, they'll never find us there."

"No," Michael said gravely. "Living among a million people would mean living among a million pairs of eyes."

"Then where? Los Kralice, Fort Campion, the City of Leaves?" Larissa tried frantically. "Hüntesgaard, the Northern Territories, Whitehaven, Silverwater, Solitude?"

"No, Larissa," Michael said again. "It won't work. For the selfsame reasons."

Larissa looked lost. "We'll live on the move then. Travel like nomads from one place to the next. Evade the Narrowers and their agents at every turn."

"And spend our lives looking over our shoulders, sleeping in shifts, fear shrouding every moment? What kind of life is that?"

The last vestiges of hope seemed to drain from her body.

The sight almost broke him in two.

"We stay," Michael told her. He struggled to keep his words steady, even. "We stay and, when she turns thirteen, we let the Narrowers test her and leave everything in the hands of fate."

"Fate? Never," Larissa erupted. A pink rash bloomed on her chest. "I will never—"

"There's nowhere to run," Michael said. "And nowhere to hide."

Larissa hung her head. "I won't let them, Michael. Not again. That's one mistake I will never repeat." A cold determination filled Larissa's eyes. A look Michael had never seen before. "I promise you, as long as there is air in my lungs and blood in my veins, the Narrowers will never take another daughter of mine!"

Boiling water cascaded over the pot and sizzled on the stove.

Michael flicked the burner off and lifted the pot from the heat.

Larissa rested her hands against the basin and stared out the window.

"Sadie?" she said.

Michael cleared the condensation on the window with a tea towel. Snow-dusted evergreen trees rose above the high sandstone wall, mapped with vines and creepers. The once-white lawn now the colour of candyfloss.

"Larissa? Are you okay?"

"Sadie?" she whispered again, unsure. "There."

"I don't see ... anyone."

Larissa turned and rested her back to the basin. She pressed her hands against her eyes and took a long breath.

"No. Look," Michael said. "Sadie's in the hall."

Larissa blinked.

Turned ghostly pale.

She took several steps towards her daughter.

"Larissa?"

Sadie smiled as she unzipped her coat and kicked off her boots.

"Mother?"

She staggered back to the kitchen window and glared down the garden. "She's there, Michael." Spun, pointed. "And there."

Larissa launched herself towards the back door. Michael darted after her. She tore up the stone steps to the garden and paced in chaotic circles in the pink snow, fingers knitted through her hair. Larissa looked terrified yet, somehow, hopeful.

"What's going on?" Michael asked, catching his breath.

"She was here," Larissa said. "And inside." She ran her fingers along the frame of the garden swing, took a seat, and rocked gently.

Michael squinted. "Who?" he asked, fishing his spectacles out of his cardigan pocket and pushing them up his nose.

"I saw Sadie. Inside. And outside. Two places at once."

Larissa started shaking.

Michael knelt in the snow and wrapped his arms around her.

"It's okay." He stroked her face gently. "It's all going to be okay."

A lock of golden hair fell across Larissa's face. Her eyes looked wild, frantic.

"It was her. It must be her."

"No," Michael protested. "She's ... gone."

"It was Sofia."

"Ridiculous," he whispered, moving closer.

"She's just like Sadie. But different, ever so slightly different," Larissa said, her words sounding nervous, afraid. "She's here, Michael. Sofia is here."

The Madison children had gathered in the garden.

"Mother?" Natalia asked.

But Larissa's gaze fell on Sadie, scared and confused.

"Father?" Sadie asked. "What's—?"

And then they all saw it.

Natalia screamed and dropped to her knees.

Eli buried his face in his sister's shoulder.

Sadie froze.

Michael and Larissa turned and there, written across the high wood panels in psychotic blood-red lettering, was one single word.

Murderers.

THE GIRL
WHO DIED

Larissa stared helplessly at the fence. Michael ordered Natalia and Eli inside.

Sadie rounded on Oliver. His scarf inched up his neck. "This was a dream," she told him. "It was the girl with the dark markings. She led me to the garden. She made me watch as she cut her wrist and wrote that *word* with her blood."

Oliver looked uneasy, more skittish and nervous than usual.

"It was a dream, Oliver. Wasn't it?"

He swallowed hard. Shook his head.

"It was you."

"Me?"

"You did it in your sleep."

"No. It was—"

Oliver shook his head.

"But ... whose blood? It's certainly not mine."

"It is paint. I watched you take it from the kitchen. I was unable to stop you. Unable to wake you," he conceded. "I can feel the discomfort in your dreams, your nightmares, I—"

"Stop. Just stop it. I can't hear any more of this."

She swept away from Oliver and approached her parents.

"Look away," Michael instructed her. "Childish vandalism. Nothing more."

Sadie stopped by the swings. Her mother rocked gently. Together they studied the large chaotic letters that ran the length of the garden. She could leave it, let her father blame the local kids, blame Cale and his crew, but—"It was me," she said. "I didn't do it on purpose. I was ... sleepwalking."

Larissa looked up. Her eyes flooded with emotion.

"I thought I dreamt it," Sadie added. "But it wasn't a dream. It was real."

Michael's hands fumbled for a handkerchief. "If you were asleep, how could you know?"

Snowflakes nestled in Sadie's hair. "Oliver told me."

Larissa hauled herself out of the swing. Her face deathly pale. Larissa was never ill. Never so meek and frail. A foil to her skittish father. She thought back to the horrid faces at the Palace of Light, the putrid, repulsive expressions that hung before her as she played.

Alexsy, Helene, Father.

But not her mother, not Larissa Odessa Madison. Either she was impervious to the music, or she truly had nothing to hide.

Larissa's lips parted, quivered from the cold. "Who's Oliver?"

"He's my friend," Sadie replied, glancing at the boy in the crimson scarf.

"I ... erm ... hello, Oliver."

"It's okay, Mother. You can't see him. It's fine. You don't have to pretend. Oliver says hello too, by the way."

"Um ... Okay ... How long have you and Oliver been ... friends?"

"A week or so, but also forever. Does that make sense? He's always been with me. He's part of me. In a weird way. It's hard to explain."

The word on the fence filled Sadie's vision.

"Who is Sofia?" she asked.

Larissa nodded towards the fence. "Get rid of it," she snapped at Michael. "Burn it if you have to."

She leant forward and tucked Sadie's erratic hair behind her ears.

A sad smile played on her lips.

"Mother?"

"Sofia was a special little girl," Larissa whispered. Her body shook. "A very special girl indeed."

"Like me?"

Her mother took a sharp breath. "Yes. Like you. Like you in so many ways."

"What happened to her?"

Larissa caught a tear as it left her eye. "She died."

"That's horrible. Was she ... murdered?"

"No!" Larissa erupted. Her fingers coiled tightly around Sadie's arms.

"There were complications," her father broke in. "Suffice to say, your mother and I miss her terribly."

"How did you know her?" Sadie asked. "Who was she?"

Larissa swallowed hard. Her eyes found Sadie's once more. "She was born seven minutes before you," her mother admitted. "Sofia was your twin sister."

The words had barely touched Sadie's ears before a feverous chill gripped her. It felt as if somebody had thrown her bedclothes back and left her lying naked in the dead of night. Michael and Larissa became a watery blur. A slow-motion, silent cinefilm version of her parents.

She stumbled. Inched away from her mother's outstretched, desperate hands.

For a moment, everything unravelled. Family, friends, Iron Bridge, the River Myr, the Carcassus Mountains, the sky and moon and stars above. They broke apart in her head, shattered, like an almost finished jigsaw being swept unceremoniously to the floor.

"I'm a twin. I had a sister. A twin sister," she whispered.

A million questions surfaced, fighting for attention.

A million voices replied.

They echoed around her skull, deafening, agonising.

"Sofia," she uttered as her eyes rolled back in her head. "*Murderers.*"

☀ ☺ 🎞 ✂ 🏛

Oliver felt like he was falling. Tumbling end over end into an abyss. A vile sickness washed through him. Everything hurt. Everything ached.

His world spun as Michael sprang forward and caught Sadie before she hit the ground. He swept her into his arms and carried her inside. Oliver followed them. The walls around him quaked. The sickness came in wave after wave.

Sadie was placed on the living room sofa. Her head against a pile of cushions.

"Sadie," Michael whispered. "Come back to us."

"We're so sorry," Larissa added. "We should have told you. Should have told you everything."

But Sadie remained as still and silent as a mummy.

Oliver dragged his long, grey fingers through his hair.

Larissa covered her with blankets and pressed a damp towel to her forehead.

"Come on, darling. Time to return."

Sadie's eyeballs performed cartwheels beneath her eyelids. Her body twitched. Larissa clasped her tightly—taking several knocks for her trouble—until Sadie became heavy and limp, like a dead cat.

Michael checked her breathing. "She's okay. Calm. Resting."

"What happened?" Larissa asked.

"I think she had a seizure, although I cannot be sure."

"A seizure! Good Gods!" Oliver exploded. He swung his fists. Anger and frustration charged his veins. He stormed across the room, punching and kicking wildly. And, as he threw a fist towards one of Larissa's display cabinets, his hand connected with a vase and ornamental elephant.

Oliver stared, shocked, at his hands, examining them as if for the first time.

The vase lay broken beside the elephant.

I did it. I touched them. I moved them.

Michael and Larissa stared at the fallen knick-knacks.

Sadie's eyes opened.

"Sadie," her mother said in a calm, breathy voice. "Are you okay?"

Sadie grimaced. Her gaze fell on Oliver.

"I moved a vase and an elephant," he told her, waving his fingers like ten wriggling serpents.

A tired smile played on Sadie's lips.

Her eyes closed again.

"Stay with us," Michael urged. "Have some water."

He managed to force several sips down before Sadie turned away.

"Sadie. Dearest, Sadie. I'm so sorry. So very sorry," Larissa said. "We should never have kept Sofia from you."

"We did it with the best intentions," Michael added.

"Best intentions?" Oliver spat. "There is no good reason to hide the death of her twin! Why did you do it? In the name of the Gods, why?"

Oliver's words were lost on Sadie's parents.

"Sofia," Sadie whispered softly.

"We love you, Sadie. We care for you more than you know. We'll do—we've done—unimaginable things to keep you safe. We've sacrificed a lot. More than you know."

Sadie looked up at her parents. "I don't want to be here. Not anymore," she said, swallowed hard. "Complications. During birth. Is that so?"

"Yes," her parents said in unison.

"Or … did Rhiannon kill Sofia?"

Michael hesitated.

"She was supposed to kill me. Did she kill my sister first?"

"You're asking complicated questions, Sadie."

She tried to sit up.

Oliver stumbled, giddy and nauseous.

"It's not complicated, Father. It's a simple yes or no."

"You need to rest." Sadie opened her mouth to object. "You

245

must," Michael ordered. "And I'll have no more talk on the matter."

"Did she kill my sister?" Sadie whispered. "I *need* to know. I deserve the truth!"

Michael wandered to the window. Hundreds had congregated on the iron bridge and flowed up Leviathan Crook, awaiting Sadie's next recital. Among them, Ryndai moved soundlessly beneath the eerie glow of their crystal lanterns.

"You have to forgive us," he said, not turning. "We did what we thought best."

"Mother," Sadie managed, her face wracked with pain. Her eyes threatened to close again.

"Rest now, Sadie," Larissa said. "Sleep. We'll talk later."

Oliver's fingers tore at his crimson scarf.

And Sadie drifted into sleep.

★ ☺ ▤ 𝔸 𝔪

Oliver and the headless Lorntide mannequins stood guard. Decorations twisted playfully as something churned inside. Something malicious, wrong.

Larissa brought hot blackcurrant cordial. She bent over and ran a hand down Sadie's face, flattening her hair and wiping away a tear.

The afternoon passed slowly. Sadie's mother popped in and out, sometimes watching her sleep, other times to check she hadn't slipped out of the house. Sadie remained motionless for the most part. Occasionally her fingers would flex into claws or tighten into fists. Her teeth would grind. Her eyes spun in their sockets.

Oliver watched, and waited, not knowing what any of this meant. All he could do was feel the pain of her dreams, her nightmares, her mind sinking to dark, fathomless depths.

Frosted faces bobbed beyond the window.

Hands pressed to the glass.

Lanterns flickered, jostling to and fro as the crowds shifted like a creeping tide.

The grandfather clock struck six times.

On the final chime, Sadie's eyes opened.

She sat upright, placed her feet neatly on the floor, hands on thighs.

"Sadie?" Oliver said, moving towards her. "What happened? I was so worried."

She looked him over as though he were a curiosity.

Oliver inched away, his skin like ice. "Sadie?"

Her stare lingered, unblinking.

Oliver stopped, frozen. It was only when Michael Madison drummed playfully on the back of the sofa that the sensation diminished.

"Sadie. My dear. Thank the Gods. You've returned to us."

Sadie didn't acknowledge him.

Her eyes were locked on Oliver. An eyebrow rose.

"People have been gathering outside," Michael went on. "But I've said you won't be performing tonight." Sadie began to hum. "To be honest, I think it's best if you stop playing for the time being." She directed the melody at her father. "I've told them you need some time off from the music, considering all that's happened." But his eyelids flickered. His pupils clouded. His breath became slow, purposeful.

Her melody transferred to his lips.

No, Oliver thought. *Michael's right. You cannot play again. Not after the horrid faces. Not after the news about Sofia.*

Sadie turned to him. Her brow furrowed over dark, scolding eyes. Slowly, she shook her head and bared her teeth like a wild animal.

Can you hear what I'm … thinking?

Sadie nodded. A cruel grin etched on her lips.

She took her father's hand and led him into the library. Sliding onto the piano stool, she stretched her fingers over the keys and slowed her breath.

Bolts on the front door slid back.

The door opened.

People swarmed through the house.

Happy people, bright eyes and smiling.

Every arm brandished the Broken Moon.

Excitement coiled through each room.

Oliver hovered beneath the library arch, nervous, detached. *Do not do this. You cannot do this. You saw what happened. You know what is coming. It is darkness, Sadie. It is horrible darkness. Cruelty and rage and betrayal—*

Sadie's gaze found him through the crowd.

Smiling wickedly, as though his words meant nothing to her, she pressed down on the keys. The first notes rang out, clear and crisp, like the innocent snow beyond the window. A gasp of relief swept through the house. The music spoke to her audience. It recalled wondrous things, weaved stories, conjured joy and magic and memory.

But as she played, Oliver began to stutter and flicker.

He could feel her pulling him in, drawing on her fear. Horrors from the depths of her mind flashed before him, surrounded him. He knew of these things, for they consumed him. Monsters and phobias and cruelties she'd read or heard or experienced under Cale's hands and his devotee's cruel tongues. Despite the monstrous onslaught, Oliver saw tears in Sadie's eyes. Her smile turned from one of cruelty to despair.

The temperature in the room dropped.

Lanterns flickered.

The world outside turned grey.

No.

The dark notes sounded.

Those same notes she had played in the music room at school. The same notes that incited Danver's psychotic rage. The same notes that transformed all the smiling faces into bloated, ghastly masks of torment and hate at the Palace of Light.

The sound split the room. A pulse from an atomic blast.

Everyone stepped back. They grabbed one another as the shockwave enveloped them. Their faces changed. Joy and colour and happiness bled away.

Sadie played on.

Oliver looked down. He hadn't vanished. He wasn't stuttering or flickering either. He was whole. And yet the dark notes, the music conjured by her fear, poured from the piano in waves. She could do it without him. She could summon fear from somewhere else, some other place, and weave it into her song.

Sadie played on.

Her audience's shoulders slumped. The skin around their eyes became dark and sore, like they'd been rubbed for a hundred years. They moaned, low and raw.

Sadie played on.

The darkness spread.

The hordes gathered down Leviathan Crook, to the iron bridge and beyond, were transformed. Her joyous music had played for days. But no more. Their hearts had become dependent on her song, buoyed by the bliss and warmth it had once conjured. But slowly, like a weed ravaging a bountiful garden, she stitched malice and cruelty into her song. Tears of remorse bled from their eyes as the dark notes cascaded down the Shadow Valley, into every soul, and every home.

For hours she played, opening a black hole of desperation and woe.

When, at last, she finished, there was no applause, just a hollow silence.

The space before the last gasp of a dying thing.

Silently, Sadie closed the lid and sat motionless, staring out the window.

Her audience departed in cold, brutal silence.

Returning to their homes, they lit their fires and huddled together for warmth, but there was none to be found. They prayed for their hopes and dreams to be restored. Withering traces of her song yearned in their hearts, but the darkness plunged its wicked fingertips into their souls, and seeped with the malevolence and ruin of all.

Iron Bridge fell silent.

Nothing stirred.

It was as if everything had died.

THE PRINCESS IN THE THREADBARE GOWN

Almost a hundred years ago, Toseland and Alice met on a busy flagstone courtyard in the underground city of Los Kralice. The star-crossed lovers stared at one another as dancers celebrated the Evenlight Festival all around. But, instead of this being a story of love and romance, it sparked the origin of something that should never have been.

Alice was the daughter of Edvard Mistery, a wealthy doktor who had preordained her entire future. A first-rate education, an apprenticeship in the Healing Halls at San Cristophe, a position at his practice in Los Kralice, marriage to a man of position and power, and a litter of intelligent, obedient children.

Toseland, however, earned a meagre wage as a hawkshaw. A lowly detective and spy. Not the sort of man Doktor Edvard Mistery had in mind for his precious daughter.

Since that first encounter, they met in secret every day behind the bandstand in the Royal Park. They whispered romantic notions to one another, their fingers entwined, and shared hard candies and fudge.

Until one fateful day.

The day Doktor Mistery discovered their secret love.

Confronted by the doktor, Toseland confessed his undying devotion for Alice, pleading for her hand in marriage.

"You? A detective, a spy! Never, sir. You shall never marry my daughter, my princess. I promise you, no man nor beast, ill-wind nor treacherous sea, shall stand between me and the death of this love."

And then, to Toseland's surprise, the doktor went limp, and collapsed to the ground.

Alice Mistery stood over her father.

A bloodied rock quivered in her hand.

Toseland and Alice abandoned Los Kralice and travelled for many days until they came upon a village set the far side of a vast river. A farmer offered them food and shelter in exchange for a day's work. They agreed and began herding cattle, weighing corn, and ploughing fields. Alice and Toseland collapsed into bed that night, and every night for the following one hundred nights, exhausted and happy.

Alice Mistery married Toseland Jeremiah AppleGarth on Lorntide in the village square beneath the moon and the stars and the gently falling snow. Together they built a warm, humble home. By day they worked the farm. By night they sat together, hand in hand, arm in arm.

And, with each passing sunrise and sunset, thoughts of Doktor Edvard Mistery's dark promise to destroy their love drifted further and further from their minds.

It had been a year to the day since their union, when a distressed cry tore through the streets. Villagers awoke to discover half a dozen men exhibiting signs of infection. An abominable skin disease of fetid, infectious pustules that bubbled with pus and corruption.

The disease spread rapidly, targeting only the men.

Every woman sat and watched as her husband, father, brother, or son, came down with the ghastly affliction. With horror in their eyes and desperation in their hearts, they pooled their money and sent word to Los Kralice for aid.

Now, Alice worried this decision might bring her father directly to her door. But, looking into Toseland's yellowing eyes, the virus swarming through his veins, she knew it was worth the risk.

Two days later, as most of the women had taken to the fields, three doktors appeared on horseback. They dressed from head to toe in black robes. Heavy waxed overcoats, masks with circular glass eyelets, and a nose shaped like a raven's beak to hold incense and spices.

They harnessed their horses, slung rifles over their shoulders, and took a small boat across the water. They swept through each dwelling, inspecting man, father, brother, and son.

"There is little hope," the doktors announced. "These men are victims of a vicious plague that sweeps the Shadow Valley."

The women protested vehemently, insisting something *must* be done.

"Nothing remains," the doktors said and reached for their rifles. "Except a swift end to their suffering."

At gunpoint, the doktors forced the women back. "Bring them out!" they ordered. "Bring out the infected."

The women refused.

"The plague must be eradicated, burned from existence, by order of the Pharmacon in San Cristophe!"

The women held fast, resolute.

"Move aside. Or you leave us no choice."

Gunfire echoed across the fields.

Again and again and again.

Crows took to the wing, cawing portentously.

Those women working the fields dropped their scythes and sheers and ran like thunder for the village.

They returned to find the village ablaze. A gruesome bonfire raged at the centre of the square, men and women piled high, wreathed in smoke and fire and death. The three doktors sat on horseback across the river, watching silently, their masks removed.

The women cursed and screamed, wailing bloody vengeance. But, as they collapsed, sobbing like children, one woman stood amidst the smouldering ruin.

Alice Mistery locked eyes with her father.

Doktor Edvard Mistery.

He saw Alice through the fire and haze but dismissed her at first, for she was covered in dirt and clad in a threadbare gown. Then, as the smoke began to clear, and she spoke, he recognised his daughter, his hope and joy, his princess.

"Our husbands are gone. Our fathers, brothers, and sons, too. I for one cannot live in a world without my love."

The other woman agreed, sobbing sorrowfully.

"We must go to them," Alice went on. "The river will have for us. The tide will pull us down and we will let it. Water shall fill our lungs and we will welcome it. We shall not struggle. We shall not fight. We will make Death afraid to take us!"

Alice and the other women joined hands by the water's edge. They inched forward. Perched on the riverbank. Toes curled over the lip.

"Alice!" Doktor Mistery screamed. "Don't do this. Get away from the edge."

Alice gave her father an empty smile then led them down into the water.

Not one of them struggled.

Not one of them fought.

They simply dwindled and vanished beneath the swell.

Edvard Mistery jumped from his horse. He knelt by the bank and thrashed around in the water for all he was worth. Tears filled his eyes. Shivers of dread stalked his bones. A dark chill hardened his veins and cloaked his heart with venomous shadows.

The river turned a sickly grey.

Ominous clouds formed, urgent and prickling with energy.

A dark wind whipped at the three men.

Doktor Edvard Mistery became frozen in horror as a dozen figures rose silently from the colourless water. They hid their faces behind soiled hair, congealed with mud and moss. Their once-white clothes, now ragged and stained with filth. They glided to the river's edge. Mounted the banks. Stretched their clawing fingers.

"River Wraiths," Edvard whispered, backing away.

The creatures gathered speed, like a howling wind. They scooped up the doktor's colleagues and dragged them screaming into the violent water. Doktor Mistery scrambled to escape but the last River Wraith pressed a foul foot on his chest. She angled her head and glowered through her sodden hair.

"Fa-ther," she hissed.

The doktor's skin turned to ice. "Alice? What have you done?"

She said nothing.

"Be gone, River Wraith!" He pulled a hallowed relic from beneath his robes and shook it at her. "Be gone, Demon Child!"

The River Wraith kicked the artefact away, gnashed her teeth, and growled like a beast.

"Return to the depths where you belong!"

Alice smiled cruelly. "You did this," she snarled, dripping with foulness. "I am nothing—"

"No!" the doktor screamed. "I love you, Alice. I will always love you."

"How can you love this?" she asked. "I am anger. I am revenge."

"There is love in you," he urged. "I know it."

"My love is dead," she replied. "You killed him."

The doktors face twisted with fear.

"If we cannot have love, then none shall have it," Alice decreed. "On this day—the shortest of each and every year—we will return to these shores and destroy all that love has built."

"I will always love you," the doktor told her. "For as long as I live. Your hatred will never consume this world. My love will endure."

"But one day you'll be gone," she snarled. "All will be gone, and all love will die."

The River Wraiths laughed darkly as they retreated from the shore and slipped beneath the surface, chanting, "One day! One day! One day!"

So, on the eve of the shortest day of the year, the eve of Lorntide, it is said the River Wraiths return to the banks of the River Myr to destroy love and happiness. But the people of the Shadow Valley protect themselves with their jongeliers, their wooden effigies of Doktor Edvard Mistery who returned to the water's edge every year to look into his daughter's eyes and use his love to force the River Wraiths back into the cold, dark, forgotten depths of the River Myr.

PART FOUR
SHADOWS

*"Through dark storms and deadly seas,
a sister is a constant light that never goes out."*
—ROSALITA BATISTA,
Le Tambour Cassé, Ville de Feuilles, 1409

THE
COMPANION

Dawn threatened to break. Eli rocked on the garden swings. The tired chain-links groaned. His feet dragged in the snow.

Oliver sat beside him, gazing into the middle distance. He could see Sadie's lamp flickering against the window. Her face suddenly appeared. She pushed the pane open and jabbed her elbows into the sill.

Everything was okay. The sun was rising, the darkness was clearing, and everything was fine with the world. The way it always should be.

"What's with the dawn patrol?" Eli said, fiddling with his Monster Magnifiers.

"I wanted some company," Oliver replied.

"And you thought you'd have a nice little chat with me? The boy who doesn't speak."

Oliver frowned. "Well, no. Not really. I thought—"

"You thought you might be able to get through to me?" Eli asked. "Make me see the irrelevance of my silence. Thought I might open up to you. Man-to-man, so to speak?"

Oliver felt awkward.

Eli smiled.

The swing creaked.

"Nice try."

Oliver looked at the faded snow where the red paint had fallen.

Eli followed his gaze. "What is it?"

"I have been thinking about the dreams. Thinking about the girl in the mirror with the dark markings. I think it is Sofia. She spoke to Sadie, calling to her, asking to bring her home."

"But Sofia is dead, Oliver. Larissa said so."

"But they are twins. Two halves of a whole. Their souls are connected. Even in death."

Eli snorted. "Why did Sadie survive when Sofia did not?"

The word *Murderers* hung before them on the fence.

Oliver shook his head. "I do not know, Eli. I honestly do not know."

"What about the music?" Eli asked, kicking a clump of snow. "Is that connected to Sofia? Is that her fault, too?"

"Perhaps. Music connects us all in some way. A universal language." Eli shrugged. "You think I am going mad. You think I am going mad like ..." Oliver paused for a moment. "Like Danver."

"Danver?" whispered Eli.

The word echoed around the garden in an unearthly way.

"Sadie told him the story of Grandfather William. She played the piano. The music made him attack Cale Boswick and got him sent to Hurtmore House. It is a horrible place. Sadie told me. A place to send children who have lost their way, or been driven mad, or whatever. Danver is still there. Sadie used to talk about saving him ... before everything changed."

Eli stopped swinging. "You know," he started. "I'm not actually here. Neither are you. You do know that, don't you?"

Oliver took a moment, then nodded slowly. "This is a dream?"

"Of course," replied Eli. "I don't talk. You're imagining it all, Oliver. You need to wake up. Things are happening. You need to be there. Wake up, Oliver. Wake up NOW!"

Oliver found himself on the edge of the bed, one hand resting on the cold iron frame.

A dream? I had a dream? I fell asleep? That is not possible.

But his thoughts were swept away by the sound of music playing downstairs.

Oliver materialised beneath the library arch. To his left, beyond the library window where Fable perched—a motionless, ice-white ornament with roving eyes—the sky had turned a cloudy, coal scuttle grey. Snow came down in thick columns. In every house, lamps were lit, fires were burning. Chimneys smoked merrily, but all memory of warmth and contentment was a long-forgotten dream.

Sadie sat at the piano. Music poured out of her as naturally as blood from a wound. The house appeared to have stopped—time suspended—as her intoxicating melodies found every secret corner.

The Madison family were drawn into the library.

Unbeknownst to them, Larissa and Natalia stood close to Oliver, as the music enveloped them. Michael glided behind and put his arms around their waists. Eli ambled past and sat beside his sister at the keyboard.

Sadie glanced at him. A mask of soulless indifference on her face.

Oliver observed each Madison in turn.

They looked like ghosts—not the ones like AppleGarth or the others in the Glade—but ghosts of their former selves. Their expressions seemed roiled, marbled, faraway. His eyes finally came to rest on Atticus. The old wolfhound had curled up in front of the fire, head resting on his outstretched legs.

Beside him sat a girl of Sadie's age.

Oliver's mouth fell open, gasping for breath, trying to summon a warning, but something rendered him useless. The girl lovingly stroked the dog's long snout, but Atticus seemed uncomfortable with her touch. She took a deep breath, imbibing the music, drinking the notes down.

Despite this new presence, the dark notes were absent, and the house resonated with a renewed hope. The girl watched the Madison family. The bliss and euphoria of Sadie's music lifted their souls.

But none of them saw her.

Their other daughter.

Their other sister.

It disturbed Oliver how much she looked like Sadie.

Sofia.

Pirouetting into the centre of the room, Sofia raised her hands high above her head. The dark etchings around her crown resembled ancient symbols, tattooed and burned into her flesh. Her entire body trembled with some uncontrollable force, before folding into a devilish bow.

Without warning, the dark notes erupted.

Lightning bolts forked the house.

Daylight evaporated, turning the world to monochrome.

A cloak of shadows.

The Madison faces dropped, hands swung apart, embraces dwindled.

"Yes," Sofia said victoriously. "It feels good to be home!"

She smiled at Oliver. Two rows of blackened teeth spread before him, twisted and rotten, like spoilt vegetables in a discarded field. "Oliver," she said gently, turning his head towards her with a cold finger. "Do not be afraid."

Several strands of his dark hair bled into shocking white.

He searched for an escape, but his feet were rooted to the spot.

"Who are you?" he said, finding his voice.

"I'm Sofia," she smiled coyly. "You know that."

"No, I mean, who are you ... *really*?"

"Did you not believe Larissa's story?"

"The one where you died at birth? The one about you being Sadie's twin?"

"That's the one."

"I ... I am not sure."

"There is a fine line between truth and lies, Oliver. You've seen the faces. You've seen the evil lurking within us all. The lies we harbour. The masks we wear." She paused, showing him her repulsive smile again. "For you wear one yourself."

"Liar!"

"Me?" Sofia giggled and fanned her face. She grabbed Oliver's throat and pinned him against the archway. "Who are *you* really?"

Oliver recoiled. "I am ... Oliver."

"And where did *you* come from?" she asked, her grip tightening.

"I—" he tried. "I am Sadie's friend. Her best friend. Her—"

"Ye-es?"

"Her Fear," he admitted. "I am all and everything she fears."

"Pathetic."

"I am part of her."

"The part she couldn't live with anymore?" Sofia spat. "The part she cast aside like an unwanted beast."

"No," Oliver wheezed, clawing at Sofia's thin, pale hands. "I am her friend, her companion. And she is mine."

"Unconditional love, is that it?"

"Yes," he managed. "I would do anything for her."

"But you're a lie, Oliver. A fantasy. And one day Sadie will come to understand."

Sofia's grip fell away.

Oliver's head spun.

He didn't believe Sofia's harsh words.

Sadie would never deny him.

"And what about me?" Sofia asked, looking around theatrically. "Where's the person who's supposed to fill the missing places in my soul? Where is the half of me that has been absent for so long?"

Sofia spun. Her white linen dress drifted outwards. Tiptoeing playfully across the room, she watched Sadie's fingers as they danced on the keys.

Dark notes cascaded around the edge of the room.

Thunder rumbled against the windows.

"We're supposed to be together. Sadie and I. I want her back."
Her wicked eyes found Oliver. "And you're going to help me."

"No," he said, massaging his throat. "I will not."

Sofia circled him now. "The basement, Oliver."

"Basement?"

Sofia nodded, her smile wider and crueller than ever.

"What basement?"

"Find the entrance, Oliver. For the truth you seek. The answers to all your questions lurk in the darkness beneath this house."

✳ ☺ ▦ ✄ 𝌆

Sadie's music deepened. Sofia watched her like a strict teacher, a guardian, a jealous rival. She drank in the dark notes, becoming stronger and clearer, taking shape, manifesting into something—*real.*

She rejoiced in the misery on the faces of the Madison family.

Friends and neighbours shambled along Leviathan Crook, scared to look inside.

The days rumbled on.

Lorntide became a distant memory, and with it went the joy in the hearts of Iron Bridge. The decorations and weirdly dressed mannequins remained, but they brought no smiles. No one thought of the New Year's celebrations and the dawn of a new century that lurked less than twenty-four hours away. Everyone fought to stay connected to the present—to the here and now—for fear they would lose touch with reality and slip, silently away.

Night descended.

Oliver watched as Sadie slept.

Her nightmares continued, dragging her further and further towards the abyss. Visions came to her in the dark.

Invading like an army of insects crawling under the bedclothes, they sank their tiny legs and claws and fangs into her pale skin. She moaned and jittered, rolled back and forth, her spine arced, fingers twisted into the sheets.

Unable to watch, Oliver found Michael asleep in the living room. An ornate torchlight and a flagon of coffee sat on the card table beside him. As gaunt and ill-favoured as he looked most days, Sadie's father now seemed to wither away. His skin looked waxy and paper thin, his backbone curving like a scythe.

Oliver had searched everywhere for the basement Sofia had warned him of. He'd found every hidey-hole and secret compartment imaginable, but nothing led below the house.

There were no secret doorways, false walls, trapdoors.

Nothing.

If only he could use his hands to press against the walls, lift the rugs and floorboards, pull the books and knick-knacks and trinkets and grimcracks and oddities from the shelves and search behind. If only he could blow away the dust and discover what lurked beneath.

Sadie's feet pitter-pattered down the stairs.

She came to rest in the middle of the hallway, searching the hardwood beams, with her bare toes. But it was her hands that really drew his attention for they were smeared with red and pink stains.

"Is that ... blood?" he asked, distressed. Shifting to get a better look, he realised Sadie was sleepwalking again. He moved to grab her, but she darted past him in an instant, flinging the front door open, and disappearing into the night.

Oliver ran after her, watching as she barrelled down the moonlit path. But the front door swung shut in his face. He closed his eyes, imagining himself on the other side—

"You can't help her."

On the arm of the chair, gently moving the thinning strands of hair from her father's face, sat Sofia.

Oliver tightened. His jaw ached. "I can. And I will," he

replied, trying to sound confident. He closed his eyes again, attempting to picture Sadie. He'd jump to her location. Wake her up. Convince her to come home.

But, somehow, she was lost to him.

He gave it another shot.

"Don't give yourself a blood clot," Sofia added. "She's gone. She'll be back."

"Did you do this?" he asked, frustrated. "Have you hidden her from me?"

"*Moi?*" Sofia said coquettishly. "You need to focus on the basement, Oliver. You have to find a way in. Don't you want to help Sadie?"

"And help you too!" he bleated.

"Yes, you'll be helping me too. But, you know, do it for Sadie."

"What is down there?"

"Seeing is believing, Oliver. You of all people can appreciate that. I could tell you all the tales in the world, try to convince you of the horror in people's hearts, instruct you where you have to go, and who you have to help, but, unless you see these things and make these decisions for yourself, then it's just words spoken to the wind."

"I do not trust you."

"That's why you need to see for yourself. I don't care how you feel. I need you to find a way into the basement. For Sadie's sake. And mine."

"But how? I have looked everywhere."

"Clearly not. For a start, I'm convinced he knows."

Sofia patted Michael gently on the head.

He snorted, wriggling in his armchair.

Like a candle being extinguished, Sofia vanished.

"Where is it?" Oliver asked, collapsing on the sofa opposite Michael. "Where is the doorway?"

But Michael continued to sleep, his coffee steaming beside him.

Oliver sighed, arms folded.

He needed help.

He could only think of one person.

米 ᗡ 🁢 ⚔ 🏛

Appearing outside the Temple of the Dead, Oliver found himself surrounded. There seemed to be hundreds, if not thousands of ghosts. Far more than last time.

They passed him on either side. Ghosts of men and women, possibly killed in war, or taken by a plague, or succumbed to old age in their beds surrounded by loved ones, perhaps alone and cold and broken-hearted. Winged ghosts swooped from one mausoleum to the next. There were songbirds, pigeons, crows, ravens, giant birds of prey with wing spans wider than an automobile, and pigs, horses, sheep, cats, and dogs.

But it was the monsters that bothered Oliver the most.

Hulking, shimmering bodies of werewolves and ogres and minotaurs stood surveying their surrounds. Nimble, sure-footed reptiles, more than eight feet tall, scurried every which way, their noses to the wind. Gorgons and deformed hybrids of men with fish tails wriggled helplessly in the hardening snow.

AppleGarth stood with his back to the railings, busying himself with a cigarette. His spine straightened. Turning, his dark eyes fell on Oliver. "What're you doin' here, son?" he said. "And all on your lonesome. Where's that friend of yours?"

"Sadie is … has … well, I have sort of lost her." AppleGarth seemed nonplussed. "But I came here looking for you. Please, you have to help me."

"Me? Well, I'll do what I can." He popped the cigarette in his mouth and began the futile task of lighting it.

Oliver fidgeted, his attention taken by the legions of spectral entities shuffling by. "Why are there so many?"

"Come down from the north, ain't they?"

"From the Winter Continent?"

AppleGarth laughed. "No, no. From the northern quarter of

the Glade. The bit overtaken by the forest. Word is, there's some ancient malice gaverin' there."

"Ancient malice?" Oliver swallowed hard. "The dark mist."

"If you like," AppleGarth shrugged. "They've abandoned their restin' places and sought solace 'ere in the south. I've never seen the like of it. Very peculiar, I must say."

"What happened in the north?"

"I dunno," AppleGarth said. "But, if I had to take a guess, I'd say they were afraid. Terrified. These lot from the north are riddled with *fear*." The word hung before Oliver. "Not sure what the dead have to be afraid of," AppleGarth continued. "Dead is dead, right? Can't fink of anyfin' worse."

"Being forgotten."

AppleGarth snorted, stopped fiddling with his matches. "Quite so."

Once again, Oliver shut his eyes and tried to find Sadie, but she remained lost. "I need you to help me hold things, move things," he said, his voice desperate. "I need to find a way into the basement."

AppleGarth considered this for a moment. He clamped his hand on Oliver's shoulder. "Come with me."

The hawkshaw led Oliver up the cobbled path to the Temple of the Dead. They slipped inside, taking a seat at one of the long wooden benches. Arranged neatly along the centre of the table were a number of ceramic dishes, each filled with uneven sugar lumps.

"Go on then," AppleGarth said.

Oliver looked down at the nearest dish. "How?"

AppleGarth extended his hand and, with the tip of his finger, nudged one of the sugar lumps onto the table. "Like that. S'easy."

Oliver extended his hand, but his finger swished through the sugar lumps and out the other side. Sighing, Oliver inspected his fingers. "Who taught you?"

"Had to teach meself." AppleGarth folded his hands together. "Give it time. Have patience. And believe in yaself." Oliver chewed his bottom lip. "You have everyfin' there is to know. It's all up here," AppleGarth said, tapping Oliver on the forehead. "You just need to uncover it. It's like a treasure hunt, son. You need to dig around a bit til you find what you're lookin' for, then pounce on it." AppleGarth flicked some dirt from his gums. "And what's all this business with a basement anyway? I thought you could, you know, see somewhere and—*Ka-Blamo!*—you're there."

"I can only jump to places I have been before: here, Sadie's house, the Palace of Light, the Steam Totem, and all. I cannot seem to jump anywhere I have never been. I do not know what it looks like, what it *feels* like."

AppleGarth scratched his dirty chin. "What would happen if ya … guessed? Took a calculated risk? An approximation?"

Oliver shuddered. "I imagine I could end up anywhere. A mile above the Sapphire Seas, at the centre of a mountain, anywhere. The chances of me guessing correctly are, well, improbable to fathom." Oliver's head dipped. "There must be a hidden door or a hatch or some way into the basement," he said. "Please, AppleGarth. You have to show me how to touch things, move things."

"It's trial and error. What works for me might not work for you. I'm no scientist. No brain doktor."

Oliver nodded.

"Come on, then. The sugar lumps. Use anyfin' you have, whatever you have. If I can do it, I know you can."

He reached out, edged his finger over the dish. Could he do this again? Could he move something in the real world with his otherworldly hands? He hovered over the sugar lumps. His heart thudded in his chest. Knees jigged beneath the table.

Tension fixed his jaw. He extended a finger and prodded. It passed through the sugar lumps, then the dish. Hissing like a viper, he shook his hand as if to reset it and tried again.

Same result.

Nothing.

Once more.

Nothing.

"Damn it!" Oliver bleated. "This is impossible. Literally, im-poss-ible!"

Oliver's face became streaked with red veins.

His eyes shimmered like fire.

"Calm down," AppleGarth said, steadying the boy. "You're gettin' all worked up. It'll never work that way. Not properly."

"I moved things once," Oliver said. "I got angry, and I lashed out, and I knocked them off a shelf."

AppleGarth dislodged something disgusting from his mouth.

Oliver took a long breath, running his hands soothingly against his thighs. His skin returned to normal, his eyes black and grey once more.

"If you need to be angry to move fings, it's going to be exhaustin'. You won't be able to keep it going for long, son. You need somefin' you can draw on easily. Somefin' that don't require you to get all worked up."

"What do you draw on?"

"Me?" AppleGarth replied. "Well, it's personal. You understand, right?"

"Is it something to do with your wife?"

AppleGarth's eyes instantly turned to tears.

"I am sorry," Oliver said. "I did not mean to upset you."

"I'm not upset," AppleGarth told him. "I'm happy."

"You do not look it."

"My wife was the greatest fing to ever happen to me. I can still remember the time we had together, every smile, every laugh, every private moment, the way she used to—" AppleGarth caught himself in a daydream. "Sorry, that stuff's for me. That's my fuel, Oliver. Find what brings you happiness, then you can do anyfin'. As I've already said." He tapped his own head this time. "It's all up here."

THE
BELL JAR

Oliver materialised in the eaved bedroom. Slinking onto the window seat, he looked out over Iron Bridge. He wondered where, amongst all the twinkling lights, throbbing gaslamps and tendrils of chimney smoke, Sadie was hiding.

He took a deep breath, closed his eyes, and tried to connect with her.

At first, the same result. But, as he tried again, pushing harder, searching, he saw flashes of light, the buzz of wireless static, and then his mind opened on a white room, tiled and clean.

Oliver opened his eyes, relieved to find himself in the eaved bedroom. He grasped his head, steadying himself.

Detergent lingered in his nostrils.

His mind flashed to the white room again.

A hospital, an operating theatre, a delivery room.

A spotless sink loaded with soap, surgical gloves, gauze, bottles of iodine, and other instruments on a metal tray.

A pair of double doors flew open.

Back home again.

He felt sick, disorientated.

What was he seeing?

He braced himself, eyes shut tight now, ready for another mind-crushing jump, but it didn't come. He ventured one eye open. The shadows of Sadie's bedroom a gloomy comfort.

Oliver jolted when Mischief sprang onto the seat beside him. She purred agitatedly, staring at the spot where he sat.

He considered the cat for a moment, waving a hand in front of her little pink nose. Mischief blinked several times before coiling herself into a pile of fur.

The vivid hospital light slapped him in the face again.

A deafening racket exploded in his ears.

Half a dozen voices yelled and shrieked as suction pumps gargled, surgical instruments rattled, rubber wheels squeaked, a woman screamed, a child balled. Streams of colour, like dancing ribbons, swirled by. The noise and chaos tried to ram its way through his eyes and ears and into his brain.

Oliver found himself stood beside the enormous Lorntide tree in the Madison hallway. Sparkling decorations of strange characters with monstrous faces twisted gently from its waxy, green-grey branches.

From the living room, Michael Madison snored rhythmically in his armchair, arms and legs arranged in an acrobatic puzzle.

Oliver collapsed on the sofa.

Fading dots of brilliant light hung in his retinas.

"What are you doing?" Sofia asked, bored, snapping into existence behind him.

Oliver took in a sharp breath.

"Visions," he told her. "Of a hospital. But it is jumbled. Confusing."

Sofia sighed. "No, I mean, why aren't you looking for the basement?"

Oliver scowled at her.

"You're wasting time."

"What does that mean?"

Sofia sighed. "Everything is finely balanced, Oliver. Imagine your little—*existence*—as a china saucer spinning on a pole. Round and round the saucer goes, wobbling at times, but corrected by pressures applied to it. On it spins, on and on, balanced precariously, but assuredly, atop the pole."

Sofia jumped over the back of the sofa and nestled beside him, inches from his face. She smelt rotten. "Someone has to keep the saucer spinning, Oliver. Elsewise it'll dwindle and die, then fall and smash into a million tiny pieces." He could taste her putrid stench at the back of his throat. "You don't want to fall and die, do you, Oliver?"

"No, but—"

"But what?" she snapped. "It only takes one saucer to fall, one little saucer, and the whole tea-set comes crashing down." She pulled away. Her disgusting teeth hung in a crooked smile. "You understand what I'm saying, don't you?"

Oliver nodded. "I need to find the basement or—"

"Everyone will die!" she squealed theatrically. Pushing in close, Sofia pressed her nose to his cheek. "But seriously, nothing is set in stone," she divulged, her breath cold against his pale skin. "But the hands of time are never on our side, and they're ticking." She slowly eased herself away, rocking her head from side to side, whispering, "Tick, tock, tick, tock, tick, tock," as she turned to vapour and shadow.

A log crackled in the grate.

The last embers glowed reassuringly.

Michael flicked an eye towards the fire, then the stairs. He mumbled something incomprehensible, glanced at his pocket watch and re-adjusted his limbs.

The fire spat out its last breath and the room slipped into a moonlit dark. A huge stone mantelpiece surrounded the fireplace. It stretched some six feet from end to end, topped with Larissa's cups and saucers, a bronze candelabra, an owl-themed matryoshka doll, a stained paperweight, and a miniature replica of the steam engine: *the Trans-Norlandian Express.*

Above the mantelpiece hung another collection of imposing paintings. The smallest of them being another canvas of William Madison. He stood in a desert surrounded by camels, wearing an orange sari, trimmed with gold, and decorated with stars and moons. He appeared to be gazing down at Oliver.

Everything went silent, except for the drumming of his heart. Oliver grew angry, frustrated. William Madison looked delighted, mocking even. Laughing at Oliver from beyond the grave, across time.

He snorted, circling the armchair where Michael slept, eyeballing Sadie's grandfather.

Anger and rage bubbled in his chest.

Oliver thrust a finger at the matryoshka doll.

It slipped straight through.

He stopped. Took a breath. Focused.

Clenching his teeth, he tried again.

Same result.

It is all up here.

Oliver closed his eyes and pictured the doll falling from the mantelpiece, its replicant contents scattering on the floor.

It is all up here.

The matryoshka doll beamed at him in his mind's eye. "You can do it," the owl said. A chorus of muffled voices yammered encouragement.

It is all up here.

Oliver swung his finger towards the wooden ornament. He knew he could do it. It was inevitable. But his finger whipped through the doll, touching nothing but air. His heart sank, anger boiled, red veins swarmed beneath his skin like parasites. Oliver lashed out in frustration. But, instead of tearing everything to the floor, his fist met the cold grasp of Sofia's pale hand.

She shook her head.

Released his fist.

Slowly extending a calm finger, Sofia nudged the doll. She connected with the wood, hard and smooth. The carved wooden owl rocked backwards, pirouetting on the mantelpiece, until it plummeted, end over end, to the floor.

Oliver jumped back, shame and disappointment burning through him.

The matryoshka doll clattered against the hardwood floor,

splitting open, spilling six smaller owls onto the threadbare rug. Sofia vanished, her disgusting smile lingering for the briefest of moments.

Michael's eyes shot open.

He sprang out of the armchair, striding towards the fireplace. Michael looked down at the dolls spinning on the hardwood. He gathered them up, placing them by the fire.

Oliver stormed away, stuffing his useless hands in his pockets. But, as he circumnavigated the room for the umpteenth time, cursing and chastising his incompetence, the boy in the crimson scarf came to a sharp stop.

Michael Madison was standing in front of the wall to the right of the fireplace. His arms outstretched, palms vertical. A rectangular line of light—the width and height of a grown man— had appeared on the wood panelling. Slowly, the rectangle filled with colourful light, changing, shifting. Opulent and wondrous.

Where once there had been nothing but a solid wall, hung a door.

The brightly painted door.

Michael reached forward, turned an iron handle, then shifted into the shadows beyond. Oliver, his heart back-flipping like an acrobat, followed nervously into the devouring gloom beyond.

✷ ☺ ▥ ⚡ ♨

Oliver followed Michael Madison down thirteen uneven steps.

Through the shadows, a gentle draft blew into his straining eyes. Oliver could sense the size of the basement. It could easily have been the size of the entire Madison house.

Amber bulbs of subtle lamplight fizzed and crackled, then gently warmed the room.

Before Oliver had time to drink everything in, Michael strode purposefully from the power switch towards a dilapidated armchair hunkering in the middle of the room.

Dust streamed between the floorboards above.

An unpleasant smell circled through the air.

"Are you okay?" Michael said. "One of Larissa's matryoshka dolls fell off the mantelpiece."

Oliver spun, wondering if Michael had addressed him directly.

A woman's voice croaked, short and venomous. "You look sick."

"I'm just … tired, I suppose," Michael replied softly.

The armchair creaked.

Oliver inched forward.

A dark figure leant into the light.

"I don't know what to do," Michael whispered. "The piano, the music, it's … unnatural."

"*She* is unnatural," the woman hissed. "You've always known."

"But I'd hoped—"

"Hope! What possible hope? You were a fool from the start. Just like your father."

"He only followed his heart … as I have done."

"Followed your heart?" she rasped. "Romanticised nonsense. And look where that's gotten you. Idiots. You and William, both."

"It's going to be okay," Michael replied, his heart clearly not in it. "Sadie will defy the Foretelling. I'll do whatever I must to safeguard her from the world."

"And who's going to safeguard the world from *her*?"

"We need to give her time," he started. "Time to prove the Foretelling wrong."

"Time? You've had all the time there is, Michael. Her hourglass is all but spent … and yours with it!" the old woman riled. "Time will only make her stronger. You know what must be done."

"I cannot," Michael said. "She's my daughter."

"You did it before. You must do it again."

"No. I cannot. I *will* not. Sadie *will* live."

She moved her weathered face into the light. "Then we are all doomed!" The words had barely left her lips when her head suddenly flicked towards the shadows. "Who's there?"

Michael turned to look. "It's just you and me. The way it's always been."

She nodded once, as if it were all the strength she had.

Michael kissed her forehead and turned for the stairs.

"I warned you," she barked after him. "I told you this would happen. You knew. We all knew."

Michael sighed.

"You should never have kept her."

Michael folded his arms. "What's done is done. You've been in the dark for too long. Your mind is twisted. You're angry. I am sorry for that."

"I see no penitence in you," she hissed. "Only shame and regret."

Michael glanced at a wooden workbench covered with cloaked objects. Turning, he walked towards Oliver, his face defiant and sad. As he came within several feet of the boy, Michael stopped and looked towards him.

Not *at* Oliver but *through* him.

It was as if he felt something but saw nothing.

"I have to go now, Mother."

Karolinja Madison cracked her jaw. "So be it."

     ❄☡▉☠♏

Oliver concealed himself in the basement's dark as Michael flicked lamps on in the living room above. Amber light bled through the floorboards in long, thin blades.

Slowly, he glanced over at the old woman.

Karolinja's eyes were fixed on him.

"Come," she said. "Come to me."

She sat in a rotten armchair, the leather worn and scarred with the claws of one, or possibly all, of the three wise cats.

Karolinja's shoulders were draped in an embroidered robe made from hessian and lined with purple silk.

"It's you," she said, as Oliver tentatively emerged. Her voice sounded coarse and strained, as if her lungs were unable to accommodate the actions required of them. "Why have you come?"

"You are Sadie's grandmother?" he replied, ignoring her question. "Why are you down here?"

"Shameful secrets are best kept in the dark, young man."

"My name is Oliver."

"That's a trifle boring, considering all that you are."

"Why are you down here?" he asked again.

"I already answered," Karolinja whispered spitefully, flicking her matted grey hair aside. "You're a curious soul. And a brave one, I might add."

"I have done nothing brave."

Karolinja raised a serrated fingernail: unkempt, gnarled, and dark yellow in hue. "Not yet." She seemed to be smiling, but it was not a comfort. "Sadie is going to leave. You need to go with her."

"Leave?"

"There's another … *girl* … in the house. She looks like my granddaughter, but her heart is cold. Vengeance and retribution burn within. You must be wary, young man."

"It is Sofia. Sadie's twin. She died during birth."

"Is that so?" Karolinja raised a bald eyebrow. "Secrets," she said, indicating a large object positioned on the wooden workbench, shrouded in a cobwebbed blanket. "Awful secrets."

"What is it?" Oliver asked. "What is under there?"

Karolinja took a long, purposeful breath.

"Sofia."

Oliver tightened. His head spun. He turned towards the blanket and then back to Karolinja, unsure if he wanted the truth he sought. The truth Sofia had promised he'd find in the dark beneath Number 5 Leviathan Crook.

"Go see."

"I cannot."

"You must," she rattled. "For Sadie's sake."

"I cannot move it," he said, nervously approaching the workbench. "At least, I cannot move it without getting angry, and even then ... I am still learning."

"Anger?" she hissed, her black eyes narrowing. "Anger leads to destruction and nothing more."

"Then how do I move it? AppleGarth said it was all up here." He tapped his head. "But I could not ... I cannot—"

"Yes, Oliver. What lurks in your mind? What controls your thoughts? What festers in your soul? What makes you ... *you*?"

Oliver scanned the dusty, cat-scratched floorboards. Spiders crouched in nooks and crannies, poised as if to flee. He knew exactly who he was. An unsettled mass of neurosis, of paranoia, of fangs and blood and shadows, wrapped in black and spun in a crimson scarf.

He shuddered as though someone had clawed his gravestone.

For the briefest moment, his eyes flashed red, his skin rippled with scales, the sensation of enormous power coursed through him. Untethered. Untamed. But, as quickly as it arrived, the sensation dissipated, leaving him cold and lost.

"I am fear," he whispered. "Sadie's fear."

"Fear made flesh!" Karolinja bit, triumphantly waving an emaciated arm.

She snarled at Oliver.

A knowing, victorious snarl.

"She did it. She actually did it. You're the first marker. You're the first evidence she is the child of the Foretelling! It's true. All of it!" the old woman bleated. "You're the proof she has the power to end it all." Karolinja seemed giddy with excitement, despite the terrible words that crossed her lips. "*For the child that takes everything we hold dear, and locks it away for all time, is the child that puts her FEAR aside, and leads the others into darkness.*"

"Me?" Oliver bleated. "I am part of the Foretelling?"

"So it is written, so it will come to pass."

"That cannot be true!"

"The blanket, Oliver. You must look beneath the blanket!"

His eyes became wild, shining like pennies, coated in tears. Oliver's hands trembled, sweaty and feverous. He tried to steel himself for what was to come, but anger gathered in his mind, like rising steam, a scalding blindfold.

Oliver's long, thin fingers clasped the blanket and cast it aside.

Dust plumed like a dynamite blast.

He studied his fingers.

He'd done it.

He'd moved the blanket.

But every element of his being wished he hadn't.

As the dust settled, a large bell jar appeared, fingerprints pasted to the glass.

Horror gnawed his bones.

For inside the bell jar, an infant floated in murky jaundice-coloured liquid. Naked and still. A circle of black symbols had been painted on her scalp.

A crown of ink.

Oliver stumbled back from the ghastly vision.

His stomach convulsed, knotted, lurched. "Why?"

"A mistake," Karolinja answered plainly.

"What kind of person mistakenly puts a dead child in a jar?"

"No! Sofia is the mistake," she replied bitterly. "And ... Oliver—" His eyes met the old woman's. "She wasn't dead when they put her in."

Sofia stepped out of the shadows.

Her filthy fingernails drummed against the bell jar.

She directed her other hand at the old woman.

Karolinja began to choke. Her malnourished hands clawed at her throat.

"A tragedy, isn't it?" Sofia said curiously, looking at the baby in the jar.

"Stop it," Oliver insisted. "You are hurting her."

"Hurting her?" Sofia replied, wrinkling her nose. "Look what she did to me."

"It ... wasn't ... me!"

Sofia swept towards the old woman. Her white dress fluttered behind like a ship's flag. She thrust her face into Karolinja's. "Not *you*?" she accused. "You knew what they were going to do to me, and you didn't stop it. You didn't raise a single one of those wizened fingers to help. You sat down here in your *grief hole* and let it all happen."

Sofia released Karolinja. "There was nothing I could do," the old woman gasped, her voice nothing but a thin whisper.

"Nothing! *Nothing?*" Sofia spat, rage taking over her entire body.

"You don't understand, Sofia—"

"Don't you dare say my name! You have no right. None."

"You don't know what happened," Karolinja protested. "I was cursed. I was under a spell. My father—"

"You were the victim of some kind of magic?" Sofia snarled sarcastically. "I wish I'd simply been put under a spell or a curse." Sofia sank to her knees and pressed her nose against the bell jar. "But no, I was murdered. Killed by your son and his stupid wife, and stuck in here for all eternity." Sofia glared at Karolinja. She raised her hand again. The old woman took a sharp breath, rising in her chair. Frozen, eyes glazed and hollow, her fingers twisted like knotted branches.

"Is that what happened?" Oliver asked Sofia.

Sofia sighed, as though defeated. "There's no point me telling you, Oliver. You don't believe a word I say, despite the evidence all around. I know you want what's best for Sadie, but the truth will surface and there, in the wake of revelation, you will come to believe."

"Believe—?" Oliver began, but the words fled his lips as Sofia's head began to spin from side to side. Her hands shook. The dark markings on her scalp ran down her face. The contours of her body expanded, vibrated. A dark face flickered in place of the young girl's, snorting and groaning like a savage beast.

"What is it?" Oliver asked in alarm. "Your face! Your … mask!"

Karolinja coughed violently as life returned to her eyes. The old woman watched Sofia's contorted face. A thin smile cracked her lips.

"I … have … to … go."

Each word came from Sofia in a different voice.

"They … are … coming!"

"Who?"

"The Narrowers. They are here!"

THE NARROWERS

Sadie awoke suddenly. Amber light twisted over the window seat, coating the eaved bedroom with dazzling radiance. Everything felt warm and glorious despite the winter's chill pressed against the glass.

She blinked, cleared the sleep from her eyes, as amber beams of light rotated hypnotically around the room.

Searching, scanning, exploring.

They moved in.

Closer.

Chalky-white light illuminated the room. It emanated from all directions, as if from multiple suns. Not even the stubbornest shadow remained.

And then she heard the first voice.

A soft whisper. Inside her. Neither male nor female. The voice shifted, faded, blended a thousand into one.

"Sadie Madison," it said. "The time is upon us."

She couldn't speak. Her jaw became heavy, palsied.

This must be a dream.

"Sadie Madison. You have the mind that cannot be unlocked."

The room began to change.

White to amber and gold.

Three silhouettes emerged. Copper-grey skeins shimmered around them.

One stepped forward, erupting with features, colour, expression.

"Do not be alarmed. You are quite safe."

His skin glowed the colour of honey. His face surrounded with auburn curls that flowed to his shoulders. It was hard to tell what he was wearing, for it glittered like treasure. His arms hung by his sides, strong and athletic. The physique of a warrior.

The silhouettes behind him transformed into two elegant women. One wore her hair loose. White-blonde needles framed her sharp features. The other had a heart-shaped face with unblemished olive skin, thick dark hair, crystal-blue eyes. They floated to the man's side, inspecting Sadie as she burrowed herself into the bedclothes.

The man spoke. "Your mind is precious."

"There is much to come," said the blonde woman.

"For your sake and the sake of the world," added the woman with the heart-shaped face.

"Are you ... the Narrowers?" Sadie asked.

Her gaze shifted from one beautiful creature to the next.

"Yes," replied the woman with the heart-shaped face. "But we go by many other names. Names that have changed through the centuries. Grigori, Watchers, Narrowers."

"The Gathering—the harvesting of memories—has existed since the beginning of time. Since anyone, or anything, had the capacity to remember," the blonde woman said. "We take away the irrelevant, the unimportant, the memories people no longer need, making space for the memories to come, space for the ones to treasure, space for the future of your life."

"Grigori?" Sadie repeated. "I've heard that name." She rifled through her memories, searching for the word. She stumbled on the next sentence. The magnitude of it rattled her entire body. "You're ... Angels?"

The man's eyes shone like twin stars. "Once, maybe. But that time is gone. We—the Narrowers—are all that remain."

Sadie took a breath, released the bedclothes and shifted

against the headboard. "You're not what I imagined. Not at all."

"Really?" replied the blonde woman, now stood at the foot of the bed. "I would propose we look exactly the way you imagined us."

"As Gods," said the other woman. "Is this not how you see us?"

Sadie shook her head.

"Do tell. How did you see us, Sadie Madison? We'd be fascinated to know."

Sadie bit her tongue as she recalled the times her father, or Oliver, or Rhiannon had spoken of the Narrowers. "I pictured many things," she said, then rallied, adding, "Darkness mostly surrounding orbs of phosphorescence. I didn't picture you as people—with heads and eyes and hands and all—just entities, spirits, ghosts. I saw my grandfather sometimes, with his crazy white hair, his strange outfits, his mischievous smile. Some part of me thought you all looked like him. I know. Ridiculous."

The room flashed gold and white.

Sadie shielded her eyes.

The Narrowers materialised into three versions of her grandfather.

"Like this?" said the one who had previously been the blonde woman.

She stood before Sadie now dressed in a loose-fitting green and brown infantry uniform, peaked hat and rifle. The man wore the camouflage outfit she had seen in the school museum. The other woman was—for no good reason known to Sadie—dressed as a ringmaster from a circus, complete with bullwhip and top hat.

"Grandfather?" Sadie muttered, staring at all three William Madisons. "You look just like him. Father said he was a Narrower. It's true, isn't it?"

"Yes," said the ringmaster. "But he betrayed us ... and fell."

"My father said he desired a mortal life, with love and companionship and adventure. He chose to leave—"

"Your father has weaved an interesting tale, Sadie Madison. Your grandfather was a selfish creature. Greed and lust flowed through him. Both in the Vents and upon this earth. His betrayal is at the heart of it all."

"No," Sadie replied. "My grandfather was a good man. Father told me so."

"Your father?" the soldier replied. "You know nothing of your father. But our concern is not with him tonight."

"The Foretelling speaks of a child whose memory cannot be unlocked," said the William Madison in camouflage dress. He moved to the side of the bed, inches from Sadie's face. "It tells of the disaster such a mind will have on the universe, on reality, on our work to keep the future free for remembrance."

Sadie gripped the bedclothes.

"Only once before has there been a mind like yours."

Her shoulders dropped. Her mouth hung open. "There was another like me? Someone else who couldn't forget?"

"But he was not the child of the Foretelling. He disappeared—"

"He—?"

"Into nothingness," the ringmaster finished.

"Because of his mind?" Sadie asked.

"Because he wanted to," her grandfather finished. "Because he could."

"Where? Who is this other? Who is he?" Gold and amber light twisted around the room once more. "What is happening?"

"You are waking, Sadie Madison," they said together. "We cannot stay."

The Narrowers returned to silhouettes.

A voice lingered in the air.

"When you leave childhood behind, open yourself to us, Sadie Madison. For it is the only way."

Sadie opened one eye and scanned the room.

Oliver stood at the end of the bed, watching.

She felt exhausted but rose slowly and walked to the radiator where she placed her hands on the copper piping. Heat soaked into her skin.

Oliver attempted a half-smile, but his expression gave him away.

"Where were you last night?" Sadie said, yanking her cardigan on and heading for the stairs.

"Me?" Oliver replied, trotting after. "Where were *you*?"

"I was here. Sleeping. Dreaming. I needed you ... but you weren't there."

"No," Oliver said, shaking his head defiantly. "You were gone. Out into the world. I tried to find you, but you were lost to me. All I could see was black and then—"

They reached the bottom of the stairs. Sounds of brewing coffee percolated from the kitchen. Sadie turned. Dark rings circled her eyes, her brow creased into angry lines. "What's got into you? You're acting ... odd, different."

Oliver stared awkwardly. "I am ... it is just ... I am—"

"Seriously," she said, losing patience. "What the devil—?"

"The Narrowers," he blurted. The words erupted like an involuntary sneeze.

"What?" Sadie said, blind-sided. "You saw them?"

"Me? No. But ... *you* saw them?" he replied. "In a dream."

Sadie froze.

"There were three of them. A man and two women. Beautiful, radiant, golden."

Sadie pulled Oliver into the library. "You can see my dreams?" she said, dropping onto the sofa.

"I do not think so," Oliver said, adjusting his scarf. "I do not know. Maybe."

"Well, that's as clear as mud."

"I mean, I saw a glimpse, a fragment. It has never happened before."

"But how did you—?"

"Maybe it is not me," he tried, looking away. "Maybe it is you. It is ... *us*. It is not crazy to think we can share thoughts and dreams, considering ..."

Sadie hugged her knees, her shoulders curled inward.

"Tell me about them," Oliver said. "The Narrowers."

Sadie pinched the end of her nose. "I think they're Angels."

"Angels?"

"They were once called Watchers, Grigori. Father's books have taught me that they were divine beings sent to earth to watch over man. Some of them must have been sent here to collect memories. To organise the Gathering."

Oliver scanned the edges of the rug.

"What about you?" Sadie asked, punching his leg. "What happened?"

"You had another one of your nightmares. You ran out of the house, disappearing into the dark. I did not go with you. I needed to stay here, to watch Michael and—"

Sadie coiled her hands inside the sleeves of her cardigan. "And ... who?"

Oliver swallowed hard. "Sofia."

Sadie froze.

"She is here. In the house."

"Why didn't you say?"

"You had gone. Ran away. I had these visions, these flashes. A hospital, an operating room, white tiles, medical instruments. Is that where you went?"

Sadie scanned the memory of her dreams. "No. My dreams were of the Narrowers and nothing more. But, Sofia ... she's here? You can see her?"

"She talks to me," he admitted. "It is ... terrifying. She is feeding on the dark music you play. You have to stop, Sadie. It is too dangerous."

"I need to speak to Father," she said. "He promised to tell me all about the Foretelling. He still hasn't. That promise is long overdue."

"I think he is in the kitchen."

"No. Not like that. I don't believe I'll ever get the truth from him with words." Sadie looked towards the piano. "I need to speak to him in a different way."

★ ☺ ▦ ⚔ ⛪

Eli sat against the arched doorway to the library, partially concealed behind an armchair and the floor-to-ceiling curtains. His eyes peeked over the embroidered fabric like an inquisitive owl. With his notebook positioned on his legs, a pen worked furiously on the textured manuscript.

Across the room, Sadie appeared to be having a full-blown conversation with, as far as Eli could tell, no one at all.

He filled one page, flipped it, continued on the reverse.

He'd covered almost three sheets when he stopped, shut the notebook, and slipped his pen into the top pocket of his waistcoat. Eli stole a glance over the armchair. Sadie was still talking animatedly with nothing at all.

Carefully, he pulled his Monster Magnifiers over his eyes and took one more peek.

Eli froze.

His breath caught in his throat.

His bones rattled.

Adjusting the levers and dials as quickly and silently as he knew how, Eli focused them on a peculiar-looking boy. He looked about Sadie's age, his hair a mix of black and silver, his fingers long, grey, and bony, his clothes a swathe of foreboding blacks topped by a blood-red scarf.

Eli yanked the Monster Magnifiers off.

His heart raced.

He tore through his notebook, searching for an empty page. With pen in hand, he began to write about this encounter with an honest-to-goodness monster. A monster, it seemed, who was friends with his sister.

Using the curtains for cover, Eli crept out of his hiding place, snuck through the hallway, the living room, and finally barrelled into the kitchen.

He waved the Monster Magnifiers in the air.

Michael turned to his son, a lopsided grin on his face.

Are you alright? he signed, putting down the teapot. You look like you've seen a ghost.

Eli's mouth dropped open, panting, searching for a word, a sound. He waved the Monster Magnifiers in front of Michael, then slid them across the table.

A monster! he signed hurriedly. In the library.

Michael nodded, mock-seriously, and scratched his chin. "Now, let me see," he said. "What sort of monster? Was it Goofang, swimming backwards to keep the water from his eyes and jumping playfully over the iron bridge? Or perhaps the Axe-Handle Hound, come to steal our tools? Or was it a skin-walking, demonic, cannibalistic half-beast Wendigo, hell-bent on tearing the flesh from our bones and feasting on our—?"

"Michael!" Larissa hissed, dragging the cup towards her. "That's quite enough."

Eli shook his head.

A boy, he signed. A boy. With a red scarf.

"A boy?"

"Where?"

In the library. With Sadie.

Michael snatched the Monster Magnifiers from the table and, snapping them onto his head, lurched towards the library. Eli hurried beside him, racing around the enormous Lorntide tree at the foot of the stairs.

They arrived beneath the library arch as Sadie's fingers gently pressed on the piano. Tendrils of beautiful music bloomed. Eli watched as his father slowed—one step at a time—until he came to a dead halt. He seemed to change, turning pale and sad as the music took hold of him.

Gently, Michael dropped the Monster Magnifiers onto an armchair.

Eli scooped them up and, tugging his father's trousers, implored him to wear them, to look through their special lenses, to see the monster at Sadie's side. But it was too late, the music had taken Michael Madison, and there was nothing Eli could do.

✷ � ▤ ✺ ▥

Sadie's music crowded Michael's head with its mastery and dominance. He'd become a slave to it, a puppet to the whims and desires of the words she weaved into her melodies.

Larissa joined them in the library, unable to defy the lure of the music. She sat on the sofa. Both hands cradled her tea.

Natalia crept into the room and sidled up to her mother. Her face a contorted mix of anger and bliss. In her hands were piles of broken lipsticks, shattered and spent. As the music seeped into her heart, her fingers relaxed, spilling the colourful vanities onto the floor.

With his Monster Magnifiers on top of his head, Eli wandered behind them, and slipped, unnoticed, into Michael's study.

The Madison family sat in captivated silence as Sadie played. But Michael experienced something else. Something more than the dark spell, more than the choking pressure that slowed his thoughts, making them stagnant, lethargic.

Through the darkness, he heard a clear voice whispering to him, echoing through his mind. *Sofia*, the voice sang, twisting between the notes. *What happened to Sofia?*

Information Michael had spent his life confining to the shadows was being dragged into the light. William Madison appeared in his mind's eye. A warning etched on his face. But the music chased William away, overpowering any ambition Michael had to fight, any chance he had to keep these secrets safe.

And then, he *wanted* to tell her.

He wanted to share all his secrets.

There was *nothing* he wanted more.

☀︎☻▥⚒♨

Sadie tumbled. Pulled violently through sheets of heavy black cloth. Submerged in dark, choking waters. Her vision blurred with images, flashing lights. Chaotic sounds flooded her ears. Every sense distorted, burning, out of control.

Then, like flicking the power switch on the wireless, everything stopped.

Above, a hundred birds of prey, flying in a gigantic column, passed a shimmering blood moon in glorious silhouette. The piercing howl of Fire Wolves drifted on the wind.

Sadie watched, disconnected, as a young Michael Madison knelt in the middle of the road. Lamplight bled through the high glass doors outside the Hospital of Santa Viktoria. Drenched with rain and tears, he screamed into the night, fists punching raindrops. He tried to scream again but his voice vanished. Michael fell forward, his palms smashing into puddles on the cobbled road. His head swung forward, defeated, broken.

"You have done what needed to be done," said a voice.

Michael looked up.

Three Narrowers stood before him, their bodies constructed of nothing more than swirling shadows. "You've done the one thing you were born to do."

"What I was born to do?" he said. "Kill my firstborn? Is that my legacy? I was born, so she might die? What kind of sick game is this? What kind of …?"

One glided forward. "You will never make sense of it, Michael. What human can? Why waste your nights ruminating on what took place here? You will only waste those hours with turmoil and torture."

"It's my time to waste," he said angrily. "I'll do as I please."

The Narrowers were silent. A fork of lightning struck the Carcassus Mountains, outlining the three ephemeral shapes with white, piercing light.

Michael's eyes thinned. "You've come for her … haven't you?"

"The twin," the Narrower closest replied. "Naturally."

Michael shook his head. "No. Never."

"You have no choice, Michael. The Foretelling cannot be denied. We will not allow it."

"*The child that wields untold power and dominion will be the firstborn, of the firstborn, fallen from the highest,*" Michael spat. "You know those words. You've read them—spoken them countless times—but they're only words to you, aren't they?" He struggled to his feet. "Those words are *everything* to me. They're who I am, they're who I *have* to be. Those words haunt me, follow me wherever I go, live inside me, reminding me every day of who and what I am."

"This changes nothing," the Narrower said. "Bring us the twin."

"She is not my *first*born. You have Sofia, you cannot take Sadie."

Rain passed through the Narrowers.

Michael raised his hands to the sky. "You're Watchers. You're Grigori! You're the Guardians of the Living, Protectors of the Light, Bringers of Day, and Castilians of Wonder," he said, the words filled with derision. "How can you murder an innocent?"

The Narrowers remained still, silent.

"I gave Sofia to *that* woman. It tore my soul in two. Broke my heart a thousand times over. Irreparably changed me. There was no argument, no struggle. But Sadie—she was the *second*—I'll never relinquish her to you!"

"Their souls are entwined, as every twin that has ever lived can attest. They are one and the same. She *must* die."

"But she is not the first," he spat once more. "That is all the Foretelling states. It fails to mention anything to do with a second, with twins. You live by the rules, by the exacting words of the prophecy! How can you bend those rules now? How can you—?"

"Enough."

Michael stared, incredulous. Rain-soaked hair plastered his face.

The Narrowers paused, as though consulting one another. Finally, the first spoke again. "On her thirteenth birthday we shall return. When the clock strikes midnight on the first day of January nineteen hundred, when Sadie Madison is a child no more, her future will be set. We will read her then and all will be revealed."

"Thirteen years?" Michael said, flat and cold.

"When the time comes, and it is proven she is to follow her sister down the darkest of paths, you will relinquish her to us. No argument. No struggle."

Michael sank back on his heals. Exhaustion and a peculiar sense of relief burned against his skin. His eyes found the blood moon hanging low over the Carcassus Mountains. The passage from the Foretelling shivered through him.

"This is real," he said quietly, as if he'd been entirely unsure of everything up until this point. "The Foretelling, my father, the Narrowing Vent ... *everything*. I wondered sometimes if it was all just a wild bedtime tale, a story to keep me entertained, something to distract my mind from the sadness in my heart. But this is a sadness beyond all measure."

Michael looked down from the blood moon and the swarm of Redkites flying over the mountains. A circle of shadows materialised around him. Hundreds of Narrowers stood shoulder to shoulder, ten or more deep.

"This is real, Michael," they told him. "This is all."

"Thirteen years?" he whispered.

Every shadow nodded in unison. "Do you agree?"

The biting rain failed to register anymore.

Michael's head stooped low. "What choice do I have?"

THE DOOR OF A
THOUSAND VOICES

While Sadie's music played in the adjoining room—and Michael let his secrets slip—Eli sat beneath his father's desk, folding sheets of paper and slipping them into an envelope. Sealing the reverse tight, he marked the envelope with a large black *D*.

Eli crawled into the alcove at the back of Michael's study, squeezing between stacks of boxes and dusty books. He stopped in front of a heavy wooden door embellished with hundreds of strange, carved faces.

The door leant against the wall. It had been there as long as he could remember. Eli found the faces a little troubling. He'd never looked at them through his Monster Magnifiers for fear they would spring to life and consume him.

For now, they remained wooden and shiny and horrible.

Slowly, he reached out and touched one. A ghoulish goblin with pointy ears, a slack jaw and thin, menacing eyes. He pushed the face until it clicked. For a moment, nothing happened. Then, a faint light radiated beneath the door accompanied by a gentle hum. Steadily the light grew, illuminating the carpet.

Eli dropped the envelope and flicked it forward. The letter sat there for a moment, bathing in light at the foot of the door, before it vanished with sudden haste, as if someone—or something—had swiped it from the other side. The goblin's face crept forward and clicked back into place.

The light stuttered, went out.

Sadie's music found Eli's ears.

Through the crack in the door, he could see his sister. She had her back to him, her arms sweeping across the keyboard.

The music tickled and tempted but didn't take Eli over. It felt strange to him, unearthly. An inner voice, a conscience, but not his own.

Something skidded along the floor behind him.

He turned, and there, at the foot of the door, sat a yellow envelope. A large letter *E* had been written on the front in wet, red ink. Eli grasped it eagerly but before he had time to open it, the study door swung wide allowing light from the library to flood in.

The music had stopped.

Michael appeared, silhouetted in the doorframe. He looked gaunt and thin, like a jongelier made of pipe cleaners. Pouring himself a glass of ziela, Michael sat at his desk. His gaze fell on the window and the world beyond.

Eli peered through the velvet curtain. He couldn't stay hidden in his father's alcove all day, so he inched forward and crawled across the hardwood floor. He'd got no further than the edge of Michael's desk when he froze. Where was the letter? Eli pulled the notebook from under his arm. A handful of other yellow envelopes protruded from the edge, but not the new one.

The latest one.

The one he had yet to open.

Slowly, he turned and crawled back.

The curtain closed behind him, causing a gentle breeze to sweep through the room. Michael must have sensed it for he swivelled in his chair.

"What are you doing back there?" he asked, throwing the curtain back.

Eli shrugged, clutching his notebook to his chest.

Michael scanned the alcove quickly. The stacks of boxes, books, the carved wooden door, and an assortment of other strange, dusty paraphernalia.

"Michael? What are you doing in the ... Oh, hello, Eli."
Larissa peered around her husband and smiled at Eli, her eyes
faint and distant, marbled with veins of grey smoke. "You
shouldn't be in here," she told Eli. "Go and play upstairs. Your
father and I have a lot to organise before tonight's New Year's
celebrations."

Eli scuttled out of the alcove. He passed beneath Michael's
outstretched arm with his precious notebook and the new letter
clutched to his chest.

✳ ☻ 🎞 ✻ 🏛

Larissa spun on her heel, heading for the kitchen. When her
footsteps had faded, Michael rummaged through his desk
drawers. He produced a long brass cylinder and, after pressing
several buttons on one end and twisting the other, a beam of
light emanated from the device.

He clambered into the alcove and pulled the curtain across
behind him. Examining the carved wooden door, he caressed
the smooth wood and sharp features of each terrifying face,
making his way from top to bottom. He stopped at the foot of
the door. His gaze fixed on the wicked goblin.

Michael shone the light onto several faces surrounding the
goblin.

They were all smooth and clean.

Untouched.

He poured the strange light onto the goblin's face and there,
clear as day, was a collection of smudged fingerprints.

✳ ☻ 🎞 ✻ 🏛

Eli had made his way onto the landing. He watched Sadie pull
on her amaranthine jacket and latch her boots. She tugged a
dark, woollen hat over her thick hair and stuffed a pair of leather
gloves into one of the zippered pockets.

Larissa drifted by, humming gently to herself.

"I'm going out," Sadie announced, "with Oliver."

Larissa faltered for a moment then waved nonchalantly over her shoulder.

Sadie flicked the latch and swung the door open. A wave of frosty air streamed into the Madison house. She hurried outside and pulled the heavy door behind her. A handful of snowflakes floated into the hallway, landing gently in the sprawling branches of the Lorntide tree.

Eli watched the snowflakes from his position on the landing, his legs dangling between the bannisters like sun-drying calamari. Fable hunkered on the large windowsill, dividing her attention between the silent boy's furious scribbling and the sight of Sadie disappearing into the white landscape beyond.

As Eli wrote, Natalia joined her mother in the kitchen and, in no time, the heavenly smell of cake drifted through the house in waves of cinnamon, lemon, raisin, coconut, pecan, toffee, chocolate, coffee, cherry, and carrot. The aroma attracted Michael from the study, followed closely by Atticus.

With the coast clear, Eli retrieved the yellow envelope.

He held it up to the light from the window. Through the thin parchment, Eli could see a small piece of paper, folded into a perfect square. He took a second glance into the hallway, checking Fable was looking the other way, then ripped it open. The folded paper bloomed in Eli's hands. He flattened the letter on the hardwood. In red ink and flowery handwritten script, it simply read: *Tomorrow.*

☀ ☽ ▦ ⚰ ♒

Sadie's pace was remarkable. Her feet drove into the snow, propelling her along Leviathan Crook like a Frost Hare. Snow fell in heavy torrents. Oliver half-walked, half-skipped beside her, his scarf pulled tight around his chin, hands buried in his pockets.

Where people had once smiled and waved—calling to Sadie with words of love and adoration—they now hid their eyes and crossed the street to avoid her.

But Sadie looked through them.

Her head wasn't on Leviathan Crook.

It wasn't even in Iron Bridge.

Behind her eyes hung darkness. Not the pinky-red darkness from staring at the back of your eyelids, but a hollow darkness. A true absence of colour.

She stopped suddenly.

Oliver stumbled forward before spinning round. "Sadie?"

"Did you see what happened?"

Oliver looked around. "When?"

Sadie immediately knew he hadn't.

She began walking again.

"Thirteen years ago."

Oliver had already fallen behind. He leapt through the snow to catch up. "You spoke to him with the music?" His dark-ringed eyes were filled with wonder and concern.

"I tried to but something else happened," Sadie told him. "I saw a memory. Father's memory. It wasn't an image or a feeling or a collection of words, but a real-life memory. I was there with him, in the rain outside the hospital, on the night I was born."

Oliver's mouth hung open.

"The Narrowers gave him thirteen years."

"For what?"

"On my thirteenth birthday—when I'm no longer a child—they'll come for me."

"Why?"

"Some sort of test. To see if I'm naughty or nice—" She half laughed and then shook her head wildly. "To see if I'm this child they speak of."

They walked in silence over the iron bridge.

"Are we safe?"

"Here?" she replied. "I don't know."

"The Narrowers could be anywhere, Sadie. We are not safe in the open."

Sadie shrugged. "And I'm not quite thirteen yet, so—"

People gathered around the Steam Totem, warming themselves on the hot air rising from iron grates, eating roasted nuts and dark chocolate. Beyond them, colourful Lorntide lanterns zigzagged along the highstreet, turning the tumbling snow into glittering multicoloured flakes. Between the lanterns, a banner rippled in the wind, the words *Iron Bridge Welcomes 1900* printed in bold black serif.

Stopping to warm her toes, Sadie attempted a half-hearted smile at the men and women beside her. The smell from the nuts and chocolate danced around her, mixing with the crisp snow. Her stomach rumbled. She'd totally missed breakfast.

"Where are you going?" Oliver called as Sadie stormed off.

"You said you saw a hospital," she called over her shoulder.

"I did?" he replied, then made the connection. "I mean, I *did*. Yes, the flashes."

"So, we're going to the hospital."

"Is it … far?"

"You tell me," she replied. "Last time I remember being there was the night I was born."

✹☽▦✵⛭

The New Year's celebrations were a much-anticipated event in the Madison house. Despite the confusion Sadie's music brought, Michael watched as Larissa and Natalia loaded the kitchen table with an infantry of cupcakes decorated to differing levels of precision: Larissa's impeccable, Natalia's in need of finessing. But it didn't matter. Nothing mattered. A new year approached. A time to make changes, for better or worse. But this year was more special than usual. Tomorrow was the first of January 1900, a new century, the dawn of a new era—

—and Sadie's thirteenth birthday.

This little fact had not been forgotten.

Larissa had prepared an enormous pancake birthday cake. The pancakes were layered—one on top of the other—with dark, milk, and white melted chocolate smothered between alternating layers. On the top, the cake was covered with whipped cream, strawberries, and fudge sauce. The pancake cake teetered precariously on a silver stand. Natalia asked her mother if it would still be standing come midnight.

Michael retreated to his study, poured a large glass of ziela and settled into his chair.

Morning light faded. His clocks ticked in a hypnotic rhythm. His heart ached, wondering what the next twenty-four hours would bring. The music still clung to his skin. He could feel it moving, caressing him, dulling his senses. His mind became a blur. Memories came and went, soaring by like runaway steam trains.

Something nagged at him, something angry. In the blinding of her music, he'd let slip a trove of truths. And now, in the wake of the music, he'd let his daughter vanish from the house, out into the snow, out into danger.

Where is she?

Michael pushed out of the chair and stood by the window.

Out there somewhere.

He took a sip of ziela.

She'll be back. She'll be back for the Candlelight Parade, and the party, and her birthday cake.

The outlawed spirit burned in his chest.

She never misses it. Never.

Arnold Tomes passed the Madison house with his dog Bailey—a playful, brindle bull-terrier—and, noticing Michael at the window, gave a meaningful nod.

Michael raised his glass.

Atticus padded into the study. He stuck his front legs on the sill and peered out. Michael ruffled the wolfhound's floppy hair with his empty hand. The dog snuffled in return, searching for a treat. "I've got nothing for you, old boy," Michael said, turning his pocket out. "Look, fluff and stitching, nothing more."

The dog seemed perturbed.

"Maybe he'd like one of these," said a voice behind him.

Framed in the study doorway, holding a perfectly decorated lemon cupcake, stood Larissa. Vanilla buttercream swirled on top, sprinkled with raspberries and milk chocolate shavings.

Michael tried to rearrange his gloomy expression into one of delight. He took the cake from his wife and sank his teeth into the soft sponge.

"What do you think?"

"Wondrous," he tried. "The best yet."

"Thank you, dear," she said, slinking out of his study and back to the kitchen.

Michael chewed the cake and, finally, swallowed. In truth, he could barely taste it. He was too worried, too anxious.

Even if he could shake the binds of the music, he knew, deep inside, how utterly helpless he'd become. Fate charged towards him like a herd of stampeding elephants. He could let it flatten him or he could stand aside and deal with the aftermath.

He had to take his mind off it.

He had to distract himself.

Michael drained his glass and went in search of a big box of decorations.

✷ ☻ ▤ ⚔ ♨

Iron Bridge's Santa Viktoria Hospital stood amidst the noise and chemical stink of the industrial district. On either side of the large off-white building were warehouses, factories, and power stations constructed of grey brick and copper piping. Steam billowed from chimneys and vents.

Sadie and Oliver stopped at the foot of the hospital steps.

A large wooden sign with iron lettering, surrounded by winter flowers, emerged from the ground. Sadie ran her fingers over the cold metal letters, trying to remember the journey she might have taken.

"Are you sure it was here, Oliver?"

"No," he answered honestly. "I never said it was *this* hospital. Just *a* hospital. A treatment room. Somewhere."

Sadie sighed. Snow scattered off her shoulders and down her back. She looked back towards Iron Bridge. "This is where it happened," she said. "This is where he made the deal with the Narrowers."

But she didn't linger.

Turning sharply, Sadie marched up the steps to the hospital.

The wind lashed her coat against her legs.

Once inside, the heavy glass and oak door swung shut neatly behind them. Sadie smelt coffee, wine, and cake. She'd expected disinfectant, lavender, infection.

The entire hallway was empty. Corridors ran in opposite directions.

"Where is everyone?"

Sadie shrugged, crossed the hallway, and rapped lightly on the reception window.

Silence.

She knocked again.

A distorted shape flashed past the frosted pane. Sadie and Oliver exchanged glances. Suddenly, the glass flew to one side and a woman's face launched out to meet them. She seemed young, yet her eyes looked as though they had seen more winters than most.

"Hello?" she said, then recoiled. "Oh my ... well ... if it isn't"—her voice suddenly louder—"Sadie Madison!"

The window slid shut again.

Voices muttered among themselves.

The glass panel opened.

"Sadie," the woman said, smiling awkwardly.

"You know me?"

"The music," the woman enthused. "And what music. Such

mastery!"

"Thank you," she muttered, staring at the old eyes in the young woman's face.

She wore a nurse's uniform. A pleated dress in blue and white, smothered by a clean apron, and a small pocket watch pinned to her breast.

"Nurse Francis," said the woman, extending a long thin arm. Dark veins pulsed beneath her pale skin. "Dorothea, to you."

Sadie took her hand.

Nurse Francis shook it wildly, her skin cold and clammy.

"Crikey me!" she exclaimed. "You're almost frozen through. Fingers like icicles. Come into the back and have a cup of coffee. Me and the girls are having an early New Year's party."

Dorothea pushed a hidden section of the desk open. Sadie slipped through and headed down a narrow hallway into a cosy staff room stuffed with embroidered chairs and sofas, framed paintings of serious doktors, a long table covered with books and pamphlets and binders bulging with paperwork, pots of tea and coffee, plates of cake and biscuits, and several bottles of plum wine.

Sadie's stomach grumbled at the sight of food.

"Coffee? Tea? Cake?" Dorothea chimed. "Drop of wine?"

"Yes," she answered promptly. "Anything hot."

Dorothea poured some tea, a small thimble of wine, and loaded a plate with slices of moist courgette cake and a fan of butter biscuits.

Sadie plonked herself into one of the patchwork armchairs, pulled her legs up to her chin and balanced the plate on her knees. She sipped the hot, spiced tea, and took a large bite of cake. She felt better immediately, sank back in the armchair, closed her eyes, and murmured with delight.

Oliver watched the faces of twenty or more nurses and hospital staff positioned around the room in a strange, motionless silence. People acting odd around Sadie wasn't entirely new, but the staff were almost without behaviour at all, like Larissa's headless Lorntide mannequins.

"Have you come to play for the inpatients?" Dorothea asked, popping a square of chocolate cake into her mouth.

Sadie flicked her eyes open, her mouth stuffed with biscuit. "Inpatients?"

"The patients that live here," Dorothea explained. "The ones that can't leave."

"What?" Sadie blurted, amazed, swallowing her mouthful. "You keep them here. Like ... like a prison?"

"Goodness, no!" Dorothea giggled. "You're a serious one, aren't you? This isn't a prison. Every patient is free to come and go as they please, but some people are far too sick to go home. We keep them, or rather, they choose to stay until they're better." She leant forward, whispering conspiratorially. "Or they die. Whichever comes first!"

Sadie gasped.

"I'm playing with you, young lady," Dorothea added half-seriously.

"And you want me to play for them?"

Dorothea smiled. "Well, yes. Of course, dear. Isn't that why you came?" She shot a look around the room. "We'd love to hear you play, wouldn't we?" Every face beamed at Sadie, eyes pinned wide, murmurs of agreement erupted at her command. "They enjoyed it ever so much last night."

Sadie stopped.

A handful of cake hovered in front of her mouth.

"Yes." Dorothea smiled. "You do remember, don't you, dearie?"

Sadie stared.

"I'm shocked ... I mean surprised ... to see you back so soon." Dorothea turned to the lifeless staff lining the room. "Well, we all are, aren't we?" she urged.

A curious ruffle of voices erupted, straining in agreement.

She turned back to Sadie and smiled.

"More tea, dear?"

THE
HORNED GOD

Sadie had no memory of the previous night.

She'd been asleep.

Dreaming of the Narrowers.

Not a visit to the Hospital of Santa Viktoria.

Had she sleepwalked here and back again? That was impossible, surely. She looked at the faraway expressions on the faces of the statuesque doktors and medical staff.

Is that how she'd looked last night?

"And you're back ... so soon," Dorothea went on. "That is surprising." She took a sip of wine. "Did you bring the Fire Wolves with you?"

"The ... Fire Wolves?"

Had they come to guide her during her dreams?

"No," she replied. "Not tonight. I have Oliver instead."

Her pale friend worried at his scarf.

Sadie placed a hand on his.

"All this attention," she told the nurse, "feels a little ... strange."

"Well," Dorothea said. "You're a little strange, aren't you?"

Sadie frowned.

"Not scarily so, my dear. Not like the terrifying creatures living beyond the forest wall, or in the depths of the River Myr, or Hershel Winter-Smith himself!"

Sadie's eyes widened. "You know of Hershel Winter-Smith?"

"Of course," Dorothea replied, taking another sip of wine. "Went stark-raving bonkers, didn't he? Slaughtered his entire family."

"Except his little sister."

"That's right. It's a good story. We're always using Hershel's name around here—what with it being a hospital and all—to keep some of the more cantankerous inpatients in line."

"It's not a story. Hershel Winter-Smith was a real person."

"Real?" Dorothea laughed, quickly swallowing a mouthful of wine and gasping for air. "Come now, Sadie Madison. I wasn't born yesterday. Hershel Winter-Smith? Hurtmore House? Load of old nonsense. Just a scary bedtime story for naughty children and cranky inpatients."

"No," Sadie replied hastily. "It's true. I know it. I read it."

"You read it?" scoffed Dorothea, throwing her head back.

"Yes."

"Where?"

Sadie thought of the cryptic black book that hid beneath the floorboards in the eaved bedroom. "A book," she said, then lied. "One of my father's."

The nurse eyeballed her curiously. "Well, if it's written, so it shall come to pass." She waved her hand at two nurses sitting across from them. "Genevieve. Edith. Sisters, listen to this. Sadie says Hershel Winter-Smith is real—"

"*Was* real," Sadie corrected.

"What?" crooned both the nurses, swivelling to face them.

Genevieve had flowing golden hair and shining cerulean eyes, youthful and vibrant. Despite their similar age, Edith looked quite different. She had short grey hair, brushed forward in a shallow fringe. Her eyes weary, glassy like marbles.

"She *read* it," Dorothea whispered, as though telling a campfire tale.

"Seems reasonable to me," Genevieve said. "So it is written, so it shall come to pass." Her hands moved theatrically as she spoke, eyes shining.

"Something written is something real," Edith added.

Sadie rested her plate on the arm of her chair and crossed her legs. Oliver shuffled nervously, watching the faces of the three women. Genevieve and Edith, like Dorothea, had the same dark veins running beneath their skin.

"We're just playing," Dorothea assured her as the three women laughed. She put a hand on Sadie's shoulder and smiled. "But you believe it, my dear. You believe whatever you want to—whatever you need to—whatever your heart desires."

Genevieve and Edith gave her toothy smiles.

A whitewashed wall and a broken fence respectively.

Huddling together, the three women began chatting. Sadie tried to listen but only gathered snippets of their conversation as a dull ache developed behind her eyes.

"Is there a bathroom I can use?"

"Of course, dear," Dorothea replied. "Back out into the hallway, turn left. You'll see it on your right."

The nurse dragged a slice of carrot cake from the table and returned to the huddle.

Sadie stood and crossed the room.

Three sets of eyes watched her leave.

She sidled through the opening in the reception desk and out into the hallway beneath the vaulted ceiling. To the left ran a long corridor. White walls, pale blue linoleum, endless doors on both sides.

Oliver appeared beside her as she walked. "Are you okay?"

"Headache."

"Again?" he said. "I had hoped those had passed."

"It's nothing to do with the Nepenthe, or the dreams, or anything," she assured him irritably. "I'm tired, that's all."

"Who are these nurses? They are behaving highly suspiciously."

"They seem … fine."

"They said you brought Fire Wolves with you last night."

"I was sleepwalking. I think. My dreams were so vivid.

So real. But they weren't of here. Not of this place. Nor of Fire Wolves."

Oliver nibbled his scarf. "Are you sure you are okay?"

"Yes!" she snapped, coming to an abrupt halt on the squeaky floor. "I'm fine, Oliver. Perfectly fine. Please stop fussing. I just—"

But her eyes rolled back.

Legs buckled.

Her body clattered to the ground.

"Sadie," Oliver cried, trying to break her fall but utterly failing. "Sadie? Sadie! Help! Somebody please help!"

But her body had gone as limp as a dead fish.

Oliver screamed helplessly, silently.

He scanned the corridor.

The three nurses now stood in the hallway, cloistered together, watching. Behind them, the low winter sun cast long shadows towards him like twisted, clawing fingers.

✹ ◡ ▤ ⚿ ⛩

Out of the darkness, the world emerged.

Sadie hurtled towards it at an incredible rate, plummeting through clouds and mist. She gasped for breath, arms wide. The ground spiralling below. Diamonds filled the horizon millions of miles away. Distant worlds, planets, possibilities.

She fell past the snow-capped tips of the Carcassus Mountains. The River Myr wound its way towards the Southern Seas like a thirsty anaconda. Iron Bridge came into focus. It looked empty, deserted. Every window dark. Every gaslamp extinguished. It didn't feel like the Iron Bridge Sadie knew.

This was some other place.

A copy.

A replica.

Her clothes rippled and flapped as she swooped over the labyrinth of roads and alleyways branching off the highstreet. With the industrial district passing beneath, her body slowed, tilted, until she landed softly outside the Hospital of Santa Viktoria.

The glass doors swung open and, straightening her clothes, Sadie entered.

❋☽▦☌♔

The nurses looked down at Sadie's body. Oliver hurried about, trying to see what was happening, but every time he found a gap to peek through, they blocked his path.

"Goodness me! She looks awfully pale," Dorothea muttered. "We should get her to a recovery room."

Genevieve disappeared through one of the many doors and emerged with a dilapidated gurney. Edith led the procession, shuffling along slowly, a cup of wine in one hand, cake in the other. Genevieve and Dorothea pushed the gurney with Sadie on top.

Oliver followed. His scarf covered half his face.

"What the devil has happened to her?" Dorothea asked.

"Looks like a mix of the cold and exhaustion," Genevieve added.

Dorothea's eyebrows dug into her forehead. "You're awfully quiet, Edith. Tell me this wasn't your doing?"

Edith made a disparaging noise. "Me? Huh! The very implication!"

Dorothea and Genevieve exchanged glances. The gurney rolled over pale blue linoleum. The poorly maintained wheels squeaked like agitated rodents. Edith approached one of the doors and, with her long fingers, punched a number into a brushed copper codex.

The lock clicked.

Edith let Dorothea and Genevieve push Sadie into the small white room beyond. She loitered in the doorway, munching her cake, watching the others work.

Genevieve manoeuvred the gurney against the left-hand

wall, retrieved a wooden table and placed it beside the bed. From a shelf, she fetched a china vase filled with a single yellow flower and an empty glass.

"She'll be fine for a while," Dorothea decided.

Genevieve nodded. "Perhaps we should get one of the doktors to take a look at her. Just to be safe."

"And perhaps we should send a message to her parents, telling them of the events that have transpired here," Edith butted in, sarcastically. "Or hoist a flag on the roof, acknowledging that Sadie Madison is in residence!"

"There's no need to overreact, sister," Dorothea replied.

"She had a little fall. She'll be right as rain in no time," Genevieve added, stroking Sadie's thick black hair.

Oliver tightened.

"As you wish," Edith croaked, concealing a dirty smile. "Come on, we've left the others to their own devices."

Genevieve smiled gently and held her hand over the empty glass on the bedside table. She uttered something incomprehensible and suddenly, to Oliver's surprise, water rose from the bottom, filling the glass.

Edith groaned from the doorway, pointing. "And what, pray tell, is wrong with the tap?"

Dorothea rolled her eyes.

Genevieve shrugged playfully. "A little practice, that's all."

"Come on, sister. Stop lallygagging around!"

"Yes, sister. No, sister. Three bags full, sister," Genevieve giggled.

She leant forward and plucked three strands of hair from Sadie's head.

"Oi!" Oliver bleated. "What are you doing?"

Genevieve wrapped the hair around her index finger and skipped into the corridor. The door swung shut. Their voices echoed, muffled, as they argued all the way back to the party.

Oliver bent down to inspect the glass. Water rippled on the surface. He attempted to prod it with his finger but, to his infinite frustration, had no effect.

He turned to Sadie.

Was she sleeping? Unconscious? He couldn't tell.

Stomping across the room, he tried the handle, but his hands passed right through. He punched the air several times, frustration getting the better of him. Oliver closed his eyes, took a steadying breath, and attempted to jump to the other side of the door.

Nothing happened.

He tried again.

Still nothing.

They were trapped.

🜨 ☋ ▤ 🜨 🏛

Sadie found herself standing in a room of white.

Nausea burbled in her chest.

Her head spun.

She was inside the hospital now. A treatment room. Everything about it felt wrong, the same way Iron Bridge had as she'd descended through the clouds.

In front of her hung a pair of double doors, frosted with glass. Beyond, the world looked white and still. She gazed around the room. Medical instruments, vials and bandages were positioned on metal tables next to a line of beds. Plastic curtains hung from a meandering array of copper piping.

Something flickered beyond the frosted glass.

No sooner had Sadie's gaze snapped to it than it vanished. She approached, and tentatively pushed the doors. On the other side was an identical room. At the far side, another set of frosted glass doors. She walked over, went through, and found herself in yet another identical room.

Sadie walked through room after room, double doors after double doors, picking up speed until she was running at breakneck pace, slamming from one room into the next. As she ran, the rooms slowly began to change. In one, the walls were decorated with paintings from the Madison house. In another, flagstones paved the floor and the copper piping dripped with amber lanterns. Another was filled with musical instruments and their respective cases. The next bustled with shelves of glass bottles, vials, and potions. The following saw each bed occupied by Ryndai, their curved swords raised and gleaming.

"Sad-ie Mad-i-son," a voice hissed.

Sadie barrelled through the doors.

The words formed around her, closed in, pushed against her.

Ahead, a solid wall.

No door in sight.

She skidded, slammed against it shoulder first, and collapsed to the floor.

She looked up.

Struggled to regain her breath.

The hospital vanished.

In its place, a black sky soared above her.

An endless void.

True nothingness.

Silence engulfed Sadie, as though all the sound had been sucked out of the world. The floor beneath flickered and vanished. Every muscle tightened as she expected to drop through the nothingness. But she remained still, floating, divorced from reality.

"Sad-ie Mad-i-son," something hissed again. "I've been waiting for you."

✴ ☽ ▥ ☎ ⛩

A small square of glass—hatched with black wire—pierced the top half of the door. Oliver stood on tiptoes and peered through. His view of the corridor beyond was replaced by two shimmering blue eyes and a mound of knotted blonde hair.

"Rhiannon!" he gasped.

The door handle waggled but didn't open.

Oliver watched as the woman in black slowly closed her eyes. He could hear her fingers moving on the smooth buttons of the codex. Behind the lids, her eyes shifted frantically in their sockets. A moment later, she woke from her trance and punched four numbers into the lock.

The handle dropped.

The door flew open.

"Quick," she said, staring at Oliver. "We don't have much time. They'll know I'm here."

Oliver looked down at himself.

"Yes, Oliver," she said, moving past him and kicking the locking mechanism on the gurney. "More people know about you. Believe in you. You're becoming clearer. I can see an outline, a shimmer. And if I can see it, so can *they*." She heaved the gurney away from the wall and through the open door. "You're more handsome than I imagined ... for a shimmer."

Oliver blushed.

"Come on! We have to go. Now!"

High-pitched shrieks erupted through the hospital corridors, followed by the beat of ferocious wings. The noise ricocheted off the walls, reverberated through the floor, zeroed on Rhiannon and Oliver.

"We have no time," she said, scampering away at breakneck speed. "No time!"

"Where are we going?" Oliver said, catching Rhiannon and the heavy gurney. "Rhiannon?" But she kept running. She launched the gurney left, then right, through a pair of double doors. "You still cannot hear me, can you?"

Haunting shrieks formed around them like ravenous wyldfire. Rhiannon stopped at an intersection. She spun in circles then pulled Sadie off the gurney, hitched her over one shoulder and kicked the trolley away.

Sadie bounced like a rag doll.

Oliver ran beside them.

They took several erratic turns and burst through a set of batwing doors. Rhiannon yanked a maintenance closet open and slipped inside. The door clicked shut as the sound of wings and screams turned to footsteps and agitated chatter.

Oliver stood in the dark with Rhiannon and Sadie's prone body.

The smell of chlorine invaded his nostrils.

＊ ☽ ▥ ☆ 益

Sadie spun in circles. Surrounded by darkness.

The voice hissed at her from every conceivable direction.

"Welcome to the Nyx."

Sadie frowned.

"The ... Nyx?"

"An empyreal dimension. Entirely empty, yet filled with infinite things."

Sadie walked forward. Hands outstretched as if blindfolded. She stood on nothing, surrounded by nothing. But neither fell, nor floated. It was a deeply peculiar sensation, something from a dream, a nightmare.

"Everything that has ever been, or ever will be, begins here."

A man's voice, ancient and knowing. It hissed like a sea of snakes, then boomed like a ship's cannon. Sadie tried to pinpoint the source of the voice, but it was hopeless.

"Everything is nothing to begin with," he continued. "Only when something is thought of, created, desired, can it be seen, understood, made real."

Sadie tried to speak but nothing came out.

"The Nyx is everywhere ... and nowhere at all. The Nyx is impossible for most people to see, for it exists in a world behind them."

Sadie could feel his breath on her skin. She turned but saw nothing.

"Think of it like this. Your eyes are a torchlight that can only be pointed in one direction. You can turn left, right, up, down, widdershins, turnwise, but you can still only see what falls under the beam of the torchlight. Everything else is shadows. Everything else is the Nyx."

Sadie found herself standing in front of the Steam Totem. The moon hung low in the sky, surrounded with stars veiled by passing clouds. The highstreet stretched out before her. Completely deserted. Silent as the grave.

Sadie's nose wrinkled as she looked down the promenade on the west bank. The gaslamps were lit, glowing eerily in the evening mist. Spray rose from the river. Leaves and litter scurried like rats.

"You cannot see what is behind you by simply turning around," he went on. "The Nyx is always behind you, behind your eyes. Seeing into one's own self is ... rare." Something brushed past. Sadie's hair trailed in its wake. "But what if you could see the nothing behind others?"

Sadie's skin prickled, aware of the voice's proximity.

"To see the Nyx of others would require the inverse of a torchlight. A blacklight, if you will. There you'll find the past, secrets, instinct, power passed on through the centuries, through words and action and song and blood. If someone could see into the Nyx behind other people, they'd be able to see everything. Everything that makes them who they are and who, someday, they'll become. Their hopes, their dreams, their secrets, their lies. The Nyx surrounds the Vents—the Living, the Dead, and the Forgotten—a place between the places, the darkness between the stars. A dimension surrounding all others, knitting them together."

Sadie knew what it was like to remember everything that had ever happened to her. To wallow in the glorious memories of childhood, Eosters and Lorntides, ice-cream sundaes, and thrilling adventures. It was the sadness she wished she could live without. The heartbreak, the goodbyes, the betrayals. They were there too, stored forever. The idea of recalling every single memory of another life made her shudder.

"How would you feel about seeing the Nyx of every person that has ever lived?" he went on. "How would you like to see into their Vents?"

Sadie's eyes caught a fleeting shadow as it dashed in and out of her peripheral vision.

"I'm sure there are things you do not understand. Things you would like to know," he teased, revealing himself for a moment before vanishing again. "I'm sure you'd like to understand why Eli doesn't talk, where Natalia came from, why your father really gave you the Nepenthe, what's waiting for you at Hurtmore House, and—the most tempting secret of all—what truly happened on the night you were born."

Sadie circled the Steam Totem, searching for the illusive shadow.

"You could see through the eyes of others," the voice hissed triumphantly. "Through the memories of those around you. You have the mind that cannot be breached, Sadie Madison. The power is yours, and yours alone. You … are the blacklight."

Sadie ran a hand along the base of the Steam Totem. The five faces stared down at her. Steam curled playfully from their mouths and nostrils.

"You are the child of the Foretelling, Sadie Madison."

The shadow of a horned creature with mighty wings materialised beside her.

Sadie shuddered with fear.

"Seeing into the Nyx may not be something you would relish," the horned shadow said. He swept forward. His abhorrent face hovering above her, twisted and corrupt. "But there are those who would pay a heavy price for a glimpse of the past," he whispered, "and kill to save the future."

THE PENNY
WHISTLE

The three women paced outside the door. Oliver hardly dared breathe. He prayed Sadie would remain dormant long enough for the danger to pass.

"She was there," shrieked Edith. Her voice rang clear and crisp outside the maintenance closet. "Right there. In my head. The dirty little rat was poking around in my thoughts."

"Sadie Madison—?" Dorothea and Genevieve said together.

"Gah!" Edith croaked her disapproval. "The girl? Hell's teeth! Are you joking?"

Dorothea and Genevieve fell silent.

"She has no power," Edith went on. "Sadie Madison ... *the firstborn, of the firstborn, fallen from the highest?* Pah! A whiny careless child, obsessed with bedtime stories and adventure. Always playing the hero rather than truly being one. I see no greatness in her."

"Then who, sister? Who was in your thoughts?"

"*Her*," Edith seethed. The word slipped from her lips like a curse. "The Living."

"If the Living has come to her aid, Sadie Madison *must* be the child of the Foretelling," Genevieve said.

"Falsehood!" Edith snarled. "I touched her myself. Do you think these hands would lie to me?"

"No, sister," Dorothea replied. "But my hands have touched her too and they told me a different story. They showed me a

318

strong child, with willingness, guile, potential. She *is* one of the Candidates. I have no doubt. After that, things were unclear."

Edith coughed wretchedly. "And you, sister? Do tell. What did you see?"

Genevieve quietened. "I saw it all. Everything she will become. I saw her standing over the world—before a dying red sky—glaring down on every living soul. I saw her fingers stretched out, plunge into man, woman and beast. Destruction and desolation poured from her like blood from a wound. She *is* the one. My doubts on this matter—albeit contrary to yours, my sisters—are unwavering."

"How can this be?" Edith replied. "Her future is so unclear, muddled. Even among us."

"She is yet to turn thirteen, sister," Genevieve added. "There are some hours yet."

"Hours? What will hours change that millennia cannot?"

"We must find her," Dorothea said. "We must read her again."

"We should take her before ..." Genevieve said, her voice thinning to a whisper. "... Him."

"We cannot trouble Him with this," Edith told her sternly. "He is abroad—a masquerade—he must not be disturbed."

"Let us find her. Stow her away until she is of age. Then read her, once and for all."

Edith croaked her approval, adding, "Search every room in this forsaken building until the girl and the Living are found."

"Agreed," Genevieve said. "I'll start here." In the gloom of their hiding place, Oliver could see the door handle turn. A crack of lamplight slashed Rhiannon's face. She turned her eyes away, burying them in shadows.

"No," Edith rumbled. "We need to secure the perimeter. Genevieve, make your way to the southern entrance. Dorothea, the western doors. I shall bind the northern entrance and then make my way to the east. We'll convene there and conduct a sweep."

Three pairs of footsteps became mighty wing beats.

The door to the closet remained open, just a sliver. There was no sign of the three women. No sign of anyone. Not one soul.

"What the hell is going on?" muttered Oliver to himself. "Who are these three women? These sisters? Who is … *Him?*"

"Oliver? Is that you?" Rhiannon said, looking towards the shimmering outline of the boy. "You're whispering. Speak up. I can almost hear you."

"Rhiannon. Oh, Rhiannon. What is happening?" he barked at the top of his voice. "What were those women talking about? How are we going to get out of here? Is Sadie okay? What did they do to her?"

His questions were so faint, like someone muttering from the other side of a mighty ballroom. "Sadie? Yes, I think she's okay. They've drugged her with something." Rhiannon propped the girl up against a bucket. She lifted Sadie's eyelids. Her pupils rolled back in her head, darting out of reach. "Looks like some sort of mobility opiate."

"A Nepenthe?" Oliver tried, almost yelling.

"A what? Nepenthe? No, it's not a Nepenthe—" Rhiannon gleaned from his frail words. "There's only one person who still deals in those."

She pushed the door open and glanced down the corridor. Oliver fidgeted as she surveyed the area. Stepping back into the maintenance closet, Rhiannon scanned the shelves. Flicking several boxes and jars aside, the woman in black grabbed a small vial filled with clear liquid, studied the label, then slipped it into her pocket. She turned and rifled through the boxes on the opposite wall. At the bottom of an archive box lay a copper and glass syringe. Rhiannon held it up to the lamplight. "The Mistresses of the Horned God are not to be trusted," she said, rounding on Oliver. "We have to go. Now. They'll be back. If you see them, any of them, run as fast as you can. They're out there somewhere, binding the doors with their Words of Shadow."

Oliver mouthed *Horned God* and *Words of Shadow*. A chill

crept over his bones. He saw demons and hellfire all around, circling, laughing. Screams echoed in the dark. Pitiful, helpless, haunted screams.

"Oliver!" Rhiannon said sternly, waving a hand at him from down the corridor. "Come on! We're leaving!"

He snapped out of his nightmarish daydream and tore down the pale blue linoleum. Rhiannon set a good pace with Sadie hoisted over her shoulder, but soon began to labour. Oliver, feeling no fatigue, became more and more fraught the slower their progress became.

Rhiannon slowed to a walk.

She shifted Sadie from shoulder to shoulder.

"We have to get to the eastern doors before Edith has time to bind them. It's not far."

Oliver skipped ahead, turning left and right, seeking the external glass doors and the falling snow beyond. "This way," Rhiannon called. "Oliver, please. This way."

She kicked a pair of double doors and emerged into a large square room. A dozen armchairs, a large table, potted plants, and thick woven rugs occupied the space. Most of the armchairs were filled with scared inpatients. One of them let out a woeful cry.

The doors clattered shut.

"There is nothing to fear," Rhiannon assured them. "At least, not from us. Be calm. This will soon be over."

Oliver scurried back and forth as Rhiannon hoisted Sadie into an empty armchair next to a cabinet filled with dog-eared board games.

"What are you doing?" Oliver implored her, as loudly as he could. "They are coming!"

"I know," Rhiannon bit. She fumbled around in the pocket of her dress and pulled out the copper and glass syringe, the small vial filled with clear liquid, and a rosewood penny whistle. She dropped the musical instrument onto Sadie's lap, clutching the syringe in one hand, the vial in the other.

"What is that?"

"Epinephrine."

"What does that do? What are you doing with it? You are not—"

Rhiannon had already removed the silver cap from the vial and submerged the needle. She retracted the plunger, filling two-thirds of the syringe. Kneeling beside Sadie, she unbuttoned her dress to the base of her sternum and pressed the needle against the skin.

Oliver's desperate finger swished helplessly. "What are you doing?" he wailed. "Stabbing her in the chest?"

"Straight into the heart," the woman muttered, dragging the needle across Sadie's flesh. "She should be back with us in moments."

"And then what? They will be upon us with their Words of Shadow. Sadie is no match for them. They will take us all. Rhiannon!"

Screams of terror rippled through the air as all three doors to the room burst open in symmetry.

The three young nurses were no more.

A foreboding figure stood in each doorway, cloaked in black. "The Living," they hissed in unison. Fire and electricity crackled in their upturned hands. Skeins of black vapour encircled them like rampant tornados.

Rhiannon raised the syringe into the air.

✷ ☻ ▤ ⚒ ⛩

Sadie sat up with a start. Sweating, breathing heavily.

Her hands and feet tingled as the eaved bedroom became swirls of gold and amber. The Narrowers stood before her, hooded and cloaked. One of them knelt by her side and pulled back his hood, revealing a beautiful, radiant, flawless face. "Sadie Madison, you have been dreaming."

"A disturbing dream it would appear."

"You are still dreaming."

"A dream within a dream?" Sadie uttered.

"Like a memory within a memory."

"A shadow," Sadie muttered. "With horns and wings."

Everything stopped including the snow beyond the window. "Malmortem."

The word drifted slowly through the air, laced with an ancient fear.

"The Unknown is among us."

✹ ☺ ▥ ⚔ ♨

Sadie lurched forward, gasping for air.

Her chest burned, heart thundered.

Her tongue felt like sandpaper.

Rhiannon stood between her and the three sisters. "The Wretched," she said, discarding the empty syringe. "That's close enough."

Edith laughed cruelly. "I hardly think so. One against three is a fool's errand."

Genevieve snickered darkly.

"That's right ... *Rhiannon*," Dorothea added. "You're clearly outnumbered."

"And outgunned," Genevieve added. She balled her hands together. Bolts of iridescent light crackled menacingly.

"New magic," Rhiannon snorted at Genevieve's display. "Child's play."

Genevieve's fingers bloomed. A ball of white-hot energy shot across the room. Rhiannon raised a hand, deflecting the pulsing mass into a noticeboard crammed with paperwork and pictograms.

In the blast, Rhiannon swivelled. "The penny whistle," she urged, pointing at the small wooden instrument in Sadie's lap. "Play the whistle. Use the music."

"What?" Sadie trembled as her body reverberated from the

blast and the epinephrine swarming through her veins.

Her eyes stung.

Her skin on fire.

"You have to remember," Rhiannon urged her. "Touch it. Remember."

The smoke from the explosion cleared.

Rhiannon spun to face the Wretched.

Genevieve snarled furiously, seeing Rhiannon still on her feet. Her hands flew over her head. Her fingers distorted like upturned roots. A venomous cloud began to form. It spiralled, gathered speed, pulled the chain lamps towards it. The cloud descended, concealing the young witch. Papers, playing cards, and board games flew into the gathering mass.

The inpatients were screaming, crying out to Rhiannon. They waved frantically as their chairs shifted across the floor towards Genevieve.

With a cataclysmic *Boom!* the cloud burst outwards in every direction, orbiting the edge of the room.

They were all trapped in the maelstrom.

Inside the eye of the storm.

The Wretched stood with their hair whipping against their faces like shredded rags. Dorothea raised her hands. Half a dozen inpatients soared into the air, suspended, floating in the chaos, howling like stricken wolves. Their faces became wracked with fear. Their legs kicked wildly, struggling to swim back to earth.

Dorothea watched for a time, her head cocked.

She shrugged.

Clicked her fingers.

Six inpatients disappeared into the spiralling vortex, like folding fruit into cake mixture.

Sadie clutched the penny whistle. She ran her fingers over the holes—six in total—and a carved mouthpiece. She had no idea how to play it. Sure, she could blow into it and cover the holes with her fingers to produce some sort of sound, but she had no knowledge of the instrument's finer intricacies. Turning it over, she noticed that the back had been engraved with twine, leaves, and flowers. Sadie traced the carving with her index finger.

Touch it. Remember.

The noise of the tornado increased. Sadie gripped the sides of the armchair as it tried to leave the floor. Rhiannon put a hand backwards, steading the chair.

"Enough!"

The three women laughed, snorted, sneered.

"Or what?" Edith goaded. "This is but a fraction of our power."

"Relinquish the child and you can save their lives," Dorothea said, nodding at the helpless inpatients caught in the looping storm. Genevieve's fingers tightened and the tornado shifted gear, hurtling chaotically.

"They have nothing to do with this," Rhiannon yelled over the deafening storm. "Leave them be!"

"As you wish."

Rhiannon's face grimaced as the six bodies dropped from the cloud, landing cruelly. They lay still. Twisted at improbable angles. Their screams suddenly silenced.

Sadie shut her eyes.

She could feel the epinephrine tearing through her, prickling her skin, drawing every drop of moisture from her mouth. Shifting the penny whistle into both hands, right at the top, left below, she placed the instrument to her lips.

🜨 ☽ 🎞 🦂 ♒

Silence. The smell of cinnamon and gyrseed.

Sadie found herself sitting cross-legged on a brass bed covered with a butterfly-patterned quilt. Concertina blinds decorated red and gold, low oak tables, and hard-worn chests filled a roomy canvas tent. Decorative fans and swords hung from tent poles overhead.

Looking down, Sadie wore a white silk nightgown

embroidered with dragonflies and jasperflies. In her hands rested the penny whistle.

Everything was strange, wrong. Like she was somewhere off limits. But this wasn't a regular place—like the library, or the museum, or the music room at school—but somewhere deeply personal.

Somewhere forbidden.

Taboo.

She flexed her fingers against the delicate whistle. Something in the movement registered as familiar. The wood and the holes beneath her fingers felt like an old friend.

Comfortable.

Natural.

She took a long breath.

And blew.

☀ �'☀ 🎹 ☀ 🏛

"What did you do?" Rhiannon screamed at the young witch. "They were no threat to you."

Genevieve shrugged, nonplussed. "I have six more," she said, glancing down at the terrified faces of the remaining inpatients.

"No!"

"Relinquish the child and all this will end."

"Never." Rhiannon glanced over her shoulder at Sadie who sat with the penny whistle in her mouth, her eyes closed. "Come on, Sadie," she whispered. "*Remember.*"

Oliver crept behind the chair, his hands playing with his scarf. Remember.

"Enough with the delay," Edith snarled.

Dorothea whipped her hands into the air.

Genevieve laughed.

The remaining inpatients rose.

Rhiannon stood her ground, shielding Sadie from the Wretched.

"Last chance," Edith bleated, as the noise of the storm reached an agonising crescendo.

Genevieve barely waited for Rhiannon's denial before sucking the remaining inpatients into the maelstrom. Edith twisted her hands into a ball, conjuring an orb of seething smoke and gas. It grew in her fingers. Licked and hissed like serpents. She opened her hands, balanced the dark sphere, and curled her lip to reveal two putrid rows of teeth.

From either side, Dorothea and Genevieve threw balls of blue fire at Rhiannon. She deflected the first. The second knocked her off-balance. Edith took her chance and released the smouldering black mass. It hit Rhiannon square in the chest, sending her flying.

Engulfed in smoke, Sadie's eyes opened.

She stood.

The penny whistle rested on her lips.

And then, the most beautiful music began to play.

Screams exploded from the Wretched.

Their arms flailed above their heads as shards of magic fizzed in their hands, stuttering, smoking.

The notes from the penny whistle cut through the chaos. The storm spluttered and stalled. The inpatients clattered to the floor, hurt, alive.

The Wretched clamped their hands over their ears, groaning and shrieking.

Genevieve became black feathers and retreated through the nearest door.

Edith shrieked, casting futile spells, as the music penetrated her mind.

Dorothea stood transfixed. The music had already taken hold.

Finally, defeated, Edith let out a vile rasp. The old crone grabbed Dorothea by the arm, croaked her Words of Shadow, and vanished in a spiral of sickly black vapour.

THE CANDLELIGHT PARADE

"Excellent, Sadie," Rhiannon said, picking herself off the floor and dusting down her skirts. "Beautifully done."

Sadie turned the strange wooden instrument in her hands. "What happened? And where did this come from?"

Rhiannon smiled. "It's mine," she said simply. "I know the basics. The rest was all you."

Touch it. Remember.

"You used my knowledge of the penny whistle to help you play."

Half a dozen terrified faces stared at them. The other six lay strewn between broken chairs and tables, books and destitute board games.

Taking Sadie's hand, Rhiannon led her out of the day room and headed for the eastern doors.

Corridors that had once been silent and empty now teemed with doktors and nurses and hospital officials, their faces tight, eyes bleary. Wails from the inpatients chased Sadie and Rhiannon down each corridor, distressed and forlorn.

"Where have those *women* gone?"

"They're called the Wretched," Rhiannon corrected her. "The witches three, Mistresses of the Horned God. Genevieve escaped before the music reached her, but Edith and Dorothea were not so fortunate." Rhiannon set a strong pace. Her boots pounded with each footfall. "You vaporised them."

"Vaporised?" Sadie shook the penny whistle in her clenched fist. "With this?"

"Yes. And keep it close," Rhiannon replied. "Genevieve may still be in the hospital. We cannot be too careful."

"Where did the others go?"

Rhiannon shrugged. "Back wherever they came from. Some dark, horrid place, I shouldn't wonder. It makes no matter. They're gone. For now."

Oliver hurried along behind them, listening intently.

"Perhaps they went back to … the Nyx," Sadie suggested.

Rhiannon took a dozen steps before saying, "How do you know of the Nyx? I've never spoken of it and I doubt your father had the guts."

"I don't know who he was," Sadie said, her eyes on the back of Rhiannon's head. "The Narrowers were there. A dream within a dream, they said. Is that possible?"

"Of course."

"They told me his name. The Unknown. Malmort—"

"Don't." Rhiannon said quickly but the words were already uttered. "Don't say his name. Any of them."

"Why not?"

They arrived at the eastern doors. Rhiannon stopped abruptly. Her pale fingers pressed against the cold glass. She looked down the corridor. No sign of Genevieve or her dark sisters. Rhiannon seemed older, tired. "It gives him strength," she said. "Saying his name makes him real."

"He's not real?"

Rhiannon looked at the shimmer standing next to Sadie. "Oliver came from nothing. The more people that know of him and say his name, the more real he becomes. The same is true of the Horned God."

Rhiannon took a deep breath. A million thoughts seemed to rush behind her eyes. The dreadlocked woman forced the heavy glass door open and shepherded them into the cold.

They trotted down the stone steps.

Oliver took Sadie's hand.

"I am so glad you are okay," he said. "You were completely out of it. I did not know what to do. If Rhiannon had not come along—"

"Don't panic, Oliver," Sadie said, quietening him. "I'm here. It's all okay."

"For now," he mumbled. "Those witches …"

"Yes," she answered, seeming to know his thoughts. "The Wretched. The three from Father's story about the Witch Tree at San Cristophe?"

Rhiannon flicked her eyes at Sadie. "Yes," she conceded. "The very same. They are three, yet they are one. A dark Goddess. A triple-headed monster."

Oliver paled. "Triple-headed monster?"

"But Father's story said they were killed and buried in the Snake Plains," Sadie protested. "They grew into a horrible, evil tree that ate the king."

"Killed?" Rhiannon said. A fearful laugh followed. "If anything, the king made them more powerful than you can possibly imagine. The Witch Tree is evil reborn. Evil ever-living."

"Where is the tree?" Sadie asked, her face becoming numb.

"Hidden. Protected. Worshipped by many. In San Cristophe, for sure, but the exact location of the Witch Tree is a closely guarded secret. No doubt Minister Craven and select members of the Eighth Day Assembly are familiar with its whereabouts. It is a dark place, concealed, forbidden."

"Has no one thought to destroy it?" Oliver asked.

"The king tried to cut it down with his Moonblade Axe," Sadie said, turning to her friend. "But they sucked him in, laughing and cackling."

Oliver shuddered. A burst of hot steam erupted from a tangle of copper piping on a nearby factory. He jumped, sinking his chattering teeth into the scarf.

"But the king did not die," Rhiannon added. "He is alive—as

alive as anything can be trapped inside the roots of that tree—tormented by the three."

"How do you know that?"

"I can feel him."

Sadie looked at her sideways. "Who?"

"The king," Rhiannon said, striding purposefully across snow-covered cobbles.

"You can feel him? How?"

Rhiannon pulled her long coat tight around her waist and flicked her matted hair off her face. Sadie and Oliver followed her into an alleyway between two large warehouses.

"You can tell how Oliver feels, can't you?"

"I can sense him. I know when he's close. And he can see into my mind. He saw the Narrowers."

"It's the same for me," she told Sadie. "I can feel the king. I know what he is feeling, what he is thinking. I can see what he sees. I see the tree, and the Wretched, and the dark place where they are hidden."

Sadie looked confused. "Is he your ... brother?"

Rhiannon let out a breathy laugh. "No. Not at all. I've never met him."

"Then what connects you to him?"

"He's alive, Sadie." Rhiannon's voice sounded different. Imposing, heavy, as old as time herself.

"The Living," Oliver whispered through his scarf.

"What?" Sadie said. "What's ... the Living?"

"I am," Rhiannon said. Her voice made Sadie's skin tingle. "Guardian of the Living, Protector of the Light, Bringer of Day, and Castilian of Wonder, if you want my full titles."

Sadie looked at Rhiannon anew. "A Guardian. A Protector. Of—?"

"Of all that lives, and all that inhabits the Light. Of all that is good, and all that shines."

"You were an Angel?" Sadie said slowly. "You *are* an Angel."

"You are a Narrower," Oliver added victoriously.

"Yes, a Narrower," Sadie echoed her friend. "A Watcher. One of the Grigori."

"True. On all counts. I am one of three, much like the Wretched. But my place is for the Living of this world. I am inexorably linked to all that lives. Linked to their eyes, their minds, their memories."

Sadie had almost forgotten the cold. "Do you know what everyone is seeing? What they're all thinking?"

"Not all at once. But, yes, Sadie. Every man, woman, and child. Every cat and dog, every rabbit, mouse, raven, elephant, spider, whale or fish, and every monster."

"That's amazing."

"To many, yes. But to you and me—"

"What?" Sadie said. "I cannot do what you do. I cannot see the memories of every cat, dog, rabbit, mouse, raven, elephant, spider, whale and fish, or monster."

Rhiannon raised an eyebrow. "What do you think your music is?"

Oliver's fingers tightened on Sadie's arm.

"My music?"

"Where do you think it comes from?"

"I don't know."

"Yes, you do."

Sadie swallowed hard. "It's not mine … the music. Is it … other people's?"

"Yes."

"How do I—?"

"You'll understand more with time, Sadie. The music you play belongs to others. The melodies are part of their happiness and joy, their broken hearts and sorrows. You reach out to them, connect, perform. You bring their emotions, their memories, out into the real world. It's truly captivating to behold. I can only see these things. I cannot interact. That skill is yours, Sadie." Rhiannon paused. "I can see the memories of all living things. Except one—"

"Me," Sadie said, her eyes wide in amazement. "You cannot read me."

Rhiannon took a deep breath. "Yet you, Sadie Madison—daughter of Michael Madison, granddaughter of William Madison—looked into my mind and learnt to play the penny whistle. You can read *me*. Guardian of the Living, Protector of the Light, Bringer of Day, and Castilian of Wonder. Now that, dearest Sadie, is a mighty power indeed."

There are those who would pay a heavy price for a glimpse of the past ... Sadie remembered *... and kill to save the future.*

Across the street, two Ryndai stood sentry outside the Eighth Day Assembly garrison. A handful of others patrolled the battlements. In the distance, several people headed for the highstreet and the Candlelight Parade.

"You've had quite the day, Sadie," Rhiannon said. "And this is only the beginning. Oliver has seen much and heard more. But we should get you home with your family. As quickly as we can. The dark is coming, and with it, a new century."

"And my birthday."

Gravely, Rhiannon agreed.

✳ ☡ ▤ ✻ ♨

Multicoloured sheets of sailcloth, embroidered with gold and copper stitching, had been pinned to the walls and ceiling of the Madison house with clamps and nails, like an iridescent mountain range. Lamplight from the landing shone through the fabrics, casting an evocative blend of hues on the hardwood floor.

Beneath the impressive awning, Michael busied himself hanging lanterns and decorations. Every surface in the Madison house had been cleared of trinkets, knick-knacks, vases, plates, enamel spoons, and Larissa's cups, saucers and teapots. All packed away neatly in boxes and piled high on the landing. In their place were row upon row of lavishly decorated cakes, puddings, cookies, jellies, brownies, gateaux, cheesecakes, and tarts. And in the dining room, the polished mahogany table held the pièce de résistance, Sadie's pancake birthday cake.

It smelt magnificent.

Larissa and Natalia were awash with it.

An aromatic sugar high.

"Mother, the house has never looked so good."

"It's never looked so delicious!" Larissa added. "Remember to pop the spiced apple and blackcurrant pies into the oven when we get back from the Candlelight Parade, Natalia. Then, our work will be done."

"This is quite exceptional," Michael said, standing amidst the sweet treats, his hands nestled in his cardigan pockets.

Larissa put her arm around him and gently squeezed his waist. The grandfather clock struck five times. Larissa clapped her hands. "Come on, only an hour until the Candlelight Parade. Natalia, is Dimitri gracing us with his presence this evening?"

"He's going to meet us by the Steam Totem at six o'clock," Natalia replied, blushing. "I believe Alexsy and Helene are coming too."

"The Rubinovs? In Iron Bridge at New Year?" Michael muttered to himself.

Larissa shrugged. "Michael, fetch Sadie and Eli. We need to get going if we're to be on time for Dimitri and his parents."

Michael nodded. Sadie still wasn't home. He'd studied the world beyond the window all afternoon. But his worries and anxiety were eradicated in an instant as a sharp, icy breeze rippled over the back of his neck.

"Wow! It looks like a Trevastian cake bazaar in here."

Sadie stood in the open doorway, gawping at the decorations and the endless puddings and desserts. Snowflakes drifted through Natalia's multicoloured lantern lights on the porch.

Michael turned at the sound of Sadie's voice.

He dashed forward and slid onto his knees.

"Sadie," he gushed, wrapping his arms around her. "Where

have you been?" She opened her mouth to speak but Michael got there first. "It doesn't matter. You're home. Safe. That is all."

He beamed brightly and kissed her frozen cheek.

✶ ☽ ▤ ☌ ▥

Eli sat listening from his position above the colourful canopy. He positioned several loose sheets atop his notebook. He wrote about the music Sadie made, about the way it made his family turn into creatures resembling his mother's Lorntide mannequins. He wrote about the boy in the red scarf. The boy he'd seen through his Monster Magnifiers. He wrote about Sadie taking the boy into the cold and snow. He wrote about the endless baking and his father decorating the house for the New Year's celebrations.

He tapped the fountain pen against his lip then signed the letter.

Looking forward to seeing you tomorrow.
Your friend, Eli.

He folded the letter and placed it inside a white envelope.

On the front he scribbled a large letter *D*.

✶ ☽ ▤ ☌ ▥

Michael herded his family into the cold and closed the front door, concealing the treasure trove of cakes, puddings, and delectable delicacies. Snaking down Leviathan Crook, the Madisons joined the hordes heading for the Steam Totem. The chill evening air became filled with lively chatter and excitement.

"Is this safe?" Larissa asked her husband. "Should we be out tonight?"

"You mean, should Sadie be out?"

Larissa nodded.

"Sadie isn't safe anywhere. Out here, at home, in the depths of Los Kralice, or perched on the precipice of Paladin's Tower. But she doesn't turn thirteen until midnight. She won't leave my sight."

Larissa nestled into her husband. Her fingers worked their way around his waist. "Don't lose her, Michael. Don't lose our daughter."

He bent down and kissed the top of her head. "I won't. I promise."

In front, Natalia held Eli's free hand—the other clutched his notebook—steadying him as he negotiated the slippery cobbles. Sadie and Oliver walked quicker than the others, despite the adventures they'd already had, but Michael's eyes never left his daughter, no matter where she wandered.

"Don't get too far ahead," Michael told her. "We need to stick together. Remember, it's easy to get separated. I'd hate to lose you—any of you—in the crowd."

The Madisons joined hands in a human daisy chain. Warm bodies and cold fingers pressed against one another. Music played all around, jaunty and whimsical. They swarmed around the Steam Totem, headed up the highstreet and joined the tail of the Candlelight Parade.

As they passed *Doktor Puttock's Apothecary of the Bizarre*, Sadie peeked into the window, hoping to see Rhiannon, but found nothing but shadows.

"Look. The Iron Candle," Larissa announced.

Michael raised Eli onto his shoulders for a better view. All eyes were fixed on the foot of the highstreet—on the Steam Totem—where Mayor Robert McKendrick—a retired Historian and veteran of the Norland Armed Forces—stood on a small wooden scaffold between the Steam Totem and the sprawling masses.

The Iron Candle featured a long grip and pommel, like a sword, emblazoned with the five faces of the Steam Totem. Above sat the cross-guard which protected the bearer of the candle from the flames. Where the blade would have been rose a basket of weaved iron, stuffed with wood and tinder, and dowsed in oil.

The mayor hoisted the Iron Candle into the air.

Below, the crowd cheered and hollered, readying their shop-bought or handmade fire-torches and candles. McKendrick turned his gaze to the Carcassus Mountains. He watched as the winter sun disappeared, only to be replaced by a ghost of the moon.

He pulled out a brass pocket watch.

Almost six o'clock.

Holding the Iron Candle as high as he dared, the mayor muttered a small prayer. He teetered for a moment, his old limbs straining under the weight of the Iron Candle. And then the Steam Totem erupted in a violent breath of molten flames.

White-hot and choking, like dragonfire.

Those standing closest covered their faces and leant away from the scalding heat. Even those halfway up the highstreet felt the fiery wave as it washed over them. A lull, a soft silence. The fire broke into long burning tendrils, spiralling up into the sky above the Steam Totem, evaporating in black wisps and dancing fireflies.

All eyes turned to Mayor McKendrick as he stood upon the scaffold, holding the blazing Iron Candle.

Pictographic flashes exploded around him.

Below the scaffold, people inched forward, their candles outstretched, ready to share the Steam Totem's magic fire. Mayor McKendrick plunged the Iron Candle low, setting off a chain reaction from the Steam Totem to the top of the highstreet.

Sadie thrilled at the magical sight.

Thousands of individual fires burned in the failing evening light. They floated as if on a lake. Shadows flickered on triple-storeyed shops, stores, and boutiques.

Sadie watched the firelight spread onto the makeshift candle in her hand.

Mysterious fire danced.

Alive and dangerous.

She'd held the same candle every year. Hers was similar to the Iron Candle in many ways, except for its grandeur. The thin iron pole had rusted horribly where the pommel had fallen off. The basket was dented and damaged but burned as furiously as any other. Sadie held it as high as she could. Orange flames decorated the faces of her family.

The crowd began to move.

Shifting like a singular animal.

The Candlelight Parade had begun.

Sadie could see dozens of candles beginning to congregate around the monument to the Victorious Dead from her position high on the hill. It normally took an hour or more for the entire parade to gather.

Sadie didn't mind. She loved being among the candles. A sensation like no other. Magical, eerie, romantic. The fire from the Steam Totem was the best part. The mysterious column would spit out hazardous jets of fire every hour, on the hour, from six o'clock until midnight every New Year.

"A fire that hot must come from the centre of the world!" Michael had told her in one of his stories.

She wondered if the new century would bring something different from the Steam Totem—some new excitement, some new extravaganza—but, for now, it was fire as usual. Thunderous, magical fire.

✶☽🏛🐉🏚

Oliver stared at the Steam Totem. Wisps of fire flickered around the eyes and nostrils of the five faces. "Rhiannon said we should be home ... where it is safe."

"I know," Sadie replied. The blue in her hair glowed in the firelight. "But Mother and Father and everyone are here. We'd have been home alone. I feel better here in the Candlelight Parade."

"I get it. Safety in numbers."

"No, you don't. You want to be at home, and that's fine." Sadie knocked him lightly on the arm. "We're surrounded. No one can get us. There's no need to be afraid."

Oliver trudged down the cobbles. He held out a hand for Sadie, but she was busy passing the heavy candle from one hand to the other. He slipped it back in his pocket and stared at his feet.

How can I not be afraid?

An icy shiver ran through him.

I am frightened. I am afraid. That is what I am. I'm all the things that make her scream, all the things she runs from, all the things that wait for her in the dark, the things that keep her from sleep.

He watched Sadie. She marvelled at the burning candle and the dizzying stars twinkling a million miles above.

I am spiders. And monsters. And being ordinary. And the Unknown, the Wretched and the Foretelling. I am everything she fears.

The Madisons passed the Steam Totem. Mayor McKendrick sat on the edge of the platform. His legs swung playfully. The Iron Candle burned brightly in a sconce above. He waved as they passed, wishing them glad tidings and happiness for the new century.

But everywhere Oliver looked he saw terror.

Danger.

Things that should not be.

His head snapped to all manner of vicious, blood-curdling monstrosities that slipped in and out of the masses. He saw Vulpes, Genevieve, Rhiannon, the Fire Wolves, and Karolinja. He saw Sofia, clad in white, the dark mist swirling around her, making her whole. One moment they were there, the next they were gone. At first, he tried to avoid them, deciding they were illusions. But every turn he made revealed a new danger. He was pulled in circles. Spun in a knot of confusion.

He refocused and bound through the masses, dodging from side to side, as though obstacles were something he had to consider.

Sadie's eyes shone as he arrived beside her.

"It is not safe," he told her earnestly. "We are not safe. They are ... everywhere."

"What are you talking about?"

"Dangers," he said. "Unnumbered."

"We're in the Candlelight Parade, Oliver. Everyone is here."

"Yes," he bleated. "Vulpes, Genevieve, Sofia ... monsters of all kinds."

"Calm down."

"I can see them. All of them."

"Oliver," she said soothingly. "I'm here. Right here. And you're with me. There's no safer place in the world."

Oliver stared, unblinking.

Sadie took his hand and gave it a gentle squeeze. "I won't let anything happen to you."

The Rubinovs emerged from the crowd at the foot of the Steam Totem. Dimitri appeared at Natalia's side. His brothers, Branislav and Erik, watched the procession with mild curiosity, while Alexsy and Helene approached Sadie and asked her about her New Year's promises.

The boy in the crimson scarf scanned the masses as they trudged by, like an army bound for war, bearing spears of fire. Carnival music wheezed and popped overhead. Firelight flickered on every surface, casting feverish dancing shadows.

Oliver saw faces in the shadows.

Malicious, devilish faces.

Horned and hoofed.

Snorting with rage.

Cackling with hateful spite.

Horrified, he turned away.

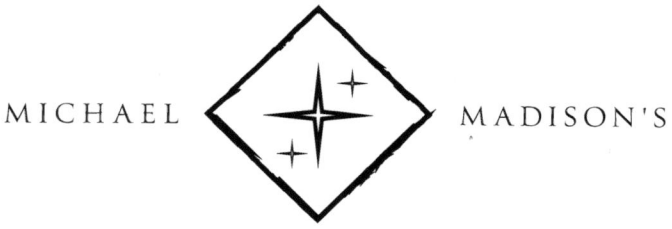

MICHAEL MADISON'S

THE EIGHTH DAY
OF CREATION

In the beginning there was nothing.

Less than nothing—if you can imagine such a thing.

But, out of the nothing, as if conjured by a sorcerer at the peak of her power, the Gods appeared and stood in the vastness of the nothing that surrounded them.

There were seven in all.

Together they created everything we know.

And everything we are yet to understand.

On the First Day, Aurora—the God of Light—tore the darkness in two. This rent of the nothingness spawned infinite shards of light that exploded, multiplying across the darkness, giving it depth and scale.

On the Second Day, Paladin—the God of Spheres—organised the light into stars and life-giving suns, orbiting them with barren worlds, gaseous worlds, and worlds of precious water. Between the stars and the suns, he created a vast labyrinth of dimensions known as the Vents—a place to look after all that had been forgotten, and all that was to come.

Upon the Third Day, Terra—the God of Earth—pulled the water back on infinite worlds and exposed the land where trees and plants grew in colossal numbers.

On the Fourth Day, Epoch—the God of Seasons—split each earth's orbit around its sun into four distinct phases, differentiating them with rain, and snow, and wind, and glorious sunlight.

On the Fifth Day, Oceania—the God of Sealife—made the whales, and the fish, and all that lives beneath the waves.

On the Sixth Day, DeMenza and DeForna—the Twin Gods of Animals—created cattle, and birds, and snakes, and every living thing that inhabits the sky or creeps upon the land.

On the Seventh Day, the Gods rested—for the universe was complete.

The Seventh Day lasted for billions of years.

Peace and harmony reigned on every Earth between the fish, and the birds, and the beasts. But, as time passed, the Gods became restless. They argued and tormented and dared one another to alter one of the perfect worlds that they had so lovingly created.

DeMenza and DeForna—the Twin Gods of Animals—acted first.

From the billions of galaxies and solar systems, they picked a single planet and created a woman and a man in their own image. They gave them dominion over the fish, and the cattle, and the birds, and the snakes, and every living thing that inhabits the sky or creeps upon the land. The Twin Gods created the Kingdom of Heaven above for them to worship and the Rings of Hell below for them to fear.

They created love, kindness, and compassion.

Wickedness, jealousy, and hate.

Tentatively, DeMenza and DeForna sat back and invited the other Gods to admire what they had achieved. For generations they worshipped the Gods. Women and men thrived, expanding their dominion across the earth and the seas. They built townships, and cities, and great roads to join one to the next. Language spread and transformed, cultures developed, music, literature, trade and business. Land borders were formed, patrolled, and militarised. Empires rose and fell, and with them came war and destruction.

To the Gods' dismay, worship ebbed, belief in their creators turned to ash.

For the first time in a million years, the Gods returned and stood over the continents of the Earth. They demanded an end to warfare and murder, to sorrow and suffering, to intolerance and devastation.

But the women and men of Earth stared up at the Gods, their faces filled with contempt and hatred. And then, as the sun rose on the Eighth Day, they took up arms against the Gods and vanquished them all.

PART FIVE
SEVERANCE

"To confront and defeat a monster, we must remain true to our hearts, lest monsters we become ourselves."
—ORISIS RÄKÄNTEUR,
Angel District, San Cristophe, The Dawn of Whispers

THE
REQUIEM

Thousands of floating candles surrounded the monument to the Victorious Dead. A wreath of fire. Alive and magical.

Sadie held her candle in one hand. Oliver's in the other.

He looked paler than usual. He pulled his crimson scarf over his nose, protecting him from the horrors of the world. His eyes darted through the crowd, never resting for more than a moment on each passing face.

Michael stood shoulder to shoulder with Alexsy Rubinov, and Eli tucked under his other arm. Behind them, Natalia and Dimitri shared secrets and playful touches while Larissa and Helene exchanged pleasant smiles, but nothing more. Branislav and Erik loitered nearby looking stony-faced and bored.

Mayor McKendrick stood upon a new platform. This one had been erected in the schoolyard adjacent to the monument to the Victorious Dead. He waved his hands above his head, quietening the masses. Once every soul had arrived and shuffled into position, a gentle hush swept through the crowd, leaving nothing but the crackle of fire and the smell of smoke.

The mayor bowed his head and pressed his hands together in prayer.

Hundreds mirrored him.

One by one, each man began to sing.

A low murmur.

A low breathy note.

Each voice joined together in an intoxicating vocal embrace, increasing in volume, the timbre shifting beautifully, ungoverned and wild. Oliver opened his eyes to see who led the performance, but every head was bowed, every eye shut.

Female voices joined the chorus.

The sound grew wider, louder, brighter.

It seemed to spread through Oliver's body—ghostly and intangible as it was—chasing away his anxiety and replacing it with hope.

And when the sound stopped, it came strict and sudden.

Voices dropped out of the sky like dying birds.

The crackle of candles fed into Oliver's consciousness.

He took a breath and risked a glance. Positioned regimentally around the schoolyard stood the enigmatic Ryndai, their eyes open, staring, hands hanging beside their curved blades. Oliver had never got used to them. Who could? Silent eyes on every street corner, observing, watching, waiting. He wondered how they let this sort of thing occur. Praying surely contravened the laws they were sent to uphold.

The mayor was next to open his eyes.

Oliver watched as he observed the faces of the masses. The mayor smiled, nodding his head, and then began to sing. He was only a couple of syllables in when everyone joined him in song.

VICTORY AND DEATH, LIKE LOVE AND REGRET.
TRIUMPH AND LOSS, LEST WE FORGET.
ALWAYS DEAD. ALWAYS REMEMBERED.

BURDEN AND FORFEIT, KEPT AT ARM'S LENGTH,
SURVIVAL AND HOPE, STRENGTH BEYOND STRENGTH,
ALWAYS DEAD. ALWAYS REMEMBERED.

LIFE FOLLOWS LIFE, IN LOVE WE TRANSCEND,
DEATH FOLLOWS DEATH, OUR GLORIOUS END.
ALWAYS DEAD. ALWAYS REMEMBERED.

Voices soared around the schoolyard and local neighbourhoods and down the Shadow Valley. Sadie opened her eyes and looked at Oliver. A sombre smile played on her lips. "Are you okay?" she whispered, giving his hand a squeeze.

"Of course," he replied. "That was beautiful, yet sad. I felt transported."

Sadie smiled softly. "The Divine Wars left their impression on everyone. And now it's left something on you too."

"Norlandians, residents of Iron Bridge, ladies and gentlemen, boys and girls of the Shadow Valley." The mayor's voice rang in the cold night air. "Welcome to the last Candlelight Parade of the nineteenth century."

Riotous applause broke through the crowd.

Whistles and enthusiastic cheers shot up like fire-rockets.

"It is my honour and humble duty to lead you into the dawn of a new age. An age of science and technology. An age of peace. A town has stood here on the banks of the River Myr for over a thousand years. Iron Bridge, as we know it, has only stood for sixty-eight of those years. Sixty-eight years since the Divine Wars. Sixty-eight years since our grandfathers and great-grandfathers took up arms. Sixty-eight years since blood spilled in anger. Sixty-eight years of peace and harmony. The twentieth century beckons with hope and adventure. A shining age for Norland, for Iron Bridge, and the Shadow Valley. Tonight, let us celebrate our freedom, the peace we adore, the victories of the past and the achievements to come."

The mayor took the Iron Candle and thrust it into the air three times.

Each thrust met with a communal *Hoorah!*

"Thank you, Norlandians, residents of Iron Bridge, ladies and gentlemen, boys and girls of the Shadow Valley. Return to your homes, to your parties and gatherings. Bring in the new year—the new century!—with style and honour and pride. Be at peace, one and all."

Cheers and applause rang through the night.

The mayor waved as the circle dispersed. Orbs of flickering light bled away from the monument to the Victorious Dead, over the river, up the hill, into streets and alleyways, coming to rest outside every shop, restaurant, and home in Iron Bridge.

☀ ☽ ▦ ✻ ⛲

Michael Madison walked beside Alexsy Rubinov. Their candles burned brightly. They wandered through the school gate, engulfed in the hubbub of excited chatter, and began the long climb up Leviathan Crook.

"I feel awkward to ask," Michael began. "But I was under the impression you and Helene—and your boys, of course—return to San Lundkvistburg to see in the New Year."

"Clearly not," Alexsy said, prodding himself comically. "I believe I'm here. Do you not concur?"

Michael managed a slim smile. "Of course, I meant—"

"It's okay, Michael," Alexsy reassured him. "We normally return home at this time of year. Have you been to San Lundkvistburg? It's simply mesmerising—magical, even—in winter. The people, the architecture, the festivities. A place like no other."

"No, sadly, I've not," he replied. "You called it *home*, yet you live here."

Alexsy considered this for a moment. "I was born there. I became who I was there. It will always be a home for me, as I'm sure the place of your younger years is for you. My home is also where Helene and my sons are. They love it here—as do I—so we stay in Iron Bridge, in the Shadow Valley, where happiness surrounds us. Behold."

Dimitri and Natalia walked together, hand in hand, a look of urgent longing on their faces.

"That is why we stayed this year, Michael."

"For Natalia and Dimitri?"

Alexsy put a strong arm around Michael's shoulder and

squeezed vigorously. "Of course," he said. "Iron Bridge can be magical too. There's something in the air. Looks like love to me."

Michael nodded in agreement but glanced over his shoulder, looking for his other daughter. Branislav and Erik trudged purposefully behind. He smiled pleasantly and they nodded in return. Michael found Sadie walking quietly beside Larissa, her arm outstretched, holding an invisible hand.

Michael returned to Alexsy. "Really? You stayed for Natalia?"

"In part. And to experience the Candlelight Parade. I've neither seen nor heard anything quite like it in my life. Truly exceptional."

"Not Sadie, then?"

"Whatever do you mean?"

"You didn't stay for Sadie? You didn't stay here in Iron Bridge because of her?"

"Not at all," Alexsy said. The characteristic fun in his voice faded. "Are you accusing me of something?"

Michael stared at the billionaire. "No," he said. "Of course not. Ignore me. Just a little … you know—"

"Do you worship the Gods?" Alexsy said, his gaze turned to the stars.

Michael almost tripped mid-step. There were two Ryndai ahead. One at the outside edge of Leviathan Crook's first curve, the second behind them at the school gates.

"Does it look like I wear the Broken Moon? No. We are a Godless family," Michael whispered, collecting himself. "I'm a man of science. The Gods have either been killed or driven from this universe."

"Then why did we all pray at the monument? Why did we all bow our heads in solemn prayer? Ryndai were everywhere, yet we prayed."

"Tradition, Alexsy. The hands clasped in prayer, the long drone—"

"Ah yes," Alexsy cut in. "The Calling of the Dead, I believe."

"The *Victorious* Dead," Michael corrected. "And then, of

course, the Requiem."

"This sounds awfully religious to me," Alexsy added, returning to his point.

"And, as I say, it's tradition. We're speaking to our dead, not the Gods," Michael replied, wondering where Alexsy was going with this. "Do you worship—?"

"What is God?" Alexsy said, as if he'd been dying for Michael to ask. "There are all kinds of secrets in the world. And all kinds of truth. What is God if not magic, and mystery, and miracles? Secrets and truths. An unknowing beyond all others." He gesticulated towards Sadie. "A thing as intangible as music." Then Eli. "Or wonder." And finally, Natalia. "Or love." Michael looked perplexed. "I'm not advocating some super-being sat up in the heavens commanding angels and condemning demons, but the notion of things beyond our fingertips. Things that fill us with joy. Things that move us, carry us, give us purpose, and ease our hearts. That's a divine thing in my eyes. That's God to me. As for the Ryndai and the Eighth Day Assembly, I doubt they even care a jot."

Helene appeared at her husband's side, her arm locked through his. "I'm sorry, Michael," she said. "Is he going on about the magic of the universe? I knew he'd get like this after the Candlelight Parade ... and the blackberry wine!"

Alexsy opened his mouth, feigning contempt. "I've barely touched a drop!"

"No, it's fine," Michael said. "It's ... very interesting."

Helene kissed Alexsy on the cheek. "Now, that's enough of this nonsense. We're at the Tomes' house. It's time for the appetisers. Is that right, Michael? This is ever so exciting. We don't have this tradition in San Lundkvistburg. Highly unusual."

"But utterly thrilling," Alexsy added. "And not a moment too soon. I'm famished."

THE BOY WHO
WAS FORGOTTEN

Flickering candles covered the Tomes' lawn. Each one buried deep in the snow-packed earth. Sadie added hers, thrusting the metal pommel into the ground like a fiery spear.

The Tomes' house was smaller than the Madisons' but rose to accommodate two bedrooms over three floors. Inside, vines and leaves, bark, roots, and flowers from a hundred gardens decorated the house. Sadie and Oliver milled in the crowded hallway, struggling to find a place to stand and admire the decorations. Michael seemed relieved to be inside. His roving eyes found Sadie every five seconds.

Alexsy and Helene disappeared into the kitchen in search of the first course, a customary glass of champagne or thimble of brandy.

"Are you okay, dear?" said Larissa, putting her hand on Eli's head.

He looked up at her with his Monster Magnifiers and nodded.

Have you seen Natalia? she signed.

Eli thumbed towards the front door then went back to checking the Tomes' residence for dangerous threats.

Larissa squeezed over to the window and peered into the night. Natalia and Dimitri were standing on the porch holding hands. Natalia smiled uncontrollably as Dimitri filled her ear with sweet words. She seemed to slip into a daydream but returned as Dimitri moved close and kissed her. Larissa blushed and spun away.

Arnold Tomes erupted from the kitchen, followed by a wave of delicious aromas.

"Appetisers are served!"

A roar of approval swelled through the house.

Larissa rapped gently on the window, urging Natalia and Dimitri inside.

A huge selection of finger food filled the kitchen counter. Chilli prawns, pigs in blankets, fried cheeses, pork and mango cubes, pastry parcels, miniature egg pies, beetroot wrapped in bacon, and an army of sandwiches: peanut butter; smoked trout, horseradish and rocket; brie and cranberry sauce; corned beef and sweet pickle; shawarma; mature cheese, cucumber and black pepper; roast beef, mustard, mayonnaise and watercress. They all came on white, brown, and wholegrain bread—regular and toasted.

Sadie began to salivate at the sight of such an epic spread.

"Don't go crazy," Michael said. "This is the starter."

Sadie filled her hands with an assortment of treats, popping them eagerly into her mouth one by one. Eli edged up beside her, his spectacles still in place. He settled on a single miniature egg pie and vanished rapidly into the party.

Hands dived into the food all around. Oliver looked uncomfortable with this level of proximity. Sadie nodded towards the hallway. Michael's head spun on his shoulders as she scurried away. "Stay inside," he called, getting swept along by the hungry hands. "Stay close."

But Sadie and Oliver had darted upstairs. There were three doors off the landing. The master bedroom, bathroom, and access to the attic stairs where Danver's room waited. Sadie turned the handle to the latter and entered.

"Should we be up here?" Oliver asked, climbing the narrow staircase.

Sadie flicked a switch. "Of course. This is Danver's room.

I've been in here loads of times—" But as lamplight bloomed, she saw that this room wasn't Danver's. At least, not anymore.

A table ran along the wall, covered with journals and paperwork. A large high-back chair faced the window. Positioned in front of it, angled at the sky, was an expensive-looking brass and copper telescope. The sloping walls were covered in charts and maps. Sadie ran a quivering hand over them as a tear welled in her eye.

"Look at all this stuff," she said, flipping through some of the books and lifting the paperwork to inspect beneath. "It's all maps of the stars and astrological charts and cosmic symbology."

"Was Danver into all that?"

Sadie gave him a hard look. "Of course not." She snapped a journal shut and tossed it aside. "He was into adventure books and heroes, aircraft and puzzles. He had no interest in the night sky. Not like this, anyway." Sadie looked exasperated. "And where's his bed, his pictures, his toys, his clothes? What have they done with *everything?*"

"You shouldn't be in here," came a strict voice. "Arnold's observatory is off limits!"

Fisher Tomes stood in the doorway.

Thumbs sunk into her hips.

"Arnold's *observatory?*" Sadie echoed, glaring at Danver's mother.

"There's lots of expensive equipment in here. Arnold would be mortified if anything got damaged."

"Mortified?" Sadie said, almost in shock. "About his *stuff?*"

"Sadie, dear. Are you okay?" Fisher said. "You look ill. You should get more to eat before it all goes. Oh goodness me. You've dropped some on the floor."

"What have you done?" Sadie asked. "What have you done with him?"

Fisher knelt to pick up the abandoned food. "Arnold? Why, he's downstairs—where you should be, young lady—pouring drinks and serving food."

"No," Sadie snapped. "Not Arnold. Danver. Where are Danver's things? Where have you put them all?"

"Not this again, Sadie. I told you before."

Sadie's eyes filled with tears. Her top lip quivered. "He's your son. Danver. My best friend. Danver." Sadie's breath became quick, shallow. Her hands shook. Then, without warning, she ran at the maps and charts and started tearing them from the walls.

Fisher dived forward, grabbed Sadie's flailing arms, and pinned her to the ground. "Arnold! Michael! Help!"

The abstract rhythm of feet pounded up two flights of stairs. Michael exploded through the doorway. "Sadie! Sadie, are you okay? Was it the agents? Was it the three?"

"What nonsense are you talking, Michael? You make less sense than your daughter!"

He joined Fisher on the carpet. "What happened?" he asked, breathlessly. "What did you do to her?"

"Me? I did nothing," Fisher exploded, still restraining Sadie. "She was asking me what I'd done with him. What I'd done with all his things and then she started destroying Arnold's room."

"Whose things?"

"Danver's things!" Sadie barked. "They've destroyed them all!"

"It's this *Danver* business again, Michael."

Michael looked at his daughter. She stared back. Sadie waved an accusatory finger at Fisher. "She's forgotten all about him. The Narrowers must have come and taken Danver from her. From her and Arnold."

Fisher frowned.

"Sadie," Michael began. "Quiet now, you've—"

"No, Father. Look. Look at his room. All his things are gone. Every last trace of him. Just like ... like the Nepenthe was supposed to do to me. Was it Vulpes? Did he give Arnold and Fisher a Nepenthe? Is he working with the Narrowers? Father? Answer me!"

Fisher looked panicked, afraid. "Your daughter's having a strange turn," she said.

"And Sofia too," Sadie went on, wriggling under Fisher's grip. "Did you let the Narrowers take Danver away like you did my twin sister?"

"Michael?"

"Childish stories, tall tales," he lied. "It's my fault. Always filling her head with fantasy and make-believe. She's tired, that's all. Dreams and faerie-tales and reality all blended into one."

"I'm not a child," Sadie snapped. "I'll be thirteen in a matter of hours."

Fisher released Sadie. "We shouldn't be in Arnold's observatory," she said again. "Come back downstairs. Bring the child with you."

Michael stood, hauling Sadie to her feet like a rag doll.

Sadie yanked her hands free, straightened her skirts, and pushed the hair from her eyes.

Fisher disappeared out the door, muttering to herself.

"Not a word of this to your mother."

Sadie went to object, then thought better of it.

Larissa, Eli, Natalia and Dimitri were huddled in the hallway picking nibbles off each other's plates and chatting away absent-mindedly when Michael and Sadie returned.

"Where did you go dashing off to?" Larissa asked. "Is Sadie okay?"

Michael took a moment. "She's fine. Being a sneaky nose," he said, looking at his daughter. "Fisher caught her poking about in Arnold's observatory. Seems he's a bit of a stargazer."

"Sadie," Larissa said admonishingly. "What have I told you about creeping around other people's houses?"

Larissa had never spoken of any such thing. "I'm sorry," Sadie said, fighting the urge to correct her mother. "I was just ... looking for someone."

"Stay close to your father and me. Understand?"

"I think it's probably time we headed out," Michael said.

"Four main courses to come before our turn with the desserts. So much food, so little time." Michael pulled his pocket watch out to underline his point. "Time is never on our side."

Sadie pictured her father kneeling in the rainstorm on the night she was born, the Narrowers surrounding him on all sides.

Time is never on our side.

He'd had thirteen years.

Time was almost up.

People were starting to leave the Tomes' and heading down Leviathan Crook. Next stops on the New Year's banquet were the Wrens', the Claus-Pritchards', the Pendragons', and the Boswicks' serving chicken, fish, pork, and beef, respectively.

Footstep trails led from the Tomes' towards each.

Eager feet carried hungry mouths.

The Madisons crossed the street and entered the Claus-Pritchards' first.

Throughout the house were trays and dishes filled with fish and seafood: baked salmon, grilled monkfish, scallops, roasted crab, boiled lobster, lemon sole, yellow fin tuna, skate, plaice, oysters, muscles, king prawns in garlic butter and a vat of paella. Michael guarded Sadie by the foot of the stairs as the rest of the family darted off in search of the next tantalising mouthful.

Sadie's gaze fell on her father. The anger and betrayal still burned inside. She wondered if it would ever go out. If she'd ever find a way to forgive him, to understand why he'd done such diabolical things.

Michael turned, seeming to sense her cold, hard stare. "Lots of things have happened, Sadie. Lots of things are about to happen. I don't have all the answers."

"You're my father," she said, her voice disappointed. "You're supposed to know *everything*."

"I'm just a man," he said, his voice sad, defeated.

Sadie shook her head. "No, you're not," she said. "You're the son of a billion-year-old spirit—an Angel, a Narrower—from an empyreal dimension. I have a mind that cannot forget. A mind somehow connected to the Vents and embroiled in a terrifying prophecy spanning millennia. What happened to you? Did the strange powers and prophetic riddles skip a generation?" Sadie's eyes widened. "I don't believe that. I cannot. You *have* to be more than *just* a man."

"I'm sorry," he said nervously. "There's less than four hours until the Steam Totem signals the new year, your thirteenth year. Everything will change. *Everything.*" Michael swallowed nervously. "Perhaps you are *not* the child of the Foretelling, and our lives will take us down a new path. One filled with possibilities, free from fear. But if not, then … well, I hate to think of it." William Madison's parting words found themselves on Michael's lips. "The future is coming, Sadie. The unknown is coming for all of us."

Sadie wiped her eyes.

"The future is always unknown, Father."

🔥☽🚃🐒🏛

By the time they reached the Boswick household—having feasted on both chicken and pork platters at the Wren and Pendragon residences—the Madisons were full to bursting, except Sadie who'd lost her appetite.

They loitered in the hallway, surrounded by tranches of steak: rib-eye, sirloin, T-bone, fillet, mountains of chipped potatoes and gravy boats brimmed with steaming sauces: peppercorn, spicy barbecue, blue cheese, béarnaise, mushroom, and garlic.

Sadie's stomach rumbled.

Acid roiled on her tongue.

The rest of the Madison family lined up to sample the generous fare.

Oliver stood beside his friend.

"I cannot get over what they did to Danver," she said. "It's as though they erased him from existence."

Oliver swallowed hard, shifting uneasily from foot to foot.

"Go on," Sadie said grumpily. "What is it?"

"Did he?"

Sadie snapped her head towards him. Her nose wrinkled. "Did he *what?*"

"Exist?" Oliver said, his voice wavering. "Did Danver ... ever exist?"

Sadie felt as though someone had impaled her with a spear. "You too, Oliver?"

"No," he said quickly. "I believe you. If you say he was real, then he was real."

Sadie folded her arms. Her head shook slowly from side to side. Her jaw set.

"Do not get mad with me," he said. "I am only playing ... What is it called? Devil's—"

"Advocate," she cut in sullenly.

"It is not a big leap, is it? I mean, look at me. I am here and I am real to you. It is not so crazy to think Danver was like me."

"Oliver. Stop it. Just ... stop." Sadie crushed her thumbs inside her fists until they hurt. "Danver was real ... is real. He's at Hurtmore House—in some horrid dungeon—with Doktor Merrick and goodness knows who, or what, else. We *have* to get there and bring him back. If we do, everybody will remember him. The Narrowers can't do anything about that. Seeing is believing. I know that much."

Oliver stared at his friend, but his eyes weren't the only ones on Sadie.

Through the candlelit gloom burned another pair of eyes, a mix of honey and green fire. His head shifted into the light, the same way the Fire Wolf had in Darachna Forest. But this creature was no wolf. He was a frightened, vengeful boy.

Cale Boswick ran a quivering finger over the scar on the side of his face. The injury had almost healed but a thin, red line remained. The eye immediately above, swollen and half closed, twitched. He turned away and sank into shadow.

Sadie caught a glimpse of him as he vanished. She could pick out Cale Boswick from his awkward frame, the way he lumbered rather than walked.

He'll remember Danver. Cale Boswick will definitely remember Danver.

She considered ploughing through the party and confronting Cale when Michael came striding over. "Your mother needs to head back and put the pies in the oven. Do you want to stay here, or shall we go with her?"

Before Sadie could answer, the door burst open and Alexsy and Helene Rubinov toppled into the house, a handful of others in tow. Alexsy staggered like a seasoned pirate, slapping Sadie's father on the back. "Mr Michael," he opened with. "Iron Bridge certainly knows how to celebrate. Am I not wrong?"

"You are not wrong," Michael said slowly, pronouncing every word. "Perhaps some coffee?"

"Coffee! Bah!" Alexsy roared. "Wine! Women! And song!" He looked down. "Sadie Madison. Sorceress of … the music. A song, if you would be so bold."

"We were about to leave," he told Alexsy. "Perhaps, when you've had your fill here, you would like to join us for dessert. And wine. And"—he gazed back at Sadie—"perhaps we can find a song for you on the wireless."

Alexsy nodded vaguely. Helene thrust a glass of champagne into his hand. His eyes lit up. "Fustran Exemplar!" He snorted, raised the glass, swayed sideways into his wife. Helene gathered him expertly and ushered him towards the kitchen.

"It's okay," said Michael. "You don't need to play for anyone. Not anymore."

But Sadie wasn't looking at him.

Across the hallway, cloaked in shadows, were the three who'd arrived with Alexsy Rubinov. Their faces seemed familiar, but she couldn't make them out. For the briefest moment, they huddled in a circle and then slipped into the party.

Gone.

"Sadie? I said you don't need to play—"

"I know," she replied, craning her neck to find the three. "I heard you."

Michael stiffened.

"I thought I saw someone. Three someones."

"Three?" Michael spun, his voice low and hushed. "Where?"

"They've gone now. It was probably nothing."

"Come on," he said, manoeuvring Sadie out the front door. "It's time to get you home. The hour is upon us."

THE CLOCKWORK UNIVERSE

Being back in the Madison house didn't make Michael feel much better. He knew the Narrowers themselves couldn't get to Sadie directly, but their agents—flesh and blood and bone—definitely could.

He closed the door and thundered the deadbolts into place.

"Michael," Larissa said curiously. "What are you doing?"

"The agents," he whispered. "Sadie thinks she might have seen ... something."

Larissa looked at Sadie, her face pale. "Did you? Did you see them? Who were they?"

"They were stood in shadow," she replied, shrugging. "I couldn't see them properly. To be honest, it could have been anyone."

Larissa squared her shoulders, smiled, and turned for the kitchen. "We've prepared for a party, and a party we shall have," she said, heading off to put the fruit pies in the oven. "Unlock the door, Michael."

He watched her cautiously, unsure if she had all her senses intact.

A fist pounded the door.

Then another.

"Hello," called a voice. "Anyone home?"

It was madness to let this go on, to let people into the house, to let them near Sadie.

"We're here for dessert!"

"Come on, Sir Michael. Lower your drawbridge!" This last voice, the tipsy slur of Alexsy Rubinov.

"Michael," came Larissa's voice again. "Open the door."

"Get upstairs. Now," he told Sadie, sliding the deadbolts back.

No sooner had the latch flicked open than a gloved hand crept around the edge and a face peered in. "Oh my, look at this place!"

Michael had almost forgotten about the colourful canvases and decorations that swept through the house. Wrens, Claus-Pritchards, Pendragons, Boswicks, and Tomeses flowed past him like water around a stone.

He watched Sadie fly up the stairs, her hand outstretched, still holding on to something that wasn't there. She vanished from the landing, heading for her room.

As the initial rush subsided, Michael pushed the door shut, stemming the invading flow of icy wind and snow. The house teemed with people gorging on the cornucopia of sugar and pastry and icing and chocolate and colourful sprinkles.

Michael scanned each face on his way to the foot of the stairs. Slowly, he climbed, leaving the party and the intoxicating sweet fragrance behind. When he arrived in the eaved bedroom, Sadie was sitting on the bed looking lost and confused.

Mischief perched beside her, whiskers twitching.

"We're almost there," Michael said, unease knitted into his voice.

"Don't worry, Father," she said comfortingly. "What will be, will be."

Michael shooed the cat off the bed. "That's your grandfather talking."

Sadie's eyes narrowed. "Grandfather William?"

"Yes, Grandfather William. He was a big believer in fate and destiny. Everything happening for a reason, cause and effect. The Clockwork Universe—"

"*The Clockwork Universe?*" Sadie asked. "Like the painting in the hallway?"

"Yes. It's an ancient theory. One that many religious leaders and deists believed in and perhaps still do, in some dark corner of the world, away from Minister Craven, and the Ryndai, and the Eight Day Assembly. The theory drew the universe as a mechanical clock, ticking along, gears whirring around inside. The universe—the clock—was predictable, predetermined in its task. Like fate and destiny. It was believed the Gods made the clock, wound it and sat back, letting it tick into infinity."

Sadie smiled. "I like the idea of that," she said. "The sun and the moon and the stars all spiralling around the world like the hands on a clock. Time moving on inexorably."

Michael rubbed his chin. "Well, yes. I suppose it has a certain sensibility."

"Do you not, Father?"

"It's not that I don't, it's more I cannot," he said. "I have to believe my future, all our futures—especially yours—are in our own hands. Not in the hands of the universe or a clock made by the Gods. And, even if the universe is some divine machine, I need to know we can disrupt the workings of the machine, just for a second, enough to change everything. Do you understand?"

"Of course," she said, smiling. "You want to defy the universe. Simple."

Michael grinned. "Me? No, I'm just a—"

"Yes," Sadie glowered. "What *are* you, Father?"

Michael ignored her. "But you, Sadie. You can do—"

Larissa appeared at the door. "Michael," she whispered. "We have a problem."

Ice lanced his bones. "A problem? What sort of problem?"

"Natalia."

"What's she done now?" Michael sighed, his fear subsided. "Can you deal with it, Larissa? I should stay close to Sadie."

"No, I cannot deal with it. She's hysterical, Michael. Threatening to walk out, leave, run away. You *have* to help me."

"Someone needs to stay with Sadie," Michael said, rising.

"She'll be fine," Larissa replied. "Close the door after you."

"Is this how it begins?" Sadie asked as her mother vanished.

Michael checked his pocket watch, a little over an hour until midnight. "Stay here with Mischief and … Oliver … I'll be back soon."

✸ ☺ ▤ ✻ 🏛

With Michael gone, Oliver emerged from the shadows.

Mischief stared at Sadie, her whiskers rigid, her nose twitching.

Sadie joined them on the window seat. Mischief purred manically, flopping on her side and playfully clawing at Sadie's forearm.

The faerie-lights around the window flicked from red to green to yellow.

"What happened to Natalia?"

Sadie shrugged. "Probably Dimitri," she said, then shook her head. "I don't know. How could I? I'm up here with you."

Oliver's chin sank into his scarf.

"I'm sorry," Sadie said.

"It is fine. I can feel your nervousness, your anxiety."

"I'm taking each minute as it comes."

Sadie's skin rippled.

Shadows dressed the wall.

Feet shuffled on the carpet.

Her head whipped about, her eyes darkened.

"And the next minute belongs to us!"

Three angry boys stood inside the eaved bedroom. The last time Sadie had seen them, she'd been desperately trying to prise Danver off Cale Boswick in the schoolyard.

"Get out of my room."

She spoke slowly, composed.

They moved closer.

"Get out. Now!"

"I don't think so," Tobin said, grinning.

Verden pulled a book from the shelf, leafed through it, then discarded it on the floor.

"Stop that," Sadie growled.

He ignored her, dropping another, then another.

Xander opened her dressing-up trunk. Sadie's skin prickled as he plunged his hands inside. He flung her costumes and props over his shoulder, like a dog digging for a bone, until they were strewn like garbage. At the bottom, beneath her princess gown, he found a tiara. Putting the sparkling costume jewellery on his head, Xander spun in badly executed pirouettes to the delight of his friends. "Look at me. I'm Princess Sadie. Aren't I pretty?"

Tobin and Verden roared with laughter.

"Put that back. Put them all back!"

Tobin launched himself at her. Pressed his face against hers. "You hurt my friend. Hurt him bad. Scarred for life, so they say. Ugly-looking thing it is," he whispered, tracing a line down the side of Sadie's face with a dirty fingernail.

"What?" Sadie said. "I didn't hurt anyone."

Tobin sneered. She could smell beef and tuna in his teeth, blackberry wine on his breath. "You remember Cale Boswick, don't you, Sades?"

"Of course, but I didn't hurt him."

"Really?"

"It was Danver. You know that. You were all there!"

Tobin pulled away. "Danver?"

"You've forgotten about him too, haven't you?"

Verden leant close. "Have you seen Cale's face?" he asked. "Well, have you?"

The boy clasped Sadie's throat and thrust her against the window. The cold bit into her shoulders. Mischief darted between the boys, seeking refuge under the bed. But Xander snatched the cat and lifted her high. Mischief's legs kicked wildly, claws unleashed.

"No, I haven't seen his face. Not properly," Sadie said. "I didn't think Danver hurt him that badly."

"Danver ... *Danver* ... who? Cut it out, Sades! There's no such person. Sounds like you pulled him out of thin air. Is that who you were just talking to? The incredible, invisible Danver! He's nothing. He's nobody! Figment of your imagination."

"Lies!" Sadie spat. "Why doesn't anyone remember him?"

"Have you forgotten what happened?"

"Of course I haven't!"

"*You* attacked Cale Boswick. We all watched you do it."

Sadie went limp. Oliver clutched her arm. His eyes wild with terror.

"I did no such thing. I pulled Danver away. I saved Cale from Danver's rage. Blood. So much blood."

Xander shouldered Tobin and Verden aside, holding Mischief tight to his chest. The cat struggled desperately. "Is this yours?" he asked, looking at Mischief's little face, the tiara twinkling in the faerie-lights.

"Yes," Sadie said nervously. "Please don't hurt her. She's just a cat."

"Yeah, and Cale Boswick is *just* my friend, but that didn't stop you, did it?"

Verden produced a slim brass case from his pocket. He flipped a catch on the bottom and a small blade sprang forth. He thrust the blade millimetres from Sadie's eye.

"You wouldn't dare," Sadie said. "Not here in my bedroom with my parents downstairs."

Verden smiled cruelly. "You're right. I wouldn't hurt *you*."

Sadie let out a long breath.

"But this cat on the other hand—"

"No!" Sadie screamed as the knife closed in on Mischief's twitching face.

The cat squirmed again, more fiercely than before, but Xander's grip held fast. Sadie lurched forward. Her hand flew towards the knife. But something knocked her back. She landed on the window seat. Her head cracked against the window, breaking the glass.

Verden dropped the knife and clattered into the bookcase. He groaned and twisted onto his side. Xander struggled to keep hold of Mischief. Her claws found his hands and arms, ripping the tiara from his head. He cursed as she rent his cheek with three red lines.

Oliver clung to Sadie.

His gaze glued to the incredible sight before him.

Mischief began to bulge and expand.

Xander screamed, released her. The pulsating mass of fur dropped to the floor.

"Wh-what is it?" he said, scrambling into the corner. "Get it away from me!"

The playful tortoiseshell cat was no more.

She became a turbulent storm of black fire, acrid smoke, and arcing sanguine vapours. Spinning like a top, she transformed into a slim column, touching the floor and ceiling, no more than a foot wide. The column descended, shifting, forming the shape of a woman.

A young woman with bone-white skin and cerulean eyes.

"Boys, boys, boys," Genevieve croaked. "Didn't your mothers ever warn you about playing with cats?"

THE HORRIBLE TRUTH

Michael and Larissa loomed over their distraught daughter. Dimitri sat beside her on the bed, his arm around her shoulders. His eyes nervous, confused.

"Natalia," he tried. "It's okay. Everything will be fine."

But Natalia curled her arms around her waist and wailed. She rocked horribly as though she might be sick.

Michael lowered himself onto his haunches.

Gently, he touched Natalia on the forearm.

She recoiled.

"Tell me what happened."

Natalia sniffed. Tears trickled onto Michael's hand.

"You know what happened," she said bitterly. Her eyes were bloodshot, her make-up on the brink of destruction. "Both of you know." Michael and Larissa looked at one another. "Sadie told me," she added. "She told me everything." Natalia's chin dropped to meet her chest. She gulped for air. "Why didn't you tell me? Sixteen years. *Six-teen* years!"

Michael looked at Dimitri. "Can you give us a minute?"

"Natalia?" Dimitri said. "Do you want me to stay?"

She waved him away, as if nothing could console her.

"I'll be with my brothers … should you need me."

"Well," Natalia said, before Dimitri had left the room. "Is it true?"

"Is *what* true?"

"Am I ... an orphan?"

The word hung in the air like poisonous gas.

Larissa took Dimitri's place at Natalia's side.

"We never meant for you to find out this way."

Her affirmation caused Natalia's chin to tremble. A fresh flood of tears ruined what remained of her make-up.

"We love you, Natalia," Michael said. "The same as we love Sadie and Eli. To us, you're our firstborn child. Nobody can take that away from us ... away from *you*."

"Firstborn?" Natalia wept. "First *bought* more like!"

Larissa tried to hug her daughter, but Natalia brushed her aside.

"I always knew something wasn't right," she said. "I always felt like an outsider, but I told myself I was being silly. Silly old Natalia. Worried she wasn't as important, or clever, or as interesting as her siblings."

"Natalia," Larissa tried. "Stop that."

"But I was right all along. Sadie told me about the Foretelling. *The child that has untold power and ... something or other ... will be the firstborn fallen from the sky.*" She shook her head. "And that's who Sadie is ... that's who you are, Father. She told me so. You're all magic and mystery and—" Tears fell in heavy droplets. "It's like one of your horrifying bedtime stories."

"Sadie told you about the Foretelling?" Michael said. And then, almost to himself, "Why would she do such a thing?"

"Why wouldn't she?" Natalia bit. "Why wouldn't *you?*"

Michael searched in vain for the right words.

"So, I've managed to stumble over two big secrets, have I?" Natalia went on, her face hard and filled with disbelief. "I suppose Eli is all tied up in it, too. What with him carrying Madison blood!"

"Don't say such terrible things, Natalia," Michael said, his heart breaking.

"I'm nothing to do with this family, this history, this life. What am I? *Who* am I?"

"You're our daughter," Larissa said, turning Natalia's head to face her. "You're a Madison. Your father and I don't see you as anything else."

"Well, I don't *feel* like a Madison." Natalia pushed off the bed. She dragged her fingers over her eyes, smudging her make-up down her face like two muddy tyre tracks. Staring beyond her parents, Natalia said, "Have you seen what she did?"

Michael frowned. "Who?"

"The *Winter Wonderchild*, of course. Sadie bloody Madison!"

Michael and Larissa turned.

The pristine white walls surrounding her bedroom door were no more. Using Natalia's bright lipsticks, the word *Imposter* had been written hundreds of times across every square inch in chaotic, psychotic handwriting.

"I ... Natalia ... This is—" Larissa tried.

"I'm going to get a drink—a proper drink—and I don't believe I need to ask your permission anymore," Natalia told them, blustering out of the room.

Michael grabbed Larissa's arm. "Leave her," he said soothingly. "Give her time."

"Sadie Madison, what did you do?" Larissa hissed.

"When did this happen? When did Sadie tell her?"

"Just now," Larissa replied. "Outside on the porch. Natalia and Dimitri were last to arrive and then Sadie was there. I didn't hear the door, but she was outside on the porch. I could see them through the library window. I was ... watching. She and Dimitri reminded me of us when we first—"

"And you saw her? You saw Sadie's face?" His voice tight, anxious.

"No. Not her face. The back of her head, but I'd know that hair anywhere."

"But I've had Sadie in my sight ever since we got home," Michael said. A fresh sheet of sweat coated his skin. "She came in with me. Went up to her room. I followed her. She never went back outside."

"Then who—?" Larissa began, but Michael had already bolted out the door.

With Sadie slumped unconsciously against the window, Oliver watched as Genevieve considered the three terrified boys before her. Each of them tried to speak but nothing audible came out. She turned to Xander. Her eyes attracted to the pocket knife. Uttering some beguiling words, the knife glowed white-hot. His skin smoked. The abhorrent smell invaded Oliver's senses. Wailing, the boy tore the blade from his flesh and tossed it onto the carpet.

"Threatening a poor little cat?" Genevieve purred. "Disgraceful."

"I'm sorry, I didn't—" he tried, but Genevieve raised a hand and his voice vanished.

"Where's the other one?" she asked. "Cale Boswick?"

Xander, grasping his burned hand, managed, "At home. His home. He was too afraid to come."

"Too afraid? Of who? Sadie Madison?" Genevieve laughed.

"Yes," he winced. "She did something to him. Something more than the scar, more than the punches. She … changed him."

Sadie floated in darkness. A long thin darkness. A tunnel of black. Was she falling? Ascending? She couldn't tell. His face drifted into view through a curtain of shadow. He smiled. It was her friend. Danver. Somehow, she had found him.

"Changed him? How?"

Tobin risked, "Black magic. Voodoo. Wicca. Dunno."

"Hush," she said, not bothering to meet his eyes. "You—with the burned hand—tell me what she did."

"I don't know." Xander trembled. "But he's not the same. He's quiet, brooding, introverted. Stays inside. Hides in the dark. Never turns the lamps on. And the way he talks—"

"Talks?" Genevieve enquired, an eyebrow raised.

"Mostly, he's fine—"

"Ye-es?"

"But sometimes," Xander said, looking to his friends. "Well, it's gibberish ... most of it. Noise, sounds, not words. At least, not any words I understand."

Genevieve smiled gleefully. "He sounds perfect."

🐛☺▦🕸🏛

Danver's face was exactly as she remembered it. His hair seemed longer. His eyes tired.

The darkness ebbed away to reveal a gloomy dungeon. Torches burned in sconces. The smell of damp and filth filled her nostrils. Sadie moved closer. Iron bars materialised. She took his hands, cold and shivering. Her heart thudded with joy and desperation.

Am I really here? she thought. *Are you here, Danver?*

His face stayed the same. Blank and unblinking.

Sadie grabbed the iron bars and gave them a helpless rattle.

🐛☺▦🕸🏛

Xander, Tobin, and Verden watched as Genevieve opened the bedroom window.

Fable and Puzzle slipped inside.

They scampered onto Sadie's bed and shook the snow from their coats. The witch muttered something incomprehensible to the cats before turning to Xander. He scuttled away like a nervous crab.

"Give me your hand," she ordered.

Xander looked for help but his friends' faces were white, frozen. Tentatively, he stretched his damaged hand towards her. Genevieve licked her index finger, uttering more unfathomable words, then pressed it to the wound. Xander let out a small squeal in anticipation of the pain, but there appeared to be none. He pulled his hand back and examined it, disbelievingly.

The wound had gone.

"Now," she said. "Let's go and see about Cale Boswick."

The bars were solid, cold and wet. The more she shook them, the more they refused to break. Danver smiled at her. A soft, reassuring smile.

Danver's smile.

I need to get you out of here. You don't belong here. You belong with me.

The misery of the dungeon soaked into her bones. She tried to imagine how Danver felt. She'd only been here minutes but was already consumed by pain and confusion.

Everyone's forgotten you, Danver. Your mother and father. Cale and his followers. Everyone. I'll come for you, Danver. You're real. I know you are. No matter what everyone says. I'll find you. No matter what it takes.

Danver pointed to Sadie's chest. She looked down and there, hanging from a thin brass chain, was a rusty key. She plunged it into the lock.

Click.

Sadie opened her eyes to find Michael shaking her lightly by the shoulders.

"Sadie. Wake up. Are you okay?"

She gave him a thumbs-up, still half in the dream. She reached for the key around her neck but clutched nothing but the buttons of her black cotton dress.

"Sadie," Michael said, his voice urgent. "Did you speak to Natalia?"

She looked around the room. The boys had gone. Mischief too.

"Natalia?"

"Yes. Did you speak to her this evening? Did you tell her about … about being adopted, about being an orphan?"

The last traces of her vision were wrenched from her. "No. I would never do that."

"And the Foretelling—?"

"What makes you think I would—?"

But Sadie had already joined up the dots.

"Sofia."

꙳ ꙶ ▤ ꙴ ꙲

Laughter and celebration filled the Madison house. The delicious smell of Larissa's hot apple and blackcurrant pies erupted from beneath the sailcloth awning.

Eli perched by the landing window, staring down Leviathan Crook with his Monster Magnifiers strapped to his head, his notebook on his lap.

He turned the small yellow envelope in his hands.

Tomorrow, it had said.

Tomorrow was *today*.

Only an hour remained.

He would be here soon. He had to be. He said so.

Snow fell past the window the same way it had for what seemed like years but was only weeks. Fire candles burned on the front lawn and every lawn throughout Iron Bridge. Below, the sound of the Madison jongelier clicked and clacked as the wind twisted beneath the awning.

Something sparkled on the snow.

Something weaved its way up Leviathan Crook.

Eli adjusted his Monster Magnifiers, zeroing in on a long, black, important-looking automobile.

It pulled up outside the Madison house.

A tall man got out.

He stood in the street looking up at the darkened window.

Eli reached for his pen.

THE
CONJURING

Genevieve stood in the living room of the Boswick's enormous house, surrounded by half-finished plates and glasses stained with greasy fingerprints, wine, and lipstick. On a plush, velvet couch sat Xander, Tobin, and Verden. Their faces like ash.

Beside her sat Fable and Puzzle. Both cats seemed agitated, restless. "I suppose you'd like me to begin," the witch said to them, her blue eyes shimmering through the gloom.

Puzzle flicked her ears.

Fable mewed helplessly.

Genevieve turned to Cale Boswick. The boy squirmed in a leather armchair facing a grand fireplace. With his head bent towards his chest, the scar on his face glistened in the dying embers. "So lovely of you to join us, Cale," Genevieve said. "You have your *friends* to thank for the introduction."

"What do you want?" he asked timidly, shielding his face. "Take whatever you like. My father has money, and gold, and antiques from every corner of—"

"Hush, boy," she bit, like an impatient headmistress. "I have no need of your father's worldly goods and chattels. Keep them … for all the good they'll do. They'll outlive the lot of you." Puzzle screeched impatiently. "Calm down, sister."

"What do you want then?" Cale rumbled.

"*You*," she said, giving him a wicked stare. "Well, I want your body."

Cale looked confused. A sheen of panic glazed his skin.

"A vessel," she added.

"Like ... a boat?"

"Yes, boy. Exactly like a boat. But a boat for one passenger. And one passenger only."

Cale looked at his friends. Their eyes were aching, streaming, wild with fear. "Who?" he asked. "What passenger?"

Genevieve smiled gloriously. "The Horned God, of course."

Cale shuddered.

Genevieve watched his face. "You're thinking of some devil or demon scribbled down in an ancient text."

Cale nodded.

"And you'd be wrong. Wrong, wrong, wrong," Genevieve said, her voice becoming almost contrary. "He goes by many names, and by none at all. He is everything. And nothing. The Horned God, the Lord of the Nyx, the Unknown, Void, King Nothing. And Malmortem—to those who know him best." She turned from Cale and looked at the terrified trio on the couch. "I'm sure you'd all like to meet him."

They shared a reluctant nod.

"Excellent," she said. "Then I shall begin."

Outside, latecomers made their way towards the Madison house. They sang cheerfully, dreaming of something sweet and tasty. Cale didn't look the least bit cheerful or hungry. He looked afraid. Deathly afraid. His stomach audibly churned with fear.

Genevieve opened her black robes and produced Sadie's tiara. Yanking out several strands of her own hair, she fastened two black feathers to the costume jewellery, forming a pair of horns. Then, with outstretched arms, she lowered the dark crown ceremoniously onto Cale's trembling head.

"Lovely," she enthused, admiring her handiwork. Both cats meowed, low and sorrowful. "Very Lordly."

Genevieve closed her eyes, her hands raised high. She began to chant, uttering noises in the back of her throat. Gargling, dark noises. Malformed, disfigured, broken. Whatever light remained in the room slipped away. A darkness took them all. A darkness thicker than shadows.

Cale's face twisted. It looked as though somebody had jabbed ten thousand needles into every inch of his skin. He opened his mouth to scream but the needles punctured his tongue. He gagged, choking on his own voice. He retched, clawing at his stomach, his chest, his throat.

A passenger.

Genevieve opened her eyes and stared at Malmortem.

He sat awkwardly in the armchair, stretching Cale's arms and legs as if to test them, flicking his tongue against the roof of his mouth. After inspecting the dark crown with mild curiosity, Malmortem turned to the witch.

"Genevieve," he rumbled. "You do realise what time it is?"

"Yes, my love," Genevieve said. "It's my sisters."

Malmortem stared at the two cats. "What of them?"

"It was the child. She banished them to the Nyx." Genevieve's fingers trembled on her folded thighs. "I've returned them to their animal form, but further transfiguration magics require the power of three. I alone cannot—"

Malmortem moved his head slowly, observing Fable and Puzzle—Edith and Dorothea—as black filaments from his feathered horns fell around him. "Yes," he said, almost bored. "Cats have never fully mastered the Words of Shadow, have they?" He laughed then, coarse and empty. "And who are these three?"

Malmortem turned his head to the boys. The unearthly look in his eyes made them cower, whimpering, desperate to escape. "Agents of the Gathering Order," Genevieve replied proudly. "Verden Wren, Tobin Claus-Pritchard, Xander Pendragon. I caught them closing in on the girl."

"No," Malmortem replied, studying each in turn. "These are no agents. Bullies, ignorants, spoilt children of a wealthy house."

"An offering then," Genevieve countered, flustered. "To do with as you see fit."

Verden let out a whimper.

"Boys?" Malmortem snorted. "Nothing but weaklings and cravens."

Genevieve's jaw quivered. "But loyal, my love. They would bend to your will. If they were so inclined. And three ... I know how pleasing threes can be."

Malmortem steepled Cale's hands, pressing the index fingers to his bottom lip. "And what of the child?"

"We've watched her for almost thirteen years at your behest. We shadow her on wings and paws, except in the Glade beyond the schoolyard for it is sacred ground. Lately, she leaves the house for hours, using music to distract and confound her family. She returned to the hospital where it all began. The Living was there. We were exposed. She saw us all. The child used her music to vanquish my sisters."

"Yet somehow you escaped," Malmortem said, an eyebrow raised.

"Barely."

Malmortem ran Cale's fingers over the scar on his cheek. "Enough," he whispered.

Dorothea and Edith instantly appeared next to Genevieve, huddled on all fours. They adjusted themselves before Malmortem, smoothing their hair and straightening their black robes.

"Thank you, master," Edith and Dorothea said, their voices hoarse.

"Thank you, my love," Genevieve added.

"The hour is upon us," Malmortem said. "Return to the house, watch her vigilantly. Do not let her slip through your fingers. The agents of the Gathering Order are still at large. Find them. Destroy them. Bring me the child."

"And you?"

"My movements are none of your concern, witch," he fired scornfully. "I am in many places and none at all."

Genevieve dropped her head. Her fingers jittered on her lap.

"Go. Now." His voice thinned to a whisper. "I will take care of these … boys."

She took her trembling sisters by the hand and led them off the sofa. They swept across the living room, to the door. Edith and Dorothea were already outside when Genevieve looked back at the Horned God, the Lord of the Nyx, the Unknown, Void, King Nothing, the one she knew as Malmortem.

Cale's body stood before Xander, Verden, and Tobin. The Horned God swarmed through every artery and organ, smothering the boy's mind, controlling every atom. He spread his arms, opened his mouth, and drowned the three boys in a terrible, blinding light.

✸ ☡ 🗎 ⚚ ⛫

Michael and Larissa worked their way through the party, making small talk, accepting endless compliments on the desserts, all the while searching desperately for Natalia.

Sadie brushed against the window by the front door. Outside, at least two dozen Ryndai had gathered on Leviathan Crook. Sadie had never seen so many together in one place.

No one had.

She wondered if the infamous Storm was among them.

Drawing the curtain, she zigzagged through the library and found Natalia pouring ziela into a tumbler in Michael's study. "Here you are," she said, leaning against the doorjamb. "Mother and Father are sick with worry."

"What do you care?" Natalia said, not bothering to turn. "Only an hour and it'll be your birthday. You'll be thirteen, a teenager. The first *true* Madison teenager. You won't show any concern for me when all the attention is on you." She took a large gulp from the glass and raised her eyebrows at Sadie.

"I know you're sad, Natalia. Angry, of course. Betrayed. I know how that feels."

"You?" she scoffed. "What could you possibly know?"

Sadie sighed and moved into the room. "I know what it is to hurt. I know what it is to lose something you care about. That's why I have Oliver."

He stepped out from behind her. Natalia took another hasty mouthful. "What *are* you?" she asked, staring at the strange-looking boy. "Both of you?"

"We're your family, Natalia."

"Really? We're nothing alike. I cannot ace all my exams. I cannot suddenly play the piano like a seasoned master. I cannot create people out of thin air. I'm not part of some scary prophecy. I don't even have the famous chaotic Madison hair! We're not family, Sadie. We're just two people who live together. Two people who grew up together. Two people that couldn't be more different if they tried."

"Natalia," Sadie moved forward. "You *are* my sister. We may not share the same blood, but we share the same memories, the same childhood, the same days together, here, in this house. Lorntide, Eoster, Atticus, the three wise cats, the Candlelight Parades, Father's stories, our nightly parlour games, and the birthday parties. There's a party going on right now. A party to remember, a party to serve as the backdrop for more amazing memories."

Natalia drained the glimmering red ziela.

"You're my big sister, Natalia. Always have been. Always will be."

Natalia shifted her weight, the effects of the ziela were clearly faster and stronger than she'd expected.

"And we're connected," Sadie added. "The Nepenthe. You can see Oliver. That's not something any sisters share, is it? That's something truly special."

Recklessly filling the tumbler again, Natalia collapsed into Michael's chair. "It's not special, Sadie. It's downright odd," she said. "And what happened to the other one—to Danver?"

Sadie's eyes widened. "You remember him?"

"Of course. I saw him in that horrid dungeon. The smell,

Sadie. It was disgusting."

"But you remember him here? In the house, having breakfast with us, at school, the fight with Cale Boswick?"

Natalia shook her head. "What? No." She sighed. "Just the dream. The dungeon."

"No. He was here that morning. We were having pancakes."

Natalia shook her head. "I don't remember that. All I know is the dungeon and the smell, and you talking about him incessantly, but I don't know his face. I can't picture him, not completely."

Something painful ran through Sadie's chest. "He's fading," she whispered. "Erased … from existence."

Oliver put a hand on her shoulder.

"He's not real," Natalia countered.

Sadie fought hard to quell the anger that rose inside, yet traces still bubbled to the surface.

"Lies," she seethed.

A tear bloomed in her eye.

"It's pretend, Sadie." Natalia sighed. The alcohol slowed her words. "Like all the clothes and toys in your dressing-up trunk. They were all made in some factory. They weren't worn by princesses, and evil sorcerers, and knights on white horses. But that's all there seems to be with you. One big drama. A theatrical nonsense, a badly plotted farce, a soulless play with callous words and empty promises!"

Natalia shrugged and took another gulp of ziela.

Tears spilled down Sadie's cheeks. "I know they're costumes. I'm not a child. Why are you being so horrid?"

"Me? Horrid? No, Sadie. I'm being honest. I'm telling you the truth, the same as you did when you told me all about Michael and Larissa and how I wasn't their daughter. How I was an imposter. Now, *that* was horrible."

Sadie desperately wanted to tell her it wasn't her doing, that Sofia was the one to rip Natalia's life to pieces, but she knew her sister would think it another fantasy, another Oliver, another—*Danver?*

Sadie cursed herself for such a horrid thought, for questioning her belief in her friend.

"I'm sorry," Sadie said, taking the blame for Sofia's meddling.

Natalia stared. "Why?" she asked. "Why couldn't you leave things the way they were? Why did you have to go and ruin it all?"

Sadie had no answers. "Is there no small part of you that feels relief to know the truth?"

"Yes, Sadie," Natalia began sarcastically. "All those doubts, and anxieties, and feelings of inadequacy that you and Eli made me feel have now been resolved. I feel so much better knowing I was right all along."

Sadie retreated a little. "I'm sorry," she tried. "This is the most honest conversation we've ever had."

"Is that right, Sadie? How clever of you to notice. Does this make you feel any better about everything? About what you've done?" Her eyes were thin and angry, cool yet luminescent. "You'll repent for everything in that place. They'll make you remember every last thing you've done to this family. There's no better place on earth for you than Hurtmore House."

"What?"

"You're going, aren't you?" Natalia said, knowingly. "You're going to Hurtmore House. To that dungeon. To look for Danver. I can tell. We may not be sisters, but we are, as you said, connected."

"I *am* your sister."

"Not in my eyes, Sadie." She drained the last of her drink before adding, "The fight, the music, the awful truth. My sister left a week ago!" Natalia shouldered passed Sadie. Turning in the study doorway, she added, "Perhaps I'll finally find happiness when you're gone for good."

Natalia was right, of course. She had changed a week ago. Everything she'd known or cared about had revealed itself to be something else. Music had found her, the dreams, the nightmares, and Oliver. She turned to the long window and stared out into the night.

Lightning cracked above the industrial district, causing Sadie's shadow to strobe against the wall. Her reflection glimmered in the windowpane for a moment. Her face looked sad yet purposeful. She sighed deeply. Rain peppered the glass.

Sadie smiled.

But the reflection did not smile back.

☀☽▤⚒⛰

Sofia lingered at the window. A lopsided, mischievous grin stained her face. Her hair plastered to her ink-stained scalp. She flattened a finger against the glass and etched a thin line with a ragged nail. Sadie blinked and her ghostly twin darted into the darkness.

She moved to follow but Oliver blocked the doorway.

"We should stay here," he said. "In the study. Where it is safe."

Sadie could feel her legs gearing up to run. The restless, nervous energy spread through her body. "But *she* is outside, Oliver. I have to know what happened to her."

"Sadie. Wait!"

A tumultuous storm gathered in the heavens. There was little protection from it under the porch. Rain came in sideways, hard and true, like falling bullets. Lightning cracked the sky. Thunder rolled down the valley like an avalanche. Oliver pursued Sadie to the end of the porch, beyond the window where Sofia had stood, and vaulted the fence.

Oliver took her arm and tried to spin her around.

"What is it?" she said, agitated, searching for signs of Sofia.

Oliver paused. The silver in his hair had almost overtaken his entire head. Only a thin band of black remained. "I know."

"You know what?"

"I know what happened to her."

Sadie rolled her shoulders. "You? How do *you*—?" She bit

her bottom lip. The rain drilling against her skin. "She told you? She told you what happened?" Sadie said, raising her voice above the storm. "Was it like Father said? Did she die at birth? Why is she here? Why now?"

Oliver tried to calm her, but she looked angrier with each passing moment. "She died. That is true. She died and you lived. There is no changing the past. Sadie, please. Come inside before whatever is about to happen happens."

"Oliver, tell me."

Her unruly hair lost its fight with the rain.

"She is still here, Sadie," he admitted. "Sofia. She is ... in the basement."

"No, Oliver. She went running down the side of the house."

"Not *that* Sofia. The real Sofia."

Sadie dragged her hair off her face.

A gust of wind knocked her off-balance.

"What?"

"She is ... She is in a ... She has those dark markings on her head. They did something to her. Something to do with the Foretelling."

Sadie struggled to hear him. "What did they do?"

"I do not know, Sadie." He tried to reach out and take her hand, but she forced him away.

"You lied to me," she said, backing up. "You, Oliver, lied to me. How can that be?"

"I did not lie—"

"You kept secrets from me. You're no better than Father ... and Vulpes!"

"That is not fair," Oliver said. "I was protecting you. I was trying to be your friend. Trying to shield you from the horrors of your past. I was just—"

Sadie's face told him to stop. "So, tell me—*friend*—what happened? What happened to me and Sofia thirteen years ago?" Oliver tried to give nothing away, but Sadie could feel the truth seeping from him. She could see his thoughts, tinged with her anger, as they developed in her mind like a pictogram.

She saw a basement, an old woman, a bell jar and the infant encased in formaldehyde. She saw the dark markings etched around the child's scalp. And then she saw her father standing next to the caged child, emotionless and cold. "Sofia. Father. Oliver—?" Her words formed slowly, fragile, ready to snap.

"I am so sorry, Sadie," he said. "It was too much for me. I could barely think of it myself. I had no idea what it would do to you. They had hidden it from you for so long that perhaps it was better left that way."

He shook his head, soaking wet, lost.

"They?" Sadie said. "My father and—?"

"Sadie. The old woman. It is—"

"Karolinja?"

Oliver nodded.

"Your grandmother is alive."

THE MAN
WITH NO FACE

Oliver became shredded, torn. Something inside had broken. Something that could never properly be repaired. Sadie could feel it. She knew he'd feel this way forever. That he'd carry it with him until the end of all things.

Sadie marched up the side of the house.

Oliver followed.

She placed an untied boot onto the slush-covered lawn and froze in wonder. Music swirled through the winter air. She turned her head, wondering where it had come from.

It wasn't from her.

Someone or something else was doing this.

Caught in the music, Sadie imagined that this wondrous, magical, transcendent sensation was how the people of Iron Bridge felt when she played.

She crossed the snow-packed lawn, turning in circles.

The music called to her.

And then, where there had been nobody at all, Sadie bumped into a tall, well-dressed gentleman. She smiled and looked up at his face.

He wore a dark purple suit—which might have been brighter had it not been soaked through—and a jauntily placed top hat.

She looked at his face again.

He wore white gloves, possibly velvet, and in one hand he held an ebony walking cane with a silver terminal. She squinted, the rain running into her eyes, and concentrated on his face.

A moustache, perhaps a beard.

And, on his left lapel, he wore a shiny broach. The initials W.S. sat proudly over a floral wreath in silver and gold.

She looked towards his face once more.

Something forced her eyes away.

"Don't worry," he said. "Nobody can see my face. Well, not my real face anyway. And especially not here."

Sadie took a step back. A strange warmth touched her, as though sitting in the afternoon sun, but all around the rain persisted. The world became quiet, like someone had twisted the storm volume dial down to zero.

"Why can't I see your face?"

"Does it matter?"

"Sort of. I've never been unable to see someone's face before. Apart from the Ryndai as they cover theirs with shemaghs."

"What do you think I look like," the man said. "Describe it."

"Describe it? Why?"

"You can imagine a face, can't you? It's not hard. I was always imagining things when I was a boy."

"Of course I can. Danver and I are always—" The words caught in her throat. "I'm brilliant at imagining things," she countered, and closed her eyes. "Well, you have a long, thin face—like a fish—and chestnut eyes beneath bushy eyebrows. A long, twisted moustache sits below a pointy nose. You have a protruding, knobbly chin covered in rough stubble and, despite the unkempt nature of the rest of your face, your teeth are crystal white."

She opened her eyes and found him kneeling before her.

His face was exactly the way she had described it.

"Hello, Sadie Madison," he said, as their eyes connected. "My name is Doktor Robey Merrick."

Sadie shuddered. Her arms crossed her chest. Fire burned through her. Disgust and hate boiled her blood. This was not the face of the man who stole Danver away to Hurtmore House. This was a kind face. A silly face. A face that made Sadie smile just by looking at it.

"What's the matter, my dear?"

She backed away. "I should hate you, but—"

"Hate me? Whatever for?" He twisted his moustache theatrically between long, gloved fingers.

"You took my best friend away. You took Danver."

"Well," Doktor Merrick said, now towering over Sadie. "That is a matter of some conjecture."

"Conjecture?"

"Yes, a matter with insufficient proof—"

"I know what conjecture means," she replied hotly. "You came to Danver's house after the fight in the schoolyard and took him away in that long black automobile of yours."

"That's what *you* say," the doktor replied. "Others might say differently."

"Others? You mean all the people who forgot about Danver. Arnold and Fisher. Xander, Verden, and Tobin. Mother, Father, and Natalia. The Narrowers have been at them all, clawing their memories away. Just like Father and Vulpes tried to do to me. Eradicating every last ounce of him. But I know the truth. I *know* Danver is real."

"Others might say that … *you* … were the one to fight with Cale Boswick."

"Others are liars!"

"But if they weren't, Sadie." He spread his hand expansively. "If they weren't liars, can you imagine what that would mean?"

"Of course I can."

"Do tell."

Images of this other reality—this lie—tumbled through her imagination. "If I was the one that fought Cale at school, then it would mean Danver never existed. It would mean Danver wasn't real. That I imagined him. That I made him up all along."

"Do you think, in the deepest, darkest reaches of your mind, this could be true?"

"No," Sadie replied immediately. "Not at all. We've been friends forever."

"But you can *imagine* it not being real?" the doktor pressed. "You said you were brilliant at imagining things."

Sadie shook her head.

She didn't want to think of it—but she *could* picture it. The same way she could picture herself as a princess in a tower, or a cosmonaut being fired into space, or a thirteen-year-old girl without a trouble in the world.

"I can see it," she said, agitated. "Of course I can see it. I can see everything, anything. I see things in the night, in daydreams, with my waking eyes. Things I shouldn't know about, things I should never have seen. I don't know where they come from. They're just ... there."

The doktor smiled. "Good," he said. "I'm not trying to upset you, Sadie. Everybody remembers things in different ways, true? Everybody sees things differently, so everyone's memory of the same event will be slightly, and sometimes dramatically, different. Not wrong, just unique and personal, that's all."

"So?" Sadie said. "Are you saying everyone else remembers seeing me fight Cale Boswick and only I remember Danver doing it?"

"That's one explanation. And you believe the Narrowers changed—or rather, took away—everyone else's memory of Danver? Even his parents."

"I don't know. Yes. That seems the most likely. I don't know why they'd do such a horrible thing." Sadie looked at his long, thin face. "What do you know of the Narrowers?"

"As much as I need to," he replied curtly, shifting his top hat forward. "Now, prepare yourself." Doktor Merrick swung his ebony cane in a wide circle overhead. The silver terminal glowed white. A plume of soft sparks showered from the end like a firework.

Everything vanished.

The garden, the house, the rain, the snow.

Everything.

Sadie glared into the utter darkness around her. "Is this the Nyx? I've been here before," she said. "But only in a dream. This is … real?"

Doktor Merrick laughed. "Only as real as you want it to be, as real as you can imagine."

"I'm imagining this?"

"Yes," he said. "But then we imagine everything, don't we? Have you ever thought where everything comes from? All the people and places, the animals, trees, houses, the sun and moon? We see them, yes, with our eyes. But it's our minds telling us what they look like. So, if we have a certain type of mind—one like yours—then we can make things appear however we want. We can see people with eyes in the back of their heads, with forked tongues, or fifteen ears. We can see a black sun in a tartan sky. We can see monsters. We can *be* monsters. We can talk to animals. We can do whatever we can imagine. We are limited by that, and that alone."

Sadie stared into the darkness.

"The Nyx is an imagining of utter nothingness," he went on. "As well as being the place where all things come from. It's a place to keep unwanted things. A metaphysical oubliette, if you will. The Vents, Sadie. A place for the lost, the dead, and the forgotten. The unknown and the unknowable."

"Malmortem."

"Yes. Quite," the doktor said. "You've learnt much, Sadie Madison."

"But I haven't learnt what happened to Danver. Did you take him? That's all I need to know. The rest I'll figure out for myself." She sighed. "Doktor Merrick? Did you take my best friend from me?"

He stared at her.

His bushy eyebrows twitched.

Instead of answering, he used his cane to produce a circle of light over her head.

✻☺▤⚐♨

Larissa was making pancakes. They smelt amazing. Eli was halfway through his stack.

Doktor Merrick and Sadie stood to one side and watched the scene.

Heavy footfalls clomped down the stairs.

Sadie felt lightheaded to see herself wander into the kitchen and smile at her brother.

Michael and Natalia quickly joined them.

The lure of pancakes never failed to deliver.

"It's the morning after you first heard the story," Doktor Merrick said. "Over a week ago."

"I know," Sadie answered, staring at herself. "I saw one of my father's memories. That was painful, not just for what I saw, but being there. In that place. Inside someone else's memory."

Doktor Merrick nodded.

"But this—seeing myself from another point of view—is singularly the most peculiar feeling in the world."

"You'll get used to it."

Sadie jumped up from the table and ran to the door.

Her family seemed puzzled.

Sadie watched herself open the front door, conduct a short conversation, and then invite Danver into the house.

But Danver was not there.

Not a shimmer, nor an outline.

Nothing.

"Where is he?" Sadie asked. "Why can't I see him?"

"This is their collective memory of that morning, Sadie. This is how your family remembers these events."

"They don't see him? They're just … playing along?" She nibbled her bottom lip. "They don't know he's there."

The doktor twirled his cane and Danver appeared, standing by the kitchen table brandishing a ripe red apple. Both Sadies smiled at their friend. Doktor Merrick spun his cane once more and Danver melted away, along with the kitchen and the Madison family.

Sadie found herself in the music room at school. It was wildly disorientating to switch locations in this way. She wondered if it was how Oliver felt when he jumped from place to place.

Her other self pulled the dust sheet from the piano and began to play.

Sadie listened in awe and amazement at the dexterity and precision of her fingerwork, the beauty of the melodies, the maturity of her phrasing, and the magic the performance evoked. Eli stood at the end of the piano, smiling brightly. He looked astonished by his sister's skill. His notebook gripped tightly between his fingers.

"This is Eli's memory," Sadie said to the doktor, who nodded. "Does he know Danver is there?"

"He believes Danver is there because he watched you talk to him under the piano, but not enough for him to see your friend. There, look. A shimmer. A twist in the light."

It was true.

She could make out a boy-sized shape standing next to Eli. The wall and bookcases behind him were skewed and distorted, as if viewed through a heat haze. Sadie's music grew in magnificence and splendour, until she hit the dark notes.

The notes that changed everything.

Sadie watched closely.

As the dark notes spiralled, the girl at the piano looked unhinged and ragged. Her head shook from side to side as the dark notes died in the air. She slammed the piano lid, then bolted for the door.

Eli tucked his notebook under his belt and tore after her.

Sadie and Doktor Merrick were in the schoolyard before the attack on Cale Boswick took place. Cale and his friends were stood in the snow discussing Lorntide and the forthcoming New Year's celebrations. They seemed genuinely excited about the winter season, almost human. Something Sadie had not expected.

The schoolyard shook with commotion, like a gathering storm. Sadie barrelled down the front steps, knocking two girls and their books flying as she pounded towards Cale and his friends, her face distant, oneiric, her fists clenched.

"What am I doing?" Sadie said, gripping the doktor's sleeve. "This isn't what happened."

He put a gloved hand over hers and stroked it soothingly. "This is what everyone remembers, Sadie. This is what everyone else saw. This is what they believe."

"Well, look who's come to play—" Cale snorted.

Sadie's fists connected with his face.

Cale crashed to the ground.

Eli sprinted across the schoolyard as Sadie's blows rained down on the stricken boy. He dived on his sister.

Knocked her onto the reddening snow.

Sadie buried her face in Doktor Merrick's coat. She couldn't bear to watch any more. "It's too much," she burbled from somewhere in the purple suit. "I did this? Did I do this? Did I hurt Cale Boswick?"

"You needed Oliver," he began. "Even then, at the start. Whether you knew it or not, you were destined to put your fear aside and do all the things you could never do without him."

"Really?"

"You needed to make space for Oliver. You could never do that while Danver stood at your side." The doktor paused. "It was you that sent him away."

Mischief sat on the window seat of the eaved bedroom, shifting her attention between the outside world and the bed.

A lantern flickered as Sadie slept.

A strange man stood beside her.

Sadie had to steady herself at the sudden change of location.

"Who's that?" she asked, staring through bleary eyes.

They were sat on the window seat next to Mischief.

The cat didn't appear to notice them.

"Well," he said. "That's me."

"No, it cannot be. He's small and round." Sadie looked at the tall, thin doktor. He raised a bushy eyebrow. "I don't remember this. I mean, I don't remember him ... you ... being here."

"You were asleep, Sadie."

Standing slowly, Sadie wandered to the other side of the room. Her other self lay asleep. The bedclothes tucked under her chin. The doktor had his podgy fingers pressed to her forehead. He shook his head and muttered incomprehensibly to himself.

"What are you doing?" Sadie said to him, but he did not answer.

"It's useless, Sadie. This is a memory. You cannot interact with it."

She looked around the room. "Whose memory? There's no one here." The cat yawned noiselessly, filling the air with the stench of old fish. "Not Mischief's?"

"This is your memory, Sadie. A subconscious memory. You'll find it if you search hard enough. Subconscious memories are exactly that. Things you don't know you know. Or, rather, things you know, but you don't know that you know them."

Sadie waved a hand in surrender. "So, I can remember what happened to me even while I'm asleep?"

"In part. The memory might be fractured, incomplete. Like trying to recall a dream in the moments after you wake. It only lasts an instant and then ... gone. Piecing them back together can be difficult. For most of us it's utterly impossible."

The small, round doktor spoke. "Now, Sadie. Tell me what happened. From the beginning. Everything. Spare no detail."

His hand pressed lightly against her forehead.

Sadie's eyes were suddenly open, but glazed, faraway. "It all started with the story. The one about the Narrowers." Her body shuddered beneath the bedclothes. "And the Vents, and Grandfather William. I told Danver about it." Again, she shuddered. "He didn't believe me. Danver said my father was making it up, but I knew it was true because I've never forgotten a single thing. Not one thing."

"Tell me about Danver," he asked, his fingers shuffling about on her forehead.

"Danver went crazy after hearing the story and the music. He attacked Cale Boswick. I hope he's okay. I hope—"

The small, round doktor withdrew his hand and rested it on his lap. "Danver needs to go away for a little while. He'll be perfectly safe. He's not well. Not well at all. He cannot be around you and the music. You need some time apart."

"No," Sadie protested. "I need Danver. I need him more than anything else in the world."

"This is not true, Sadie. There is another you need."

"Another?"

"When the time is right, you and Danver will be reunited." He smoothed her eyelids shut. "Fear not. I'll take excellent care of him."

Watching by the bedside, Sadie experienced something worse than death.

True loneliness.

THE
WITCHING HOUR

Angry cloud raged overhead, ominous and vengeful. Oliver emerged from the shadows as Sadie and a tall, thin man flickered in and out of the stormlight.

"With Danver around, you would never have seen the things you've seen or learnt the things you've learnt," the man was saying as Oliver approached. "But most importantly you would never have created Oliver." The doktor smiled at Oliver. "He is the most important thing you have ever done."

"He's my Fear."

"Of course he is."

Sadie stared at Oliver.

A mix of anger and relief welled in her eyes.

"Without Oliver you would never have escaped the museum pursued by Hobbsworth. You would never have followed the Ice Fox through the brightly coloured door. You would never have run with the Fire Wolves. Never sat opposite Vulpes. And as for the Wretched, well, your fear of them would have been your undoing. Oliver saved you from all that. He is more powerful than you could possibly imagine."

Twirling his cane like a baton, the doktor led Sadie down the garden.

The air fizzed. Electric. Alive.

Something moved in the shadows beneath the sandstone wall.

It shifted awkwardly.

Lurched forward.

"For example," said Doktor Merrick. "May I present, for one night only: Goofang, Glawackus, Hodag, the Cactus Cat, the Winter Witches, the Axe-Handle Hound, Wendigo, and Ratchet Owl—monsters from your father's bedtime stories—and a legion of your other favourites too, Sadie."

Her father's creatures shambled, lurched, and slithered into view. Behind them came a mighty throng of others— abominations from her nightmares, from her penny dreadfuls and horror grimoires, things that should never have been. A sea of leathery wings, horns, teeth, and burning eyes. The smell of blood, decay, and death weaved its way around her.

Strobes of lightning cut through the rainstorm, illuminating the monsters. They seemed far bigger than Oliver had ever imagined. More foul and murderous. Radiating with silent dread.

Panic overwhelmed Oliver.

The creatures were upon them.

Nightmarish beasts all around.

The doktor held up a white-gloved hand and they stopped. Their chests rose and fell. Hot vile breath streamed into the night.

"Choose one," the doktor said simply.

"For what purpose?"

"Not you, dearest Sadie," he said.

His gaze fell on her terrified friend.

"M-me?"

"Sooner or later we must all confront our fears." The doktor adjusted his gloves. "What scares Sadie more than anything else in the entire universe? What's her biggest fear?"

Oliver could barely look at the monsters, much less decide on one to confront. What did that mean? Was he supposed to engage them in combat?

"Shall I pick for you?" Sadie said. "I think I know what it is."

"No," the doktor instructed. "Oliver *must* choose."

"But how? Why?" he protested. "I am nothing. Her Fear, and that alone."

The doktor laughed. "You're much more than that, Oliver."

Sadie unzipped one of her pockets and pulled out a piece of folded paper. She flattened it against her thigh. Held it up. Oliver scanned the paper as it became dotted with rainwater.

There were three words.

Repeated over and over and over.

Leave Me Alone. Leave Me Alone. Leave Me Alone.

"You did this, Oliver," she told him, shaking the soaked manuscript. "You did something beyond anything I can explain. You did magic. *Real* magic."

Oliver took a deep breath and turned to the wall of terrifying creations. "Okay, okay," he said, his voice as small as a woodlouse. "I will do it."

He closed his eyes and tried to picture all the monstrosities in his head. To see why each frightened Sadie, why they were part of her fear. Why they were part of him. Each face soared into view. Snarling, growling, whispering, screaming, scheming. It seemed too much. There were hundreds. No, thousands. Brutal, reckless creatures waiting to rip him apart. What good was he against the prowess of Glawackus, the strength of a minotaur, the cunning of the Winter Witches, the speed of a vampire?

Vulpes lurked in the throng. His bald white head and bejewelled teeth gleamed menacingly. A green vial of Nepenthe twirled through his fingers. The Wretched stood beside him, smiling and laughing darkly. A shadow, shaped like a winged devil with long, twisted horns, rose above them all, claws outstretched to the sky.

Were they actually here—this legion of monsters—stood in the Madison garden? Or was this some dark magic, a cheap trick, an illusion? Perhaps, but wasn't that him too? That was Oliver's origin—an illusion, imaginary, pretend, like all the characters Sadie had pulled from her dressing-up trunk.

The last lock of Oliver's black hair turned silver-white.

"The choice is made," announced Doktor Merrick.

The sea of creatures parted. They groaned and jabbered as a much smaller, human-sized figure emerged. She stood six feet from them. Her chaotic hair blustered in the wind.

"She's my biggest fear?" Sadie whispered, the question directed at both Oliver and Doktor Merrick. "That cannot be. I do not fear *Sofia*."

"Quite so," the doktor said. "For this is *not* Sofia."

"Then who—?" she began. "It's me? But ... I'm not a monster."

The Sadie Madison standing before her, surrounded by hulking shadows, glided forward. "But you are scared of the monster you might become," the girl said, looking down at herself. She clicked her neck and crunched her knuckles. Twisting her body in a dark pirouette, she spiralled and transformed all at once. Her clothes melted into a simple black gown. Her unruly hair instantly styled with intricate plaits. Her eyes wild and fierce. She snickered darkly. "This frightens you more than anything in the entire world. A dark future. A life of destruction and death. The Foretelling." She balled her hands together, then ripped them apart to create an orb of white fire. It spun above her open palms, fizzing and crackling. Whipping her arms through the air, she launched the fireball into the Madison house.

Sadie's childhood home exploded in a deafening roar of splinters, shattering glass, and deadly fire. Horrified screams erupted inside and echoed through the night.

"You can feel this future, Sadie. I know you can. The end of everything. It's right there. One false step away."

Sadie shielded her eyes from the inferno.

Flames licked the frame of her bedroom window.

"No," she said defiantly. "This will never be." The roof of the Madison house yawned, buckled, devoured by the flames. "*You* will never be my future."

Her dark self sneered. "A future with nothing but happiness and love is impossibly close, too," she said floating back to earth. She clicked her fingers and the fire vanished. The Madison house reappeared. Intact and undamaged. "Both futures are almost upon you. Don't become me, Sadie Madison. Don't fear me."

"I don't."

"False," her dark self snapped. "You cower before me. Your *friend* is all the proof you'll need. Look at him. Small and weak and wracked with fear."

Oliver's eyes were frantically trying to avoid the stare from Sadie's dark self.

"You have a great power, Sadie. The greatest power the world will ever know. To read another's mind, to see their thoughts, their memories, their future. To see them, use them, manipulate them, as if they were your own," her dark self continued. "Conjuration, alchemy, and magics of a terrible kind. These things have been studied to the highest levels. Much has been risked for a glimpse at the power you will wield. A power that will come to you as naturally as breathing, as laughing, as dying."

Oliver began to shake.

He sank his fingers through his white hair and gripped his scalp.

AppleGarth's words hung in his mind's eye.

Find the thing that brings you happiness—then you can do anything.

What brought Oliver happiness?

What made him whole?

It was Sadie.

Always Sadie.

Her happiness was all he cared about. He looked at the army of vicious horrors standing before him. But they no longer scared him.

For they *were* him.

As confidence surged, Oliver took a single step forward and stood in front of Sadie.

His perfectly silver hair rustled and shimmered in the moonlight.

"Hear me now!" he yelled at the sky. "I am her fear! Grand

and trivial, robust and fragile, brutal and cunning. I control you. For you are me. And I am you! Come to me now, make me whole. I am her shield. Her protector. Her fear put aside!"

Oliver lifted his arms.

A choking cloud of black vapour rose from the earth.

A dark mist.

It enveloped the monsters, swept them into the blustering storm, screaming and moaning with despair. Sadie's dark self struggled to remain rooted to the earth. The dark mist pulled her legs from beneath her, wrenched her body into the air, and swallowed her whole.

A wave of deafening screams rose from the legions above.

A call to arms.

A hideous war cry.

Sharp claws exploded from Oliver's fingertips, only to retract beneath the skin. His arms flashed with iridescent scales before returning to pale grey flesh once more. A forked tongue shot from his mouth and licked the air between two rows of gnashing fangs. His spine arched like a crook and stretched him towards the sky. His entire body expanded until he towered over Sadie and the doktor, throbbing and shaking and terrible to behold.

And then, as if he could hold the transformation no longer, he shrank back to normal.

Oliver bellowed at the monsters around him. A jet of fire—like that from the Steam Totem—erupted from his mouth, reeking of sulphur and death.

The monstrous legions merged with the spiralling dark mist.

It descended, knitted itself into Oliver's crimson scarf, then evanesced into his skin.

For all his fear of monsters—even the mention of the word—Oliver was one himself.

Sadie's monster.

Her fear incarnate.

A blinding bolt of lightning tore the sky.

Thunder shook the ground.

The rain eased, slowed, stopped.

Stars broke through the clouds.

Doktor Merrick sniffed the air.

"A fantastic display," he nodded with satisfaction, like a scientist overseeing a successful experiment. "You are one of five, Sadie."

"Five?" she replied, somewhat blind-sided.

"You've heard of the Candidates, true?"

"Yes ... but I know nothing of them."

"You all share a birthday, Sadie. Each one a year older than the next. Each one the answer to their own prophetic riddle. Each one special in so many ways. And, Sadie, each one has a unique friend." He glanced at Oliver. "You are the final piece to the puzzle. A puzzle I've been trying to complete for many years. Come with me to Hurtmore House. For there, in that place, you will learn all you'll ever need."

"And Danver? Will I get to see Danver?"

"He's waiting for you." Doktor Merrick smiled. "Come."

The doktor left the garden swinging his ebony cane merrily. Sadie trotted behind like an obedient dog. "But what of my father?" she asked. "And Mother. Natalia and Eli?"

"Why do you care?" he replied. "Your father betrayed you. He and your mother kept painful secrets your entire life. Your sister is, well, not even a sister. And Eli—" He turned on his heel to face her. "There's always an innocent bystander, isn't there. It cannot be helped."

Doktor Merrick was off again, skipping down the driveway. They stopped next to the long, black, important-looking automobile. Leviathan Crook felt eerily quiet. Not a soul wandered the street. Every light out.

Even the Ryndai had vanished.

Sadie glanced down the hill, then back at the house.

On the porch, even Natalia's lanterns didn't dare move.

Gradually, one by one, lamps ignited and shadows swept past every window. People were dancing and singing and celebrating in every room. Despite the darkness Sadie's music had conjured, the house had never seemed so alive, so full of life and happiness and joy. Oliver could tell she wanted to run back inside and hug her parents, and kiss her sister, and wrestle Eli to the ground, giggling and laughing the whole time.

"I wish I could go back in time. Back before the fight in the schoolyard, before the story, and the music. Before my world changed forever."

"That's only possible in dreams and memory," Doktor Merrick told her.

"I know."

Oliver caught his reflection in the black paint of the doktor's automobile. For the most part, he still looked the same as he always had. But his hair had become the most brilliant white and sprouting up his neck and hands were thin strands of electric red. Monstrous fire that glowed in his veins.

"And someday soon, you can bring Danver home," the doktor added, tossing his top hat and cane onto the passenger seat. "You can show them all how real he is. You can show them you were right all along. You can be part of something truly amazing."

Sadie looked at the house again.

Doktor Merrick bent down, opened the rear door and spread his fingers, gesturing her inside. "So, Sadie," he asked. "What'll it be?"

✳☻▥☆⛫

The Madison family grandfather clock struck midnight.

People gathered in circles. They sang and hugged and exchanged kisses.

Champagne corks popped.

Glasses chimed.

Michael moved towards the study where he'd left Sadie. He hurried inside. Senses on high alert. But, as he scanned the room and found nothing but shadows, his heart froze.

Sadie had gone.

Michael skirted his desk and slid the velvet curtain along its rail. He found nothing in the alcove beside stacks of boxes, paintings, books, and the carved wooden door. He spun frantically. His gaze caught the window. Beyond the glass an automobile pulled away from the kerb. Brake lamps flashed red against the snow.

"Michael, where is she?"

It was William Madison.

"She was right here," Michael said, steadying himself at the sudden appearance of his dead father. "No more than two minutes ago. There's no way they've taken her. They cannot get into the house. And she wouldn't be foolish enough to go outside."

William stared at an automobile disappearing down Leviathan Crook. "She's a child. Children are prone to ignoring the requests of their parents and making breathtakingly reckless decisions. *You* certainly did and look what happened?"

"Now is *not* the time for recriminations."

"All you had to do was keep her in the house, keep her safe." The old man looked around the room and spread his hands animatedly. "So, where is she?"

"I don't know." Michael removed his spectacles and rubbed his eyes. "Gods know where she is now."

"I'm right here."

Michael turned, dropped to his knees.

Sadie stood in the doorway.

He pulled her close and wrapped her in his arms. She was shivering from the rain and the cold. But she was here. She was safe.

"Who were you just talking to?" she asked.

Michael hesitated. "Just ... to myself ... I suppose. I panicked a little when you weren't here." He looked over Sadie's shoulder, but his father was no longer there. "Where did you go?" he said. "You're soaking. What were you doing outside?"

"I thought I saw Sofia," she said. "I know what happened to her. I know about Karolinja. And the basement. I know everything."

He pushed the wet hair off Sadie's face and stared into her eyes. They seemed diminished, like a light had gone out. His daughter seemed different, changed.

"I'm sorry," he said. "I know that's not enough. That will never be enough. But it was the only way. It was the only thing we could do to make you safe. Sofia was the first. The Narrowers gave us no choice."

The pain of that awful night bloomed in his gut.

"You always have options, Father," she said. "So much has happened. I guess we're all a little different now."

The grandfather clock fell silent. The last echoes of its twelve chimes died into the rugs and carpets and curtains. Larissa appeared behind Sadie. Her anxiety rash had bloomed on her chest and neck.

"Thank goodness," she said, grasping Sadie in her arms. "And happy birthday, darling."

"Yes, happy birthday," Michael added.

He looked out the window again. Lights shone in every house on Leviathan Crook. Shadows danced past each window. The sound of music and feverous rejoicing filled the air. Fireworks streamed into the sky, lighting the world with huge florets of colourful fire and smoke.

Michael closed his eyes and drew a long breath.

The hour was upon him. Upon them all. He held the breath in, frozen in the moment. Part of him prayed it would last forever, that his father had bestowed him with the power to hold time, but he knew fate and destiny were closing in on him.

Slowly, Michael opened his eyes.

The sight chilled him to the bone.

At the front gate, where there had been nothing but icy sludge and a fine drizzle, were three figures draped in black.

"Michael?" Larissa said, seeing his face. "What is it?"

"The Wretched," he said, almost surprised.

Larissa gasped. A hand shot to her mouth.

"Sadie, the time has come. Stay close to me. Do *not* go outside. No matter what happens. Please obey me this time. I beg you." He tapped his fingers nervously against the window sill. "But the Wretched would never align themselves with the Narrowers and the Gathering Order."

Larissa grasped the frame and stared at the three women.

One of them waved forebodingly at her.

"Don't worry, Larissa. The Wretched can never enter this house. My father's wards and glamours prevent any spirit from the Vents crossing the threshold."

"They're from the Nyx, Father," Sadie added helpfully.

Michael frowned. "How do you—?" But this wasn't the time. "The house is warded against that too," he said. "Unless somebody has changed the symbols, we are quite safe from the Wretched here."

The three women didn't approach the house. They simply stood at the front gate and stared at the study window. Michael shooed Sadie and Larissa away, through the library, the hallway, and into the kitchen as New Year's anthems and choruses boomed around them.

"Where's Natalia?" he asked.

"In her room. Crying. Broken-hearted."

"And Eli?"

Larissa found him in the dining room, feeding Atticus strawberry sponge cake.

"Okay, everyone's here. Fine. Good." Michael tried to control his breath. He needed to stay as calm and controlled as possible. He had no idea what the coming moments would bring, what the Wretched had planned, where the true agents of the Gathering Order were, who they were, and when they might strike.

He needed to be ready for anything.

For everything.

He shimmied through the kitchen, shook hands and

exchanged pleasantries with his guests. He rattled the back door. Locked. He looked out into the garden beyond.

His heart shuddered.

His breath came harder, faster.

Three figures lingering on the lawn.

"The Wretched at the front. Agents at the back!"

"We're trapped," cried Larissa.

Sadie didn't appear to be at all concerned with their desperation or the shadowy figures waiting for her at the boundaries of the Madison property.

"What do we do?" Larissa said, pulling Sadie close.

"Stay here. Stay in the crowd," Michael said as he rushed out of the kitchen. "And make sure no one opens that door!"

Michael avoided dancing party guests and plates stacked with cakes and puddings as he launched himself into his study, closed the door and jumped into the alcove. Hoisting the carved wooden door over towers of books and boxes, Michael manoeuvred the door into the study and leant it against the wall adjacent to the window. With a nervous finger, he twisted several faces.

The minotaur six points turnwise.

The siren three points widdershins.

He pressed them forward.

Each clicked as it sank into position.

He froze, unsure. "The griffin, the bullfrog, or the firefly?" he whispered. His fingers twitched over the grotesque faces. A thin line of amber light shone around the edge of the door. The final face eluded him.

"Michael. Stop."

An ancient voice.

His finger hovered over the firefly. "Please be right."

"Michael," the voice came again, more urgent this time. "Please. Stop."

Outside, shadows swarmed against the glass. "You cannot run, Michael," they said, the voices sounded as though inside the room. "The future is inevitable."

"I have your agents and the Wretched at my door," he said. "What other choice do I have?"

"None," they answered. "Our agents are here for your protection. They can keep the Wretched at bay while we reveal your daughter's future."

"Why are the Wretched here. Who do they serve?"

"Another."

Michael's stomach churned.

"The Horned God, Michael. The Lord of the Nyx. the Unknown. The one they call Void, King Nothing, Malmortem."

"Malmortem." He laughed nervously. "Impossible. A bedtime story. Nothing more."

"He has come for her. To harness her power as his own."

Michael looked at the Narrowers in disbelief, ashamed of the thought that hit him. "But Sadie would live," he said. "Even bound to this creature—to Malmortem—she would live. How is it you cannot offer such a future?"

"What possible future?" they answered. "She is too dangerous. With the child of the Foretelling alive, the future is clouded in uncertainty. The Foretelling is a prophecy, Michael. A divine declaration. Not a tarot reading or a hand of black gimlet. Bring us the child. Let us test her—as you promised thirteen years ago—once and for all!"

Michael shook his head.

"We made a deal. A solemn vow."

"You cannot make me," he hissed.

"True," they replied. "But disciples of the Unknown are at your door. They will not give you this option. They will take the girl and lay waste to everything else. Michael, we are running out of time."

One by one, the carved heads in the wooden door clicked back to their starting positions.

The amber light died.

"Michael," they urged. "Bring us the girl. Do it now. Before it is too late."

THE GIRL WHO CAME HOME

Larissa still had both hands locked on Sadie's shoulders when Michael returned to the kitchen. She looked pale, scared and unsure. "What's happening, Michael? Where have you been?"

"It's fine," he lied. "Everything is going to be fine." His eyes hardly met hers. "The door," he said. "I thought ... maybe ... we could use the door."

"The door?" Larissa said, surprised. "You said running away was futile. You said they'll find us no matter where we go."

"What door?" Sadie asked. "The carved one with all the interesting faces?"

"Yes. That door."

"Michael, where are you taking us?" Larissa implored. "Shall I fetch Natalia? Is Dimitri coming too? I don't know if she'll come without him. To be honest, I doubt she'll come at all."

He levered Sadie away from Larissa.

"We should all go together. Michael? Wait!"

But he swept away from his wife and guided Sadie towards the hallway. "Yes, yes," he said over his shoulder. "Get Natalia and Eli. Atticus too."

"Where are we going, Michael? San Cristophe, Los Kralice, Ville de Feuilles. Where, Michael? Where? What about clothes, a suitcase, money?"

Instead of fetching Natalia and Eli and forcing them to run away from everything they knew, Larissa followed Michael patiently through the library, smiling at her guests and twirling to the music on the wireless.

The study door clicked shut as she arrived.

She turned the handle, shouldered the door. It was locked tight. She knocked calmly, smiling awkwardly at the room. No answer came. "Michael," she called, her voice strained and anxious. "The door's locked. Do open up."

An almighty crash filled the house.

The tear of splintered wood.

And shattered glass.

Rent from its hinges, the front door lay in the middle of the hallway.

Dust and snow plumed at its edges.

Three women dressed in black flowing robes stood on the stricken door.

The Wretched spread their hands. Balls of dark fire flecked with skeins of scarlet, indigo, and turquoise formed above outstretched fingers.

Party guests screamed and scrambled.

They dived for safety.

Ran each other down as they fled.

The Wretched laughed wickedly, smiling and leering at Larissa.

"Move aside, woman," Edith croaked.

"Give us the child," added Dorothea.

Larissa clutched the doorframe and pounded on the door with her heel.

"La-rissa," Genevieve purred. "Step aside. We only want the child. We'll leave the rest of you to your ... *lives*."

The witch sneered. Her cerulean eyes glowed.

"Don't make us hurt you."

Guests scrambled past the three women as Natalia barrelled down the stairs.

"Hello, dearie," Dorothea croaked, reaching out a malformed hand and pulling her close.

Natalia screamed as the witch's fingers bit into her skin.

Larissa's breath became ragged. She flattened herself against the study door. Pounded again with her heel, her fists. "Don't hurt her," she pleaded. "She has nothing to do with this."

"Then give us the child," Genevieve said. "Give us ... your *real* daughter."

Natalia struggled. Limbs flew. "What *are* you?"

Larissa slammed on the study door with everything she had. "Michael!"

Edith strode forward impatiently.

Dark magics fizzed at her fingertips.

Larissa's body relaxed, softened. Her fingers caressed the red cuff bracelet that circled her wrist. "Michael," she said evenly, eyeing the three witches and her ashen, sorrowful daughter. "If you can hear me, seal the door. Open it for no one!" She pulled herself to full height. Set her jaw. Folded her arms. "Do your worst!"

The Wretched hissed.

Throwing their arms wide, balls of dark fire expanded, reverberating with immense power. Larissa's eyes fluttered shut in expectation of the devastation from their magics. But, instead of dying right there in the library, a young man's voice broke through the confusion.

A voice Larissa knew.

"Move aside, witch!"

Standing beyond the Wretched, clad in carnelian knee-length gowns trimmed with gold, were three boys. Each held a long, thin blade that shone under the flickering lamplight, cold and deadly.

"I said, move aside!"

He dashed forward. Sword sliced the air.

Dorothea dodged the blade as he tore Natalia from her grasp.

"Dimitri?" Natalia cried as she clattered over the back of the sofa. "What are you wearing?"

Turning to the Wretched, Dimitri added, "The child is ours.

The Foretelling will not be denied."

Screeching, the Wretched unleashed balls of dark fire. Dimitri, Branislav, and Erik—Agents of the Gathering Order—raised their weapons to deflect them away. Furniture splintered, bookshelves disintegrated, sparks and smoke and cindered pages choked the library. Staggering to regain their balance, the sons of Alexsy Rubinov hoisted their weapons above their heads.

And charged.

✷ ◡ 🖩 ⋇ 🏛

Michael could feel the explosions and fighting through the wall. The sound was so deafening he could have sworn he was standing in the middle of it. His hands pressed against the door. The handle lay inches from his grasp, calling to him.

Michael knew that each passing moment of indecision changed the future. Endless possibilities came into line, then drifted into nothingness.

The Wretched were in the house. He could hear them. But how? His father had warded the building decades ago. It was impossible for them to breach his ancient spells. As one panicked thought drifted into the next, Michael staggered across the room and gripped the frame of the window.

Beyond, the Narrowers swarmed against the glass.

"How did the Wretched get inside?" Michael stuttered. "The wards? The glamours? Have they been broken?"

"Release the child," the Narrowers said. "The clock has passed midnight. We must perform our tests."

Michael clasped Sadie tight. His head spun. "What are you going to do to her?"

"Nothing invasive, Michael. We cannot touch her—not in any way you'd understand—but we need to look into her mind. We need to see her future. She is a child no more. It will all be laid out for her now. For good or ill."

"And you'll release her back to me," he said. His fingers

clasped Sadie's shoulders.

"We have no real power here, Michael. We can observe and nothing more."

The door pounded ominously. The clatter of steel and raging fire seeped around its edges.

Michael's gaze shot to the window.

Row upon row of Ryndai stood in the front garden.

Swords glistened.

Lanterns glowed ominously.

"Michael," the Narrowers insisted. "Break the seals. Let us in. Give us the child before she's taken from you."

Michael's gaze switched from the shifting shadows of the Narrowers, to the Ryndai, to the sound of violent conflict beyond the study door. Dropping to his knees, he swept a dozen silver figurines and curios off the windowsill. He slid his fingers around the edge and raised the dark wood. Beneath, etched into the outer wall of the Madison house, were a complex series of symbols, tokens, and markings—like the ones on Sofia's scalp. Grabbing a mother-of-pearl-handled letter opener, Michael scratched the edge of the nearest symbol. The symbols shone, radiant and golden, then, as if they'd never existed, vanished into nothing.

The Narrowers were inside, circling the walls, moving over furniture and knick-knacks like purposeful smoke. They congregated in the centre and morphed into three figures built of shadow.

"Hurry," Michael said, nodding towards his daughter.

Sadie stumbled forward, fearless and blank.

Michael turned to the carved wooden door. He frantically punched the faces of the minotaur and siren with his index finger. Amber light shone around the edge once more. Finally, he pressed the face of the firefly and, with a gentle *whoosh*, the door swung open.

A grey room with bare, dusty floorboards appeared. A large bay window filled the far wall. It framed a park, lined with trees of orange and gold, glowing with soft lamplight.

Michael whirled around his desk. He crouched beside the drawers and pulled the tiny silver key from beneath his shirt. He slid it into the lock and the drawer glided open effortlessly, revealing the *Book of Whispers.*

Sadie watched her father as he took the iron-clad tome and disappeared through the carved wooden door. Michael rushed to the bay window and stared out over the park. An enormous New Year's celebration was underway. Thousands of people were singing, embracing, dancing to music emanating from a huge carnival. Sweet aromas filled the air. Candyfloss, hot donuts, roasted cinnamon apples.

"What are you going to do to me?" Sadie asked.

The Narrowers said nothing.

From three dark, extended arms, hung three sets of long, shadowy fingers. They dangled over Sadie's head for a moment before descending through her unruly hair and onto her pale skin. The Narrowers' ghostly fingers sank effortlessly through her flesh as though it were water.

Slam!

The study door shuddered on its hinges.

A sound like churning machinery and ancient chanting emanated from the Narrowers.

Slam!

Michael dashed back into his study, clutching the book.

"They're coming," he said, wedging himself against the study door. He tried to picture the scene on the other side. Were Larissa, and Natalia, and Eli okay? They could be hurt, injured, dead. He shook the thought away and focused on Sadie. Three figures loomed over her.

Slam! The study door almost collapsed into the room.

It took what remained of Michael's strength to resist the urge to open the door and rush to help his family.

Sadie had to come first.

Slam! A crack of light streaked the hardwood. The door

splintered. Michael forced himself against it, holding back whatever raged on the opposite side.

Slam! The top corner of the door fell onto Michael's head. His clocks and collectables clattered to the carpet. He collapsed, back to the door, feet pressed hard against his desk. The entire house shook in its foundations. His sight blurred. Was it the force of the battle? Was it tears? Was it ... the end?

An almighty flash filled the study.

The Narrowers screamed and howled like tortured animals.

Michael flattened himself against the floor.

The Narrowers tore their fingers from Sadie's head.

"*She—is—not—*" they wailed disbelievingly, their voices shrill and piercing.

"Not the one?" Michael said, astonished. He scrambled to his knees. The *Book of Whispers* fell to the floor as his fingers clawed Sadie's waist. Tears tumbled down his face. "Sadie is *not* the one?"

The Narrowers convulsed. They twisted into odd shapes and colours. Crackled with fierce energy. Sadie watched them thoughtfully as they spiralled like windmills. A dark watery void materialised on the floor, pulled at them, sucked the Narrowers and their screams into the nothingness. As they disappeared— one tortured voice after the next—the void fizzed, choked, and frothed shut behind them.

A scorched circle remained.

An acrid, metallic scent.

The slams stopped.

The study brightened.

Michael glanced into the grey room beyond the carved wooden door.

"Are we going through there?" Sadie asked, peering in for the first time.

Michael stared at the scorched circle then shifted his gaze to the *Book of Whispers* lying beside him.

"No," he said, finally. "Not now. Not ever."

"That room," she asked. "Where is it?"

He retrieved the Book of Whispers.

Closed the carved wooden door.

The amber light faded.

"It doesn't matter. Not anymore." Michael shuddered. He wiped the tears away with the back of his wrist. "You're not the one. It was Sofia. It was always Sofia."

Michael gulped lungfuls of air, steadied himself, and swung the study door open.

Framed in the doorway, Larissa held Sadie's towering pancake birthday cake topped with thirteen candles. Behind her, the entire population of Leviathan Crook swelled, waiting for a glimpse of the birthday girl. Natalia and Eli flanked their mother, beaming happily.

Michael blinked several times, wondering if it was a dream, wondering if he'd died to this eternal torment.

Everything appeared to be in perfect order.

The door, the library, the entire house.

Where were the Wretched and the Agents of the Gathering Order?

His eyes found the window.

The Ryndai had dispersed too.

Only one remained outside.

What happened to the destruction and chaos he had heard from the other side of the door? He dragged a shoe against the hardwood floor. The scorched circle had gone. His clocks and collectables were back to their rightful place, ticking, unbroken. The wards and glamours beneath the windowsill were remade.

Michael slipped the *Book of Whispers* back in its drawer.

The grandfather clock in the hallway began to chime.

He checked his pocket watch.

Midnight. Again.

"Happy birthday, Sadie," said Larissa, beaming inanely.

"Thank you," she replied. "And a happy New Year, one and all."

✳☺▦�

Eli shuddered as the entire congregation of the Madison house burst into song around him. They sang loudly and in several different keys. Alexsy Rubinov being the loudest and most off-key of them all.

Sadie took a short bow and blew out her candles.

A cheer rang through the house as the last one flickered and died.

Candle smoke wafted into Eli's face, thick and pungent.

He slipped his Monster Magnifiers on, clasped his notebook, and let his fingertips brush the secret letters inside. Letters from his mysterious friend beyond the carved wooden door. From D. Had that been him in the long black automobile? Had Eli missed him? Or had he failed to show? Either way, Eli hoped his friend was okay.

"You have to cut the first slice," Larissa insisted.

Sadie took a kitchen knife from Natalia and expertly drove it through the cake. She grabbed a dense wedge of pancakes and chocolate and stuffed it greedily into her mouth.

Eli watched through his Monster Magnifiers.

Sadie chewed hungrily on her birthday cake.

Dribbles of chocolate ran over her chin.

Crumbs caught in her hair.

But, to his horror, what stood before him was not his sister.

She looked like Sadie in almost every way, but her teeth were gnarled, yellow and forsaken, her eyes languid black pools, the crown of her head stained with dark cryptic writing.

THE JOURNEY HOME

Doktor Merrick's long, black, important-looking automobile smelt of cinnamon, stale cigar smoke, and gasoline. The seats were well-worn and comfortable. The door pockets stuffed with maps and well-thumbed atlases.

Doktor Merrick exchanged his white gloves for parchment driving ones and placed his top hat on the passenger seat beside him. He fiddled around with a wireless. Sadie had never seen one inside an automobile before. After a few seasoned tweaks he found a signal and, with it, music. It was not a piece Sadie recognised but she sat back and enjoyed it all the same.

Leaving Iron Bridge far behind, they followed the River Myr towards the Southern Seas. Michael had taken the Madison family this way one summer for a week at Fort Campion, a large fishing town at the tip of the Shadow Valley. Sadie remembered the excitement of that family holiday with fondness. Larissa had been pregnant with Eli, and Natalia was high on childhood dreams. Sadie spent her days sat among traders and crafters on the floating market reading *Papas and Ghouls* comics, a precursor to her penny dreadfuls and horror grimoires. She loved to watch the water rise and fall as ships glided in and out of port beneath the dazzling sun.

Doktor Robey Merrick took the Fort Campion turn-off and manoeuvred the automobile through dark twisty streets and onto a crescent harbour. A catacomb of steep, winding alleyways and overhanging balconies sprouted around them. The boardwalk buzzed with New Year's celebrations. Lantern light reflected in the automobile's windows as they glided past busy taverns, hotels, and restaurants. Doktor Merrick took the coast road, leaving Fort Campion behind, and headed west.

"I'm doing the right thing, aren't I?" Sadie said, breaking the rhythmic monotony of the thrumming engine.

"Are you asking *me*?" the doktor replied. "Because it's a little late to be having second thoughts. You know, whatever you choose to do will be the right thing—if you believe in fate and destiny, *The Clockwork Universe*, in the Foretelling." He looked over his shoulder. "It'll be fine, Sadie. Hurtmore House is the *only* place you should be right now."

"Is that so?"

"Yes, your father thinks he can protect you. But he's a mortal man, Sadie. Flesh and blood are such fragile things."

"I happen to disagree," she said. She wondered about her father again. She wondered what he was. The son of a billion-year-old spirit from the beginning of time had to be something more than just a man, more than mere flesh and blood.

"What do you think your father would have done if you'd stayed?" the doktor said. "The Narrowers would have done their tests on you, concluded that you *are* the child who will bring about the end of all things, and have their agents dispatch you without a second thought."

The wireless crackled. The music became broken, distorted. A voice struggled to get through. Doktor Merrick twisted the dials. Finally, a woman's voice came forward. "Merrick? Do you have her? Tell me you have her."

Sadie recognised the voice immediately.

"Yes. I have her."

"Oh, thank the Gods," Rhiannon said.

Sadie jumped forward in her seat and stared inexplicably at the wireless. "How are you doing this? How are you speaking to each other through the wireless?"

The doktor glanced at her in the rearview mirror. "It's a sort of two-way wireless. A voice transmitter, if you will. Much like a FarSpeaker."

"In an automobile?" Sadie said, astounded.

"Hello, Sadie," said Rhiannon. Her voice crackled and wheezed through the speakers.

"Why didn't you tell me any of this?" Sadie said. The sensation of talking to a wireless was impossibly awkward. "Why didn't you tell me I could get to Hurtmore House in an automobile with the doktor?"

"It's not that simple, Sadie. I told you everything you needed to know," Rhiannon explained. "You had to *want* to leave. You needed a reason—one far bigger than Danver—to leave your family behind. You needed to see your family for who they really are. You needed to see them differently. Doktor Merrick and I couldn't make you. We couldn't bundle you in a blanket and whisk you off against your will. That's not how it works."

Sadie slumped against the worn leather and gazed out of the window.

"What happened at the house?" the doktor asked, turning his attention to the wireless.

"An almighty fight. The Agents of the Gathering Order and the Wretched. Ryndai saw it all. The witches' magic was dark, unknowable. As we feared, their allegiance lies with the Lord of the Nyx."

"Malmortem," the doktor hissed under his breath. "The Unknown walks among us?"

"I didn't see him," Rhiannon said. "But I fear he is close." The wireless crackled. Distant melodies feathered the edge of hearing. Rhiannon added, "There was a timeshift, Robey."

"A timeshift?" the doktor replied. "I didn't feel anything."

"Fifteen minutes or so. To a moment before the confrontation."

The doktor nodded to himself.

"There's ... something else."

"Yes."

"There's another child here."

"I know, I know. The boy with the goggles. Eli. Or do you mean the adopted girl?"

"No," Rhiannon said. "I do not know who or what she is but—"

"It's Sofia," Sadie said, jumping forward again. "My twin."

The wireless buzzed and whistled horribly.

"And ... she's there?" Doktor Merrick asked. "In the house with the family?"

"Yes," Rhiannon said. "But I cannot read her. I cannot see what she sees or feel what she feels."

"Why ever not?"

"She is not of the Living, Robey," Rhiannon told him.

"A ghost?"

"I fear she may not be of the Dead either. She is ... something *else*."

Doktor Merrick took a moment. "I understand. Remain where you are," he instructed. "Remain at the house. See that Michael and his family—and Sofia—are watched closely."

"As you wish," Rhiannon replied. "Godspeed, Robey. Godspeed to you all."

The wireless crackled, died.

"Turn the automobile around," Sadie ordered. "We have to go back!"

"Back? Whatever for?"

"My family are in danger! Sofia is in the house. She's pretending to be me. There's no telling what she'll do. Doktor Merrick, please. Turn the vehicle around."

He lifted his hands off the wheel and swivelled in his chair.

Sadie's eyes widened.

"I'm sorry," he said.

"Hands on the wheel," Sadie insisted.

But the automobile negotiated the curves in the road of its own accord.

"You see, I'm not actually in control. There's nothing I can do. We're bound for Hurtmore House, and there's nothing you nor I can do to change that now."

The steering wheel eased from side to side.

Sadie watched it for a time, convinced that, sooner or later, the doktor's illusion would crumble and the automobile would certainly plunge off the coast road and onto the ragged rocks below.

A tiredness billowed through her. An exhaustion beyond anything she had known. She closed her eyes and instantly returned home.

She saw her family—Michael, Larissa, Natalia, and Eli, the three wise cats, and the soft, loveable Atticus. Her heart ached for them passionately. Each one of them. Not because she wasn't with them, but because she *couldn't* be with them. She wondered if they would remember her. She wondered if the Narrowers would eradicate her from their memories, the same way they'd done with Danver. Sadie wondered where Rhiannon watched her family from. She hoped the Living would keep them all safe until she could return.

And what did she mean by a *timeshift?*

"You cannot save them all," Oliver said.

His long grey fingers rested on her knee.

"I can," she said. "And I will."

The boy in the crimson scarf looked anxious.

"Father, Mother, Natalia, and Eli. I'll save them. Even Sofia, whoever or whatever she is. I *will* save them all."

"How?"

Sadie looked deep into his aching eyes. "One by one."

The doktor opened a small, nickel-plated tin and tipped out a handful of mints. He offered them to Sadie, but she shook her head. Doktor Merrick stretched his legs onto the dashboard. He cradled the back of his head with one hand, the other rested on the steering wheel. The automobile trundled down the brightening road. Towering mountains fizzing by on one side, the endless Sapphire Seas on the other.

Hours passed.

The horizon became streaked with morning light.

Dark cherry and papaya.

"Ah, here it is," the doktor said suddenly.

He yanked the wheel to the right, taking them off the coast road. They dived down a small, unmarked carriageway between the Carcassus Mountains, the opening of which shone with bright, shifting colour. The road seemed to turn through hundreds of ninety-degree corners, making the distance far longer than it ought to be.

The subterranean shadow slipped away and the road expanded onto an enormous plain surrounded by a vast ring of mountains. There were no hills, no high ground, no distinguishing features of any kind. This place was barren and flat and wholly unpleasant.

Sadie looked out the back window. To her dismay, the carriageway between the Carcassus Mountains had gone. Vanished. As if it had never existed.

Ahead, a huge building materialised through the mist. A mighty galleon of stone upon a sea of grass and thickets.

The doktor rolled his shoulders as the automobile passed between two gargoyle-topped stone pillars and fizzed along a gravel approach road.

The long, black, important-looking automobile eased into a parking space with *Doktor Robey Merrick* emblazoned on the wall.

He sighed deeply.

Stretched his arms.

Swivelled in his chair.

"Welcome home."

THE GIRL WITH MISMATCHED EYES

Steam hissed angrily from the engine. It swirled around him like dark spirits. "You *must* get on the train, Serafine!"

She stared at her father with nefarious, cold eyes.

Her cold stares were nothing new. Sometimes he imagined she was trying to crush his skull with her mind or attempt to read his thoughts. He smiled and stared back. "Now is not the time for your childish games, Serafine." He grabbed her arm and dragged her towards the train. "We've been travelling for five straight days. My patience is all but spent."

A horn erupted.

Another torrent of steam.

"The train is leaving," he told her, eyebrows raised. "Like it or not, so are we."

He pushed Serafine up the steps, through the door, and into the carriage.

The wheels began to roll.

"Find a seat and get comfortable. It'll be morning before we arrive."

He dabbed his brow with a white handkerchief.

Serafine shuffled her tiny frame down the corridor. She peered through glass-panelled doors at passengers in each compartment. There weren't many people travelling. Most were single travellers, sitting alone, searching for sleep. The occasional couple chatted excitedly. The effects of New Year's champagne still alive in their veins.

She found an empty compartment and slipped inside. Her father, hauling their luggage, joined moments later.

"Perfect," he said, heaving their bags into the racks overhead.

Serafine failed to acknowledge him. She turned her eyes to the window. A vast canvas of mountains and stars clung to the glass.

The man took his seat and, as the train gathered speed, slipped a hand into his pocket and grasped a small disc. Cast in gold, the disc was set around an equilateral triangle. Cradling it in his palm, he etched his thumb over its contours. It was something he'd done a hundred times a day for as long as he could remember. His flesh found tiny indentations in the gold. Words engraved along the circumference.

Something Forgotten Is Never Lost.

The train plunged into the western edge of Darachna Forest, leaving San Cristophe and the Snake Plains in its wake. Sandarac trees rushed by—metres from the window—concealing the horrors that dwelt within. He wondered what Serafine would make of this new, exciting world. She had never seen anything like it.

But the world had never seen anything quite like Serafine either.

The girl had an ill-favoured look. Although pretty, she had heterochromia—one blue eye, one green—and a claret birthmark that covered the left half of her face. Conversely, her hair was mesmerising, like gold thread. It would turn every head she passed and set minds wondering about the reward for such a prize.

Serafine was acutely aware of this and kept her golden hair hidden from the world. She wore a leather flying cap over her crown and ears which fastened beneath her chin with a brass buckle.

The compartment door swung open.

"Sorry to disturb, I know it's late," said a ticket inspector.

"Can I see your papers?"

Resting his briefcase onto his knees, Serafine's father retrieved the necessary information.

The inspector scanned the paperwork. "Very good, Mr Davidian."

"It's Father Davidian," he corrected, tapping the Broken Moon armband encircling his right bicep. "Father Morqash Davidian."

"I see," the Inspector said, shifting uneasily. "Don't meet too many people of faith in these parts."

"Serafine Davidian," the ticket inspector said, turning to the girl. She too wore the armband. "What a charming, yet most unusual name."

Serafine smiled, masking the left side of her face with a pale hand.

"It means *Burning One*," Father Davidian told him, taking the documents from the inspector and slipping them into his briefcase.

The inspector nodded and backed out of the compartment. Serafine watched him with her blue eye, the green one hidden behind her fingers. "Best get some sleep if you can, young lady," he said before closing the door. "It's a little over seven hours to Iron Bridge." He looked at the Broken Moon on Serafine's arm once more. "Be careful when you arrive. Keep yourselves to yourselves. I hear the town is crawling with Ryndai."

Father Davidian nodded in appreciation.

The inspector slid the door shut after him.

Serafine turned back to the window.

"We're out into the world now. A place full of distractions and temptations."

Serafine used her index finger to draw a circle on the window around the moon.

"We're on a divine mission. A search for a miracle worker. A child—one not much older than yourself—who channels a power which the world has never seen."

Serafine faced her father. She locked both eyes on him, revealing her dark birthmark. She opened her mouth to speak— her teeth jagged and pointed like a shark—but Father Davidian held up a finger.

"Sadie Madison is a descendant of the Grigori. An earth-bound angel. The world will come to know her, love her, worship her. Once her music plays in every country, in every city, in every home and heart in this world, belief will return. Her music will transcend flesh and bone, emotion and memory, time and space."

He ran his fingers over the warm gold disc in his pocket.

"Something Forgotten Is Never Lost," Father Morqash Davidian muttered to himself. And set his determined eyes on the star-ravaged sky.

THANK YOU

Thank you so much for reading *Sadie Madison and the Boy in the Crimson Scarf*. I hope you enjoyed it!

If you have the time to write a brief and honest review on Amazon, GoodReads etc, that would help me enormously to reach new readers.

I have a growing mailing list with exclusive news, writing tips, and giveaways. Scan the QR code above or visit **www.neiljhart.com/sign-up/** to get **FREE** downloads including *Michael Madison's Bedtime Stories* and Erin's *Book of Scarecrows* from *'The Last Scarecrow'!* You can unsubscribe at *any* time.

I'm also active on Facebook, Twitter, Instagram, and TikTok. If you have a question about this book, or my writing, you can get in touch with me there or follow for updates and news about future books and promotions.

Once again, thank you for reading *Sadie Madison and the Boy in the Crimson Scarf*.

Best wishes, **NjH**

ABOUT THE AUTHOR

Neil J Hart has won awards for his haunting
fantasy novels *The Last Scarecrow* and *Sadie
Madison and the Boy in the Crimson Scarf*.

Neil also works as a graphic designer.
He fosters for Cats Protection. Relies on coffee.
Adores cheese and cucumber sandwiches.
And collects Tomb Raider memorabilia.

More info and links to Neil's social media at
www.neiljhart.com

THE LAST SCARECROW

Erin loved to build scarecrows. She made a dozen in all. Her Pa showed her how. But he's dead now. Everyone is dead. Well… *almost.*

The Many Years Storm flooded the world, swept Erin's brother out to sea, and turned her hilltop farm into a rapidly shrinking island. While hope remains, Erin must take her chances on the open ocean and find her brother. But she doesn't have the knowledge to build a raft and there's no-one to ask except the last and most terrifying of all her scarecrows… Number Twelve!

Erin needs help. Scratch that. **Erin needs a miracle.**

OUT NOW!

THE SPIRALVERSE SAGA
HARPER HALE

AND THE
CRYSTAL OF SHADOWS

While intergalactic forces conspire to destroy the **SpiralVerse**, **Harper Hale** struggles to get to class!

Quirky sci-fi fangirl Harper Hale is the first Earthling to enrol at the Galactic Institute—the most prestigious finishing school in the SpiralVerse. But her dreams of becoming a mystical Caster disintegrate when she is classified: VOID.

Heartbroken and lightyears from home, Harper struggles to make the grade with unreliable support from her gelatinous digital EduHelper and a misfit gang of alien friends. Then, when two rival classmates are abducted and a ferocious civil war erupts, blame launches in her direction.

Can Harper find a way to rescue her classmates, clear her name and ace her exams, before all light in the SpiralVerse is snuffed out?

THE ADVENTURE BEGINS MAY 4TH 2025

ACKNOWLEDGEMENTS

This book would not be possible without an army of amazing people who helped shape and mould the story of Sadie Madison from a children's short story into the saga it is today.

A sharp salute to Christopher Jenkins and Nicki Cater for being so impossibly giddy with excitement after reading an early draft (claiming, 'Better than Potter!'), for writing music inspired by the book, and championing me to others. My wonderful family for their encouragement, support, and love. To Elana A. Mugdan, Jen Moss, Sam Ashurst, Matt Bates, and John Repplinger for beta reading this book and providing tough, thoughtful feedback. My editor Manda Waller for her thorough examination and polish of my manuscript. And to Scarlet Frost for inventing ziela, allowing me to cast the Ryndai 'Storm' in her image (*sort of!*), and for being the best human I know.

'Sadie Madison and the Boy in the Crimson Scarf' won the Wattpad Award 2022 for Fantasy and since then has received a breathtaking avalanche of reads, votes, and comments from the Wattpad Community. You guys are amazing.

And enormous thanks to YOU for buying, borrowing, recommending, lending, and reading this book. I hope you enjoyed it as much as I enjoyed writing it. There is more coming in 'The Madison Chronicles'. I hope you're eager to continue the adventure into music, magic, and memory...

MUSIC

Like millions the world over, I'd be pretty lost without music.
What other magic can transport us through time, connect us
to memories—that stir every emotion on the spectrum—with a
handful of notes, a melody, a rhythm, a voice, a lyric?

I always write with music playing. I use specific playlists for
characters, scenes, locations, emotional pinch points and action
sequences to help guide and influence the writing. This book
is littered with song and album titles, nods to music acts and
performers, and even the names of musicians I've met and
played with across the years.

Music defines us. Links us. Binds us.
Reminds us who we are. Who we were.
And who we aspire to be.